About the author

Carol Coffey was born in Dublin and now lives in County Wicklow. She holds a Master's degree in Education and has taught in the area of special education in both Australia and Ireland. This is her fourth novel. Her previous novels *The Butterfly State*, *The Penance Room* and *Winter Flowers* are also published by Poolbeg.

Acknowledgements

Firstly, I'd like to sincerely thank Laura Trigo Sanroman-Lyster for her meticulous Spanish translations and for generously offering her valuable time to this book.

Thanks also to Paula Campbell, Kieran Devlin, Sarah Ormston and David Prendergast for their on-going support. Thanks also to all of the accounts and warehouse staff of Poolbeg Press for the important part they played in getting this novel from my laptop to the bookshelves.

As always, a heartfelt thanks to Gaye Shortland for her expert editing, generous guidance and seemingly endless patience.

For my late parents,
Catherine and Michael

Chapter 1

Brendan Martin rose from his bed and looked through bleary eyes at the view of Dover town, which fell steeply away from the small hill where his uncle's house stood. He turned on his radio and looked back through the window, from where he could make out the neat town grid and the picturesque steeples of the many churches. He could see the park at the edge of town, the red tiled roof of its pretty gazebo and the expanse of pink cherry blossoms that trailed along the river's edge each May. From this height, he could not hear any of the town's traffic or the voices of the children in the school that stood three blocks below him. He took in the tranquil panorama, knowing it would be the only serenity he would enjoy that day.

Brendan looked at his watch. It was almost twelve and he knew his Uncle Frank would, at any moment, come bellowing down the narrow pathway to the small granny flat Brendan had come to live in only six days previously, although to him it seemed like a lifetime ago. It was hard to believe that New York City, where he had lived and worked in blissful isolation for the past twelve years, was less than forty miles from the New Jersey town in which he stood and where he had been born. That was before his mother decided to pack up and return to the dead-end Irish midland village he had

1

grown up in. When he lost his job and his licence following his second Driving While Intoxicated, his Uncle Frank had travelled to New York for the court hearing. Even though his retired cop uncle still had a few friends in the New York police force, he couldn't save his nephew from doing eight days' jail time and receiving a six-hundred-hour community-service order. Brendan knew the sentence could have been much longer and that the judge had only agreed to a more lenient sentence on the condition that Brendan was released into his uncle's care and that Frank would oversee Brendan's community service until a New Jersey probation officer had been assigned to him. With his savings gone, Brendan had no option but to accept his mother's brother's help and to return with his uncle to Dover where he'd at least have a roof over his head.

Brendan heard the squeak of the screen door of the main house and quickly pulled on his jeans. He smoothed down the white T-shirt he had slept in the night before and, after throwing water onto his thick, wiry black hair and washing the sleep out of his deep brown eyes, glanced quickly into the mirror. His dark looks and Irish accent got him a lot of attention from American women, who told him he looked like that Irish movie star whose name he could never remember.

Brendan heard a knock on his door and immediately began to finger the mole on the left side of his face, a nervous habit he had developed in childhood which resurfaced sometimes when he felt anxious. He rubbed his hand over his unshaven face and rushed to open the door. Instead of his uncle, his meek-mannered cousin Eileen stood before him, her small eyes trained on her shoes. She looked up at him for a second then lowered her gaze again to study her footwear. Brendan glanced over his cousin. She was the eldest of Frank's five daughters and the only one to have remained at home. Eileen, who was only two years older than Brendan and just shy of her thirty-seventh birthday, was also the only one of his cousins that he liked, even if she did remind him of his mother. She had the same pale grey eyes and thin brown hair that took on a reddish hue in the sunlight. She was also about the same height as his mother, about five foot he assumed,

2

as he stood almost a foot over her. Unlike most American women he knew, Eileen dressed like a woman twenty years older. Despite the warm spring air, his cousin wore a heavy green winter coat, buttoned up to the neck, small black court shoes like the ones he had often seen his mother wear and an oversized canvas shoulder bag that looked too heavy for her slight frame to carry.

"You ready?" she asked quietly.

Brendan nodded and followed her down the path towards the side entrance, relieved not to have to go into the house this morning. He could avoid his uncle for the one-hour round trip it would take to walk his cousin to her volunteer work. Why she couldn't walk there alone, in broad daylight, he wasn't sure, but until he had arrived his elderly uncle had walked her there and had returned to collect her when she'd finished. Brendan had heard whispers from Eileen's younger sister Orla of an incident at college which had happened almost twenty years before. Orla had told him that after "it" happened, Frank drove all the way to Philadelphia and brought Eileen home where until recently she had spent her days doing nothing. What she hadn't told him was what exactly the incident was. He couldn't imagine his docile cousin getting herself into any trouble but he didn't really care enough to query the matter further. It had nothing to do with him. All he wanted was to get enough money together to return to his life in New York where he would be free from his disapproving uncle and needy cousin.

As they walked down the driveway, Brendan looked at the polished silver car that Eileen owned and which he had never seen her drive. The homeless shelter where she volunteered was about a twenty-five-minute walk and he wondered why she didn't just drive there, especially if her father wouldn't allow her to walk there alone.

He briefly thought about asking her but, as if she read his thoughts, she said, "I always wanted a car. Just so if I wanted to go somewhere, I could."

Brendan looked at her, an expression of confusion spread across his lightly tanned face.

3

"I'm going to take lessons . . . some day. If I can get someone to teach me."

"You can't drive?" he asked incredulously.

Eileen blushed and looked away. Brendan took himself by surprise when he laughed out loud at the irony. He didn't mean to be cruel – it wasn't in his nature – but he didn't know which of them was more pathetic. He, who wasn't allowed to drive for one whole year, or his cousin, who spent Saturday afternoons polishing a car she didn't even know how to drive.

He shook his head and caught up with his cousin who had walked on ahead of him. When she struggled to keep up with his long strides, he slowed his pace and wondered if today she might actually talk to him.

From their house on Watson Drive, the pair turned left onto Salem Street and left again onto East Blackwell, the town's main boulevard, which reminded Brendan of a scene from *It's a Wonderful Life* where Jimmy Stewart runs down the picturesque parade waving at friends and passers-by. He took in the quaint surroundings. On either side of the main street, brightly coloured awnings adorned the town's many shops whose names portrayed the town's long history of migration: DiBartolo's and Nardoni's, Fitzgerald's and Rodriquez'. Locals sat comfortably at the lunch counter of the five and dime, having an early lunch or queuing for a coffee to go. Older people sat on wooden benches reading the day's news and catching up with friends in the small, tightly-knit community. A group of pre-school children crossed the road with their teacher, each carrying a small bag of breadcrumbs, presumably to feed the multitude of ducks and pigeons in the park.

Brendan liked this town and often wished his mother had stayed here. In the years since he'd come to live in New York, he hadn't visited his relatives often. He preferred city living and wasn't especially close to his uncle anyway. Even before his traffic violations, Brendan had sensed Frank's disapproval of him and believed that the less time they spent together the better it was for both of them. He had been twenty-three when he'd finished college and returned to the country of his birth. He had instantly fallen in love with the huge city, happy to lose himself among its noise and confusion. His love of books had led to him taking a degree in literature, which his mother only agreed to fund on the promise that he would get a job as an English teacher when he'd finished. But Brendan knew even back then that he could not see himself discussing his beloved books with spotty teenagers who couldn't care less about the work of Joyce or Wilde. Instead, he had found work labouring on building sites for an older Irish man, Colm Mooney, who taught him everything he needed to know about carpentry. Brendan hadn't ever realised that he could work with his hands and he really enjoyed it. At Colm's insistence, he went to night classes to complete his carpentry qualification. He loved the solitude the job offered while he worked alongside others, rarely speaking but listening to the banter among his workmates. He knew that when he wasn't around they would talk about how odd he was but he didn't care. The city offered him a life which was the opposite of the one he had known living above his mother's grocery shop in a small hamlet outside Mullingar. The old-fashioned store had been left to his mother from a maiden aunt he did not remember and sold basic provisions to the small population of the dying midlands village.

Brendan had been a dreamer as a boy and spent lonely hours sitting alone in a field at the side of their shop, reading the adventures of Tom Sawyer or Huckleberry Finn. When his mother was annoyed at him, which was very often, he would climb over the wire fence and run as fast as his legs could take him to the other side of the field where he would lie down in the grass and escape from her disapproving eyes and her tight, angry mouth. He was not allowed to roam the countryside during the long summer like other village children were. His mother always wanted to keep him where she could see him. When lunch was ready she would close the shop and open the back door for him to come in. She rarely called him. In fact, she rarely spoke to him at all and he had grown up under the weight of her oppressive silence. He knew that this was the reason he could not bear the quiet and he kept a radio on in his apartment all the time. In those years he often lost himself inside those adventure stories and imagined himself wandering the expansive prairies during the day and then returning home to a mother who told stories and hugged him at bedtime. He had not known his father, but had never given much thought to the man who had separated from his mother shortly before his birth in America.

Brendan glanced at Eileen who, as usual, had said little since they'd left the house. From Blackwell they had turned right onto Mercer Street and had walked several blocks downhill before turning right again onto Locust and then onto Oak. When they finally turned left onto Maple Street, Brendan felt like he was in a scene from the movie *Groundhog Day*. Each day he would try to walk Eileen all the way to the shelter as per his uncle's strict instructions but each day she would quietly refuse. She would stop about a block from her destination and thank him for walking her there, following which she would look at her shoes and wait patiently for him to turn and walk away. On the second day, he had walked behind her for a few paces but she stopped moving and leaned against the wall, staring out at nothing in particular until he gave up and walked away. Each day he had returned to his uncle's house and lied to him, telling Frank he had walked Eileen up the path and had waited for her to go inside the house before turning around. Yesterday he had promised himself that today he would walk her all the way no matter how much she refused. For now, he had nowhere else to live and he couldn't afford to get on the wrong side of his uncle.

Eileen tilted her slim back into the garden wall of a house and looked at the ground. He could see her swallow hard, as if she instinctively knew this was the day he would insist on following her father's instructions. He saw her chest rise as she took a deep breath in.

He sighed heavily and said, "Look, Eileen . . ."

He thought he saw her chin tremble and he cowered a little. Oh God, please don't cry, he thought to himself.

"It's just a few more steps –" he started but she turned to face him and he could see tears in her eyes. "Jesus!" he said aloud as he looked away from her. "Why . . . why do you . . . why can't I?"

Heavy tears had begun to roll down her narrow face. He wondered how often this scene had occurred between his cousin and her father and if it occurred on this very spot. He looked at her and peered down the street. On each side, mature oak trees shaded it and large, well-manicured gardens led up to well-maintained clapboard houses. It was a good neighbourhood where he felt nothing could really happen to her. He briefly wondered if his retired cop uncle was being over-protective of Eileen. He relaxed a little and nodded.

"Okay . . . but . . . if Uncle . . ."

"I'll tell him you walked me to the door," she said flatly, recovering so suddenly from her tears that he wondered if they had been real.

Brendan watched as Eileen walked away. He stood for a moment until she sensed him watching her and turned to look at him. Her eyes were now dry and her face wore its usual serious expression. He looked at her for a moment longer and knew that there was more to his shy cousin than she pretended. He turned and walked back towards the house, wondering what it was that she was hiding and also wondering what work Uncle Frank had in store for him that day. Whatever it was, he knew he'd spend the time thinking how to get himself out of his job baby-sitting his cousin and back to his life in the city he used to call home.

Frank Dalton's house on Watson Drive was one of the few remaining old houses in Dover. It was an old two-storey clapboard that was in a state of complete disrepair when he bought it over forty years before. Over the years he had restored the house to its former glory. It was a labour of love, with Frank doing as much of the work as he could, only paying contractors whenever he could afford them or for work he could not do himself. He had almost driven his Irish-American wife Coleen to distraction in the process, spending much of their paltry savings and putting off starting a family until the house was suitable to bring a baby home to. Coleen had been born in the town and had met Frank while he was a young policeman in New York. As soon as they married, he secured a transfer to the Dover police force in the hope that they could raise a family in a safer environment.

Frank's then-teenage sister, Patricia, who had come to America with him, moved to Dover with them at his insistence. He had promised his mother he would look out for his wayward sister and couldn't do that if she remained in New York. Frank now realised he had been a fool to think that he could control his sibling. As soon as they'd arrived in Dover she rebelled against him at every opportunity, including mixing with people he did not approve of. He had been lucky to spot the same traits in his eldest daughter early and was thankful that she was now living under his watchful eye where she could come to no harm. His other daughters had turned out well. They had all married good men, hardworking lads with Irish backgrounds. But Eileen was different. She needed to be protected from herself.

It was too late for his sister. He had tried his best to control her but before he could pack her back off to Ireland, she was four months pregnant, secretly married to Brendan's useless, waste-of-oxygen-on-this-earth father and had run off to New York with him. Patricia's elopement did not last long though and she had returned to Dover, shaken and penniless and about to give birth, the child's father nowhere to be seen. He could see the same character in the boy, the careless attitude, the living of life without purpose or plan. It didn't help that the lad looked just like his father. He felt that he could never tell what was going on behind Brendan's dark eyes.

Frank had only seen the boy once during his childhood, when he returned to Ireland for his mother's funeral. He had stayed with his sister and the boy for a week during which Brendan hardly spoke to him and spent his time sitting in his room or in the field beside the shop, reading books when he should have been playing football with his friends. His sister had changed too. No more was she the boisterous, defiant woman he had so often fought with. She now rarely spoke except to bark at the boy for making noise. It had worried him for months after his return to America and he had even considered asking Patricia if Brendan could come to live with him – but by then he had his own growing family to worry about and he had put his concerns to the back of his mind. Now he could see he had made a mistake. His nephew was as silent as a mute, yet seemed unable to bear the quiet and kept the radio on so loud Frank could hear it from his bedroom when he tried to sleep at night. He had hoped that his nephew's forced return to Dover might bring them closer but, now that the lad was here, he doubted that would ever happen.

As he weeded his front lawn, he could see Brendan coming up the street. He cringed as he watched him walk with the same swagger his father had all those years before, the strut of someone with too much time on their hands.

He hoped none of his neighbours could see his nephew and rose to his feet as quickly as his hip replacement would allow.

"Brendan, come on for Christ's sake, move it! You drop Eileen off okay?"

Brendan nodded.

"To the door? Like I said?"

"Yes, sir."

"She do any of her whinging? Like asking you to let her walk on alone?"

"No, sir."

Frank looked into Brendan's eyes. He didn't believe that Eileen hadn't started any of her nonsense on him. His work as a police officer for forty years meant he could always tell when he was being lied to, but he could see nothing in his nephew's dark pools.

"Okay, get the lawnmower out. There's work to be done around here."

Chapter 2

When Brendan woke at ten, it was with the realisation that he had dreamt all night about his mother and, upon waking, he could not get her out of his mind. In the years since he had come to America, he had not contacted her often. At Christmas he would send her a card and on her birthday, which was the day before his own, he would phone her and engage in an awkward ten-minute phone conversation during which they would discuss the weather, his work, whether he'd managed to find a teaching job yet and if he was going to Mass regularly. He would dutifully tell her what he felt she wanted to hear and cringe for the last two or three minutes of the phone call where neither of them knew what to say.

This morning he found himself worrying if she was okay and he couldn't understand why. He briefly wondered if seeing how Frank bullied Eileen made him wonder if his uncle had also bullied his mother when she was younger. The similarities between the two women amazed him, except his mother had often been cruel to him and, as far as he could see, Eileen was a gentle person who could do with standing up for herself more often. He couldn't imagine his mother being easily bullied yet the thought now weighed heavily on his mind. He remembered an argument between her and Frank when he came to Ireland for their mother's funeral and how uneasy she had been during his visit. Until Frank arrived, Brendan, who was seven at the time, hadn't even known that he had a grandmother or that she lived a mere fifty miles from their shop in a town they had visited often.

One evening, Frank had arrived back at the shop wearing a dark suit and a black armband on his left arm. He'd climbed the stairs and called Brendan out of the kitchen onto the narrow landing. Frank went inside to where Brendan's mother sat and shut the kitchen door, leaving Brendan on the other side.

Brendan heard his uncle shouting at his mother. He leaned his ear against the door and waited for her voice but in the few minutes that passed he could only hear his uncle bellow that because his mother had not attended the funeral, she had disgraced him in front of the whole town. Before Frank had finished yelling, he heard his mother clear her throat. He thought that his acerbic mother would snap back at her brother but instead she spoke so quietly that he had to strain his ear further into the door to hear her voice above his uncle's.

"You expected me to go? After all that happened when I came home! Her being dead doesn't change the fact that neither I nor my son was welcome there."

Brendan moved back from the door, the shock of her words making his heart beat so fast he was afraid they could hear it on the other side. He squeezed his eyes shut, trying to understand what she was saying. Why wasn't he welcome at his grandmother's? What was wrong with him?

He moved to the door again and thought he heard her crying which seemed to soften his uncle for a while.

"Well, it's your own fault. If you weren't such a –"

"A *what*?" he heard his mother ask sharply, her voice louder now than before.

"So . . . so goddamn headstrong! Always shouting about what *you* want. You've never listened to anyone else. Never cared what others thought. You've always been the same."

He could hear his uncle's heavy footsteps moving towards the door but before he could react, Frank yanked it open so unexpectedly that Brendan fell into the room and landed at his mother's feet, bruising his hands on the rough wooden floor. His uncle pushed by him and went into their tiny sitting room on the other side of the tiny landing, slamming the door behind him. Brendan looked up at his mother and gave her an appreciative smile for standing up for him, even if it was with relatives he didn't know existed, but his happiness was short-lived. She leant down and slapped the backs of his legs hard and walked down the stairs to her shop where she remained until Frank went to bed.

Brendan tried again to shake his mother from his mind. He had not thought about that argument between her and Uncle Frank for a long time, yet he could remember every little detail of what they said. When Frank said his mother was always shouting it had puzzled him at the time. He had rarely heard her raise her voice. He rarely heard her speak. Even when customers came into the shop, she would nod and say the odd word but he could not imagine his mother the way that her brother had described her. Neither had he ever found out why he wasn't welcome at his grandmother's but he had pushed this from his mind and tried to forget about it.

He turned over in the bed and thought about the events of the previous evening, wondering if they had triggered the depressing memories that had surfaced this morning. He groaned as he tried to find a comfortable position. He hadn't done manual work for weeks before arriving in Dover and his back ached from the hours of weeding his uncle had asked him to do the day before. When it was over and he was leaving to walk Eileen home, Frank offered him fifty dollars but for some reason Brendan refused payment even though he could have done with the money. He wondered if it was because he felt guilty for lying to his uncle about Eileen.

The previous evening over dinner, Frank had chatted with Coleen about the day's work and then the couple talked at length about their early years at the house and how they had enjoyed planting the saplings that were now mature trees, shading the garden during summer and blocking off the north wind that swept up along the side of the house during winter.

Even though Frank's wife was nice to Brendan, he felt she tried to mother him which, for reasons he could not fathom, made him feel like screaming out loud. Often he would find her looking at him with an expression of sympathy and she would startle him by hugging him for no reason as she passed.

When the conversation died down, Frank looked directly at Eileen, who like Brendan rarely spoke during dinner, and asked her if Brendan had walked her all the way to the house. His question took Brendan by surprise especially as he had already answered it earlier that day. Brendan felt his throat constrict as he watched his nervous cousin put her dessertspoon down while she prepared her answer. His heart began to beat loudly as he wondered what Frank would do if he found out he had lied to him.

His shy cousin slowly raised her eyes upwards to meet her father's and confirmed that Brendan had indeed insisted on walking her to the door. She had even managed to fake an annoyed inflection in her voice which seemed to please her father. What was even more clever was the fact his cousin hadn't actually lied to her father. Brendan *had* insisted on walking her to the door but had given in to her protests and let her go on alone. His uncle hadn't even noticed this prevarication. When the conversation moved on to another subject, Brendan, who was seated beside her, could see Eileen's hands shaking on her lap. He watched as she clasped them together in an attempt to stop the tremor and then, deciding that it was useless, excused herself and retired to her room where she spent most of her evenings.

As he reflected on the previous evening, Brendan found himself getting annoyed about the effect his uncle had on his cousin. Eileen was a grown woman so why was she so afraid of her father? Why didn't she just leave? He got up and turned the radio on, then started to make a pot of coffee. He knew that until a few years back Coleen's mother used to live in the apartment until she had to go into a retirement home and that she had since died. He looked at the small cooker and wondered if the old lady cooked her own food here as he would prefer to do. Coleen insisted that he came inside for all of his meals. His knew it was useless to say no as she would badger him with her warm smile and friendly eyes until he accepted. Twice a day he would go into the kitchen, for lunch and dinner. He preferred to be alone so after dinner every evening he would make his excuses and retire to the apartment where he would read until the small hours of the morning, keeping the radio on to drown out the silence.

Brendan sat down on a small armchair and read until it was time to walk Eileen to Maple Street. He walked to the kitchen door and found Coleen alone in the kitchen, washing dishes. Before she could ask he told her that he'd already eaten even though he hadn't. He could never eat in the morning.

"Uncle Frank up?" he asked, even though he didn't particularly want his uncle's company.

"Yes, honey. You want me to call him?"

Brendan shook his head.

"Coleen?"

"Hmmm?"

"Was my mother . . . em . . . talkative . . . or you know . . . argumentative?"

His aunt turned from the sink and faced him for a moment, a rare serious expression washing over her face. She shrugged her shoulders and masked a smile.

"Your mom!" she said in her high-pitched voice. "She never stopped talking! Oh boy, you should have known Patricia when she was a teenager – your mom was quite the tiger! Oh, the rows in this house!" Shaking her head, she returned to her dishes.

Brendan leant against the patio door and watched his aunt. She looked nervous. What she said didn't add up. The Patricia he knew rarely spoke, let alone shout. What had happened to his mother?

"So what happened? Why is she so different now?" he asked.

The serious expression returned to Coleen's flawless face. She pushed back a bang of chestnut-brown hair from her deep-set blue eyes and smiled nervously at him. Despite her years Frank's wife was still an attractive woman. She had a slim figure and wore more fashionable clothes than her eldest daughter.

"I haven't seen your mother in . . . well . . . since she left here with you. Eileen was a toddler and I was expecting Orla. It's more than thirty years now but Frank says . . ."

She stopped talking and seemed to choose her next words carefully.

"Well, honey, people change," she said slowly. "Sooner or later, we all get sense, don't we?"

Coleen shook the soap bubbles from her hands, drying them with a small kitchen towel for longer than she needed to. Brendan saw her glance out the kitchen door and down the hallway. He followed her eyes and found that Frank was standing at the bottom of the stairs, looking at him.

Eileen came down the stairs past her father and stood in the hallway, putting on her coat, her eyes as usual downcast. Brendan knew his conversation with Coleen was over. He walked down the hallway past his gruff uncle and opened the front door. Then he beckoned for Eileen to exit ahead of him. She was again dressed in the same old-fashioned clothes and carried the same heavy bag.

"You give any thought to your community service?" Frank shouted after him but he pretended not to hear and kept walking.

As they made their way to the end of their road and turned the corner onto Blackwell Street, Brendan tried to make conversation with Eileen. At the very least he hoped he would find out what hold her father had over her.

"Thanks for not dropping me in it with Uncle Frank last night."

"Okay," she replied curtly as she turned her face as far away from him as she could.

"I have to say, I was worried for a while but the way you got around that question . . ."

When she did not respond, Brendan coughed nervously. He tried to think of something to say as they made their way silently through several small side-streets off the town's main boulevard.

"I . . . I noticed you seemed very nervous when your father asked about me," he finally added.

Eileen looked down at her shoes and swallowed.

He could feel her tense up as she quickened her pace until they reached the spot where they parted.

"Thanks for walking me," she said as she left him.

"I'll see you at six!" he shouted after her but she was already out of earshot or pretended to be. Brendan watched her until she was out of sight.

He turned around and sighed, wondering what his uncle had in store for him today.

Chapter 3

A week passed and Brendan had not got any closer to finding out why Eileen was so fearful of her father nor had he found or even looked for somewhere to do his community service, which sent his uncle into a rage whenever the subject came up. He wanted to tell his uncle that walking Eileen alone should be considered reparation for his driving offences but he didn't have the nerve to say it and he didn't want to hurt his cousin who seemed a lonely soul. He thought about how Frank's other daughters behaved around him when they visited. They all seemed to love the old man and he watched as Eileen seethed in their company. Brendan didn't enjoy their visits any more than she seemed to. Eileen's sisters were, like their mother, loud and constantly cheerful in that all-American way.

A breakthrough came one morning when, during their silent walk to the homeless shelter, the strap on his cousin's heavy canvas bag finally gave way under the weight of its mysterious contents, strewing about ten books onto the pavement on Blackwell Street. Brendan quickly bent down to help her pick them up but she pushed his hands away and began to shove the books into the bag. Despite her protests, he lifted some of them and quickly scanned their titles before placing them in the bag.

He was impressed to see the works of Irish authors Kavanagh and Ó'Faoláin as well as the great American writers Steinbeck, Hemmingway and Fitzgerald among her collection. He could see her hands shake as she lifted the remaining books, looking around as she did so to see who was watching. He briefly wondered if his cousin might be mentally ill and wondered, if that was so, why nobody would have told him.

When the last book was safely packed away, Eileen stood and lifted the bag, hugging it tightly to her chest. He stood silently and watched her as she looked nervously at him.

"You won't tell Dad?" she asked frantically.

He could see that she was terrified. "That you're carrying a small library around with you?" he joked.

He smiled at her but her odd behaviour made him feel nervous. He was now sure that there was something wrong with his cousin. A silence fell between them until she looked up at him with her pale grey eyes as though she was weighing him up, wondering if she could trust him fully. When he thrust his hands forward and offered to carry the heavy load, she cowered back at first and held her beloved books even closer before slowly relinquishing her treasure to her cousin.

"Dad says reading is a waste of time. I carry them with me because he goes through my things. He doesn't want me . . . getting any ideas."

"He won't let you have books?" Brendan asked, astounded.

Eileen blushed. "Not just books. Friends . . . a job . . . or . . . boyfriends," she said, blushing even more. "He only allows my volunteer work because Father Guinan organised it at the church."

Brendan ran his hands through his thick black hair, unsure what to say.

"I love to read," was the only response he could think of. "It stops you . . . from feeling lonely." He was astonished at the words leaving his mouth. He hadn't even known he'd felt that way.

Eileen nodded and smiled shyly up at him, revealing two deep dimples he had never noticed before.

18

For the rest of the journey she talked shyly about the books she had read, books of poetry, adventure and travel. He wanted to ask her why her father dominated her so when her sisters were living full lives outside of his control but, as he watched his cousin's face light up when she spoke of the Irish writers she grew up reading, he became mesmerised by her enthusiasm for something he also shared a passion for. Brendan told her of the days he spent as a lonely child, losing himself in Twain and Stevenson and how on Fridays after school he was usually the only child waiting on the main street in the rain for the mobile library to drive through his tiny village, hoping to find a book that would while away the lonely weekend that stretched out before him. He astounded himself by telling her that throughout his boyhood he lived in the comfort of the imaginary, but stopped short of disclosing that he did not entirely grow out of his obsession with stories of improbable worlds and fanciful places.

Brendan enjoyed the conversation so much that he was surprised when she stopped dead at the very spot he usually left her and was disappointed that their conversation was now over. He had never told anyone about his lonely childhood before and felt lighter for having shared his misery with another person. He stared after his cousin as she walked on alone in the direction of the homeless shelter.

When Brendan arrived at the house, Frank was waiting for him to accompany him to an appointment at the hospital. The heart attack he'd had two years previously had revealed a serious heart defect and, with the heart surgery he'd had and his hip replacement, he could no longer drive and even had to retire slightly earlier than he would have liked. Frank moaned about how Brendan's lack of a driving licence meant he would have to leave his car in the driveway and fork out for taxis.

Brendan helped Frank into the back seat of the cab and sat beside him.

"Drink driving!" Frank snorted as the driver looked at them through his rear-view mirror. "Goddamn stupid behaviour! I'd expect that from a teenager – but you! Thirty-five years old! Goddamn idiot!" He was shouting by this time but was unaware of it. The new hearing aid Coleen had bought him was sitting in its packaging in the living room where, as he loudly announced one evening, it would stay.

Brendan remained silent and ignored the comments about his lack of maturity. Coleen, who did not drive, had sensibly made an excuse that she had a friend calling over to see her so couldn't accompany her husband. Brendan wondered how his aunt had stayed married to his grumpy uncle but deep down he knew that they were happy together and that Coleen had learnt how to manage her cantankerous husband over their long marriage.

As they made their way to the hospital on the outskirts of town, they passed a small Hispanic restaurant on the corner where two dishevelled men stood, drinking beer.

"Bloody wasters!" Frank said a little too loudly. "No good nor ever will be."

Brendan cringed and hoped the men, who had not looked up, had not heard his uncle through the open car window. He wondered how a cop, who would have spent his years working with the entire Dover population, a high proportion of which were Hispanics, could be racist.

"Uncle Frank!" he said, immediately regretting his involuntarily outburst. He pressed his back into the leather car seat and ran his finger over his mole nervously.

Frank studied his nephew's expression of discomfort and looked Brendan up and down. His eyes fixed on the tattoo on his upper right arm. The huge tattoo had two skulls engulfed in flames inside an intricate Celtic knot. He shook his head disapprovingly at Brendan. "My own blood," was all he said as the taxi turned slowly into the hospital grounds.

Within days of their conversation about books, Brendan found Eileen would talk for the entire journey to the shelter, mostly about books that she'd enjoyed or those she had yet to read. Brendan found himself walking slower now in her company as he relished their short time together each day. He had never had any siblings and, while he'd never thought about this very much, he was now enjoying the company of his cousin.

The cousins were becoming closer but they instinctively knew to keep this from Frank who would only trust Brendan to walk Eileen each day if he was sure she would not get around him. One evening over dinner, when Frank complained about the infiltration of academics into the White House and how what they really needed was politicians who'd put their shoulders to the wheel and get the job done, an exchange occurred between the cousins, a secret smile which they hoped he would not notice.

As Brendan walked Eileen the following morning, their conversation on modern poetry slowed as they approached Oak Street.

"I guess you're wondering why I won't let you walk me the whole way?" she asked, changing the subject abruptly and startling Brendan.

He shook his head and was about to say no when she put up her tiny hand to stop him.

"It's okay. I know it's strange," she said.

She looked at her shoes and exhaled, trying to find the right words to explain her strange behaviour.

"It's because it's mine. It's the only thing I've got that is mine alone. Do you understand?"

Brendan didn't answer. He had no idea what it was like to be Eileen and didn't want to pretend that he did. He looked down at her in her oversized coat and her new bag whose contents were, as usual, weighing down heavily on her narrow shoulder. Every morning since her books had fallen onto the main street, he offered to carry her bag but she always refused.

He waited, expecting her to say more.

"Each morning before I go to the shelter, I help mother around *her* house. When my sisters visit, I look after *their* children, cook for *their* husbands. Nothing is mine except these few hours a day when I am just Eileen Dalton, volunteer. I like to keep it . . . to keep it away from there, from them. Do you know what I mean?"

Brendan nodded. He understood, or at least he was trying to.

He cleared his throat. There was something else about his cousin that until recently he had no interest in knowing.

"Why . . . why does Frank stop you from living your life as you want? I mean . . . Orla said . . . I heard something happened in college. Do you . . . want to talk about it?"

Brendan looked at his cousin who had turned bright red.

She bit down on her lip and tried to stop her chin from trembling. "That was a long time ago . . . Orla shouldn't have . . ."

Brendan stopped walking and faced Eileen. His cousin looked as though she was going to cry.

"I'm sorry," he said. "Forget I said anything. I didn't mean to . . ."

Eileen pulled her heavy bag up higher onto her shoulder and folded her arms around her body, but made no response.

As they walked on he lured her back into their conversation about literature and, while she brightened some, Brendan could see in her eyes that he had aroused painful memories.

When she slowed her pace as they arrived at their separation point, she looked up at him with her shy expression and bit down on her lip.

"You can walk me a bit further if you like."

Brendan tried not to show his surprise and just kept walking, commenting on their surroundings as they went.

From fifty yards back, Eileen stopped and pointed at a large white clapboard house on the opposite side of the road.

"That's the Domus Shelter." Then she added nervously, "You can leave me here now."

Brendan gazed at what he thought was the most beautiful house he had ever seen. He walked towards the house, ignoring his cousin's pleas for him to leave.

"That's close enough!" Eileen said but he couldn't hear her and crossed the road for a better look.

Standing at the steep verge that led up to the lawn, Brendan stared, mesmerised by the beauty of the old house. It was not the worn-down, official-looking building he had expected. The three-storey white clapboard house was surrounded by a small white picket fence and stood on a large site that swept steeply up from the road. Five wooden steps with a white wooden railing on either side led to a pretty white veranda that wrapped around the house, running down both sides. In the garden to the left, a wooden swing rocked gently in the wind. Two huge bay windows were partly shaded by two mature oak trees that stood in the middle of the expansive garden. Upstairs, three dormer windows were evenly spaced. The third floor – the attic presumably – had only one window, a round one that sat neatly in the middle of the red tiled roof.

Brendan stood open-mouthed as he took in the house and its magnificent grounds.

"It's beautiful!" he said to Eileen who stood stone-faced beside him. He looked to the right of the house and saw a row of apple trees that ran right through to the back of the site. Beneath them stood a tall white man and a small, overweight black woman.

Brendan looked at his cousin, waiting for her to tell him who the two people were.

"That's Alice Turner, the manager," Eileen offered quickly. She looked at her feet and swallowed.

Brendan looked from the woman to the man who was walking around the trees with a clipboard in his hands. He was studying the apple blossoms and writing notes furiously as the manager walked slowly behind him. What Brendan noticed most about the man was his clothes. Over a white collarless shirt, he wore an old-fashioned sleeveless jumper with beige and orange diamond shapes down its front, and dark brown trousers tucked into a pair of boots that from a distance looked like wellies. The strange man looked like he had jumped right out of the 1940's. His haircut also caught Brendan's attention – he had a shock of foppish blond hair, cut neatly around the ears. He was wearing rimless glasses.

"Who is that?" Brendan asked, fascinated by the unusual man.

"That's John Doe," she replied although she kept her eyes to the ground.

"John Doe? Like a – like an unidentified corpse?"

He started to laugh but stopped when his cousin raised her small face to look at the man. He suddenly sensed that she was upset and didn't want to hurt her any more than he had already done today.

He removed the smile from his face and adopted a more serious tone. "I mean . . . seriously . . . that's the man's name?" he asked.

An expression of sadness washed over his cousin's pale face.

"Nobody knows who he is. He likes to be called Jonathan," she replied, raising herself on her toes and rocking her body forward, as though to reach out to the man.

There was something in her expression that Brendan couldn't quite read.

He was startled when he heard the man suddenly call Eileen's name loudly. She smiled anxiously towards Brendan. He could see John Doe squinting through his glasses and grinning at his cousin like a Cheshire cat. Brendan looked from Eileen to John and suddenly realised that this man was probably the reason she came here each day. He would also bet that John Doe waited at that exact spot each morning, which was the reason she didn't want anyone walking her the whole way. He opened his mouth but the words would not come out as he intended them to.

"Is he . . . are you . . . ?"

Brendan changed his mind about asking her about her relationship with the man when she began to blush. He had probed too much today and it was none of his business anyway.

He was both amused and intrigued by the man's identity or lack thereof.

"Can't he tell someone who he is?" he asked, realising how stupid his question was as soon as he'd said it.

"He doesn't know . . . for sure. Well, he thinks . . . it's . . . it's a long story," she replied, looking away from John and returning her gaze to her feet to hide the redness that had flamed up her neck and rested on her cheeks.

Eileen walked up the drive and across the lawn to where the pair stood smiling at her in welcome.

Brendan took one more look at the man who was now pointing at the trees and involving Eileen in his conversation with Alice.

"How can someone not know who they are?" he asked himself aloud as he walked away.

Chapter 4

Two days after Brendan had walked Eileen all the way to the shelter, he found himself at the picket fence of the house in the evening, waiting for her to finish. He had stopped at their usual spot but, when she did not appear, he walked down to the house and waited for her to come out. At ten past six there was still no sign of her. He wondered if he should knock at the door but was afraid that she would be annoyed with him for intruding on what she had said was her place.

He worried that something had happened to her and felt guilty that what concerned him more was what his uncle would say to him if it had.

At half six he could not wait any longer and found himself walking up the driveway and tapping nervously on the door. No one answered and he was about to knock harder when he heard a voice behind him. It reminded him of the voices he had heard when he saw *Gone with the Wind* in the local picture house as a child. It sounded like a Southern accent. Melodious, old-fashioned, a voice from the past.

"There's a bell on the side. It rings loud in the kitchen so they'll hear you," the voice said.

Brendan turned to find John Doe standing behind him. He

looked into his pale blue eyes and noticed that close up John looked older than he imagined he would be. His blond hair was slightly greying at the temples and deep lines, accentuated by his broad smile, ran from his eyes to his hairline in even rows. On the right side of his face, a long narrow scar ran from above his ear for about three inches into his hairline. Brendan could see how the cut had been unevenly sewn and caused his hair to grow in an odd, bunched-up way around the injury. He briefly wondered if John had had a brain injury. He had read an article on it once where people woke from such injuries with no memory of who they were. Before Brendan could reply, the smile on John's face faded and was replaced by an expression of utter fear.

John jumped backwards, falling down the wooden steps and into a small bush at the side of the porch. He sat up quickly and tried to push himself backwards with his hands as though to move further away from Brendan.

"*¿Cómo . . . cómo me encontró? No dije nada. Lo juro. De verdad. No me haga daño.*"

Brendan moved forward to try to help John up but he shrank back and continued to whimper in what sounded like Spanish.

Brendan put his hand down to John to help him up. His heart was thumping loudly at the man's behaviour but, when John began to emit a loud scream, he backed off and ran up the steps, pressing the bell frantically and banging on the door. No one answered so he ran to one of the bay windows, banging on its large pane of glass and shouting for someone to come. Two passers-by stopped and watched, one of whom began to take a mobile phone from his pocket, presumably to phone the police, forcing Brendan to return to the man to try to calm him down. He reached forward and tried to grab his hand to get him to his feet.

"Look, man. Cool it!" Brendan said. "I'm just here to pick someone up. You've got me mistaken for someone else."

But John continued shouting and whimpering in Spanish.

Brendan didn't speak the language but it sounded as if he was

27

pleading for his life. Brendan had raised his hands to the onlookers to assure them he wasn't hurting John when the door opened and Alice, the manager, stood staring at the scene before her.

"What did you do to him?" she asked. She roared into the house, "Eileen, ring the police!" which brought his cousin running down the long hallway.

Eileen stood open-mouthed while Brendan tried to tell her what happened.

"This is Brendan?" Alice asked incredulously. She looked closely at Brendan and began to nod slowly as she tried to get John, who was still whimpering in Spanish, off the ground.

She stood him up and took his face gently in her large, fat hands. "John, this man is not going to hurt you. This man is here for Eileen. Okay?"

Alice's words seemed to alarm John even more and he began to wave his hands, shouting again in Spanish.

"*Va a hacerle daño a Eileen. Va a herir a mi amada para hacerme pagar.*"

Eileen went to him and visibly shook as she smoothed his hair down. She kissed him lightly on the cheek.

"It's okay, love," she said, but he did not calm down and continued to shout.

"Get Pilar," Alice ordered and Eileen hurried away, disappearing down the long hallway and out of view.

Within seconds a pretty Latina arrived at the door. Despite the furore, Brendan instantly noticed how beautiful she was and the gentle aura that emanated from her. She was small, about Eileen's height, with dark, shiny, waist-length hair, tied loosely back. She had deep brown eyes and dark brown skin that shone in the spring evening light. She gently placed her forearms over John's and spoke to him in Spanish. Brendan could hear Eileen's name in the sentence, which alarmed him. He wondered if it was a good idea for his cousin to have feelings for this man who was obviously disturbed. He looked at the Hispanic woman, hoping she'd translate.

"He thinks you have come to hurt Eileen, to punish him," she said.

She spoke again to John and he looked at Brendan sideways, as though he was still not convinced. He seemed to calm a little then and Pilar led him into the house. Alice followed close behind, leaving Eileen and Brendan at the doorstep.

Sweat had begun to run like a torrent down Brendan's back and had formed in large beads on his forehead. He had never met anyone like this man before and the incident had shaken him. Eileen's eyes settled onto her cousin's face. He knew she was worried now that he would tell her father about why she came here each day. Brendan looked away from her painful gaze, wondering what he should do.

"Come in," she said quietly.

Brendan followed his cousin inside. He glanced quickly into the two large bay-windowed rooms on either side of the impressive hallway and noticed that they were empty. A large wooden staircase stood in the centre of the hallway, the steps of which looked like they were made of marble. Despite the incident, Brendan took a few steps forward and touched them, the stone-cold feel on his finger tips confirming his suspicions. He touched the intricate railings of the stairway, impressed by the workmanship. Eileen veered to the right of the stairwell and he followed her down a smaller hallway which led towards the back of the house. He glanced quickly into the rooms they passed and saw that each was sparsely furnished with an old single bed and battered bedside locker.

"Those are some of the bedrooms," said Eileen. "They're in a complete state of disrepair. The heating doesn't work properly here so we only use the ground-floor rooms for the older clients who can't use the stairs. The house is the exact same on the other side. The large dorms, they're upstairs . . . and then . . . Jonathan . . . Jonathan sleeps in the attic." She lowered her face, raising her eyes slowly up to meet his.

A door at the end of the hallway led into a corridor that ran across the back of the house.

Eileen opened a door facing them. It led into a dining area. Five large round wooden tables, each with about eight chairs, were placed around the brightly painted room. Two large plain windows faced out onto the back garden, revealing a mixture of large oaks and young apple trees full of white blossoms. From the left of the dining room he could hear the banging of pots and pans and could smell food being cooked in what he assumed was the kitchen.

"That's the laundry," said Eileen, indicating a door to the right of the dining room. "That's mostly where I am all day, washing and drying the sheets. Sometimes cooking in the kitchen, whatever Alice asks me to do."

"Where is . . . are the homeless people?" he asked. Save for the noise from the kitchen, the house was eerily quiet.

"They come back from seven onwards. Have dinner and a bed for the night. Next morning, they eat and leave for the day. Except Jonathan. He stays here."

She sounded nervous. He could tell she had no interest in making small talk with him. She wanted to know what her cousin was going to do.

Eileen made them both a coffee and they sat down at one of the wooden tables. Her hands shook as they wrapped around her steaming cup.

"Sometimes . . ." she said hesitantly, "sometimes, when there is no work to do I sit with Jonathan outside. Sometimes we go to the library or to the bookshop or sit in the park by the river and talk."

She looked up at him and there was an expression of pleading in her eyes.

"We talk about books and our lives . . . his life before he came here. Sometimes he might hold my hand . . . or he might kiss my cheek . . . and that's all, Brendan. That's all there ever will be. He is stuck here and I . . . I am stuck with my father. I . . . I need Jonathan . . . because . . . because he understands."

Hot tears welled in her eyes and she looked away from him. She moved her gaze to the garden where she had experienced so much happiness since John Doe came to the shelter over fifteen years ago and she had fallen in love with him. It had been her secret. Until now. She knew that when her father found out, she would be taken from here for fear she would make the same mistakes she had made in college. Mistakes that to her, even now, did not seem like they were so very bad. She remained silent and waited for Brendan to speak.

He looked out the window at the empty swing that twirled around in the spring breeze, and thought about how lonely it looked swinging around there on its own.

"I won't tell," he said resignedly.

Eileen raised her hands to her face and sobbed into her closed fingers. Brendan reached out and touched her hand but dropped it when a large lump formed in his throat. He stood quickly and turned away from her in case she saw that he was overcome by her sadness, her desperation.

When she had recovered her composure he walked her to the front door and this time took her huge bag from her, slinging it easily over his broad shoulder.

As he opened the front door, he heard a voice calling him.

"Brendan!"

He turned to find Alice rushing down the hallway after them. He could hear the sound of pots banging so he assumed she had come from the kitchen and had left the doors open behind her.

"I'd . . . we'd like you to come back and visit. Would you do that?" she asked.

He turned to look at his cousin. He wanted to say no. What reason would he have to visit there? But Eileen's mouth was smiling weakly beneath her teary eyes.

"I think it would be good for Jonathan," she said.

He shrugged and wondered why she'd think he'd care what was good for John Doe. The man was obviously very disturbed.

"I'll think about it," he said and ushered Eileen out, closing the door gently behind them.

On the way home, Brendan tried to raise his concerns about her feelings for such a troubled man but, when she looked up at him, her expression was so innocent, so childlike, that he couldn't go through with it. Instead, he asked her why John Doe was so afraid of him and was disappointed when she couldn't shed any light on her friend's strange behaviour, except to say he sometimes reacted to situations like that.

When they reached the house, he excused himself at the front door and walked down the side entrance to his apartment. Knowing what he now knew, he didn't feel that he could sit at the dinner table and look his uncle in the eye.

He was worried about his cousin's infatuation with a man who could never offer her a life. His head began to hurt and for the first time in days he missed his life in New York City. At around this time most evenings he would be sitting in the pub on the ground floor of his apartment block, drinking and hopefully hooking up with one of the girls who wasn't annoyed with him for not ringing her back. They were getting fewer. And, if total abstinence hadn't been a condition of his probation, he would have found a new place to drink by now. Brendan lay on his bed and rubbed his temples to ease them from the deep throb that had settled in during the walk home.

Letting Eileen into his life had eased a loneliness that he didn't even know he'd felt until he'd come here. But it had also complicated what had been, until now, an easy existence. Until now he'd thought that they were alike, that like him Eileen found fulfilment in the pages of great prose which was dampened only by the disturbance of other people. He hadn't expected her to be so passionate about another human being and a small part of him felt deceived, cheated. As the silence settled around him, he realised that he hadn't turned on his radio. He lifted himself off the bed and, despite his headache, turned the dial up to as loud as his head could bear it.

He made himself a coffee and thought about John Doe and the fear the man had shown when he had seen him. When John had first spoken to him on the porch, his accent was definitely Southern States American and that, combined with his appearance, indicated the man was not Hispanic. He knew many white people spoke fluent Spanish but what he wondered was how, when afraid, John had retreated into it as though it was his first language. More than anything else, he wondered how a grown man did not know his own name. Surely someone knew who he was? Surely there was someone out there looking for Jonathan Doe?

Chapter 5

The following morning Brendan awoke with a hollow feeling in his stomach. He hadn't eaten any dinner the previous evening and was starving. He pulled on the crumpled pair of jeans lying at the bottom of his bed and an old pair of sneakers. He walked down the narrow pathway to the main house and peeped in through the window, hoping that no one would be there. Then he opened the patio door quietly and stepped inside. He saw that Coleen had left the usual small plate of his favourite pastries on the table. He lifted the lukewarm jug from the coffee maker and poured himself a cup before sitting down. He could see dishes piled up at the sink and knew the others had all eaten which meant he could probably enjoy his breakfast alone, the way he preferred it. Upstairs he could hear the hum of an electric shower running and hoped that no one would bother him until it was time to take Eileen to the shelter.

As he shoved the last piece of pastry into his mouth, Frank appeared at the door with Eileen close behind him.

"Oh, look what the cat brought in!" Frank said sarcastically, an obvious jibe at Brendan's failure to come inside for dinner when Coleen called him the previous evening. He had pulled a pillow over his head, ignoring her shrill cries until she gave up and left him alone.

Brendan looked away from his uncle. He had no intention of arguing with the old man. He poured himself another small coffee and stood at the counter to drink it. He didn't know why but he always felt uneasy in his aunt's kitchen and preferred to stand when others came into the room. The large space spanned the width of the house and was furnished with an antique oak dining table beside which Coleen's old wooden dresser stood wearily under the weight of her Waterford crystal collection. On the far side of the room, an odd collection of easy chairs was strewn about the large brick fireplace, giving the room an intimate ambience. It was where Frank and Coleen's family gathered during get-togethers but Brendan didn't feel like family. He felt like an imposter, someone who was pretending to fit in when it was clear that he didn't.

"You do anything about your community service? Robert Hensen phoned looking for you this morning."

Brendan frowned. "Who?"

"Your probation officer!" Frank yelled as he raised his eyes to heaven. "Brendan, listen to me. Hensen and I go back a long way. He'll cut you some slack if you get on with this. Said he'll be happy to keep in the distance, not embarrass you or me for that matter by visiting your community-service placement too often. He said if I prefer he'll drop by here and check in with me from time to time. He's gone out on a limb to keep this private, Brendan, so for Christ's sake do your bit. Bert Ingalls, he said for you to come down to help out with the kids at the community centre. Brendan, are you listening to me? Can you get this done or do I have to take you down there myself?"

"I'll do it today," Brendan answered meekly, dreading the thought of doing his community service under the watchful eye of his uncle's old police partner and bowling buddy.

When they left the house, Eileen and Brendan walked in silence, both absorbing yesterday's events, both wondering if the friendship they shared had been damaged by the previous evening's revelations.

At the shelter, John was not standing in the garden where

Brendan suspected he usually stood waiting each day. He could see Eileen raise her face slightly, looking for him on the deep-green lawn.

"See you at six," he said as he walked abruptly away.

"Brendan?" Eileen called after him.

He turned to face her, his hands dug deeply into the pockets of his worn jeans.

"Are you upset with me?" she said, sounding childlike.

He shook his head but it was true that he was. Even though he knew he was being childish, he could not shake off the feeling that Eileen had somehow betrayed him.

"Then . . . everything's alright?"

He nodded and offered her a half smile.

"See you at six," he repeated as he turned away.

Instead of calling to the community hall as he'd promised, Brendan walked to the other side of town to look in the job centres. He didn't really want to stay long enough in Dover to do his community service but knew that if he could find work in the small town, he could get a place of his own and could get out from under his uncle's feet. He knew his uncle thought that his procrastination was down to sheer laziness but the real reason he had put off starting his community work was because, as far as he could see, it would involve working with other people which was something he hated. Sartre's expression "Hell is other people" had become a sort of mantra to him over the years. He had tried the local animal shelter a couple of days after he'd first arrived in Dover and it was no surprise to him that they had more volunteers than any of the other charities in town. He had also considered cleaning up the motorways but the nearest stretch was five miles from Uncle Frank's house and he had no way of getting there without forking out for taxis he could not afford.

When he got tired of looking at adverts for jobs that he had no experience in, Brendan struggled to order a late lunch in one of the town's Mexican restaurants whose waiter insisted on speaking Spanish to him.

"*No hablo español,*" he said, which for some unknown reason sent the waiter into fits of laughter.

When Brendan left the restaurant, it was still only four o'clock, so he bought the *New York Times* and walked into the park. He moved through the regular group of dog-walkers and ball-players and found an empty bench in a popular spot beside the river. Engrossed in news from the Big Apple, he did not notice the clouds moving across the sky, blocking out the spring sunshine and releasing tiny drops of rain. Neither did he notice as park-goers ran for cover, until the weight of the quiet bore down on him. He looked up, troubled by the unexpected stillness, and focused on a woman pushing her baby in a pram through the rain. He wondered if his mother had ever brought him here. He couldn't imagine her sitting by the gazebo making small talk with other mothers but, according to Frank and Coleen, his mother was a different person then. He wondered if he would ever have the courage to ask her what had happened to change her into the bitter person she was today and had been throughout his dismal childhood.

He looked at his watch. Only an hour had passed and the Domus Shelter was only about a fifteen-minute walk from this part of town. He stood and walked slowly to the shelter where he'd wait until his cousin had finished whatever it was that she was doing there . . . he didn't like to think too much about it.

When he arrived, he stood by the neat picket fence and stared up at the magnificent house. He could see Alice standing by the door, talking to a tall, white-haired man in a sky-blue suit. She appeared to glance down towards him but continued to talk to the visitor. He watched as she pointed to various parts of the house while the man stood nodding. Brendan hoped she hadn't spotted him and sighed when she finished her conversation and waved for him to come on up the driveway. As he sauntered up the steep incline, the man drove past him in a new Mercedes which was almost the same colour as his suit. Brendan waved at the passing car, a tradition in rural Ireland that he had not grown out of. The man glanced at Brendan through the open window, his cool blue eyes taking in the stranger. He raised his hand reservedly as though he was the Queen of England and nodded at Brendan who decided to take an instant dislike to him.

Brendan glanced around the front yard nervously, hoping he wouldn't have a recurrence of yesterday's incident but John Doe was nowhere to be seen.

"*He's* friendly!" he said sarcastically to Alice, gesturing towards the departing Mercedes.

"Well, that's contractors for you!" she said in her drawling accent.

"He must be doing pretty well," Brendan added.

Alice chuckled loudly. "Lord!" she said for no apparent reason.

He glanced at her and tried to figure out her age. Close up, she had small tufts of curly grey hair about her temples but there was hardly a line on her round, smiling face. Her dark brown eyes shone with the sort of contentment he knew very few people had in life.

He looked on either side of the wooden porch to check again for John.

"Oh, don't worry! John's usually in his tower at this time of day," she laughed, glancing up at the solitary round window on the third floor.

He liked the way the woman drawled the word "tow-wer".

"Where you from?" he asked.

"Georgia originally but I've been here a long time. Most my whole life."

"You getting work done?" he asked, looking up at the windows that she had been pointing out to the visitor only moments before.

"Thinking on it. It's expensive. Costs a lot to run this house. The historical society helps us with some of the upkeep, mostly to protect what's classed as heritage, but there's plenty of ordinary things that we just don't ever have the money to pay for."

Brendan followed Alice into the house and walked gingerly into the tiled hallway. She beckoned for him to follow her up the impressive staircase to the second floor. At the top of the stairs, the door to a small room that looked out onto the back of the house stood open. He glanced inside the open door and saw a worn wooden desk and two tall filing-cabinets crammed into the tiny space.

"I only use this when I have to – I hate paperwork. Much prefer to be downstairs with the people," she said.

"These are the dorms," she added. She threw open the doors of two large rooms on either side of the landing.

Brendan followed Alice inside the one on the right. Beds covered by thin grey blankets lined both sides of the long room. Beside each bed stood a tiny wooden locker, most of which appeared to be in need of repair. Some stood on three rickety legs while others had missing doors or drawers. He looked up at the ceiling. An ornamental cornice that ran the length of the huge ceiling had been repaired at set points, revealing the room's past as several smaller rooms which were broken through when the house became a shelter. The door of the room hung badly on its hinges and there was a large hole in the wall over one of the beds.

"That was Zeb. He comes in some nights all calm and then gets crazy on us," she smiled, shaking her curly hair around her head.

"Why don't you just throw him out?"

"From a shelter? Lord, no! Zeb has his problems but nobody gets sent out of here. That was always Mr Thompson's philosophy."

She walked slowly from the room and Brendan followed.

As they descended the stairs he looked around the beautiful old house. Even though it was a little rundown upstairs, it was impressive. He ran his eyes admiringly over the crystal chandeliers in the hallway and smoothed his hands over the oak banisters. It annoyed him that someone who had come looking for help would then cause damage to such a beautiful building.

"You don't get wood like this any more," he said to himself rather than to Alice.

Then he glanced at her. "How old is the house?"

"Well over a hundred and fifty years old," she replied slowly in her Georgian twang. "It belonged to Walter Thompson. It was his home and his father's and grandfather's before him. Long history to this house." She looked about the hallway appreciatively. "I never get tired of looking round me. Even when I'm chasing my tail around, which is most of the time."

"How come he gave it to the charity?"

"Mr Thompson – that's what he made everyone call him –"

"You knew him?" Brendan interrupted.

"I had the pleasure of knowing him. I worked with him here from 1973 to 1982."

Brendan raised his thick dark eyebrows at her. "You've been here that long?"

She nodded. "Course he was an old man by the time I came here. His two sons – there's portraits of them downstairs – they lost their lives in the Second World War. He wanted to do something to make up for the waste of his sons' lives. He didn't have any other children and his wife died a long time before those boys even went to war. Anyway, he saw how some servicemen came home injured with nowhere to go or nobody to care for them. He put his money into making the house a home for them until they got on their feet again. Later, he dedicated the house to helping the homeless from all walks of life. Then . . . when I came to meet him . . ."

Brendan noticed her smile fade slightly.

"It was Vietnam." She snorted a short laugh and shook her head as if to expel a painful memory. "My fool husband always wanted to get us out of the south. As if by some miracle he'd come to another state of the US and find nobody minded the colour of his skin." She looked away and smiled again as if she was remembering him for a moment. "Well, he must have known what he was doing after all because we upped and moved to Dover. We were young and I had my first and only baby. A boy, Theo Junior. He's in New York now. An artist. I wasn't but twenty-three years old when I first came into this house. I never would've met Mr Thompson if it hadn't been for Theo's fool-headedness. Well,

Theo got drafted and before I knew it he was sending me mail from places I never even heard of. Bin Thuy and Phan Rang. Can't believe I can still remember those strange names!"

Brendan became uneasy at the personal story she was telling him. He was, after all, a stranger. He moved into one of the large bay-windowed rooms at the front of the house to look around. He knew that her story wouldn't have a happy ending and hoped she'd change the subject if he tried to distract her. She followed him and sighed.

"The men use this room?" he said, glancing around at the comfortable armchairs and large television.

"Sometimes," she replied absent-mindedly.

Brendan could see she was intent on finishing her story.

"Anyway," she continued, "my Theo never came home and I never got no more cards off him since the last one. 1972 it was. I still have it. Going to give it to my eldest grandson when I'm gone. That same year, I read in the local paper here that Mr Thompson was taking in Vietnam vets who needed a home. Not all of them were local boys – most in fact came from other places. Landed home and ended up here. Much like me. Well, I'd come down here and look for my husband among those poor men. Some had no legs, arms, some blind. Some didn't know who they were any more. So I thought, maybe he's here. Maybe my Theo remembered Dover and got himself here to look for me and our baby."

She shook her head and let out a long breath, as if the memory, despite the passing of the years, was still too painful.

"Oh, my foolishness! I looked and looked and then I got so down I let go of everything I believed in. I'd have lost my will to live if it wasn't for my child. Every so often, Mr Thompson would come out of the parlour downstairs and talk to me. He was kind and on days when I thought I could look no more, he'd phone me if any confused black men ended up on the doorstep." She laughed out loud and shook her curly hair again. "But he was just being kind because he knew Theo wasn't ever coming back. Then, after a while, I knew it too. Though they never found him. Never found my Theo's body. Probably, they said, he'd drowned on a shore with a strange name to it. But I still came here whenever I could just to talk to the men here, to find out what it was like, what life there had been like for my Theo. And you know something? I started to find love here, to find my way again. I found God here in these men, black and white. Soon I wanted to come here every day and, when Theo started school, that's what I did. Mr Thompson gave me a job looking after those men. They didn't have to wander the streets during the day like they do now. No, he cared for them around the clock until he'd spent nearly all of his inheritance doing it. I had never had a job like that before, one I loved. Mostly I worked in stores or diners before I married. Then, when Theo went to senior school, I went to college and got my social work degree. Proudest day of my life and I said Theo must've known what moving to this place would bring me. He did find me a place where colour didn't matter as much, though it hadn't mattered to me at all beforehand. I never thought about it like he did. He knew. He knew he had to leave me somewhere where I'd be okay."

Alice clasped her hands and rubbed them together. She fixed her gaze on Brendan who continued to avoid her eyes. He thumped a large wooden pillar that stood in the middle of the large living area and hoped she didn't want him to respond. He never knew what to say in these situations. While she was speaking, an idea had slowly come to him. If Alice bought the materials, he could do all of these repairs as his community service. It could be the perfect place for him to do it. Apart from John Doe, who he could keep his distance from, there wouldn't be anyone else here to bother him. Frank had a large shed full of tools that he could use so it wouldn't cost her much. He looked at Alice and noticed that she seemed to be waiting on him to say something.

"I can do all the repairs," he said, hoping that she hadn't been expecting anything remotely resembling empathy.

"Now, that's what I'd hoped you'd say," she replied, smiling once again.

"You knew I could do carpentry?"

"Mmm-hmm. Eileen told me all about her talented cousin."

Brendan grinned and wondered if Alice had told him her sad story to manipulate him into doing something to help. In fact, he wondered now if she had been manipulating him since he arrived at the picket fence of the shelter. He thought back to when he'd arrived and how he'd thought he'd seen Alice looking at him as she spoke to the contractor and how she hadn't acknowledged him but had looked away. Then the slow realisation came to him that the visitor looked nothing like a builder and that she'd known Brendan was watching her.

"That man, he wasn't a contractor, was he?"

Alice burst out laughing. "Lord, I almost lost it when you said he must be doing okay for himself. Dr Reiter is a contractor of sorts, 'cept he comes here to work on heads, not doors!" she laughed. "And, even then, he doesn't get the job done!"

Brendan walked with her towards the hallway but stopped suddenly when he saw John Doe sneaking up the stairs. He wondered if the strange man had been listening to his conversation with Alice.

He creased his forehead, wondering now if he could cope with John Doe's madness.

"Don't you worry 'bout John. He's the kindest, gentlest soul I ever met in my life and in here I've been blessed to know many."

She led to the front door where Eileen was waiting patiently. His cousin didn't look surprised when she saw him inside the house. He knew that she must have had some part in Alice's plan or perhaps she had even been the one to orchestrate it. He turned to Alice, unsure if she knew the reason he wanted the work. His probation officer would be contacting her and he didn't want to have to explain this later. It was better that she knew now.

"It's for . . . community service," he said, somewhat embarrassed.

"Uh huh. I know it. See you tomorrow," she drawled, laughing as she walked away.

Chapter 6

"Here?" Brendan asked from the top of a shaky wooden ladder that looked like it had seen better days.

"No! A little to the right!" two voices shouted from beneath him.

Brendan adjusted the outside light that had come down from the back wall of the house during a storm the previous winter.

"Here?"

"More right!" Pilar shouted while Alice squinted up at him.

"Here?"

"Yes!" the two voices chorused.

Brendan took the drill from his nail-belt and was about to start driving the fixing into the wall when he noticed John Doe hiding behind the dense scrub at the back of the large garden, watching him. Pilar followed Brendan's gaze and beckoned for John to come out of his hiding spot and join them but he moved swiftly along the boundary wall of the garden, his eyes trained forward to avoid making eye contact with Brendan.

"He will come around," Pilar said in her New Jersey accent which transformed to a rich, melodic Spanish accent when she spoke with John Doe. In the five days since Brendan had come to work at the shelter, he had learnt that the Puerto Rican beauty had come to America with her family when she was five but that Spanish was still the language she spoke at home where she lived with her brother and sister-in-law.

Brendan shrugged and returned to his work. Despite John Doe's apparent fear of him, he was enjoying the work and even more so enjoying spending time with the pretty Latina who had worked at the shelter for ten years. After his first day, she had offered to drive him home and had now taken to picking him up when she was on day shift. So pleased was Frank to hear that Brendan had not only sorted out his community service but was doing it at a charity which was a favourite of the parish priest, that he surprised Brendan by allowing Eileen to spend more time at the shelter to ensure he could continue to escort her each day. Even more surprising was his uncle's reaction when Pilar called to the door on the second morning.

As Brendan entered the kitchen he heard her in the hallway, greeting Frank warmly and calling him "uncle". Frank practically dragged the petite woman into the kitchen in a bear hug while Brendan stood open-mouthed.

"You know each other?" he asked, astonished.

"Know each other? Coleen and I practically raised this little beauty when her mom died. Pilar was in the same class as Orla. Her dad, Emilio, Lord rest him, was my partner for twelve years right here in Dover!" He excitedly lifted Pilar off her feet for another bear hug.

His uncle's enthusiasm for Pilar had thrown water on Brendan's theory that he was a racist who had no time for anyone that wasn't white and preferably Irish. That evening, when Coleen was alone in the kitchen, Brendan told her about his uncle's comment about the Hispanic men on the morning that they drove to the hospital, and asked her if he did not like Latinos.

Coleen looked embarrassed but as usual smiled sweetly, her deep-set blue eyes showing only a hint that there was something behind her husband's comment.

"Honey," she had said in her high-pitched voice, "your uncle is a kind man and no, he has no problem with Hispanics. None at all." And she walked abruptly from the room, leaving him alone in the kitchen.

But despite her insistence that his uncle had no problems with Hispanics, Brendan heard his aunt and uncle arguing about it later that night in their bedroom above the kitchen, so he knew that he had not come to the wrong conclusion. The question was why his uncle behaved that way when he clearly had no problem with Pilar. Brendan opened the patio door quietly and walked down to his apartment, sorry that he had brought up the subject at all.

After almost two weeks, John Doe finally began to show signs he accepted that Brendan was no threat to him, just as Pilar had predicted he would.

It happened one morning when he tried to pass Brendan who was carefully repairing several loose balustrades on the stairwell. Brendan stood and moved his tools to one side to allow the man to pass.

"Sorry," Brendan said but John looked away and ran down three of the marble steps before turning around to look at Brendan.

"That's okay," he said nervously, once he was safely out of Brendan's reach.

Alice, who was standing at the foot of the stairs, winked at Brendan and patted John's back as she led him down the hallway.

Three more days passed before John said another word to Brendan and, again, it happened when John had no option but to try to pass him as he continued to repair the intricate banisters.

As he moved carefully past, Brendan could hear him murmur nervously in Spanish.

"You learn Spanish in school?" Brendan asked, startling both himself and the frightened man.

He had continued to be puzzled about how this Southern-sounding man spoke such fluent Spanish but he had not intended to initiate contact with him. The question had just come out spontaneously. Things were going well at the shelter and the last thing he needed was another one of John Doe's outbursts. He had asked Pilar about it on the ride home one evening and learnt that the Spanish John spoke was different from her Puerto Rican dialect and was in fact more like the Spanish spoken by Mexicans.

John pressed his back into the wooden stairwell and eyed Brendan suspiciously.

"I don't know . . . no."

"Where'd you learn to speak it so well then?"

"I . . . I always spoke it. I didn't learn it."

Brendan could see that John was becoming anxious and knew it was time to end the conversation.

"Well, you're pretty good," he said as he returned to his work.

He heard John walk down a few more steps and halt.

"Are you really Irish?" John asked.

"I was born here but, yep, I'm Irish. I was raised there."

"And you're really Eileen's cousin?"

"Yes," Brendan replied, amused.

"You don't look Irish," John said quietly.

"I get that a lot!" Brendan laughed. He turned to look at the unusual man and noticed how very innocent he seemed.

And *you* don't look Spanish, Brendan thought, but did not articulate this for fear of affecting the man's erratic temperament.

John nodded and gave Brendan a somewhat wary smile and continued down the stairs, this time turning his back to Brendan and moving down the stairs at a slower, more relaxed pace.

The following afternoon, as Brendan set about trying to fix the old bedroom furniture in the two large dormitories on the second floor, Alice called him from the bottom of the narrow stairs that led to the attic. It was Friday afternoon and Brendan had begun to dread it as the long lonely weekend stretched out before him.

"Could you fix John's bookcase before you go? He said it looks like it's about to collapse."

Brendan went back to the dorm for his tools and then followed Alice up the creaking stairs.

"Does he know we're coming up?" he asked nervously.

"He's the one who asked for you to fix it!" she exclaimed. "And John lets hardly anyone in that room of his. I haven't been up here myself for months. Anyway, he's with Dr Reiter downstairs in the living room so . . . we'll likely expect some Spanish mumbling later. He's always like that when the doctor's been."

Brendan remembered his first encounter with the aloof man in the sky-blue suit and wondered if the psychiatrist was any friendlier to John.

He bent down slightly as he entered the tiny door that led into a large open area. The small entrance reminded him of the door in *Alice's Adventures in Wonderland*. He tried to stand but the truss roof of the attic only increased to his height in the centre of the room.

"It used to be used just for storage but John's been up here a long time now," Alice said as she pulled a cobweb from her hair.

"How come he doesn't sleep in the dorms?" Brendan asked. "Looks like you could use this space."

Alice nodded. "We could use it all right but . . . this suits him better. John's been on the street lots of times but he's not your average homeless person. Needs to be here in the quiet at times. And, Lord, we don't send him out neither. John ain't made for the street, that's for sure."

Light slanted in from the round window and from its twin which looked out towards the back of the house. Brendan looked around the dusty room which looked like it hadn't been cleaned in a long time. The old oak floor was covered with a fine film of dust and cobwebs hung in every corner. John's single wooden bed, unlike the other beds in the shelter, was not hospital issue. A toilet and sink stood behind a cheap partition at the far end of the room. Brendan could hear the tap dripping and made a mental note to come back and fix it.

A large plywood bookcase, strained with the weight of a multitude of books, stood against the wall to the left of the bed. Two of the upper shelves had given in to their burden and had broken clean across the middle, their contents hanging precariously down onto the shelf below. Brendan scanned the books quickly and reckoned the man had at least a dozen books on how to grow apples trees.

The remaining wall was surprisingly clear of any objects save for a large map of North America. Brendan, who had grown up with a love of maps, studied the chart. He had also had a large map of America on his bedroom wall as a child and had marked all the states he planned to see when he got here. He had not made it to any of the places he had longed to visit. He knew that deep down he worried that the realisation of these long-held dreams might bring him disappointment or that the solitude these quiet places would offer his troubled mind would leave him alone with thoughts he would rather avoid. Instead, he had buried his head in the noise of the big city and, apart from his rare trips to his relatives in New Jersey, he had never left the state of New York. He peered closer at the map and noticed tiny coloured pins placed in various states with a fine red string wound from pin to pin.

"What's this about?" he asked Alice.

She let out a long breath. "Poor John. Dr Reiter sees this, he'll tell him off for sure."

"What is it?"

"It's him trying to get home. Poor love. Ever since I've met him he's been trying to figure it out. Never did though. This is John's home and, for now anyway, this is where he'll be. Young Mr Thompson, that's what I call old Mr Thompson's nephew who oversees the funding for the house, he's pushing for us to get John into a housing development but we've tried before and it fails . . . it fails badly . . . and he ends up back here all down in despair. Ain't worth it. I guess though that you can't blame John for trying to get home. I'd do the same thing myself. There's times I don't rightly agree with Dr Reiter – or Pilar for that matter. She trained with Dr Reiter in New York as a psychiatric nurse. Seems normal to want to find out where you're from, don't it? Seems like everyone wants him to move forward but how can he when he doesn't know what's behind him?"

Brendan studied the pins running down the east coast from New York to Virginia and North Carolina and back again.

"How come he doesn't know? I mean, Pilar told me she couldn't discuss his history but . . . but how come no one knows what happened to him? There must be some record somewhere . . . a police record of a road accident maybe or something like that?"

Alice looked behind her to ensure they were alone.

"Well, I shouldn't be saying anything either but, that day you came here and John was so afraid of you, I thought . . . well . . . that you were sent here for a reason."

"Like Superman!" Brendan joked but the humour was lost on Alice.

"Eileen felt it too. That's why we came up with a plan to get you here. I retire this year and I'd love to see that boy sorted 'fore I go. Oh, I know you joke when you're uncomfortable but I mean it. I saw real fear in his eyes as though you had sparked off a memory in him. And maybe . . . maybe he's got something to offer you too."

Brendan tensed at Alice's suggestion that a disturbed man like John could help him. It made him feel incomplete, like there was something wrong with him. He also thought about Eileen's infatuation with the eccentric man. He wanted to ask Alice if she thought their relationship was a good idea but was afraid of what she might say, good or bad.

Alice stopped speaking and looked about the room. Her mouth moved back and forward as though she was trying to make sense of something.

"I mean . . . well, most of what that boy says is pure made-up fantasy but at times . . . at times he's said things to me that I am sure he's plucked out of a real memory. Yeah . . . he knows some things, I'm sure of it . . . but . . . Dr Reiter says don't encourage it, keep him from talking about it and keep him looking to the future. He's been working with John ever since he was found and he never figured it out. He can't do it, no one can. Pilar says he's the best there is."

"Was it . . . I saw the scar at the side of his head . . . was it an accident or something?"

"I don't think so. That scar was old when they found him. Reckoned someone had given him a good beating. No one knows for sure how old he was when he was found but somewhere between eleven and fourteen years old, the file says. He was tall but painfully thin so it was hard to tell. That was 1979. My, all those years of looking for something you ain't never found. Makes me sad even thinking 'bout it."

"Where was he found?" Brendan asked, his sense of intrigue deepening.

The front door closed loudly, sending a shudder up to the attic. Alice went to the window and saw Dr Reiter looking around the grounds for a moment, the way he did when John had run off on him. She knew they'd had another disagreement, which usually occurred when the doctor challenged John on some crazy memory. She watched the doctor frown up at the attic window before getting into his car and driving slowly down the driveway.

Brendan woke her from her thoughts. He noticed her expression had changed from sad to resigned in a moment but he could not tell why.

She pursed her lips and folded her arms about her large body. "Look, we probably better not talk about it any more. I shouldn't have said anything. Hmm, Thompson says we need someone round here with more head than heart and I told him we need someone with the same amount of both. He's right though. I love those men so much sometimes I get blinded by it. Love them like they're my own family. If I don't, who's gonna do it?" Alice let out a long sigh. "I guess all the staff get a little infatuated with John when they come here. But they leave and sometimes leave him in a mess . . . all upset again and running off on us for weeks at a time, looking. Forget I said anything. Better to do as Dr Reiter says. Better not to go along with what John says. He thinks you believe him, he'll latch onto you like you're his new best friend."

Alice looked around the room and back to the map. She smoothed her skirt and looked sadly about the room which held everything John Doe owned in this life.

"I got to tell Pilar about that map, much as I hate to. Anyway, can you fix that bookshelf? It's real important to him."

Brendan nodded and set to work. The bookcase needed two new shelves which he went away to cut from the wood Alice had ordered in.

As he cleared up his tools for the evening, John appeared in the doorway and was taken aback by Brendan's presence, as though he had forgotten about his request for him to fix the shelves. He looked at his bed as though he sorely wanted to lie on it and then back at Brendan who watched the strange man decide if it was safe to come inside.

"Come on in – I'm just finished," he said, trying to instil calm in the man who was already muttering as Alice said he would.

John stepped quietly into the room and crept slowly along the wall. He stopped at his map and checked that it had not been interfered with.

"I didn't touch any of your things," Brendan said quickly, trying to calm John down before he started any shenanigans, but the strange man simply nodded and lay down on his bed, murmuring to himself in Spanish. Brendan lifted the books to replace them on the new shelves. He noticed a book he'd read as a child: *Little House on the Prairie* by Laura Ingalls Wilder. He remembered thinking it was a book for girls but it was the only children's book in the mobile library that he hadn't read so he brought it home and read it over the weekend. He could still remember the sense of adventure the book gave him and how he imagined himself as a pioneer in the Wild West, fighting Indians and saving women and children from unchristian scalpings. He swept the dust off the cover with his hand and smiled at the memory.

"I read this when I was a boy," he said aloud, causing John to sit suddenly bolt upright as though he hadn't even known Brendan was there.

John took off his glasses and cleaned them with a white tissue that he had shoved up his sleeve, his hand visibly shaking as he replaced the lenses on his face. He swallowed and slowly raised his bright blue eyes to look at Brendan but looked quickly away again.

"It was on television when I was a child," Brendan added when John didn't say anything.

"I'm not allowed to watch television – Dr Reiter says it's bad for me," John said so quietly that Brendan could hardly hear him.

"Well, I never saw it either. I only ever read books. I grew up without a TV. My mother wouldn't have one in the house. The only films I saw were in the cinema and that wasn't often."

"Kuvic watches TV here all the time . . . and he drinks beer," John replied as he got up from the bed and took the book nervously from Brendan's hand.

"Who's he?" Brendan asked.

"He's been on vacation," John twanged in his deep Southern accent. "He's back tonight. He only ever works nights because he doesn't get along with Alice."

Brendan wondered why no one had thought of using John's accent to trace where he was from or, if they had, why this failed to lead them to his home.

"I don't rightly get along with him neither cos of the teasing. Usually stay in my room when he comes in at seven."

Brendan nodded, absorbing what John was saying to him. "You tell Alice about this?"

John shrugged. "Alice knows. There's nothing she can do. Thompson wants Kuvic to have the manager's job when Alice retires in the fall. Alice told him Pilar should get it but Kuvic, he's got an uncle, a politician, who might be able to get a lot more funding for the place. Thompson needs that more than he needs Pilar."

Brendan listened intently to John, amazed that he spoke with such clarity. He hadn't expected him to be so aware of what was going on around him.

"Of course, I'll be gone by then," John added.

"Where you going?" Brendan asked impulsively, already forgetting Alice's request that he not encourage John's ramblings.

"Home."

Brendan looked towards the door to ensure that Alice or any of the other staff were not around.

"Where's that?" Brendan asked, his fascination with the man's story overpowering the voice in his head that told him to be careful.

"Virginia."

"Have you got family there?" Brendan asked somewhat, mischievously.

"Some . . . but . . . well . . . I've been having some trouble finding them." John laughed suddenly and slapped his knee, frightening Brendan. "It's the darndest thing!" He shook his head. "I'm going to find them though. Been looking a real long time."

Brendan could see a look of desperation in the man's face. "Well, good luck with it," he replied, somewhat insincerely. "It's John, isn't it?"

"Jonathan. My name is Jonathan."

Chapter 7

The following morning Brendan woke early and went to Coleen's study to use the internet. It was still early and there didn't appear to be anyone up. He had fallen asleep thinking about the information Alice had given him and knew that someone along the way had missed something that would lead to John's true identity. The thought of being the one to solve a thirty-year mystery had thrilled him and he had slept fitfully, dreaming of himself walking John up a long pathway to his waiting family. He sat at the computer and typed in a search for children missing in 1979. He sighed when he drew a blank. Not a single site reported any missing children that matched Jonathan's description that year. It didn't make any sense. He searched some more, frantically typing in the words *boy* and *missing* and *Jonathan* with various spellings but still nothing came up.

He heard the partly closed door creak and looked up to find Eileen standing there in a quilted blue dressing gown.

"I've done that. Over and over. You won't find anything," she said as she leaned against the door jamb.

"There must be *some* record," he replied.

Eileen came in and pulled over a chair to sit beside Brendan. She shooed him over and took control of the keyboard. She typed in the name of a New York newspaper and searched the archives. Within seconds, a photo of a young John flanked by two New York policemen flashed onto the screen. The caption read "*Live John Doe found in Marcus Garvey Park*".

Brendan peered at the photo of the half-starved boy with a mop of shoulder-length white hair staring into the photo. He was barefoot and was dressed in clothes that were too short for his long body. Even though it was a black-and-white photo, his face looked deathly pale. He looked much older than the prepubescent boy Alice said he had been.

"That's when he was found. In an East Harlem park. Guess the name stuck," she said flatly.

"Jesus," Brendan said, shocked at his dishevelled appearance. "And there were no reports of children missing before he was found?"

"No one matching his description. It seems like no one was looking for him."

Brendan leant back on the chair and swivelled around, trying to collect his thoughts. "How can that be?"

"Wherever he was, he'd been there for a long time. Maybe he had no family. Maybe they were dead. There were marks on his body but none of them were fresh injuries. They were very old scars showing that he had been . . ." Eileen's chin quivered a little but she composed herself quickly, "beaten repeatedly."

Brendan leant forward and read the report on the left of the photo. "It says he led them less than three hundred metres to a basement apartment at 54 Parkview which was a rundown house where he said his grandmother lived – but, when police got there, the apartment was completely empty. The landlord said that it had been rented to an old Hispanic woman who had lived alone there and that she had died a week before." He raised his eyebrows in interest.

Eileen scrolled down to the photo of the dilapidated house. The caption said that it was a four-storey building that had been converted into several apartments. The wrought-iron railings that ran along the front of the basement areas of the adjoining houses had been removed from Number 54 and the tiny garden inside appeared to have been converted into what was presumably a parking-space, which looked like it had not been used in a long time. Tall weeds and blades of grass poked up through the uneven paving, making the house look so abandoned that it was hard to believe that anyone had been living there for a long time.

"Looks like a really old house," Brendan said, scanning the photo.

"I'd say it's gone now. Probably been torn down and replaced with a high-rise," Eileen replied as she typed in another search on the same newspaper archives.

"This was two weeks later. This report said a woman had been found in that house where they believed she'd been dead for about a week and that the post mortem revealed she'd had a lung disease. It said that the old Hispanic woman was undocumented. The newspapers interviewed some neighbours who said she lived alone and had kept to herself and that she didn't have any family. They said her name, as far as they knew, was Rosa Soto. Immigration did a check and they had no records of anyone matching that name and age. She had no social security number. Nothing. Guess she was just another illegal using a false name."

Brendan sighed and ran his hand through his unbrushed hair.

"They didn't have kinship blood-testing back then," she went on, "so they couldn't establish for certain that Jonathan wasn't related to the woman in the morgue, but his physical appearance alone suggested that he had no Hispanic blood in him so they just thought he was some crazy street kid. Also, Rosa Soto's neighbours said they had never seen him before – and when police tried to get him to bring them around the neighbourhood, he didn't know his way anywhere, couldn't name a street, didn't know anyone, nothing. The report said that John spoke with the same Southern accent that he does now so police concluded that, wherever he was from, it was hundreds of miles from where he was found."

Brendan smiled at his cousin. He could tell that she had spent long hours searching for clues on the identity of John Doe.

"And they looked, did they? In Virginia and North Carolina and all those places on his map?" he asked.

Eileen nodded. "Alice said police in four states were working on the case and came up with nothing."

"What about asking Frank? I know he'd left New York by then, but he still has friends on the force there."

"*No!*" Eileen yelled. She put her hand over her mouth and looked up at the ceiling, hoping her parents hadn't heard her. "We can't. Please! If Dad gets any way involved in the shelter, he'll know about . . . about Jonathan and me. Look, Brendan, I've looked and looked for him and it's useless. Please leave it alone – please?"

"I'd have thought you'd want him to find his home?" he asked, surprised.

"One time, yes, but now, now I think it's better if he . . . stays here."

Brendan looked closely at his cousin. He realised that if Jonathan found out who he was, he would leave this town and Eileen would probably never see him again.

"But . . . Alice said she and you wanted me to work in the shelter because I'd provoked a memory in him."

Eileen blew out a long sigh. "Yes, that's true . . . but all I want is for you to befriend him . . . for him to not be so afraid. That's all. Kuvic will have him out of the shelter as soon as he's the manager and he'll probably go into a housing development. I hope . . . I hope that he'll settle and that maybe . . ."

Eileen blushed and looked down at her quilted dressing gown. She pulled at a loose thread until the redness faded from her face.

"Please say you'll stop looking into this?" she begged.

Brendan nodded and looked back at the photo of Jonathan on the screen. He looked terrified and Brendan wondered what he had gone through up until that point.

"What happened to him after that?"

"He went into state care," Eileen said softly. "Alice says that he then went from foster home to foster home, in and out of state institutions, juvenile centres and . . ."

He noticed her jaw clench and her fingers curl up.

"Sometimes he was admitted to psychiatric institutions," she said as though those words held a painful memory for her.

"Alice said his old file is at least eight inches thick with information on the places he's been cared for and police correspondence but that the case was closed years ago. He was homeless a lot as an adult. Drifted around. Even since he came to the shelter he drifted off for a while now and then, but he always came back when he didn't find what he was looking for."

"What brought him to Dover?"

Eileen pushed her bony shoulders towards her neck and shrugged. "I guess he thought he'd find something here. Alice said she was looking out of the window one day and found him swinging on the old swing in the front yard, like a child would do. She went down and brought him inside. She took him into the kitchen for something to eat and he wandered about the house and garden looking at everything and touching things. He was convinced it was his house. Said it had the same clapboard front and bay windows but that everything else was different. The shelter has been the most stability he's ever known."

"What do you think about his past?"

Eileen turned off the computer and stared at the wallpapered wall in front of her.

"I think he has . . . or at least he did have a family at some point. I think that the house and the orchard that he remembers are real but that it got mixed up along the way with things he imagined were his own memories. He endured a terrible trauma, terrible cruelty. But . . . I really don't know why no one ever looked for him. He's so gentle and kind . . . someone taught him well. At some point in his life somebody cared very much for him. I expect they thought he was dead. I don't know why they never reported him missing but there has to be a reason for it."

Brendan let out a long puff of air and stood, stretching himself. He looked out at the front driveway and wondered what he'd do with himself that day. In the driveway stood Eileen's perfectly shiny car.

"Hey, do you want a driving lesson?" he asked.

"Are you allowed?"

"I won't drive, you will!" he replied.

A rare broad smile washed over Eileen's face. She leant forward and embraced him gently. "Thank you, thank you!" she said excitedly as she ran upstairs to get dressed.

Brendan walked down the hallway and went into the kitchen to pour himself a cold coffee from last night's leftovers. As he replaced the coffee pot onto the port, he noticed a letter on the counter. He recognised the tiny, neat handwriting as his mother's.

Without thinking he picked up the letter and moved to the table to read it. It was addressed to his aunt and uncle and began with the usual few lines asking how the family were. Brendan scanned down to read how business in the shop was bad because large supermarkets had taken over the trade small shops used to depend on. She went on to say that she had decided to sell up and had placed the small shop on the market. He moved further down the letter and read that she had decided to come to America for an extended stay while she decided what she was going to do with herself and that she hoped they could put her up for a while. He cringed when she added that she would understand if they didn't want to do that and that she'd find accommodation in town. It made her sound so desperate, so alone. So like him. Her last line read that she did not want to go to New York for "obvious" reasons. He wondered if the "obvious reason" was him and the anger that he felt towards her in his childhood resurfaced and surged through him like molten lava.

He threw the letter down on the table and buried his head in his hands. He understood now why his uncle had been so irritated last night and how quiet the normally talkative Coleen had been over dinner. It also made sense now that Frank had asked him if he had told his mother about his forced move to Dover and why he had said in hushed tones, unusual for his uncle, that he'd better tell her soon. Brendan's breathing quickened and his heart began to race. He did not want his mother here, not when his life was going well for a change. Not when he was happy. He lifted the letter again to see if she'd said when she would arrive but there were no dates given. Without thinking, he ripped the letter up and walked out of the patio door to his apartment where he lay on his bed, completely forgetting about Eileen, who had come downstairs to find him gone and the letter in pieces on the kitchen floor.

It was after eight that evening by the time Brendan finally calmed down. He had remained in the apartment for the day and had risen from his bed only twice: once to use the bathroom and then to eat a small bowl of dry cereal. He got up and walked down the side entrance and out onto the street. He felt like walking and found himself moving along the town's main street, which looked very different at night. Small groups of teenagers, many of whom were Latinos, stood on the pavement, queuing for a nightclub or talking to friends. He watched couples walk into the cinema, hand in hand, and others take a stroll through the town with their children. He suddenly felt very alone and wondered what John was doing at that very moment. He hoped that Pilar was working and that John would not be hiding in his room from this Kuvic.

With nothing else to do, he turned onto Salem Street and took the long way to the shelter. It looked very different in the darkness. The window of each room was ablaze with light, including Jonathan's single round window in the attic. Brendan glanced around the pristine lawn and the apple trees. The place looked so peaceful and welcoming. When he returned his gaze to the attic, Jonathan was standing at his window looking down at him. It was as though he knew that Brendan was standing there. For a moment the two men just stood and stared at each other until Jonathan raised his hand and waved weakly. Brendan waved back and felt suddenly embarrassed to be standing there, waving at another man in the darkness. He turned and walked quickly away from the house but when he glanced back, Jonathan was still in the window, his spectacled face pressed close to the windowpane.

Brendan was still not ready to return home and decided to take a different route along Richards Avenue. The air had not yet cooled from the July heat and he wandered slowly through the picturesque streets, trying to banish his mother from his thoughts by focusing on the beauty around him. All along the boulevard, cherry blossoms shone in pink hues under the streetlights. The moon, large and round above him, looked particularly beautiful. He stopped to count the stars but could only make out three or four of the brighter ones, the light of the others drowned out by the town's lighting.

When he finally arrived onto Watson Drive, his uncle was sitting in the dark on a wrought-iron seat in the far corner of the garden.

"Brendan, come here. I want to talk to you."

Brendan let out a sigh. He walked slowly to where his uncle sat.

"Sit down. It's a lovely night," Frank said quietly.

Brendan sat and folded his arms instinctively as he waited for the lecture on why he shouldn't read or tear up other people's letters.

"I just wanted to tell you that I'm proud of you," Frank said.

Brendan turned and narrowed his eyes suspiciously at his uncle.

"The way you've worked at the shelter, the pride you've put into the work. Coleen was talking to Pilar after Mass last Sunday and she says you've done wonders there."

Brendan nodded but remained silent. He could feel a 'but' coming.

"I know things haven't been easy for you . . . and I know I've been hard on you . . . but Coleen and I want you to know that everything we've . . . everything I've said has always been for your own good. It's because we care about you."

Brendan could see the old man's eyes moisten. He looked down, embarrassed to see his tough uncle becoming emotional.

"How do you feel about your mother coming here?"

The directness and suddenness of his question took Brendan

by surprise. He looked up for a moment and shrugged, returning his gaze to his feet much like Eileen did when she felt awkward.

Frank sighed and folded his arms across his fat body. "Well, son, you know my sister and I haven't always gotten along. There are reasons for that that are best left in the past but what I want to know is how it'll affect you. You've been a different man these past few weeks. Happier. Coleen and I don't want to see that change. If you feel that your mom coming will affect you, then we've decided to put you first. It's something we should've done a long time ago."

Brendan kept his eyes on the ground. He briefly wondered what his uncle meant by his last comment but decided to focus on the part about him being happy. He was in a much better mood lately. He was probably the happiest he had ever been but he didn't want to be responsible for shutting his mother out, not when she had no one else to turn to. There were no other family members in Ireland and, despite how he felt about her, he didn't want to see her grow old alone. Also, he planned on returning to New York as soon as he could, so he felt he had no right to insist that his mother stay away.

"It's fine, Uncle Frank," he said as he stood up.

He watched his uncle grimace with pain as he tried to lift himself off the hard bench, and leaned forward to help him.

Frank grabbed Brendan and hugged him tightly. He seemed relieved, as if he couldn't bear the thought of turning his sister away.

"You're a good boy," he said, his voice muffled in Brendan's thick hair.

Brendan moved backwards until Frank let go his grip.

"Anyway, we'd better go in now – let's get some food into you," Frank said as he moved toward the front door, embarrassed now at his show of affection.

Chapter 8

Monday morning came and Brendan walked with Eileen to the centre. Pilar had started on a week of night shifts and he would only see her if he came back late in the evenings, which he planned to do. For weeks he had tried to chat her up but the Latin beauty was having none of it. His charm had worked well on other American girls but Pilar was different. He was going to have to come up with another way to ask her out.

When he entered the hallway of the shelter he was surprised to find a tall, lean man of about forty standing in the entrance. Eileen took one look at the man and scurried off to the laundry where she would spend the day washing the sheets from the night before. Brendan had been genuinely surprised to see how hard his cousin worked each day at the shelter. It was not the picnic he had imagined and he knew she often left with tired legs and an aching back.

The man walked forward and thrust out his hand to Brendan. "I'm Kuvic. You must be Eileen's cousin."

Brendan nodded and took Kuvic's hand. "Is that your first name?"

"No," Kuvic replied curtly.

"I'm Brendan." He winced from the tight clutch. As he tried

to free himself from Kuvic's grip, he noticed the deep pockmarks in the man's face, a sign of teenage acne. He had light brown hair and sea-green eyes that seemed to be mocking him. He wore a navy shirt and trousers that made him look like a security guard instead of a social-care worker in a homeless shelter.

"It'll be nice to have someone round here who pisses standing up," Kuvic sneered.

Brendan cringed at the man's vulgarity and managed to loosen his hand from his tight grip.

"You mean apart from the clients?" he replied amiably, referring to the mostly male 'clients' that passed through the door each day. He had become used to the politically correct terminology used at the shelter, terminology that he'd once scoffed at but now embraced.

"Well, they mostly piss in the beds. The 'clients'. Don't know why I keep forgetting to call them that." Then he walked abruptly away from Brendan and into one of the sitting rooms where the television blared.

Brendan stood for a moment and tried to make sense of what had just happened. He couldn't believe that a staff member could talk about the people that came in each day in such a demeaning way. He knew that he'd been guilty of judging the clients when he first came to the shelter only six short weeks beforehand. In the beginning, he'd thought they were a useless lot of wasters, living on benefits and taking no responsibility for themselves. Then he began to see similarities between himself and the men who crossed the threshold each day and he began to recognise the simple life events that for some led to a lifetime of homelessness. He had even come to understand the destructive nature of Zeb whose dyslexia had prevented him from acquiring an education in the small town where he had grown up in the 1940's. Poor literacy and no qualifications meant Zeb couldn't find work and, when his benefits ran out, he lost the room he was renting in a boarding house and took his life's frustrations out on everyone around him. When Brendan drove for a second time while drunk, which he accepted now as a stupid, reckless act, he knew that Colm Mooney had no choice but to sack him – it was Colm's work van that he had been driving that night. In a few short weeks he had no money to pay his rent and, despite his problems with his Uncle Frank, if it hadn't been for his support he'd be in one of these shelters himself.

He had learnt a lot in what had been a new environment for him but Kuvic worked here and should know better than to talk about the clients in that way. He went to the shed to collect his tools for the day and began repairing the shutters on the side of the house.

He didn't know where Alice was but he wished she was here to keep an eye on Kuvic who had not made a great first impression on him. At lunchtime he relaxed when she appeared in the driveway in her battered Ford. She looked harried but still took the time to quickly check on Jonathan who was sitting in the garden waiting on her to return.

Brendan sat on the grass and ate a sandwich that Henrietta, the cook, had taken out to him. Jonathan, who had been sitting in the distance almost the entire morning watching Brendan work, came up and sat close beside him. He uncovered the plate of lunch Henrietta had given him also and took a swig of water. Brendan glanced furtively at Jonathan's strange clothes. He wore a different sleeveless woollen vest, this time with yellow and green stripes, over a white striped shirt. Brendan wondered where John managed to find these old clothes and why he wore them in the first place.

"Sure is a lovely day," Jonathan said.

Brendan looked up at the July sunshine. He pulled off his T-shirt to work on his deepening tan. It had been the reason Molly Keenan had followed him behind the bike shed on the school grounds one summer. She told him she loved his dark skin and eyes and had allowed him to kiss her. They were both about fourteen years old and it was the first time Brendan realised that girls found him attractive.

"You'll get skin cancer," Jonathan said as he placed a blade of grass in his mouth and lay back on the lawn.

Brendan laughed.

"Oh, I'm not sassing you. My daddy knew about that long before people were talking about it. He said too much sun is a bad thing."

Brendan laughed but then remembered the sad photo of Jonathan staring out of the newspaper's archives.

"You remember him? Your father?" he asked.

"Sure do," Jonathan drawled. "We lived on a property in Newsart, Virginia, and, boy, it was hot there each summer. You had to wear a hat, save you from sunstroke. We owned a huge apple orchard on 'bout fifty acres. Me and my daddy and my brothers worked there all year round and two Negro families came back each year at harvesting time. Yeah, Daddy said there was nothing like a hard day's work to keep a man happy."

Brendan peered closely into Jonathan's face to see if he was making the story up but the strange man stared back at him without blinking. The language he used was so old-fashioned. He was pretty sure that people of African-American heritage preferred to be called 'black' and that no one had used the term Negro since the '50s or '60s. Yet he knew that the man meant no offence. He was also sure that people in Virginia didn't use the term 'sassing' half as much as he had heard Jonathan use it when he was talking to Alice.

"Sounds nice. Sounds like a nice life," he replied.

"Yeah. It sure was. When the work was done, I'd climb that mountain beside our farm or, if I was plumb tired out, I'd ride my old mule up there and breathe in the cool air high up on that hill. It was so fresh and clean, make you want to stay up there, drinking it in."

Jonathan picked an apple from his lunch pack and polished it on his woollen vest. He took a bite.

"*Ughh!* I don't much care for these early apple varieties. You wait 'til my crop in the fall. You won't taste better apples anywhere. Course if I was in Virginia, I could harvest them at least two weeks earlier than I can here."

"What were your parents' names?"

"My dad was also Jonathan and my mother's name was Lorna."

"Did . . . did you have any brothers and sisters?"

"Sure. I have two brothers, Clay and Virgil, and three sisters, Mackenzie, Tyler and Cassie."

"They're pretty strange names, except for Cassie," Brendan replied, remembering the Cassie he had bumped into in Murphy's pub on more than one occasion.

"Yeah, but they're common names round those parts," Jonathan replied.

"Where are they now?" Brendan asked.

"I . . . I don't know. Been telling you about that. I guess . . . I guess they moved, maybe."

Brendan bit his lower lip, the guilt of probing the man about his family weighing down on him. "I shouldn't have asked. I'm sorry."

"Oh, that's all right," Jonathan replied genially. "It's nice to have someone to talk to about them. Most people try to make me stop!"

Brendan nodded and stood. He dusted himself off and lifted his plate off the grass to take it in to Henrietta.

"I can do that," John said as he took the plate and rushed inside with it.

He returned almost immediately and stood smiling at Brendan.

"Can I help?" he asked, looking down at the shutters that Brendan had taken off to plane back.

"Sure," Brendan replied.

He handed John a sheet of sandpaper and watched as he rubbed the shutter so hard that he was eating into the wood. Brendan took the shutter from him and looked around for something else for his new apprentice to do.

"Can you paint?" he asked.

"Landscapes?" Jonathan asked seriously.

"No! Shutters, Jonathan! Do you think you could paint them? They just need a fine coat, that's all. Real light strokes, okay?"

"Sure. I can do just about anything," he replied, oblivious of the mess he had made sanding the shutter.

Brendan opened a can of paint and handed Jonathan a shutter he'd already sanded. He looked up and saw Kuvic standing at the corner of the house, smiling at them.

"I see he's got you calling him Jonathan? That's not your name, is it, John Doe?"

Brendan looked at Jonathan who had frozen to the spot. He returned his gaze to Kuvic as he walked off, his steel-capped heels tapping loudly on the driveway as he moved.

"You okay?" Brendan asked.

"Sure. I don't pay him any attention," Jonathan replied nervously.

"What's his problem?" Brendan asked.

"He just hates to see anybody happy," Jonathan replied. "Word is he was put out of his job as a prison guard cos he was abusing the female prisoners . . . you know, sexually."

Brendan's mouth dropped open. "Really?"

"Yeah. I heard Pilar telling Alice and Henrietta 'bout it. Her brother's a police officer and she said even when they sent him to the male part of the prison he tried to bribe prison guards to let him into the female prison at night. The governor got rid of him but Kuvic's uncle put pressure on Mr Thompson here to give him a job at the shelter. All the women here including Pilar, Alice, Jane, all of them, they don't much care to be around him."

Brendan thought back to how Eileen had darted off like a rat when she had seen Kuvic in the hallway that morning. His fists unconsciously closed into rigid balls. If Kuvic laid one hand on his cousin, he'd kill him. He knew that Kuvic must be in heaven in a place with mostly female staff. He also knew that Kuvic's handshake this morning was really about sizing Brendan up to see if he was as big a sleazebag as him. Brendan knew he couldn't claim to be a feminist but he was way above any of the stuff Kuvic seemed to be about.

He blew out some air and returned to his sanding as he kept a close eye on Jonathan's painting skills.

"You're good at that," he said.

"Oh, I've done this before. At the farmhouse. We had a big old house with shutters on all of the windows and each spring my daddy'd take 'em all down and me and my brothers would paint them the deep blue that my momma loved so much. Daddy said it was the colour of her eyes. Of course, I'd get paint all down my dungarees and my momma would say I was the clumsiest child she ever saw!" Jonathan stopped talking and the smile slipped slowly from his face.

"We had some right good times there. In the evening, I'd swing on that old tyre in the front yard and let the breeze blow on my face and through my hair. I'd swing high and higher 'til I could see clear over the top of the trees and out to the Blue Ridge Mountains. And I'd picture the animals on that mountain going about their business. Mountain lions and black bears, possums and deer. All doing what nature intended them to do and . . . it was the happiest I felt in my whole life. Knowing I was part of something . . . of a place that breathed and was alive, you know what I mean?"

Brendan put down his sandpaper and looked at Jonathan. So beautiful was his description of his home that Brendan could imagine the place, could see himself on that swing looking up at the mountains in the distance. He was beginning to understand why his book-loving cousin had fallen in love with him.

"You could be a writer," Brendan said.

"Oh, my daddy was a writer. Expect I got it from him."

"I thought you said he owned an orchard?"

Jonathan lowered his head and murmured, "Em . . . I don't know why I said that. He had a bureau that he'd write at and I'd have to be real quiet. Guess it was just paperwork he was doing." He shook his head.

Brendan gazed into Jonathan's face and decided that he wasn't lying to him. He seemed genuinely confused by something that had popped into his mind.

"One time, I happened upon a mountain lion. I reckon it's just about my favourite animal," Jonathan continued. "I was hunting rabbit on the ridge and I surprised her. She looked real skinny, like she was sick or somethin', and she had two small cubs with her. I threw my rabbits behind me and raised my rifle but she just looked at me as though she was weighing up what to do about me. Well, it felt like an hour passed with her standing there looking at me with those eyes but it couldn't have been more than a couple of seconds. Then she just walked away, down a steep forest track with her cubs. I remember feeling glad that I didn't have to shoot her because I didn't want to turn those little cubs into orphans. That night I thought about her and realised that she had a decision to make at that moment. Either she could take a leap at me, take my rabbits and risk being shot which would leave her cubs on their own – or walk away and hope I wouldn't bother her. Sometimes I feel the same way as that lion. Dr Reiter, he says I should just look to the future. At times I think maybe he's right and I ought to take the safe path where I can keep what I've got and accept that I may never find what I set out to look for."

Brendan, who had stopped work while Jonathan told his amazing story, stood silent.

"Do you mean your family? That you should stop searching for them?" he finally asked.

Jonathan nodded and looked up into the blazing sun. "But then I think . . . I owe it to them to be able to stop worrying about me. I know there's someone looking for me, wondering all the time what happened to me."

"I could help you," Brendan found himself saying, surprising himself at his involuntary response.

"How?"

Brendan shrugged. "What if . . . what if you told me your stories, everything you remember, and I could try to piece them together? Bit by bit until the pieces fit together?"

"You want to hear my stories?" Jonathan asked incredulously.

"Yes."

"All right!" Jonathan yelled as he slapped his knee.

Brendan picked up the shutters they'd finished and placed them on saw horses to dry overnight.

"But it'll have to be our secret. You can't tell Eileen. She doesn't want me meddling into your life."

Jonathan pondered this for a moment. "Eileen and I don't keep secrets from each other but . . . okay. I'll do it."

"Great. Oh, Jonathan, do you remember what your last name was? I mean your real name. Not Doe."

"I sure do. I've told that Dr Reiter a thousand times."

Brendan stood there and waited for him to go on.

"It's Nelson. Jonathan Wyatt Nelson."

Chapter 9

The library on East Clinton Street was a pretty, red-brick single-storey building with large Georgian-style windows and an ornate cream-panelled door that stood proudly in the centre of the old building and was framed by faux Greek columns. Steps with delicate wrought-iron banisters led up to the doorway on each side, the entrance surrounded by small flowering shrubs and a water fountain with two playful cherubs at its centre.

Brendan registered with the shy librarian and glanced at the four computers which were all being used by people who looked like they had nowhere else to go that day. He decided to search for Jonathan's town the old-fashioned way and took a huge atlas down from the shelf before finding himself a table at the back of the small but well-laid-out reading room. He sat down and opened the section on America, then roughly turned the pages until he came to a detailed map of the eastern states. He scanned the index looking for Newsart in Virginia but could not find any towns by that name. He wondered if Jonathan was sure about the spelling of the town but no other town names came close to or sounded remotely like Newsart. Brendan began to look for Newsart in the surrounding states including North Carolina and Kentucky but came up blank. In desperation, he looked for

Newsart in every state of North America but there was not one single town in the whole of the country by that name. He exhaled loudly, causing two or three readers to look up at him crossly.

He looked over at the computers again but they were all still occupied. He closed the book and walked back to the librarian's desk to ask for her advice. As he approached her desk the middle-aged woman blushed, which brought a smile to his face. If only he had that effect on Pilar! The shy librarian was not a bad-looking woman and had fine, tightly cut sandy-brown hair and hazel eyes. He glanced down at her thick stockings, flat shoes and long brown skirt and decided that the woman worked hard to hide herself from the world.

She advised him to check at the local records office for towns whose names had been changed. He had no idea how old Jonathan Doe was but decided to confine his search to the past fifty years. As she handed him his library tickets, he touched her fingers accidentally. She blushed again and gave him a nervous, silly laugh like a schoolgirl. He hoped the shy woman, whom he noticed was not wearing a wedding ring, did not sit alone in her apartment each evening. He pictured her there with her cat and a microwave dinner and hoped that his image of her life was wrong and that she was not as lonely as he was. Except it was different for men. He could ease his loneliness by picking up a girl for the night but women who did the same thing were branded as sluts. It was double standards and he had often thought about how unfairly women were treated in a so-called modern society. It was, he knew, even worse at home in Ireland where a woman in a small town would get a name for herself and never manage to shake it off.

He had decided he would tell Eileen that he had gone out for some nails, and he had even picked some up on his way, to ensure she didn't suspect that he was looking into Jonathan's identity.

Back at the shelter he wandered through the house and found Pilar folding sheets in the laundry with his cousin.

"Where's Alice?" he asked.

"She had a hospital appointment," Pilar replied.

"Is she ill?"

Pilar glanced briefly at Eileen and then back at Brendan. "No. Just routine stuff."

Brendan nodded and walked outside, then around to the side of the house where he had left Jonathan painting some of the shutters.

"Right, what do you want to ask me today?" Jonathan asked immediately.

Brendan sighed. "Are you sure about the name Newsart?"

"Yep."

"I couldn't find it on the map. Couldn't find it in any other state either. The only other possibility is the town's name was changed."

"Name didn't change," Jonathan twanged, then added, "I knew you wouldn't find it."

"Then why didn't you tell me and save me the bother of looking?" Brendan asked crossly.

Jonathan tensed and dropped his brush to the ground. He moved backwards and cowered behind the saw horses.

Brendan swallowed. "I'm sorry," he said.

"You said you'd put the pieces together for me," Jonathan said nervously.

"I will, Jonathan. Look, tell me another story, okay? Tell me one about your . . . your sisters."

Jonathan relaxed and picked up his painting-brush from the ground. He returned to his work station and began to paint as he reminisced.

"Well, I've got three sisters. Mackenzie and Tyler, they're little twins – identical – and Cassie, she's a few years older than me. She's blind though."

"What happened?"

"Guess she was born that way. Me and Nella would tie a string around Cassie's waist and bring her with us down to the creek or through the woods. We'd be real careful that she didn't bump into anything. My daddy was so careful with her. He worried so much about her."

"Who was Nella?"

"A little coloured girl. Her family worked on the farm and she'd come play with Cassie and me. I think she was about a year older than me but she was tiny and skinny. I was taller and it bothered her. That girl would get so mad and keep measuring herself to me!"

"Did Mackenzie and Tyler play with Nella and Cassie?"

Jonathan thought about this for a moment and appeared troubled by the question.

"I don't think so," he drawled, rubbing his temples. "I . . . I don't remember."

Brendan looked up at the clear blue sky and wondered if he was asking the right questions. He let out a long breath and tapped his carpentry pencil on his knee.

"What about your brothers, did they play with you and Cassie and Nella?"

"I . . . I don't see them doing that."

"You don't see them doing that? What does that mean?"

"It means I'm trying to replay it in my head – and I can't." Then he suddenly shouted, "*I don't know!*"

Brendan stepped backwards, surprised by Jonathan's sudden outburst.

Within seconds, Kuvic appeared around the corner of the house, making Brendan suspect that he had been standing there listening but, before he had a chance to tease them, Alice appeared behind them, puffing and panting.

Brendan noticed how out of breath she was and realised that she had been that way for a couple of weeks.

"That's fine, Kuvic. I've got it. Come on, John," she said.

Kuvic shot Brendan a grin and walked on towards the back of the house.

Alice put her arm around John and led him to a seat in the garden, then walked back over to Brendan and leant in close to his ear.

Brendan noticed the dark circles under her eyes. He glanced quickly over her large body. She had not lost any weight but her face looked drawn, as though something was worrying her.

"That map we saw in John's room – I'm goin' to forget I ever saw it. What I got to know is if you forget you ever saw it too?"

Brendan nodded. "I didn't see any map," he replied.

"Good," she wheezed.

"Alice, are you alright?" Brendan asked as she turned away.

She turned back and smiled a huge grin at him. "Why, my plan's working already. Few weeks back, you'd never notice how another human being was feeling. Well, look at you now, interested in poor old Alice!"

Brendan shrugged and smiled at her, embarrassed yet pleased at the same time.

"It's just a chest infection that I can't shift," she said. "I'm fine and I'm gonna be even better cos I know you starting to love that man as much as I do."

She beckoned to Jonathan and led him towards the house.

Brendan watched as Jonathan walked slowly into the house, his hand raised to his head as though remembering his past caused him physical pain.

Brendan sighed heavily and returned to his work. As he sanded the shutters he thought about his next step. He would have to forget about finding Newsart for now and focus on another aspect of Jonathan's story but, right now, he had no idea what that would be.

When Jonathan reappeared in the garden later that day, it was to walk with Eileen among his rows of small apple trees that ran all the way to the boundary wall. Brendan had climbed the ladder to fix one of the shutters back onto the house and now climbed down a few of the steps to watch them. He could see Eileen smile up at the tall man as though she was a lovesick teenager. He tensed as Jonathan moved a bang of hair from her eyes and handed her a blossom that had fallen from one of his apple trees.

"You don't need to worry about them," a soft voice said behind him.

He looked down to find Pilar standing at the bottom of his ladder. Her long hair was tied into a tight bun and she wore a simple red cotton dress with matching sandals. He moved his eyes from her feet to her stunning face and noticed her blushing. He looked away quickly and returned his gaze to his cousin who was now sitting on the grass with Jonathan. He shook his head and descended to the ground.

"I wish I could believe that. Eileen is infatuated with him and I . . . I don't want to see her hurt."

"Because of what happened to her? You want to protect her?"

Brendan searched Pilar's face in the fading evening light. Her skin was radiant and her face unlined but there was a quiet maturity to her that belied her youthful appearance. Uncle Frank said she had been in Orla's class at school, which would have made her about thirty-four years old. He wondered briefly why she had not married but quickly refocused his thoughts on his cousin.

"You know about the incident?" he asked, using Orla's tactful terminology.

"I was doing my training in New York when she was admitted to the hospital. Her dad thought it was best not to admit her to the clinic here. He didn't want people to know that she had tried to commit suicide."

"What?" Brendan asked. He could hear the alarm in his voice. He'd had no idea.

"You didn't know?"

"No! Jesus. When?"

Pilar looked at the ground. "It was, I think, about . . . about 1996. Look . . . I shouldn't have said anything."

"Why? Why would she do that?"

Pilar did not look up. She pushed her hands into the side pockets of her summer dress and rocked backwards and forwards on her feet.

"I think you should ask her yourself," she finally replied.

"Please, Pilar! Was it because of a man?" he asked in desperation. He had grown to care about Eileen very much and, if his silence had placed her in any danger, he would never forgive himself.

"Yes," she said quietly.

Brendan thought for a moment. The dates didn't add up.

"But Orla said that 'it' happened in Eileen's second year in college," he said. "That would have been two years before '96."

Pilar did not raise her eyes to him. "Like I said, you need to ask her yourself." She finally looked up and rested her eyes on the lovers.

"And you think that this isn't a bad idea?" Brendan said as he gestured to the love-struck couple.

"No. It is good. For both of them. But they know that there are restrictions. Sadly."

Brendan folded his ladder and moved to the shed to put his tools away for the night. He walked back over to Pilar who had offered to drop Eileen and him home while she was on her break. A lump had formed in his throat and his heart beat mercilessly in his chest. No wonder his cousin didn't want Frank to know about her relationship. His uncle was probably worried that any emotional upheaval would send Eileen over the edge. He could feel a panic rising in his chest. If Frank found out, if anything happened to Eileen, if John left and she couldn't cope with the loss, his uncle would blame *him* and, what was worse, he would blame himself. His mind raced.

"Do you think Jonathan will ever find out where he is from?" he asked as he and Pilar moved down the driveway together.

Pilar stood by her car and shouted back to Eileen that they were leaving. She turned to face Brendan.

"No. Because there is no home. It is a fantasy, Brendan. I wish it were true but, believe me, this is the only home he has and we are the only family he will ever have."

Together they climbed into Pilar's old car and when Eileen jumped in the back seat Brendan turned and looked at her as though he had never seen her before. A wave of emotion overcame him. He wanted to put his arms around her and hold her. He wondered now if he had misunderstood his uncle's vigilance about his eldest daughter and if Frank was simply trying to protect Eileen from any further trauma. His mind raced over the possibilities of what had actually happened. He wondered if it was a broken relationship that Eileen couldn't cope with or, worse, if someone had assaulted her.

She met his gaze and, in that moment, it seemed she knew that he had found out about her past. She looked out of the car window and in the fading light he could see small tears in the reflection of the glass.

The three rode home in silence and, when they pulled up, Eileen got out and closed the car door quietly. She walked up the driveway past her father who was watering his flowerbeds in the cool evening air.

Brendan got out and leaned into the passenger window to Pilar.

"Thanks for the lift."

"You need to talk to her," she said.

Brendan nodded. "I know."

He stood back and, as her car drove slowly away from the kerb, he heard his uncle's voice.

"You're wasting your time thinking it's a regular date that girl is waiting on!"

Brendan looked back at Pilar's rear lights and shrugged.

"Oh, don't give me that look. I see how you brighten up when her name's mentioned in this house. You got to get to the brother. Those Puerto Ricans, that's how it goes. Used to be like that at home too and here, one time.

"You mean I have to ask *her brother* if I can ask her out?" Brendan asked as he walked up the driveway. He laughed loudly. "I'm *not* doing that!"

"Well, then you won't be going out with her. Your choice." Frank emptied the last of his water onto the rose-bed.

Brendan looked up as Eileen's bedroom light came on. He would have to talk to her. He would have to find out what had happened to her and he wasn't looking forward to it.

Chapter 10

When Brendan arrived into Coleen's kitchen the following morning, Eileen was not sitting at her usual place at the table. She had not come down for dinner the previous evening, saying she had a headache which Coleen had taken her up some aspirin for. He went to the hallway to look for her but the house was abnormally quiet. He returned to the kitchen and poured himself a coffee. Beside the pot was the usual small plate of pastries that Coleen left out for him. As he ate, a gnawing feeling that something was wrong grew stronger with each tick of the loud kitchen clock that hung over the doorway. It was a souvenir from Ireland and had a large map of the island painted green on the inside of the square ceramic plate. On each corner of the plate, a leprechaun with a ridiculously long pipe smiled a toothy grin. It was the type of clock that no one in Ireland would dream of hanging in their house but that Irish-Americans spent small fortunes on while on holiday in the homeland.

When he couldn't stand the quiet any longer, he climbed three steps of the stairs and called Eileen's name as quietly as he could.

He had rarely been upstairs in Frank's house. When he had first arrived he was offered Orla's old room which was beside Eileen's bedroom in the front of the house but he had opted for the granny flat where he could be alone as much as he wanted to, which back then was most of the time. More recently, he had taken to sitting in the house a little longer after dinner, talking to Coleen in the kitchen while Frank dozed on a chair by the empty fireplace. He also spent his time in a futile search on the internet for more clues on Jonathan or would retire to his apartment to mull over what he knew so far and what leads he would look into next. His life was fuller than it had ever been and he was happy, but this morning the quiet overhead had awakened an anxiety in him that he had almost forgotten about.

He called Eileen's name a few more times, raising his voice a little louder until he heard feet on the landing. He relaxed but his relief was short-lived when Coleen arrived downstairs in her dressing gown. She had dark lines under her eyes as though she hadn't slept a wink the night before.

"Frank's still asleep," she said.

Brendan raised his eyebrows at her. It was Eileen he was waiting on, not Frank.

"She's not feeling well, honey. Maybe you should go on ahead without her," Coleen said.

Brendan swallowed. Eileen never missed a day at the shelter and she hated the weekends as much as he did. Something was very wrong. He looked at Coleen and wondered if he should tell her what he now knew but she reached out and hugged him. This time he did not draw back as he normally would but placed his strong arms around her thin frame and drew her to him.

"Now, darling, don't you worry about Eileen. She'll be fine in a couple of days. She gets like this sometimes. You'll see." She patted his back.

Brendan moved away from her and nodded as he walked out the door. It felt strange going to the shelter without Eileen. He wondered how his cousin felt last night when he looked at her the way he did, with pity. It had obviously affected her deeply. Perhaps it was because he was the only one who until that point hadn't known about what happened to her. Not that he knew even now what that was, but he suspected that his cousin wanted people to look at her the way she was before she had tried to take her own life and that, until last night, he had been the only one in her life who didn't judge her by that one event, by that one action that had since defined her in the eyes of everyone who knew her. If only he hadn't turned to look at her in the car. If only she hadn't met his sympathetic gaze. If only.

When he arrived at the centre, Jonathan was standing in the garden, waiting for them. Brendan could see him push his glasses back further into his eyes as though to do so would suddenly bring Eileen into view.

Jonathan moved forward and looked down the street as if to see if Eileen was straggling behind her cousin.

Brendan looked at the ground.

"Eileen's got flu," he lied.

"In summer?"

"Yeah, well, flu . . . or something like that. She had a headache and she was coughing, I think . . ." He trailed off as he looked furtively at the disappointed man's face. "It'll give us more time to focus on your stories."

Brendan set off up the drive, then glanced back to see if Jonathan was following him.

Jonathan's eyes were still fixed on the street.

"Okay, I guess," he replied, dejected, as he followed Brendan.

"What do you want to know today?" Jonathan asked.

Brendan tried to focus on his apprentice but his mind was on Eileen. He looked up from his saw horses where he was attempting to repair some of the bedside lockers in the dorms.

He couldn't remember what he had decided to ask Jonathan about when he got to the shelter that day and said the first thing that came to mind. "Mmm . . . eh, tell me about your father," he said.

"Well, he was a tall man, about my height, and his people went way back in Virginia. Some of them were well known. I think . . . I think something to do with politics."

"Politics?" Brendan asked, surprised.

"Oh, I don't know. I think so. One time, there were election boards all over our house and a lot of people coming and going. I remember the photo of . . ."

Jonathan moved his gaze away from Brendan and stared into thin air.

"I think there was a man on them. I . . . I think I didn't like him much."

"Can you remember who he was?"

Jonathan shook his head.

"Seems kind of funny for an apple farmer to have relatives in such – well – I'm not being disparaging to your father, Jonathan, but . . . relatives with that kind of position in society."

Jonathan ran the hand holding the brush nervously across his brow. A small blob of paint flew off the brush and landed on the scar on his temple.

Brendan stood and offered him a cloth to wipe it with but he seemed oblivious to the offer. Brendan wiped the sticky paint from his face.

"You'll have to get turpentine for the rest," he said.

"I don't see too well out of that eye," Jonathan said.

Brendan looked at the scar that ran across Jonathan's temple and into his hair line. The injury seemed to have narrowly missed his eye.

"Because of that scar?"

Jonathan nodded.

"How'd it happen?"

Jonathan looked out of the window and into the distance.

"I liked it better when we were working outdoors. I can see things clearer in the open," he said.

"We can bring these outside," Brendan replied, gesturing to the lockers.

They moved outside and, as they settled down to work in the sunshine, Jonathan gazed yet again into thin air. He cleared his throat then and ran his brush lightly over the cheap wooden furniture.

"Seems like I have two memories of how I got that scar and I don't rightly remember which is the right one."

Brendan's interested heightened and for the first time that morning he was able to put Eileen to the back of his mind.

"I remember being maybe four years old and Cassie and I were walking down by the creek that ran at the bottom of our property. Nella was with us too. I don't think my daddy trusted me to mind Cassie on my own and, anyway, Cassie was maybe six and she didn't want a baby taking care of her. That's what she used to say. She didn't mind if it was Nella watching out for her though. Those girls were so close. I remember Daddy looking close into Nella's face and telling her that she was responsible for Cassie and that if anything happened to her he'd skin her hide." Jonathan smiled to himself. "Course, he was only joking. He'd never hurt a fly, my daddy wouldn't. He often said that he knew that if anything ever happened to him that he'd die happy knowing Nella would watch out for Cassie. Made her promise that one day. I just remembered that this instant!" He shook his head in amazement.

"Why didn't he think your mother would care for her?" Brendan asked.

Jonathan thought about this for a moment. "I don't know," he replied. "A lot of things I remember don't make any sense. Guess that's why Dr Reiter said I shouldn't stake too much on them and to put 'em out of my mind. Anyway, at the boundary of our property, someone was cutting down trees. That took us by surprise because it wasn't the season for cutting with the birds and all. I remember Cassie saying that. She knew all sorts of things because she could listen to things better than anyone else. Before we knew it, a small sapling came dropping from the sky towards us. Nella ran towards Cassie and threw her down into the creek. It was shallow there so she only cut her knees on some small rocks where she landed and she sat there in the water, hollering. But I don't remember anything because that tree hit me clear on the side of my head and cut into my eye."

Jonathan stopped talking and a serious expression washed over his face.

Brendan could see him shaking his head and moving his lips as though he was trying to make sense of something.

"Then I remember a part where Virgil and Clay were setting to cut some wood in the woods near the house. They were younger than me so I was in charge but Virgil, he wasn't the type to take orders, and Clay, well, he just followed Virgil's lead with everything. So he picked on this tree. It was too big for chopping but he swung and swung. Hardly made a dent in the trunk. He kept at it though until the old axe gave up and clear came off the handle and flew through the air. Darn thing cut my head open and went into my eye. Daddy just took me inside and poured homemade whisky on it and sewed my flesh there and then. Well, I yelled and yelled. Momma, she couldn't sit still until it was over. It was like she felt every bit of that needle going through my skin. When he was finished, Daddy tanned Virgil's hide good and that boy didn't sit down proper for a week."

Brendan recounted both stories in his head and decided that there was something amiss. It was like Jonathan was describing two different fathers. One who worried incessantly about his blind daughter and whom Jonathan said wouldn't hurt a fly and the other who beat his errant son and sewed his other son's head without an anaesthetic.

"How old were you then?" he asked.

"Oh, I guess about eleven or so."

"So your mother was there but you don't mention her when you were four. Four years before Virgil cut your head, your father was worried about leaving Cassie alone but four years on your mother is there. I don't understand it." He looked questioningly at Jonathan but he didn't respond. "What did he look like?"

"Virgil? He had blond hair and bright blue eyes, like me. We all looked the same. Except Cassie. She had long brown hair with auburn through it. She had brown skin and big brown eyes. She was real pretty."

"No, not Virgil, your father. What did your father look like?"

Jonathan moved his eyes upwards again, as though he was trying to picture the man. Then he moved his gaze back to Brendan.

"He was real tall like me and he wore a hat. No, he didn't . . . he didn't like hats. Just in the sun, that's all. He had . . . b-b-brown hair and blue eyes . . . or maybe he had fair hair . . . curly, I think . . ."

Brendan noticed Jonathan raising his fingers to massage his temples. He was beginning to see a pattern developing with Jonathan's headaches. It was usually when he had remembered something from his past. Something real.

"And your mother?"

Jonathan looked away again. "Em . . . she was tall too and skinny with white-blonde hair tied up messy like she had no time to fix it and clear blue eyes, almost white in parts. She had a narrow chin that stuck out and she was real pale like me."

"That's two blue-eyed parents you described."

"So?" he replied, somewhat defensively.

"Well, I don't know much about genes and I guess it's not impossible but isn't it strange how your parents had five blond, blue-eyed children and one brown-eyed, brown-skinned daughter?"

Jonathan looked away and frowned like a chastised child. "Now, I just knew you'd go and get like Dr Reiter on me!"

"No. I'm just trying to piece it together, like I promised."

Brendan sawed a broken leg off a bedside locker and threw it behind them. He picked out his tape and began measuring the length of the remaining legs to make a replacement.

"And, Jonathan, you never mention your mother when you mention Cassie. Think back . . . can you see your mother standing beside your sister?"

Jonathan looked away again and kept his eyes trained way above Brendan's head. "No," he replied and seemed amazed, as if he had never realised this himself.

"You said Cassie was older than you, and that Virgil, Clay and the twins came after. Is that right?

Jonathan nodded.

"Well, could it be that your mother died and your father remarried and then all the other children came along? Or maybe your mother remarried?"

87

Jonathan shook his head. About a minute passed before he answered.

"My momma . . . I don't see her with another man. It doesn't play that way. No, sir!" he replied definitely.

There he goes using that term *play* again, Brendan thought. It was as if he saw his memories like a movie that he'd take out and play from time to time.

"And your father?" Brendan asked.

"I don't know. I know that he loved me and my sister . . . all of us. I know he worked hard. I know he had a wooden bureau that I wasn't allowed to touch but apart from glimpses of him – small memories – that's all I can remember. Do you know what that's like, Brendan? Can you imagine what it would be like if you didn't remember much about your own father?"

"I don't know *anything* about my father."

"Anything? How come?"

"I never met him. He was gone before I was born."

"I'm sorry," Jonathan replied sincerely.

"Don't be. I've never thought about it. I suppose you find that strange?" He looked up from his work.

Jonathan nodded. It was very strange. "What was his name?"

Brendan looked to the ground and snapped his measuring tape back inside its case. "Something Martin. I never knew his first name." He leant back and fingered the mole on his face. "I never asked her. I never asked what my father's name was."

"Didn't you see it on your birth cert?"

Brendan thought about this for a moment. He had never seen his birth certificate. When he needed a passport, his mother had insisted on applying for it herself.

She said he had enough to do studying for his final exams at college and he hadn't given it any thought.

"Where was he from?"

"Ireland, but I don't even know what part. They met here when my mother was young and it didn't work out. Period."

"You're not hurt by him not staying around?" Jonathan asked.

"I can't see like it would have made any difference. If he left, he can't have been much good," he replied flatly as he began to cut a spare leg off a locker that he couldn't salvage.

"Still, it would have been nice to know his name." Jonathan stared into Brendan's face for a reaction but there was none visible. His new-found friend was already lost in his work.

"Right, let's get some of these ready for tonight," Brendan said.

Jonathan nodded but kept his eyes on his friend. Brendan's flat expression reminded him of Eileen. He had seen the same look on her a thousand times, the expression of hurt so deeply buried that it strangled a person from within, cutting them off from even knowing what their true feelings were. For once he felt lucky. He knew how he felt. He knew everything about his feelings. He just didn't know to whom those feelings belonged or where exactly he had felt them. But he would know soon. He could feel it in his bones. He was going home.

Chapter 11

The front door of Frank Dalton's house, which was rarely used, was Brendan's preferred entrance when he arrived home from the shelter that evening because he wanted to climb the stairs to Eileen's room quietly and preferably unnoticed by his aunt and uncle.

Upstairs, he tapped twice on the wooden door and heard Eileen turn in her bed.

"Eileen?" he said but his cousin did not answer.

"Eileen. I need to talk to you. Please open the door. I'm sorry if I did something to upset you. Just . . . please let me in."

Brendan waited a full five minutes but he did not hear any more sounds coming from her room. He sighed and descended the stairs before entering the kitchen where his aunt was cooking dinner and his uncle was reading at the kitchen table. He leaned back against the counter that wrapped around the lower end of Coleen's kitchen.

"You have a good day, honey?" she asked.

Brendan nodded and looked briefly at his uncle who had not acknowledged his presence.

"I tried to talk to Eileen but she won't talk to me. I don't know what to do." Caring for someone, he realised, caused pain and made him feel exposed and vulnerable. These were feelings

90

that he felt he could do without and he briefly wondered if they had been a worthy exchange for the loneliness he experienced before he came to Dover and let his cousin into his life. He fixed his eyes on his uncle whose attention he seemed to have gained.

"Leave her alone!" Frank bellowed. "She'll talk when she's good and ready!"

"Uncle Frank, I just want her to talk to me . . . so I can sort it with her."

"Sort it?" Frank sneered. "It can't be sorted. Eileen cannot be sorted, no more than your mother can. They are the way they are, so accept it."

Frank stood up and pushed his way by Coleen as she tried to get something from the refrigerator. He thrust a piece of paper into Brendan's hand as he made his way out of the kitchen. It was another letter from his mother. This time it was on one page. A brief note telling them the date and time she would arrive into JFK. The note was cold and businesslike and used none of the normal greetings a person would put in a letter. Brendan checked the arrival date. It was only three weeks away.

"So that's what's bothering him?" Brendan asked Coleen.

Coleen gave him one of her doleful smiles and shrugged. "He's just worried that . . . you know . . . there'll be trouble with your mom."

So am I, Brendan thought to himself.

Brendan took out the large notebook that he was recording Jonathan's stories in and laid it flat on his small table. He had two diagrams on opposite sides of the page. On the left, he entered all the details of the life Jonathan said he'd had on an orchard with several fair-haired siblings and two parents. On the other side of the page he had Cassie, Nella, a possible politician family member and a quiet father who may have been a writer. He scanned the ages that Jonathan said he was during the memories he had so far recalled. Jonathan had lots of stories at age four and his memories of that life with Cassie and Nella were remarkable. So far, he had not recalled any memories of

Cassie and Nella which linked up with the period when he reported living with two parents and with his brothers, Virgil and Clay and twin sisters named Mackenzie and Tyler. What could possibly be the explanation for that? Brendan quickly wrote down the few scant pieces of information Jonathan gave him that day. He undressed and went into the tiny ensuite bathroom to shower before dinner.

When he came out, he was surprised to find Eileen standing at his table, looking at the information he had collected. He wrapped the towel tighter around his waist.

"Ei-Eileen!"

"What's this?" she said, pointing at the table.

Brendan could see her chest rise and fall quickly and her voice, usually so soft and meek, was shrill and urgent.

"*You promised you wouldn't meddle!*" she shrieked.

Brendan looked away from her accusing eyes and swallowed.

"Eileen . . ." he started but she lifted the notepad and threw it across the room.

"I trusted you!" she said as large tears sprang in her grey eyes. "You're . . . you're just doing this to fill up your own empty life. You need the adventure . . . you need his stories but you'll hurt him, Brendan. You don't realise what you're doing."

"I won't hurt Jonathan," he replied.

"You will. You just don't realise it yet," she gulped.

She opened the door to leave but Brendan rushed forward and slammed it shut. He placed his back to the door and blocked her exit. She tried to push him out of the way but his broad frame was too much for her tiny body and she relented, sobbing uncontrollably into his bare chest.

"I can't lose him," she sobbed.

Brendan wrapped his arms around her and tried to soothe her. He pushed her hair away from her face and dried her eyes. Slowly her breathing settled and when she calmed Brendan led her to a chair and sat her down.

"I'm going to get dressed in the bathroom," he said. "Please don't leave. I want us to go out."

She nodded, blew her nose loudly into a tissue and looked down at her shoes, embarrassed now by her outburst.

When Brendan returned, Eileen was dressed in her heavy green coat. He looked at it and she blushed.

"I ran into the house to get it. In case . . . it was cold."

Brendan glanced out the window. There were at least two more hours to go before the sun set and it was still about sixty degrees Fahrenheit outside.

He opened the door and led her down the side entrance.

"Where are we going?" she asked.

"To the park."

The pair walked in silence to Hurd Park which was a fifteen-minute downhill walk from Watson Drive. When they arrived at the entrance gates, a large crowd had gathered by the gazebo where a brass band was warming up for a summer concert. They found a bench by the river and sat looking into the water. Brendan hoped that, like Jonathan, being outdoors might encourage his cousin to open up to him about what had happened to her.

She apparently sensed this and her chin began to tremble.

"When Dad went to New York to get you, I was excited that you were coming. More excited than anybody else in the family."

"Why?" Brendan asked.

Eileen shrugged. "Lots of reasons. I felt . . . connected to you . . . that we had things in common . . . but, mostly, it would be like I had a fresh start with someone who . . ."

Brendan looked at the ground. He knew what she was going to say.

"With someone who didn't look at me like I was crazy." She blew out a puff of air and focused her eyes on the bandstand. "Before you even arrived Dad had plans to keep you busy and that included replacing him each day to walk me to and from the centre. I begged Dad and Mom not to tell you anything – not to tell you why but they thought you should know all about me. It was only when I went into one of my depressions that they eventually agreed."

Eileen stopped talking as the band began to play loudly. She leant towards Brendan.

"Can we walk by the river?" she asked.

Eileen resumed her story as they walked along the river's edge. She stopped to pick up an apple blossom that had blown down from the trees above her. The narrow pathway was quiet except for an occasional person walking a dog or couples out for an evening stroll. They crossed a narrow wooden bridge and stood looking into the water as it washed over stones lodged on the bottom of the shallow stream.

Brendan tapped on the wooden rail and looked about himself, waiting for her to speak. She looked up from the water and turned to face him.

"I was an exceptional student in college," she said. "I worked hard and kept to myself. I wasn't wild or headstrong or remotely like . . . like Patricia. Oh, I know I look just like her and that's fine . . . but . . . I was not the same even though Dad would claim that I am. In my second year there I befriended a shy scholarship student. I noticed that he worked two jobs on campus to keep himself in college and I felt sorry for him. Orla was in first year in the same college by then. Victor was in my class studying English literature, my favourite subject. By the second semester, he was struggling so I offered to study with him a couple of evenings a week."

Eileen paused and bit down on her lip. Brendan reached forward and touched her arm lightly.

"It's okay," he said.

"After a while, he became . . . infatuated with me. I was different then. More outgoing and . . . just a regular girl. He wanted a relationship but I just didn't see him that way. I told him that I was flattered and that was true. He was a real good-looking boy. Also, I was seeing Doug at the time."

Brendan interrupted her. "*Orla's* husband Doug?" he asked, astonished.

"Yes," she replied faintly. "We were high-school sweethearts and . . . it wasn't serious or anything but when it happened and I was so distant . . . we drifted apart. Doug was at the same college studying law and Orla stayed on there. I guess they . . .

drew together for support and in time it turned into something different."

"Jesus!" Brendan said. "You weren't upset?"

She sighed and returned her gaze to the cold water running under the bridge.

"At first and, yes, maybe even now a little but . . . it wasn't even like we were in love or anything . . . it was just that . . . the life she had, well, some of it had been my life and I was left with nothing." She took in a deep breath and continued.

"Anyway, I went to Victor's dorm and tried to explain to him that I wasn't interested. I had already stopped doing grinds with him and I went there to beg him to stop sending me letters. Also, I felt that he'd been following me at night when I went to the library. But he thought . . . he said I wasn't interested because he was poor. He said I thought I was too good for him. I told him it wasn't true and then . . ."

Eileen put her hands to her throat and began to breathe heavily.

"He wouldn't let me leave his dorm room. I shouted for help and he put his hands around my throat."

Eileen's eyes widened as though she could see the horrible event unfold before her eyes.

Brendan, knowing what she was about to say, banged the railing of the wooden bridge in temper.

"Then . . . he beat me so badly that for weeks I didn't recognise my own face in the mirror and he . . . he . . . raped me."

Brendan let out a loud moan and tensed his back as her words cut through him. He unfurled his fingers that had been wrapped tightly around the rail.

"Where is he now?" he demanded. He could already visualise himself beating the bastard to a pulp.

"It doesn't matter where he is now, Brendan. What he did was not the worst thing that happened to me. Dad said it was my fault, that I had led him on, made him think that I was interested in him. He asked, what did I expect would happen going into men's bedrooms? That hurt more than any of the cuts on my body. It still does. Two days later Orla called him from the hospital and he drove down, discharged me and took me home and I've been here ever since."

"Eileen . . ." Brendan said softly.

"There's no need to say anything, Brendan. Nothing can change what happened."

"When did you . . ." Brendan struggled, unsure how to pose his next question.

"When did I try to kill myself? Two whole years later when I could no longer live the life my father expected me to. Trapped in the house like I was the criminal. My every move being watched. He wouldn't even let me file charges. He said that there was nothing to be gained from bringing it into the open, that it would bring shame on him and on me. I could have gotten on with my life. I could have finished my degree and managed to put it behind me as far as possible but instead I was caged up in the house and that seemed to me to be worse than what Victor did to me. It seemed like I was the one being punished. Then one morning I woke up and it was a beautiful spring morning. I looked out of my window and thought, there is so much beauty out there, so much life and I couldn't touch it or feel it. I could just look out my window or go shopping with Mom. I knew then that I couldn't go on living that way any more. I ran a bath and got in fully clothed. I took Dad's razor and I . . . I cut my wrists."

Eileen instinctively rubbed her wrists together and then clasped her hands in front of her. Brendan took them and turned her palms upwards. Two jagged silver lines ran across the width of her wrists. He wondered how he had never noticed them before. He ran his fingers softly over the scars.

She looked up at him and smiled through watery eyes. "Now you know why I never wear short sleeves. Anyway, after that, things got much worse with Dad. When I left the psychiatric hospital in New York, he wouldn't let me out of his sight. Once he found a book on dying in my room and he forbade me from buying any more books. It was just one of those spiritual books but he didn't understand. Little by little my world closed in until all I did was sit in my room. It was the parish priest who suggested that I do volunteer work at the shelter. Dad only gave in because Father Guinan was a friend of his. And . . . here I am . . ."

Brendan took his cousin by the shoulders and turned her towards him. He unbuttoned her heavy coat, slipped it off her shoulders and folded it over his arm.

"You don't need to hide away any more, Eileen," he said. "Come on. Let's go home."

He put his arm around her shoulders and led her out of the park. In the distance they could hear the band playing and the sounds of people singing along to the music. They crossed the street and began the slow climb together back to the house.

Chapter 12

"D'you like fishing, Brendan?" Jonathan Doe asked as he steadied Brendan's rickety ladder on the ground.

"No," Brendan replied, distracted. He rummaged around in his nail-belt as he looked for a screw to fix another shutter onto the window at the front of the old house.

"Never?"

"Never."

"Well, I got to tell you, you're missing out. There's nothing finer than catching a trout for dinner. Momma would be real pleased with us and Daddy too. He didn't have much time for fishing so I'd take my brothers after school and we'd sit by that lake for hours. Sometimes if we caught something early we'd have time to jump in and swim in that deep lake until we were almost waterlogged. Wasn't usual to see Virgil or Clay sitting so quietly but they would cos we'd have ourselves a competition to see who could bring home the largest fish for supper. My momma could fry fish better than anyone I knew. We'd have it with some fried tomatoes and potatoes."

Brendan nodded and smiled. "Sounds tasty." He was remembering the burnt offerings his mother used to dish out each evening after she closed the shop. By the time he reached the age of twelve he was cooking for them both and would have the evening meal ready when she'd creep up the stairs each night.

"Oh, it was. I can still smell the aroma of spices coming from my momma's kitchen. Yes, she could cook."

Jonathan smiled wistfully at Brendan.

"I enjoy talking to you, Brendan. And I'm feeling especially happy today."

"Because Eileen's back? I saw you two catching up this morning in the garden."

The smile faded from Jonathan's face and he looked into the distance. "She told me that you know what happened to her. I want you to know that I'd never hurt Eileen."

Brendan climbed down off the ladder and stood close to Jonathan.

"I know that," he said. He reached forward to pat Jonathan on the back but his friend hunched down and raised his hands to his head if to protect himself.

"I wasn't going to . . . hit you," Brendan said, surprised by Jonathan's strange reaction.

"I know," Jonathan said quietly. "I don't know why I do that."

"What else did you eat?" Brendan asked, changing the subject.

"Oh, my favourite, apple pie!" Jonathan replied. "Boy, they were somethin' else! She'd put a row of pies to cool on the windowsill of the kitchen and we'd sneak around the back and take a pie, run off behind the barn and eat it. Oh, she'd be so mad. She's start hollering and speaking so fast we'd pretend we didn't understand her and keep running."

"Did your mother speak Spanish?"

"No."

"Then what did you mean about pretending not to understand her?"

Jonathan frowned and looked at his upturned palms as though the answer lay in them. "Why, I don't know," he replied.

As Jonathan raised his hand to his head and scratched it, a

wave of pity flooded over Brendan as he watched his friend try to make sense of a hazy memory.

"It's the darndest thing," Jonathan said. "I can see it but then I don't."

Brendan climbed back up the ladder and drilled the last fixing to the wall.

"There. I can't do any more for today. Alice ordered some more supplies but they won't be here until tomorrow or the next day."

"But it's only twelve o clock!"

Brendan climbed down again. He stood and thought for a moment, then looked at Jonathan.

"Why do you use the name John Doe?"

"I don't. Everybody else does. They've got it wrote in big red letters on my file."

"Why do they do that then, when you can remember your own name?"

"Cos they don't believe me. Dr Reiter, he says there's no such person as Jonathan Wyatt Nelson. He said the police checked and that there was no such person. They said it was just a name that I chose. Can you believe that?"

"But . . . why pick that name?"

"I didn't pick it! *It's my name!*"

"Okay. Calm down, Jonathan. I believe you."

"Besides, I couldn't prove it. I don't have any paperwork. No birth cert. Nothing."

Brendan thought about this for a moment. "I have an idea. Do you want to go for a walk?"

"Where to?" Jonathan asked.

Brendan could hear the apprehension in his voice. "Just into town."

"I'd have to check with Pilar cos Alice won't be here until later."

"Come on, Jonathan. You don't need to ask for permission. You're a grown man."

"I guess," Jonathan said uncertainly as he looked back at the house.

"How old are you . . . roughly?"

"I was born somewhere between 1965 and 1968. Least that's what Dr Reiter wrote on his report."

The records office in Dover's health department was housed in a small squat building on the corner of Sussex Street. It was more modern than most of the town's buildings and was made of concrete columns and tinted glass that prevented passers-by from looking into the cramped offices inside.

Brendan and Jonathan entered the office where two female staff were positioned behind tall glass partitions at the far end of the room. Three rows of red plastic seats lined the room which was empty save for Zeb who was asleep on a chair in the back row. Brendan looked at him and was about to go over to him when a voice from behind one of the partitions called out.

"Oh, leave him be! He's not harming anyone."

Brendan looked over and saw a thin woman with a shock of red curly hair glaring at him.

"I wasn't going to bother him. I know him."

"Zeb comes in here for the air conditioning. He sits here most of the day."

Brendan looked at the sleeping man and felt a surge of pity. He wondered where most of the shelter's clients went during the day and was glad Zeb had found a place where people were kind to him.

"What can I do for you?" she asked.

Brendan leant into the window that separated him from her and flashed his brightest smile.

"I was looking for some birth certificates for my friend here," he said.

He looked behind him but Jonathan seemed to have lost interest in their mission and had walked away to study three large framed maps on the wall behind the seats. Brendan watched as he gingerly walked by Zeb on tip-toes and almost pressed his short-sighted eyes against the maps.

"Jonathan?" Brendan said.

"I'll be there in a minute," he replied without turning around.

Brendan looked at the woman's badge and read her name: *Maureen Logan.*

She handed him two forms to complete.

"I need seven. Thank you, Maureen," he said flirtatiously.

The woman laughed and handed him a pile of forms. Brendan could see a wedding ring on her finger and decided to believe that was the reason that his charms didn't work on this occasion. He took the forms over to the counter and filled in the names of the entire Nelson family, one on each form. As Jonathan looked over his shoulder, Brendan completed a form for Cassie, then Jonathan, Virgil, Clay and the twins, Mackenzie and Tyler. He knew that he was guessing their ages but even if he got one birth certificate it would be proof that Jonathan once belonged to the family. When he was finished, he had one form left over.

"Why don't you apply for you own and get your daddy's first name, Brendan?" said Jonathan.

"What for?"

"Be nice to know, wouldn't it?"

Brendan shrugged and wrote his name and date of birth with his mother's maiden name and married name of Martin.

"1976? You're only thirty-five? I'm not sassing you but you look a lot older than that," Jonathan said, amazed.

"I had a tough paper round!" Brendan joked.

"Huh?"

"Never mind."

Brendan brought the completed forms back to Maureen who flicked through them and then looked up at him. An expression of amusement spread over her face.

"Are you serious?" she said. She chuckled but put her hand to her mouth and tried to become serious.

"Yes, why?" Brendan asked.

"Well, these are . . . Are these are *really* his family's names?"

"Yes!" Brendan replied, irritated.

Maureen looked back at the forms. "Oh, look, you stated that these are Virginian births so we can't access them here. You need to go to the state they were born in."

Brendan sighed and looked behind him to see if his friend was disappointed but Jonathan had gone to study the maps on the back wall of the office.

"I can get this one for you though. This one is right here in Dover," she said, pulling Brendan's application from the bottom of the pile.

When she left the room, Brendan joined Jonathan at the maps. He scanned them but they were confined to New Jersey. He took a seat on the back row and glanced at Zeb who had not moved one inch. He noticed a cut above his right eye.

"Zeb got hurt," he said to Jonathan.

"Uh huh, I know," he replied absent-mindedly.

"How do you know about it?"

"He was fighting with Sam Wallace the other night over who owned what bed and Sam hit him. Kuvic came up the stairs and there was a big to-do. Kuvic said if Zeb caused any more trouble, he'd throw him out. I heard it all going on underneath me."

Brendan sighed and shook his head. He was beginning to hate Kuvic and hoped that he wouldn't have to see much of him for the rest of his community service. Maureen returned and called him to the counter.

She handed him his certificate. Brendan walked away and read it but returned instantly to the counter.

"This must be some mistake," he said.

"No mistake," she replied confidently.

"This isn't my birth cert!" he insisted.

"Check the details," she said.

Brendan turned away and let his eye run down the columns. His date of birth was correct. August 23rd, 1976. He checked his mother's name. Patricia, maiden name Dalton, birthplace Ireland. He reluctantly looked again at his father's name. This was not his birth certificate. Something was wrong.

He turned back to the window where Maureen's smile had faded and she was looking sympathetically at him.

"Are your parents divorced?" she asked.

Brendan shook his head. "Separated."

"Well, lots of people change their name to Martin. People can be narrow-minded, even here in this town."

Brendan stuffed the certificate into his jeans pocket. He would have to talk to Uncle Frank before he did anything.

"You get it?" Jonathan asked.

Brendan nodded but kept his eyes fixed on the ground.

"And?"

"I don't want to talk about it, Jonathan."

Brendan saw the look of disappointment on his friend's face but he knew it had more to do with Brendan not showing him his certificate than their failure to get information on his siblings.

"Aren't you disappointed?" he asked Jonathan. He could hear the anger in his voice, anger that had nothing to do with Jonathan's odd behaviour.

"Oh, I already knew they wouldn't be able to help us here," he drawled.

"Then why didn't you tell me that *before* we came here!" Brendan spat.

"Cos you didn't say where we were going."

Brendan looked away from Jonathan. He was right. He was a fool to think Jonathan hadn't already looked for his own birth certificate.

"I'm sorry," he said.

"What's eating you, Brendan?" Jonathan asked anxiously.

"Nothing. I've . . . I've got to talk to my uncle, that's all. Nothing to worry about."

When Brendan arrived back at the shelter, Pilar had gone home early and Alice was standing in the garden. She watched as they walked up the driveway.

"Pilar was looking for you. Better think of a good story about where you were."

Brendan nodded. He sat down on the lawn at her feet and stretched out. Jonathan walked onwards to the back entrance in search of Eileen.

"We were looking for birth certificates."

Alice nodded. "I expected it'd be somethin' like that. You find anything?"

Brendan could hear how much more laboured Alice's breathing had become. Even though she kept insisting on it, he did not believe that she was fine.

"No. Nothing," he replied. "Alice, do you mind if I leave early? There's nothing to do until that wood arrives anyway."

"That's fine, Brendan. Seems like you've nearly finished your service anyway. I'll be sad to see you go."

Brendan stood and touched Alice's arm.

"Oh!" she said. "I almost forgot. I'm having a party Saturday, three weeks' time. I'd love it if you and Eileen would come. Pilar too."

"What's the occasion?"

He noticed her eyes mist over. "Oh, just getting my friends together, that's all. My son will be there. I'd love you to meet Theo."

"My mother arrives a few days before that but I'd say it'd be fine."

"Well, bring her."

"Oh, no," he said hastily. "She's not . . . sociable."

Alice looked at him assessingly.

"I'd love to come, thanks," he said. "Tell Eileen I'll be back later for her."

Then he took off down the driveway towards home.

When Brendan arrived at the house Coleen was out and Frank was sitting slumped on the sofa in the lounge room listening to traditional Irish music. Brendan's muscles went taut as he contemplated raising the sensitive subject of his parentage with his uncle whose mood was usually low when he'd been listening to the hauntingly sad tunes. Brendan wondered why he did that, why he listened to music that upset him and made him long for his homeland.

He sat down on the sofa beside his uncle and took the crumpled piece of paper from his pocket. As he unfurled the certificate, his uncle glanced sideways and squinted at the fine print. Brendan handed the piece of paper to him. Frank exhaled loudly and slowly straightened his back into an upright position.

"I was wondering when you'd go looking for this," he said slowly. "I was hoping it'd never occur to you but I should have known better."

"Why didn't you tell me?"

"It was up to your mother. I guess she thought it was better that you didn't know."

"Because he was Mexican?"

"No, because he was no good, son."

Brendan took the paper from his uncle and looked again at his father's details.

Rafael Martinez. Place of birth: Mexico.

Frank stood and turned off the CD player beside him. He moved seats and sat on an armchair facing his nephew.

"Your father was a crook, son, but Patricia didn't know that when she met him. It was small stuff, I think – petty theft, using fake passports, that sort of thing. He was working here in Dover, just passing through for a few months. He was a handsome man, charming too, and Patricia was completely taken in by him. You . . . you look so much like him."

"Do you have any photos of him?"

Frank shook his head. "Sorry, son. Anyway, Rafael was illegal and I knew as soon as I saw him that a green card was what he was after but my sister wouldn't listen to me. She wouldn't even listen to Coleen and a lot of the time I depended on your aunt to talk sense to her. Well, when she fell pregnant with you she married him as quick as she could. She couldn't wait to get out

from under my roof. Ran off to New York with him and . . . I
don't really know what happened there. We had no address for
her and we were worried sick the whole time she was gone. When
she came back she was a nervous wreck and she wouldn't tell us
anything. You were born three weeks later and . . . well, that was
that. She never saw Rafael again and she went back to Ireland
with you. Son, if it hadn't been for the fact that we already had
Eileen to care for, we'd have kept you here. Orla was on the way
and Coleen wasn't too well so we had our own worries. It's a
regret Coleen and I will have for the rest of our lives."

"Where is he now?"

Frank let out a long sigh. "I don't know, son. I doubt if your
mother knows any more but you could ask her. I guess you've a
right to know."

Brendan looked at his feet. He felt his uncle was lying about
not knowing where Rafael Martinez was but he didn't want to
push it any more. It didn't matter anyway.

"I know what happened to Eileen," he said.

His cousin's comment that what happened to her was the
final straw for Uncle Frank now made sense. She was talking
about what happened to Patricia. He wondered if the whole
family knew about it and how many more family secrets he was
unaware of.

Frank reddened and moved his gaze out of the window.
Brendan could see his chin tremble and knew the memory still
upset him greatly.

Frank eased his heavy body up from the armchair and patted
his nephew's leg.

"You going to be okay?"

Brendan nodded. He'd just found out that there was a whole
other side to his background that he knew nothing about, a
whole other race of people whose language he did not speak and
whose country he had never been to. He had never given any
thought to his father because he had just thought of him as a
useless man who'd abandoned his mother and he had been able

to put him out of his mind. He guessed that knowing his father was Mexican did not change any of that.

He checked his watch. It was only three o'clock and he had three hours to kill before he picked Eileen up. He went to his apartment to shave and change his shirt. A short time later, he pulled open the patio door of the main house and shouted to Frank that he'd be back later. There was someone he wanted to see.

Chapter 13

Pilar Diaz's house was a low-roofed single-storey house in the middle of Crystal Avenue, a quiet cul-de-sac about a twenty-minute walk from Watson Drive. The front door stood to the extreme left of the house with two long windows to its right, set low on the beige clapboard wall. A small wooden gate opened onto a narrow pathway to the door of the house and a two-vehicle carport sat to the side. Two children's bikes lay abandoned beside a small herb garden on the right of the uncut lawn. From where he stood on the opposite side of the road, Brendan could see a man pouring oil into one of the cars in the carport. It was a pale green Ford and was parked beside Pilar's small blue car. Brendan focused on the man and decided he must be her brother. He had followed in his father, Emilio's, footsteps and was dressed in a New Jersey police uniform.

Brendan stood a while longer, embarrassed to be carrying the small bunch of flowers that had seemed like a good idea until he actually arrived on Pilar's street. He clenched his shoulder blades back and heard his tense vertebraé crunch. He moved his head from side to side until a similar crack occurred in his neck. He had not felt so tense in a long time and he couldn't believe he was actually going to ask this man for permission to ask his sister out.

When the man suddenly moved from the carport and looked his way, Brendan almost lost his nerve. Guido Diaz was a not a tall man but he was well built and Uncle Frank had joked with Brendan one night that he had better bulk up if he decided to face Pilar's brother head on.

He threw the flowers onto the grass verge and began to nervously massage the mole on his cheek. He put one foot onto the road but lost his nerve and was turning back when a child called out to him in Spanish. The girl was about six years old and was standing there holding the flowers he had thrown down.

"Shoo!" Brendan said.

She laughed and began to call across to Pilar's brother – probably her father.

"Get lost!" Brendan said but Guido was looking directly at him and had moved down the car port to greet him.

The girl stuck her tongue out at Brendan and followed him across the road, holding the flowers and placing one foot in front of the other like a bride.

"*¿Puedo ayudarle?*" the man asked.

"*No hablo español*," Brendan said and for the first time he understood why so many Hispanic people found this amusing. When they looked at him, they saw a fellow Hispanic, not an Irishman.

Guido Diaz looked him up and down for what seemed to Brendan to be an eternity.

"I said – can I help you?"

"I'm . . . I'm Brendan. Brendan Martin. I'm here to see Pilar . . . with your permission." He cringed as he said those last few words. If the lads in Murphy's could see him now!

"You the DWI guy?" Guido asked in a broad New Jersey accent.

Brendan sighed. "Yes."

"You do time for it?"

"Eight days," Brendan replied in humiliation.

"And you want to see *my* sister?" He spoke as if the very idea was ridiculous.

110

Guido Diaz finished wiping the oil off his hands but did not move his gaze from the visitor who had begun to sweat in the sweltering summer heat. Guido moved back to his car and threw the rag onto the ground.

"Listen, man," he said, "if it were up to me, I'd send you packing right now, but Pilar makes her own decisions." He looked him up and down again. "Well, come on in."

Guido led him into a narrow tiled hallway. He opened a door to the right and introduced Brendan to a heavily pregnant woman who was sitting under a fan trying to cool herself.

"This is my wife, Isabel."

Brendan shook the woman's hand and followed Guido out of the room and down the long, dimly lit hallway. He glanced quickly at the paintings on the wall. A small oil painting of the Virgin Mary hung to the side of a large tapestry of the Last Supper.

"You Catholic?" Guido asked when he caught Brendan staring at them.

"Yes," he replied even though he hadn't been to Mass even once since he had come to America.

"Good."

They entered the small kitchen at the back of the house.

Brendan lowered his head to enter the room and found Pilar sitting at the kitchen table feeding a little boy in a high chair. She stood and blushed.

"You've got a visitor," her brother said sourly. He turned to Brendan. "You don't look nothing like Frank."

"I know. I'm half Mexican."

It was the first time he said it yet the words rolled off his tongue like they had always belonged there.

"Huh!" Guido said while Pilar's mouth dropped open.

Brendan wondered if this would change anything, if being half Hispanic would gain him any brownie points with Guido or with Pilar herself.

"Well, I'll leave you two alone. I've got to go to work in a few minutes."

Brendan understood his meaning. Guido was telling him that he'd better be gone by then.

Guido walked out of the room but glanced back at Brendan and gave him a look that said 'don't mess with her'. Brendan understood it. If he had a sister he would do the same thing himself.

He stood awkwardly in the room and waited for an invitation to sit but Pilar stayed standing and crossed her arms around her body. She was wearing a light cotton dress with purple flowers and was barefoot. Her hair, which was normally tied up tightly, hung loose around her shoulders and fell down to her tiny waist.

"Are you really half Mexican?"

"Yes, I just found out today that my father was Mexican. I . . . haven't even absorbed it yet. It strange to know that there is a half of me that I know nothing about."

Pilar nodded pensively. "Is that why you are here? To tell me that?"

Brendan could hear an unusual intonation in her voice. She sounded annoyed but he had no idea why.

"I . . . just wanted to see you." His instincts told him not to mention his conversation with her brother.

"Where did you go with John today?" she asked in the same tone.

Brendan blew out. So *that's* why she's annoyed, he thought to himself.

"Just . . . just . . . well, I'm trying to help him find out where he's from."

Pilar raised her eyebrows in surprise. "What? Do you know how dangerous that is for him? Do you know how – how affected he will be when you find nothing? He is sick, Brendan. John is mentally ill. You don't know what you're doing."

Brendan glanced down and then moved his eyes to the kitchen window. An invisible mosquito buzzed outside the fly screen as it tried to find a way in.

"I'm just trying to help him," he said.

"Then leave him alone. Brendan, I've seen you with him and you care for him. That's good, really it is, but you don't know anything about him. Maybe you're interested in him because of your own background. You just said that it was strange not knowing anything about your father."

"I don't care about my father. I was referring to my background," he replied sharply. "And what do *you* know about Jonathan?" It was rhetorical because he didn't believe she knew any more than he did.

"*How much do I know?*" she shrieked.

He had never heard her raise her voice before.

"I know that when he was found he was half starved and that he had old injuries that showed he had been beaten for most of his childhood. He had three fractured ribs and a broken arm that had never received medical attention. Some of his teeth were missing. There were marks on his back that proved he had been beaten with a belt. He had a form of rickets called antirachitic. That means that he saw very little sunlight because he was probably kept locked indoors for most of his life. Brendan, John doesn't remember his past because he has blocked all of that out. His family must have been responsible for that. What other explanation is there? Have you considered that those evil people thought he was dead? That he escaped and he is now safe? And you want to help him find them? If they did know that he was alive, the reason they never came forward and claimed him is because they knew they'd be charged with child abuse."

"You don't know that. He's told me lots of stuff. He has a lot of happy memories with his brothers and sisters."

"Jesus, Brendan! It's all fictitious. Don't you know that? None of that is real."

A voice came from the other room. "Don't blaspheme!" Guido shouted.

Pilar glared at the wall separating her from her brother and then sighed. "None of it is real, Brendan. Please believe me. Please promise me that you won't encourage him."

Brendan looked away from her. He did not want to give up on Jonathan. His friend's quest had got into his bones and made his blood pulse through his veins like it hadn't done in a long time. But he couldn't refuse her, even though he already knew that he would not keep his word.

"Okay. I promise."

A door slammed and Pilar's brother came into the kitchen. He had his gun on his hip and was letting Brendan know that his time was up. Brendan couldn't take his eyes off the weapon and swallowed hard.

"Well, are you going to turn him down and make me happy?" Guido joked. "What's your answer? I have a right to know – isn't that so, Brendan?"

Brendan cringed.

Pilar looked from Brendan to her brother.

"You came here to ask for my brother's permission to ask me out! In 2013!" she bellowed. "¡El permiso de mi hermano! ¡Estamos en 2013! ¿Cómo se atreve? ¡Yo decido con quién salgo!"

"Pilar!" Brendan pleaded. "Please speak in English. I can't understand what you're saying."

"You don't ask for my brother's permission. It is 2013 and I decide who I date!"

"I'm sorry. Frank said –"

"Frank!" she growled. "Probably that was how it was when he worked with my father a long time ago, or maybe how it is in Puerto Rico now, but not here, not in America!"

Guido laughed and made his way out of the room. "Too bad, man – you heard her."

Brendan heard the front door slam and the car rev up in the driveway.

"Look, I'm sorry. I can see I've made a mistake. Forget I ever called." He was already wondering how he would face Pilar in the shelter the following day. "See you."

Brendan left the kitchen, walked down the hallway and opened the door to let himself out. He closed the door behind him and stood for a moment on the pathway with his face buried in his hands in embarrassment. He'd had plenty of rejection before but it was always in a dark crowded pub and he'd usually have had too many drinks to fully remember the details the following day.

As he walked down the pathway he could hear Isabel and Pilar talking in raised urgent voices as if they were arguing. The door opened and he turned to see Isabel pushing her sister-in-law out and closing the door loudly behind her. Pilar stood rooted to the spot and did not raise her eyes to meet his. Her face was burning red.

"Brendan . . . I'm . . ."

"Look, you could have just said no. End of story. No need to make an opera out of it!" he said angrily.

She kept her eyes on the ground. "I'm sorry. If you were here to ask me out . . . you should have asked me directly, that's all."

Brendan sighed. He hadn't been sure what to expect when he came here but he hadn't expected this. He felt like a fool now and it would take him a long time to get over the humiliation. He looked at his watch. It was ten to six and he had to get to the shelter for Eileen. He thought about how beautiful Pilar had looked when she was so angry, shouting at him in Spanish. He looked at her now, all cool and calm. She had returned to the Pilar he knew.

"Pilar," he said.

"Yes?"

"When you're angry or – or afraid, do you speak in English?"

She frowned at him. It was not the question she was expecting. She thought about it for a moment.

"It depends but, I guess, no, I usually speak in Spanish."

"Because it's your first language?"

"Yes," she replied, confused.

"Pilar?"

"Yes," she said.

"Do you think in Spanish?"

Pilar screamed. "*Sí, sí, pienso en español. ¡Ahora lárguese!*" she roared, reverting angrily to her native tongue. "*Get out!*" she screamed again in English to ensure he got the message.

Brendan frowned, unsure why she had become angry again. As he opened the gate, the hinges squeaked loudly.

"That needs oiling," he said.

Pilar lifted a small ceramic pot plant and threw it at him, narrowly missing his head.

"¡Agghh, *bastardo!*" she screamed.

"I understood that!" he shouted as he headed out of the cul-de-sac towards safer ground.

As he walked towards the shelter, Brendan thought about the first time he had seen Jonathan up close. He remembered how the strange man spoke in Spanish as he cowered in fear on the steps of the shelter. As though it was his first language. But none of Jonathan's stories mentioned his family speaking Spanish. It was yet another mystery surrounding the man who had had become so important to him, another mystery he was determined to solve.

Chapter 14

"You sure Alice said we could go all the way to Mountain Park?" Jonathan asked.

Brendan nodded and stopped to catch his breath. He bent over and placed his hands on his thighs. He had no idea he had become so unfit until he attempted the steep incline through the forest walk of the park's Blue Trail which would lead them to a magnificent lookout over Dover town.

"The view from the top is supposed to be nice," he said. "Think you'll like it. I think you'll feel more relaxed talking up here."

After twenty more minutes of hard ascent, the pair arrived at a large open area which was too rocky for trees to grow on. Together they walked to the edge of the rock and looked out over the entire town.

"Wow, that sure is pretty!" Jonathan said. "I've never been up here before."

Brendan placed his backpack down and sprawled on a large boulder to the side of the rocky outcrop and panted loudly. He thought of Alice and how each day she seemed more out of breath. On more than one occasion, he had almost asked her what was wrong. It was clear that she was sick but he decided that if she wanted to tell him, she would have done so, and that she was obviously keeping her illness to herself for a reason. He took out two bottles of water and threw one to Jonathan.

"We used to come to a place like this when I was a boy," Jonathan began.

Brendan took a large swig of water and sat up to listen.

"Once a year we'd meet on this high point of the mountain and give thanks for the harvest. It was like our own private Thanksgiving. I think my great-great-great-great-grandfather started the tradition and the family kept it going. He was a pioneer from the old country. We'd meet up with our cousins, aunts, uncles. Everybody would be there and we'd bring honey-glazed hams, sausage, fresh pies and potatoes. We'd stay there from sunrise to sunset, my two favourite parts of the day. When I was small, I loved to see the sunrise. I loved to watch its red and yellow glow light up the land and spread out across the sky. I thought it was the most beautiful thing in the world. Always felt sorry that Cassie couldn't see it but I'd try to tell her what it was like and she'd smile and thank me. That big yellow sun would go down right before our eyes at the clearing. My daddy said that clearing was there long before us Nelsons settled there. He reckoned it was an Indian place of worship and I could see how it would be. It sure was beautiful. It's one of the first things I'm going to do when I get home – climb that ridge and look out in time to see that sun rising. I'll take Cassie with me and explain it to her like I used to."

Jonathan stopped speaking and squinted into the sun as it climbed over the town. He raised his hand over his eyes to shield them from the glare.

"You can only just about hear the wind up here. It's so quiet. I love the quiet, don't you?"

Brendan shook his head. "No. I can't stand it. It . . . it makes me . . . nervous." Brendan didn't want to talk about himself and the heavy silence his mother had raised him in. He preferred to hear about Jonathan's incredible life, to listen to his extraordinary stories.

"I need the tranquillity, the peace that silence brings to my heart when I am alone with my thoughts," Jonathan said. "Sometimes at night it takes a long time for the men in the dorm to go asleep and I lie there and wait for the silence to rise up from their rooms and settle in my head. When it finally comes I think about my family and imagine where they are, maybe keeping the tradition going in that clearing and wondering where I am. Maybe they set a place for me. I think they would do that. Yes, the quiet lets you see into your heart, into your soul, lets you listen to your thoughts so you can know who you really are. You can't do that if you fill your life with noise." He paused. "That's what I miss most of all, you know, the things that I know were important to me. Like big family get-togethers around the table, sharing a meal and talking about the day."

Brendan thought about this for a moment. He looked at his friend. Jonathan was wearing his old woollen vest with the orange diamonds and the same faded corduroy trousers. His pale face and clear blue eyes gave the man an air of innocence but there was a depth of maturity behind those rimless glasses. He was a man who had experienced a lot of things, but which of those memories were real and which were, as Pilar put it, fictitious, was anyone's guess.

"I'd like to know more about how you speak Spanish."

Jonathan shrugged. "I told you. I always spoke it."

"Always?"

Jonathan nodded.

Brendan stood and threw a stone over the edge of the rocky outcrop as he tried to think of more questions.

"When you were found, did you speak English?"

"Yes."

"And read and write English?"

Jonathan frowned. "No. I remember someone would come to the hospital and teach me to read and write. A lady. She was real nice. Then I was sent to a foster home, four actually, but none of them really worked out for me."

"Why?"

"I kept running away, looking for home. Couldn't see how I needed a foster home when I had my own family to get back to."

Brendan bit the side of his lip as he absorbed this.

"So you went back into that hospital, the one Dr Reiter was at?"

"Yes, until I was an adult because I couldn't run away from there. Everything was locked. When I left, I just drifted around looking. When I finally settled at the shelter, Dr Reiter agreed for me to stay on in Dover because he was sick of me running off and felt I'd be a lot happier there."

"And you definitely couldn't read or write English when you were found?"

"Definitely."

"What else do you remember?" Brendan asked, anxious for more.

"Well, that clearing I was talking about, I went up to there on my own one day. I was about fourteen and I was upset. Can't remember what it was about now. Seems like I can never remember the things that made me sad. I just know that they're there, somewhere in my mind but something just won't let them come out. Maybe I'm lucky to be that way. I don't know. Anyway, I made my way to an old shack and it was empty. I didn't really plan on going there. I just found myself outside that hut and I let myself in. I knew it was empty cos the old Indian woman who died there, well, she was the last of her people. I wonder what it is like to be the last of your people, to be the only one left. Well, I slept there for three whole days and just ate whatever I could find around the small clearing she had dug out for herself. At night I swear I heard her moving around, making her medicines and humming the way she used to. My momma said that old Indian had a cure for snakebite, said she saw her save a man when she was a young girl. But I wasn't afraid. I was more afraid of going home."

Brendan wondered if he should ask Jonathan if he was sure about his age in this story. The newspapers reported that when he was found he was anywhere between the ages of eleven and fourteen so he must have been younger in the story than he remembered. He decided not to interrupt the flow of the story and made a mental note to ask him about it later.

"You were afraid to go home? Why?"

"I don't know."

"Were you afraid that your father would beat you?"

"Oh, my daddy never beat me. No, sir! Now Virgil and Clay, they got tanned lots because they were always looking for it. But me, no, sir, I stayed out of the way and did as I was asked."

Brendan took a blade of grass from the ground and began to chew on it.

"Jonathan?"

"Uh-huh?"

"Did Virgil and Clay look like you? I mean, a *lot* like you?"

"Guess so. Why?"

Brendan leaned back and propped himself up on his elbows and thought about the upset his suggestion might cause Jonathan. "No reason."

"What did happen when you went home?"

"I don't remember." Jonathan looked away and squinted into the sun again. "I love the sun." He began to rub the side of his head the way he did when Brendan's probing became too much for him.

Brendan stood and walked over to the edge of the rocky surface, aware that it was time to change the subject.

"There's a big lake down there. Do you fancy a swim? It might cool us down."

"Sure."

Together they slowly negotiated the steep descent and stripped down to their underwear.

Brendan walked slowly into the lake to gauge its depth. He looked back at Jonathan who was still standing at the water's edge.

"Careful, it's cold and real deep!" Brendan shouted and waded on through the ice-cold water.

He glanced back. Jonathan was still standing at the edge.

121

"Come on in!" Brendan shouted, and dived into the water.

He swam vigorously across the lake which was about three hundred yards wide. When he got to the other side, he turned but could not see Jonathan anywhere.

"Jonathan!" he called out but there was no reply.

He swam back to the middle of the lake but still could not see his friend. He shouted again and could hear his voice echo off the rocks surrounding the lake. He swam back towards the water's edge.

About twenty yards out he put his head under the water and swam around in circles, looking to see if Jonathan was mischievously hiding under the water to frighten him.

He swam closer to the shore, in line with the place he had last seen his friend, dived under and swam forwards a little. He came up for a breath and dived again.

And then he saw him – floating lifelessly in the water.

He came up for air, then dived again. Placing his arm around Jonathan, he dragged him upwards before pulling his limp body to the water's edge.

Brendan laid him on his face on the rocky surface and gasped at the sight of the long, narrow scars that ran the length of Jonathan's back. He turned his motionless friend over and checked but he was not breathing. Brendan tried to remember the lifesaving he had learnt during school swimming lessons and winced at the thought of putting his mouth over another man's. He shivered, opened Jonathan's mouth and blew air into his lungs. He repeated the sequence until Jonathan began to splutter, his hands instinctively rushing up as he tried to push Brendan off him.

Brendan turned him over and helped him to his knees. A gush of water flowed out of Jonathan's mouth and ran onto the silvery rocks as he coughed up the fluid from his lungs.

Once he was sure his friend was okay, Brendan lowered himself onto the rocks and sat motionless in shock.

"I thought you could swim!" he gasped. "You said you swam in the lakes at your home!"

"I thought I could too," Jonathan replied weakly.

"What? What the hell does that mean?"

Brendan placed his head in his hands and groaned loudly as he imagined himself telling Eileen that her reason for living had drowned in his company or telling Pilar who had no idea that he had even taken Jonathan out for the day.

"I saw it. I saw myself swimming," Jonathan finally said.

"What?"

Jonathan moved his lips as he tried to speak and explain himself.

"Jesus, never mind," Brendan said as he rose to his feet. He quickly dressed himself.

Jonathan tried to stand but stumbled forward, falling onto the rough rocky ledge. Brendan moved to steady him and squirmed again as he stared at the disfigured flesh on Jonathan's back.

"Did your father do that to you?" he asked.

"No!" Jonathan yelled. "My daddy never raised his hand to me. I already told you – he is a good man. Why don't you believe me?"

"Then who did it? Who did that to you?"

"I can't remember."

"You can't or won't?"

"I can't."

Brendan stared at his companion for a moment and the irritation he felt slowly evaporated.

"Jonathan, you must remember something about it. Even if you've suppressed it, there must be some trace of memory there. Can you remember anything about it? Anything?"

Jonathan put on his trousers and pulled his shirt and woollen vest over his wet body. He fumbled around the rock in search of his glasses and squinted as he pushed them tightly up the bridge of his nose.

"I've tried. Each year of my life, I have tried. Dr Reiter would show me photos of when I was found and he'd say 'Tell me what you see' and I saw nothing. All the things I am afraid of, Dr Reiter felt they were connected to what happened to me but even exposing me to those things didn't make me remember."

Jonathan shook his head. He leaned on a rock as he put his socks and shoes on. "Sometimes I think it's useless," he said.

Brendan had never heard his friend sound so despondent. "Don't give up, Jonathan. Something will happen, you'll see."

As they made their ascent back up to the forest pathway Brendan stopped to catch his breath.

"The mountain, I don't suppose you remember its name?" he asked doubtfully.

"No, but it was about a five-mile hike uphill. I know because I had to haul some of that food up there from our house."

"What did your house look like?"

Jonathan stalled and stared out at the view. Brendan took a rest and stood behind him, waiting.

"I told you – it looked a lot like the shelter. Guess that's what made me stop there. Seems like I always had the name of this town in my head, like Dover should mean something to me, so I came here – looking. I walked the length and breadth of the town and, just when I'd almost given up looking, I found myself on Maple Street and there it was – my home. Least, it looked a lot like it. Our house was made of white clapboard too but it didn't have the attic room. It was at the end of a long driveway and, until you drove up that dirt road, you couldn't even tell there was a house in there. The first thing you saw when you got to the top of that driveway was an old tyre swinging from a huge oak tree. My daddy said that tree was as old as the Declaration of Independence. He built a tree-house in it just for me and I'd sit there for hours listening to the birds singing and sometimes I'd see an airplane flying slowly through the clouds over my head. There was a row of old apple trees in the middle of our lawn. I can remember someone lifting me up in a little yellow coat I wore and letting me pick a red apple from its branches. I remember that the house had a screen door that always squeaked when you opened it and that it had a pretty wooden porch that wrapped the whole way around the house. It had a swing that was suspended from the porch roof by two chains and Cassie and I used to fight over it. There were hens and I remember a black-and-white cow and a cat that didn't drink milk and spat at you when you passed. But the house I've described is like a million other houses and Dr Reiter thinks I saw it in a book or something. I didn't though. It is real. I am sure of it."

Brendan moved forward and looked into Jonathan's face.

"Maybe you were very young when you left there which is why you don't remember the names of places. Maybe you were taken somewhere else to live and something bad happened there," Brendan offered.

Jonathan shrugged. "That's a lot of maybes."

"It would explain why you have such good memories at age four and why you cannot remember anything from then until you were a teenager. Wouldn't it?"

Jonathan shrugged again. "I'm tired," he said as he began to climb again. "Can we talk about it tomorrow?"

"Sure," Brendan said, disheartened.

They reached the forest pathway and began their descent of the mountain.

"Don't tell Pilar that you almost drowned," Brendan said. "Or Eileen," he added.

Jonathan turned and grinned. "You promise that you won't give up on helping me and I promise not to tell Pilar. I won't even tell Eileen that you kissed me!"

Brendan let out a huge laugh. He raised his hand and touched Jonathan on the shoulder. He noticed that for the first time his friend did not recoil from his touch.

"I promise."

Chapter 15

"Come in, son!" Frank hollered from the lounge room where he was sitting alone in the dark.

Brendan entered and sat down facing his uncle who had not come to dinner and who, according to Coleen, had been moping about all day.

Frank had a small glass of amber liquid in his hand.

"I'd give you one if you were allowed," he said.

Brendan waved his hand dismissively. "It's fine, really."

His enforced sobriety had not bothered him as much as he'd thought it would. He didn't know anyone in Dover with whom he could go drinking anyway.

"I don't drink much but I've got a lot on my mind," his uncle said.

Brendan could hear the slurring of his speech which suggested Frank had been drinking for the better part of the day.

"Oh?"

"Just your mother. I'm worried – worried that it'll all come up again. I mean, I don't want to see Eileen hurt."

"My mother knows what happened to Eileen?"

"I had to write and tell her. Felt she ought to know. Told her I'd handle it. She phoned me all upset, crying."

126

Brendan couldn't imagine his mother crying about anything and wondered why his uncle felt the need to tell her about it.

"Well, just tell her not to mention it," he said matter of factly.

"Ha! You ever try to tell your mother to do anything? She'd do the goddamn opposite to what I say. You'll see. She'll start trouble in this house. Won't agree with how I've managed things."

Brendan looked away and smiled to himself. The whiskey was obviously causing his uncle to exaggerate. His mother had very little interest in her own son, never mind poking her nose into Frank's family affairs. He stretched his feet out onto the deep pile carpet and wondered if this would be a good time to ask for his uncle's help.

"Frank, did you ever come across any live John Doe's in your time on the force?"

"What the hell do you mean *live*?"

"I mean people who were found by the police alive but didn't know who they were."

Frank thought about this for a minute.

"Yes, there was one case. I remember. This pedestrian, oh, it happened further along on the highway out of town. Emilio and I were called out to it. She was out walking and was run over by a car. Hit and run it was. She didn't have any identification on her – seems her handbag was stolen – and when she woke up in the hospital, she had no idea who she was. We checked the area, brought her photo around and no one knew her. We had to put her photo in the newspaper here. She had a New York accent so we put it out there too. Anyway, her sons identified her, said she was passing through Dover on her way to visit a friend but that her rental car broke down in the dark. She had phoned one of her boys from the highway but she must have got run over shortly after that. It ended up okay. They came and took her home.

"There was this other one. Oh, this is much more interesting. There was this guy from Cleveland down here on business. Well, while he was here, he hired a boat and took in some fishing on Lake Hopatcong. The water was a bit choppy and I guess he fell in and hit his head off the side of the boat as he fell. Lucky for him another boat was passing and pulled him out. When he woke up in the hospital, we thought he was on holiday here because he woke up talking with a sort of British accent. It was the strangest thing. Difference was, when he was well enough to talk to us, he was able to say he was American and knew all his details, address, phone numbers etc. The doctors said it was some kind of rare brain damage from the knock he got. Oh, some specialist came down from New York to see him. Boy, when his wife arrived she thought it was strange hearing him talk like he was a tourist. I wonder if he ever got his own accent back? Guess we'll never know."

Brendan looked out of the window and thought about this. Maybe Jonathan was wrong about the state he was from. Maybe his accent was also brought on by a blow to the head and he had been looking in the wrong state for all of these years.

"Did you ever find anyone . . . like a child . . . that no was looking for? You know, that no one ever claimed?"

"A child? God, no! I've heard of a few cases in the big cities but, no, I never saw anything like that here. Every child's got a mother, right?"

Brendan nodded.

"Why are you asking me about this? Is this about your father? Are you wondering about him?"

"No."

Brendan's answer was so immediate, so resolute, he began to wonder why he had no inclination to find out about his father. He knew he should be longing to know more or should even want to meet him, but he had looked as far into his heart as he knew how to and found that that longing simply wasn't there.

He stood and closed the lounge door to ensure Eileen didn't hear him. He was running out of ideas and felt he had no option but to use Frank's expertise in the search for Jonathan's family.

He pulled his chair closer to Frank and he told his uncle everything he knew about Jonathan Doe, with the exception of his relationship with Eileen.

When he finished Frank poured himself another whiskey and thought about it.

"Seems to me like you have to go back to the scene of the crime," he said.

"Which is?" Brendan asked.

"Goddamn it, Brendan. Good job you didn't go into the force. Embarrass the life out of me. That house in New York, of course. Take the man there. See where it leads."

Brendan nodded. It seemed like a really good idea. He wondered why he hadn't thought of it before.

"It's good to have a man-to-man chat like this," Frank slurred.

"Coleen wants you to come in for your dinner," Brendan said, only now remembering why he had come looking for his uncle in the first place. When he didn't answer, Brendan moved closer and heard a low wheeze emanating from his uncle's nose. He grinned at his sleeping uncle and took the whiskey glass from his hand, then took a blanket from the sofa and threw it over him.

Okay, he said to himself, New York, here we come.

Chapter 16

Brendan was already showered, shaved and waiting in the kitchen when Eileen came downstairs.

He had phoned Alice the night before to ensure she was on the following morning. Brendan had not seen Pilar since their row and was relieved that she would not be on day shifts for another few days. It would give them both a chance to cool down and hopefully put the sorry event behind them. When Eileen arrived in the doorway, she was wearing a green cotton dress and fashionable sandals. The dress, which had long sleeves, made her grey eyes look green and set off the red in her hair in the sun-filled kitchen.

Brendan stood up. "You look lovely," he said.

She smiled shyly and sat beside him.

"I haven't worn this dress for years. I took it out the night we had our talk and I've been looking at it hanging on the wardrobe door ever since. Brendan, you were right when you said I was covering myself up and you were also right that I don't need to do it any more. But . . . I wasn't doing it because I was ashamed or embarrassed about myself. I did it to shut the world out, to protect myself, and it occurred to me that in a way I was helping

Dad to shut myself away, to block out the world. I'm not going to do that any more. What's more, I am going to Alice's party."

Brendan put his coffee cup down and stared at his cousin. "How are you going to talk Frank into that?"

Eileen took a deep breath. "I am going to ask and, if he says no, then I'll go anyway. If you're going, he might be happy for you to escort me. You are going, aren't you?"

Brendan nodded. "I was hoping to ask Pilar but . . ."

Eileen grinned. She had known that her cousin was interested in Pilar but wasn't sure if he had taken it any further.

"Will I be in the way?"

"No, she threw a pot plant at me so I doubt she'll be interested in going anywhere with me."

Eileen laughed. "That doesn't sound like Pilar!"

"Well, you should have been there."

Brendan looked at his watch. It was nine and he would need to hurry if he was to catch the 10.07 train which would get him and Jonathan into Penn Station a little after eleven thirty. He hurried Eileen and walked as quickly as she could keep up with him.

When they arrived at the shelter, Kuvic was signing for a delivery of wood in the hallway. He looked at Eileen from head to toe and wolf-whistled as she ran down the hallway to the laundry.

Brendan reached forward and caught him by the throat, pinning him to the wall and sending the delivery dockets flying about the hallway.

"You ever look sideways at my cousin I'll kill you," he said.

Kuvic sneered and jerked free from Brendan's hold, pushing him with full force across the hallway.

"How many weeks you got left here, Paddy? Might have to tell Thompson to cut them short. I can keep a closer eye on Eileen for you then. Or Pilar. I see the way you look at her but, don't forget, I saw that little border-hopper first."

Brendan lunged forward and grabbed Kuvic by the shirt collar, pushing him hard into the wall again.

"She's Puerto Rican, you stupid bastard. That means she's an American citizen."

Kuvic raised his arms to loosen Brendan's grip and punched him, knocking him into the hall table. Brendan lunged forward and punched Kuvic in the face, sending him flat into his back on the polished tiled floor. He stood over him and was about to punch him again when he heard Alice shouting from the landing.

"Stop that!"

He looked up and backed away from Kuvic who clambered to his feet and dabbed his bleeding lip with a handkerchief.

"See what he did?" Kuvic asked Alice who glared down at them.

"Kuvic, where is Zeb?" she demanded.

Brendan grinned as the smile on Kuvic's face slowly faded.

"I had to throw him out last night. I warned him about fighting but that dumb son of a bitch just kept on starting rows. Couldn't get a moment's peace."

"That's a lie!" another voice called from the upper floor.

Jonathan walked down the stairs, followed close behind by Alice. His blue eyes were ablaze with anger.

"Zeb was shouting all right but you didn't give him a chance to settle down. Said he was interfering with your favourite TV programmes. I heard you from my room. You just dragged him down the stairs and threw him out. The other men were afraid. There was hardly a word in that room until morning. They were even afraid to come out to use the bathroom."

Kuvic looked at Alice who was now standing in the hallway with her arms folded about her body.

"Are you going to believe this nutcase over me?" Kuvic asked in disbelief.

"Don't you dare ever refer to any of the clients with those words again!" Alice replied. "Do you hear me? I won't only be going on what John says. I'll be asking the other men this evening and I'll ask Zeb when he comes back tonight. If what they say is true, you'll have some explaining to do. Don't forget, I am the manager here."

"Not for much longer," Kuvic murmured as he turned on his noisy heels and walked away.

Alice sighed and stood for a moment in the hallway. Brendan noticed that she looked deflated, spent.

"Are you okay?" he asked.

"Yes, but you two get on out of here now. Time is running out."

As they took their seats on the train, Jonathan squinted nervously out of the window and remained in a trancelike state for the next twenty minutes of the journey, occasionally glancing at Brendan with narrowed, suspicious eyes.

"Aren't you going to ask where we're going?" Brendan said at last.

"I can read!" Jonathan responded sharply.

Brendan leaned forward and touched Jonathan's knee. "What's the matter?"

"Why are you taking me to New York? I want to go to Newsart, Virginia, *not* New York City!"

"Do you trust me?"

Jonathan looked out of the window and swallowed. "Are you taking me to see Dr Reiter? Cos if you are, I'm getting off at the next stop. I mean it, Brendan. He can't help you anyway. He only knows what you know."

"I'm not taking you to Dr Reiter."

"You promise?"

"Promise."

Brendan flushed when he noticed several amused-looking passengers had become interested in their conversation and were staring at them. He quickly took his hand off Jonathan's knee and leant back into his seat for the rest of the journey. He relaxed to the sway of the train as it made its way noisily along the tracks and began to imagine the two of them standing outside that old rundown house in Harlem. He could see Jonathan standing there, remembering everything about how he came to be there, remembering who he was and where he had come from. He imagined himself returning victorious to Pilar who would apologise, tell him he was right all along and might even go with him to Alice's party. More pleasing than any of these thoughts was a vision of himself standing on that mountain clearing in Virginia with Jonathan, looking out at the Blue Ridge Mountains and walking through the orchards. He could see the old Indian woman's hut, the mountain lion with her cubs and the swing on the porch of the homestead Jonathan had so vividly described. He didn't expect Jonathan's parents to be alive but he could hear his brothers and sisters thanking him for bringing their brother home and he would sit at their table as they explained how Jonathan had become lost to them and put the last piece of the jigsaw into place.

When the train pulled into Penn Station, Brendan led his companion outside into the bustling city. He noticed Jonathan become ill at ease in the noise and confusion of the crowded city and mused over how two very different men could become good friends. Brendan relaxed into the hustle of the noisy crowd and moved with them, dragging Jonathan along as he went. Twice he gently pulled Jonathan's hands from his ears as he tried to block out the noise of voices shouting and of traffic beeping.

Then a traffic cop blew his whistle at jaywalkers, causing Jonathan to rush inside a diner to hide. Brendan followed him and, knowing it was useless to try to move him for a while, ordered coffee and pastries, and they sat looking out at the crowd as they ate and drank.

"We have to go back out sometime," Brendan said at last but Jonathan did not answer him and kept his eyes focused on two Latinos who were standing outside the window, smoking.

"Are you afraid of those guys?" Brendan asked.

Jonathan nodded.

"Do you know them?" he asked hopefully.

Jonathan shook his head and placed the diner's large menu on the window ledge to block them from his view.

"Then why are you afraid of them?"

Jonathan looked frantically around the busy diner and did

not answer. Brendan noticed his friend's hands had begun to shake and sweat had begun to bead on his forehead. A feeling of panic began to rise up in him as he contemplated the possibility of Jonathan having one of his outbursts in the restaurant but he focused his mind on the purpose of their trip and the happy ending he knew that this journey would achieve.

"I want to know where we're going," Jonathan demanded.

Brendan sighed. "You won't know where it is until you get there. I mean, you won't recognise the name until you see it. Trust me."

Jonathan began to tap the salt-and-pepper set on the table nervously.

"I need to use the bathroom," he said. He left his seat and made his way down to the end of the long narrow diner.

When he returned Brendan had paid the bill and was standing with the door open to encourage Jonathan to rejoin the crowd.

The pair walked to the bus stop and caught the M10 to Harlem which would take them down Frederick Douglas Boulevard.

"Tell me when you recognise anything," Brendan said.

"I've never been here before, Brendan, and you want me to tell you if I recognise anything?" Jonathan replied, exasperated.

"You *were* here, Jonathan. This is where you were found, this is where you were in the hospital – and what about your foster homes? They were all in New York, weren't they?"

Jonathan nodded and looked around himself doubtfully. "I don't see anything that I know."

"You will," Brendan promised.

As the bus approached West 125th Street, Brendan signalled to Jonathan that they would be getting off.

They continued their journey on foot down Martin Luther King Boulevard then swung right down Lenox Avenue. Brendan took out the map he had printed off the internet and rechecked how many of the small side roads they'd pass before they'd reach Parkview where he hoped the house would still be standing.

When they arrived there, the street did not look at all as

Brendan had imagined. He'd thought that the old city houses would have been mostly replaced by high-rise apartment blocks but the narrow street was still lined with a long terraced row of four-storey houses. The top three floors of the stone houses were fronted by large windows, each with mounted air-conditioners suggesting that the large houses were now divided into smaller apartments. Black wrought-iron railings ran along the front of the basement areas which were accessed through a small gate. Some of the houses had removed the basement railings and used the little gardens inside as parking spaces.

Brendan turned to look at Jonathan whose face registered no emotion.

"Do you see anything to recognise?"

"No. I – I don't remember any of this," Jonathan replied anxiously.

Brendan began to walk faster down the long narrow street, anxious to stand in front of the house and watch his friend remember. He glanced back at Jonathan as he stumbled along with less enthusiasm.

Brendan stopped halfway down the street where workmen were renovating three of the houses simultaneously. The railings of the houses had all been removed to make way for three large skips and long tubes ran from the top floor to the skips which the construction workers used to dispose of rubbish.

Brendan stopped and peered at the numbers on the doors: 50 . . . 52 . . . 54.

It was the last of the three houses.

Brendan moved Jonathan forward and stood him squarely in front of the house which looked like it had been abandoned for years. He moved his body sideways so he could watch Jonathan's face as he began to remember.

"Well?" Brendan asked.

"Well, what?"

"This is the house that you brought the police to, the night they found you in the park. You told them that your grandmother lived here."

Brendan waited and watched Jonathan's face crease and fold as he tried to make sense of the sight in front of him. He looked up to the top floor and slowly moved his eyes down the house. Brendan thought he saw a flicker of recognition as Jonathan trained his eyes on the basement but then his friend closed his eyelids tightly and stood motionless on the pavement.

"Anything?"

Jonathan opened his eyes and shook his head. "No. I *told* you. I've never been here before!"

Brendan moved closer to the house and sighed. There had to have been a reason for Jonathan to bring the police to that house. He looked into the open basement door. There didn't appear to be any workmen inside. He shouted up to a worker on a scaffold in the next house.

"Hey! I used to live here!" he lied. "Mind if we take a look inside?"

An Irish voice replied, "No problem, but help yourself to two of them hats there and don't be long. The boss'll be back soon."

Brendan took two hard hats from a box beside the skip and handed one to Jonathan. He inched his way past the huge skip which almost blocked the driveway and headed towards the basement. He looked back to find Jonathan still standing on the pavement outside the house.

"Come on!" he said.

The basement of the house was remarkably small considering the overall size of the building and consisted of two small rooms and a tiny bathroom. The first room was completely empty. The walls were painted in dark blue paint which hung loose in sections in the damp, musty room. Across the hallway, a tiny bathroom with a small round window faced out to the front of the house and had an old-fashioned shower cubicle, sink and broken toilet bowl.

Brendan moved to the second room which was slightly larger and faced out onto the back of the house. An old wardrobe stood inside the door and a wooden kitchen counter, rotting with damp and mould, sat under the window. He peered through the filthy glass and could see the tall trees of Marcus Garvey Park in the distance. The walls of the room were stained with grease and the ancient floorboards creaked under his feet as he moved about the room, looking for what exactly he didn't know.

He returned to the front room where Jonathan stood, looking out the window. He searched Jonathan's face but his friend was in a trancelike state. Brendan raised his arm to touch Jonathan but he flinched and raised his hands to his head.

"It's me, Jonathan, it's Brendan! I'm not going to hurt you. What can you see?"

Jonathan turned to stare at him as though he had been woken from a dream.

"*No me escaparé otra vez. Abuelita ayúdeme. Abuelita. No lo haré,*" he said in agitation.

Brendan moved backwards. "Jonathan, what's happening to you? Tell me!" he asked, more urgently now.

"*No me lastime,*" he whimpered. "*¡Seré bueno!*"

"I won't hurt you, Jonathan. I'm your friend. Please, please, tell me what you can see?"

But Jonathan was locked in some memory, lost in some dark, murky place in his mind. He waved his hands in the air as though he was trying to open something that once stood by the window. Brendan moved forward to try to calm him.

"I'll get in, I'll get in," Jonathan said in English.

"Get into what?" Brendan asked.

Jonathan was now cowering under the window.

"Jonathan, calm down!"

He needed to wake Jonathan from his memory, he needed to know what he could see.

"Tell me!" he demanded.

He saw the terror increase in his friend's eyes.

Jonathan stood and backed slowly into the corner of the room. His eyes looked huge and wild, as though he feared for his life.

"Please, please!" he begged as snot and tears ran down his face.

Brendan moved forward again. "Jonathan," he said gently.

But Jonathan's eyes darted sideways and focused on the open door. He ran, knocking Brendan over onto the dusty floor, and fleeing onto the street.

Brendan jumped up and chased after him. The skip slowed him down as he tried to inch his way down the narrow driveway. He heard the screech of a car and a loud bump.

"*Jesus, Jonathan!*" he yelled as he squeezed past the end of the skip and ran out to where a car was stopped in the middle of the road.

"Did you see that?" the driver asked as Brendan stood panting at the car. "Some maniac just ran out in front of me. I hit him hard but he just got up and kept running!"

"Which way?" Brendan panted and ran in the direction the man was pointing. When he reached 5th Avenue, he stopped and tried to catch his breath. He leant against a building and looked right as hordes of people left their office buildings for lunch. He looked to his left where the street, which led to the park, was much quieter. But his friend was nowhere to be seen. Jonathan was gone.

Chapter 17

Brendan ran his hands through his thick dark hair and tried to calm his breathing as he stood on the corner of 5th Avenue and 119th Street. He tensed the muscles in his legs as he tried to control the tremor that had begun to move in painful waves up his body.

"Jesus!" he said, shaking his head at the hopeless situation he was in.

He had no idea which direction Jonathan had gone, so searching for him would be like looking for a needle in a haystack. He glanced again at the crowds of people spilling out from their offices to his right and reasoned that it was unlikely Jonathan would have willingly run towards them. He looked left at Marcus Garvey Park in the distance. It was the place Jonathan had run to all those years ago. Maybe he had gone there now.

As he ran forward, he pushed several people out of his way and ignored their insults as they caught up with him at the pedestrian crossing. Sweat had begun to pour out of him, plastering his white T-shirt and his heavy denim jeans to his body.

Brendan tried to get into the park at the 5th Avenue entrance but there was a queue of parents and small children in front of him. He ignored the line and hopped over the small fence beside the monument. He pushed through the crowds, calling out Jonathan's name. He stopped at a section of thick, overgrown trees and shouted out again.

He swung left towards the baseball arena and entered the recreation centre in the hope that his friend had taken shelter there from the searing New York heat but he was not there. In the distance he could see two mounted police but he did not want to report Jonathan missing yet. He stopped running for a moment and bent forward to catch his breath.

"Jesus, where *are* you?" he said aloud.

He checked his watch and it was almost two o'clock. Jonathan had been missing for nearly half an hour. He was pretty sure that his friend didn't have any money on him so the likelihood of him returning to Penn Station to get home was nil. Also, he did not believe that Jonathan would have recovered so quickly from the stupor he had been in and felt that he was somewhere in this park, hiding from some memory that had been sparked off in that basement room.

Brendan sat down on a park bench to think. He tried to get into his friend's tortured mind and figure out where someone like Jonathan would hide in this big park.

He returned to the gate and took a map from a teenage ranger whose voice had not yet broken. He studied it for a moment and walked quickly northwards to the pool area, hoping his friend had not jumped in. When he got there, all three pools were filled with screaming children. He walked along the side and stared in as he looked for an adult among the rubber rings and arm-bands. Several mothers, concerned by his agitated appearance, glared at him until he moved off towards the basketball courts. He had no reason to believe that Jonathan would be there but he was running out of options.

Only one of the courts was being used, by about five black youths.

Brendan stopped and wrapped his fingers around the green wire that surrounded the court.

"Did any of you see a tall white guy, about 6 foot, blond

hair?" he asked. Brendan could hear the anguish in his voice, the sound of sheer panic.

The youths stopped dribbling the ball and came close to the fence.

Brendan swallowed as they stood close to him on the other side of the wire. They were all big and it had only now occurred to him that they might not welcome questions from a white man in their neighbourhood.

"Yeah, man," one answered in a strong New York accent. "Came in that gate there and ran right through the court 'til he realised it was fenced all the way round. We tried to show him the way out but he looked like he thought we were goin' to kill him. He was limping bad and his head was cut open. You chasing him? He do something on you?"

Brendan shook his head. "No. He's my buddy. I'm just trying to find him."

"Better do it fast. He's bleeding down his face bad. Might be dead by the time you catch up with him," another youth added excitedly.

"Which way did he go?"

Brendan frowned as two of the youths pointed westwards and another pointed north. The two remaining youths shrugged as they passed the ball to each other.

Brendan bit down on his lip as he decided his next move. He had already been down as far as the recreation area in the eastern part of the park and he had run through most of the northern section. He had entered the park through the southern gate.

He decided to make his way towards the centre and then follow the pathway to the western end of the park.

He walked along the long narrow pathway which was quieter than the other paths he had been down. He passed a tall metal tower on his way. He looked up at it and reckoned it was about fifty feet high. He remembered reading once that the hollow, iron-framed structure was built as a fire-watchtower in the mid-1800s when New York's buildings were mainly built out of wood. He leant against one of the metal stanchions and thought about his next move.

Maybe Jonathan was no longer in the park and was somewhere on the streets of New York, alone and without any means to buy a drink in the cruel heat. He wiped the sweat off his brow and walked to a food cart to buy a bottle of cold water. He drank quickly and poured the remainder of its contents over his head.

"Where *are* you?" he said quietly to himself.

He looked at his watch and a whole hour had now passed since Jonathan disappeared. He tensed at the thought of what could happen to someone like Jonathan in the big city. According to the kids playing basketball, his friend already had a head injury that was bleeding heavily. As he left the park for 5th Avenue, he reddened at the thought of phoning the centre to tell them what had happened and decided that he would not give up yet.

He took the map out of his pocket and found his way back to the old house. Slowly, he began to comb the area in outwardly-moving circles, looking initially in small parks and diners and then anywhere else that his friend would think of hiding. With no success, he walked through Central Park in the direction of Penn Station, hoping that his friend might have calmed down and would be waiting there for him but Jonathan was nowhere to be seen. His friend had simply disappeared.

By six thirty Brendan had no option but to phone the shelter and come clean.

He sat on a park bench and stared at the public phone on the corner of 33rd and 8th and thought about what he would say. He slowly made his way to the phone box and, unsure what the call would cost, he jammed several fifty-cent coins into the slot.

He almost hung up when Pilar answered but took a deep breath and told her what had happened. When he finished, her silence cut through him much worse than if she'd hurled another one of her pot plants at his head.

"Pilar?" he said.

"Go back to the park. You'll find him in there, probably near the tower – or up the tower."

"This has happened before?"

"I told you, Brendan. I told you to leave it alone. When you find him, don't try to talk him around. And if he is on the tower, do *not* go up after him. Do you hear me? Do *not* climb it. He may panic. Just stay with him. I'm on my way. I'll have to get Kuvic to come in and cover for me – Jane is here but she wouldn't be able to manage on her own. Cathy is away this week and Alice is out looking for Zeb. It's best that she doesn't know about Jonathan anyway until we find him. I'll phone Dr Reiter and organise to have him taken to him when we've found him."

"I promised him I wouldn't take him to Dr Reiter," Brendan said worriedly.

"It's a little late for keeping promises," she replied curtly and hung up, leaving Brendan standing on the sidewalk with the receiver in his hand.

He felt like an idiot. Why hadn't he listened to her and to Eileen? Why couldn't he have left well enough alone? Jonathan was out there somewhere, alone. He could hear Alice's voice telling him that Jonathan wasn't made for the streets and Eileen's remark that Brendan was living his life through the man's amazing stories and it was true. He had endangered his friend and all he could do was hope that no harm would come to him.

Brendan was not a praying man but he looked upwards and promised that if Jonathan got out of this unharmed, he would never again try to find out the man's identity. As he replaced the receiver, he longed to give in to his exhaustion. He felt like he could lie down there right on the pavement and sleep and found himself looking longingly at the grey concrete. His shoulders ached and his stomach growled from hunger.

He hailed a cab back to Marcus Garvey and, despite his exhaustion, he ran quickly through the park which looked ominous in the fading light. He looked upwards to the sky which was still bright but the tall buildings surrounding the park blocked out the sunset and dipped the lush green area into premature darkness.

He made his way to the tower and looked up at its immense columns.

"Jonathan?" he called softly even though the park was now almost empty save for a couple of homeless people lying on nearby benches.

He looked up but he could not see anyone on the metal structure. Brendan lowered himself down onto the dirt and leant against a tree where he sat motionless for an hour and a half until Pilar arrived.

She did not look at him but walked directly to the tower and touched the cold steel with her hand.

"Jonathan," she said softly. "*Por favor, baje. No pasa nada. Ahora está a salvo.*"

Brendan came to her side. "What are you saying?"

"I am telling him to come down, that it is safe."

Brendan could see her eyes moisten and he looked away, painfully aware now of the hurt he had caused and the damage he had done.

"*¿Abuelita? ¿Es usted abuelita?*" a voice called out from the lookout at the very top of the tower.

Brendan winced as he realised how high Jonathan had climbed.

He saw Pilar tense and look to the ground as though Jonathan's words caused her pain.

"What?" Brendan asked frantically.

"This is not good. He thinks I am his grandma," she replied.

She answered Jonathan in Spanish, in soothing words of comfort.

After a while she walked about twenty feet away and took out her mobile phone. Brendan had never owned one. He hated the thought of people being able to reach him wherever he went. He moved closer to her and heard her speak to Dr Reiter in a low urgent voice and listened as she used terms like 'psychosis' and 'psychotic episode', words that made Brendan's blood turn cold. He heard her giving Dr Reiter directions so that an ambulance would be waiting outside the 5th Avenue entrance when Pilar managed to talk Jonathan down. When she was finished, she put her phone away and moved back to her spot by the metal pillar.

"Jonathan?" she called. "Please come down and I will take you away from here. I won't let anyone hurt you!"

Brendan noticed that she called Jonathan by the name he preferred, a name he had never heard her use before.

A silence fell as they held their breath and waited for him to reply. Slowly, they heard the sound of his feet on the metal steps. They heard him cry out in pain. Brendan looked away from her, aware now that he would have to tell her about Jonathan's accident.

"He got hit by a car – I think he hurt his foot. His head is cut too."

Pilar glared at him and he looked away. Guilt overwhelmed him and he could not return his eyes to Jonathan until the man had made it painfully down the last rung.

"Pilar?" Jonathan said.

A smile washed over her face and heavy tears flowed down her face. She wiped them quickly away and moved towards him.

"I heard my grandma," he said.

Brendan was moved by how childlike his friend sounded in the dark, empty park.

"Yes, but she had to go and asked me to take care of you. Is that okay?"

Jonathan looked around himself and appeared perplexed by his surroundings.

"How did I get here?" he asked.

"We can talk about that later," Pilar replied.

They walked together towards 5th Avenue. Soon they could see the blue flashing lights of the ambulance waiting at the park's exit.

"Jonathan, we need to get a doctor to look at your foot. Okay?" Pilar asked.

Jonathan tensed and moved backward away from them. He

began to shake his head furiously and narrowed his eyes at Brendan.

"You promised!" he pleaded.

Brendan looked away and focused on the neon lights of the bar on the other side of the street.

"It's okay," Pilar said. "I will be there too. I will drive to the hospital behind you in my car."

As they waited at the door of the ambulance, one of the paramedics prepared an injection for Jonathan.

"No!" he pleaded as they pulled his sleeve up.

"What's that for?" Brendan asked but Pilar did not answer him. He turned to face her and saw that her eyes had once more filled with tears.

As the paramedic injected the long needle into Jonathan's vein, his eyes glazed over.

"I'm sorry," Brendan mouthed but his friend's eyes had already closed and his body slumped forward. "I'm sorry."

Chapter 18

The New York State Psychiatric Institute on Riverside Drive was an enormous structure of reinforced steel which dominated the city skyline off Henry Hudson Parkway. The exterior of the eleven-storey building was clad with large panels of green aluminium and huge panes of toughened glass on both sides of the semi-circular building. Pilar swung her car onto the off ramp and parked quickly in the hospital's staff car park. She opened the door and ran to the hospital's emergency department with Brendan following as close behind as he could. When they arrived at the emergency desk, Jonathan had already been taken to X-ray.

Pilar sat down on one of the chairs in the waiting area and put her face in her hands. Brendan sat beside her but decided not to try to comfort her – she had not uttered one word to him on the rushed journey down the highway.

She clasped her hands together as though she was praying.

"He called me Pilar when he came down. That's good," she finally said aloud though Brendan knew that she was talking more to herself than to him.

Half an hour later, Jonathan was wheeled by on a trolley by two stern-looking orderlies followed closely by a nurse. Pilar jumped up and went to him. Brendan followed her and they stood looking down at their friend with his half-closed eyes. The cut on his head had been cleaned and stitched. Brendan looked closer and winced as he saw that it was in the same spot as Jonathan's old scar.

"His leg's not broken. It'll be right in a few weeks," a nurse who seemed to know Pilar said. "Dr Reiter will be down shortly to assess him."

The orderlies briskly wheeled Jonathan away.

Pilar returned to her seat and bent forward, hugging her body. Brendan instinctively put his arm around her and she did not pull away. She turned and buried her head in his chest.

"I'm sorry," he said as she sobbed loudly, oblivious to the stares of people in the small waiting area.

"You can't ever do this again," she said.

"I won't. I promise."

Two hours later Dr Reiter arrived and stood over them. His cool eyes focused on Brendan. He beckoned for them to follow him into a small meeting room and sat at the head of the small, coffee-stained table. Pilar and Brendan sat quietly on either side of the table and trained their eyes on the cheap veneer wood.

Dr Reiter cleared his throat and turned to Pilar.

"The sedative is wearing off so I was able to speak with him and find out what has been happening," he said.

He turned his cold gaze on Brendan, placing his hands flat on the table.

"So, I take it *you* are the one who is going to help John get home?" he quipped.

Brendan swallowed and waited for the lecture he knew would follow. He looked at the doctor who he had not taken to on that first morning they met at the shelter. Reiter had an air of arrogance about him which Brendan detested. The flesh on his bony face was lined with long, narrow wrinkles which ran down his cheeks like streams and gathered around his neck in loose folds. His long bony hands which rested confidently on the table looked menacing, as though they might rise up at any moment and squeeze the very life out of him.

"Do you know what a paracosym is?" Reiter asked.

Brendan shook his head and looked at Pilar who did not move her eyes from the table top.

Dr Reiter leaned towards him. Brendan saw the faint glint of anger in his eye.

"Perhaps Ms Diaz will enlighten us? She is, after all, responsible for John's *care* at the shelter."

The disdain in his tone felt like a punch to the diminutive nurse. She swallowed and focused her eyes on her hands that were clasped tightly on the table.

"No? Well, allow me to do the honours," said Reiter. "A paracosym is an imaginary world that is created by children."

Brendan noticed that his voice sounded flat and emotionless as though he was reading the text from an autocue for a television documentary and not referring to a human being.

"Many children who create these imaginary worlds have experienced severe trauma and so they create alternative worlds, worlds that are safe for them to live in. This world can include imaginary people and places they've never been to. It may even involve the child speaking an imaginary language. In John's case, it was, I acknowledge, a real language, but otherwise he presented as a classic case. Unfortunately he did not grow out of this paracosym and clings to the belief that the life he imagined he had was real when in fact it was not. This, young man, is what is known as psychosis – where a person cannot tell what is real from what is imaginary."

Brendan felt an anger welling up in him, not only because of Reiter's contempt towards him but because of his treatment of Pilar. None of this was her fault.

"He has given me clear detailed descriptions of his family and the stories he tells me never alter," Brendan said. "How do you explain that?"

Reiter suddenly began to laugh loudly. Pilar lowered her head into her hands and shook her head. Brendan watched as the smile slowly faded from the psychiatrist's face and was replaced with a scornful expression.

"What's so funny?" Brendan snapped as he looked from Reiter to Pilar.

"They are imaginary," Dr Reiter said. "All of it is – from his white-haired siblings to his blind sister to the apple-picking parents in Virginia. Believe me, the police left no stone unturned in their investigation and came up with nothing."

Brendan shook his head.

"You don't agree?" Dr Reiter smirked.

Brendan flushed with embarrassment. He knew the doctor was mocking him.

"No, I don't. He must belong to someone!"

"Of course he does or once did belong to someone, but have you considered any or all of the reasons that nobody would come and claim him?"

Brendan flushed and looked away from the doctor's piercing gaze.

Dr Reiter turned his attention to Pilar who slowly raised her head and met his glare.

"Ms Diaz, I helped secure that position for you on the grounds that you used your psychiatric training to inform and educate all people in contact with John at the shelter. You were specifically directed to tell people not to engage in his fantasies. Now, can I expect you to do your job or should I discuss this problem with the charity's management body?"

"It won't happen again," Pilar said as she looked at Brendan who nodded simultaneously.

"I take it your investigation into obtaining more permanent accommodation for John is making progress?" Reiter said.

"Yes," she replied.

He raised his eyebrows, waiting for more.

"John has appointments at the housing authority coming up. They'll be showing him a couple of apartments in the locality."

"And Mr . . . ?"

"Martin."

"Mr Martin . . . will he be . . . ?" he began.

Pilar stood and appeared to return to her calm, aloof ways. She looked at Brendan, who thought he understood what Dr Reiter was asking for, something he wasn't going to get.

"Brendan will remain on at the shelter but he won't have any more personal conversations with John," she said.

Brendan flashed a look of gratitude at her and hoped that Thompson agreed with her when he found out what had happened today.

Reiter frowned and pursed his lips in disapproval. "Well, then. I don't see that it'll do John much good to remain here, even in the short term. It might in fact cause him to regress so I'm happy for you to take him back with you. I'll be down to see him in a couple of weeks and I've prescribed him strong sedatives until he settles a little."

He handed Pilar a white sheet of paper. She looked at it and for a brief moment appeared concerned by the prescription but said nothing and placed the paper in her pocket.

Dr Reiter opened the door and stood almost in their path, making it impossible to avoid his cold stare as they squeezed by him.

They took the lift to the second floor where Jonathan lay in a bed, still sleepy from the injection. They put their arms around his shoulders and raised him to a sitting position, then helped him out of the bed. Each taking an arm, they led him from the room and to the lift, Pilar making soothing noises all the time and assuring him that they were going home.

When they reached the car, they strapped him into the back seat.

As they drove out of the car park, Jonathan half opened his eyes and began to murmur excitedly in Spanish. As she stopped at the traffic lights, Pilar looked behind her and murmured something to the semi-conscious man. She turned to Brendan with an expression of anger and hurt.

"I know," he said.

"This can never happen again."

As the car left the suburbs of New York and reached Route 78, Jonathan appeared to fall into a deep sleep and an uncomfortable silence settled inside the car.

Brendan leant forward to put on the radio but pulled his hand back when Pilar glared at him.

"He's sleeping!" she hissed.

He sighed and looked out into the darkness on either side of the highway. He couldn't see even one house on which to focus his thoughts, one house with a light that he could focus on and imagine the people living there and what they were doing up at this late hour. He checked his watch. It was almost one o'clock in the morning.

Hard as he tried he could not shake the image of Jonathan's face as he trembled in the corner of that bleak, empty room.

"He was there before, Pilar, in that house. You should have seen his face. He was terrified."

"Then why bring it up, Brendan, why torture him? Everyone knows that awful things happened to him and that no one is looking for him. So why? Why do you need to do this to him?"

Brendan did not look at her but kept his eyes focused on the darkness around him.

"Because I am no one," he replied. "I thought finding his home would help me become somebody, help me find a place I could belong. Instead, I hurt him."

Pilar took her eyes off the road and looked at Brendan as though she had never seen him before. She took her right hand off the wheel and placed it gently on his leg. He lifted his hand and placed it over hers.

When they at last pulled into the driveway of the shelter, Kuvic came out and tried to help Brendan to lift Jonathan from the car but the confused man's eyes shot open. Jane followed close behind.

"*Leave me alone!*" he shouted.

Brendan moved forward and blocked Jonathan's view of Kuvic.

"It is *you* he is angry with," Pilar said gently to Brendan.

He moved back and tried to conceal his hurt as Kuvic rushed forward, smirking, to help Pilar move Jonathan from the car.

They led him inside the house and towards the stairs.

"I'll manage from here," Pilar said to Kuvic as she and Jane slowly helped the drugged man upstairs to his room.

When they were gone from view, Kuvic dug his hands into his pockets and began to laugh out loud. In the brightly lit hallway, Brendan could see his cut lip and grazed face from their little early-morning brawl. It was hard to believe that their tussle had happened less then eighteen hours ago.

"You've done it this time, Paddy!" Kuvic said. "Oh, and by the way, I haven't forgotten about how you assaulted me. That'll look bad when I report it to the police. Not something a guy on probation wants to happen. Or maybe I won't say anything. That is, if you behave nicely." He beckoned to Brendan. "Come in here. There's something I want to show you."

Brendan squirmed but followed him into the lounge to the left of the hallway. Kuvic had one over him now, so for now he would do as he asked. He looked around the pleasant room which was scattered with several comfortable armchairs and a brown leather sofa placed under the bay window. An old television stood in the corner of the room on a wooden table. He had spent very little time in this room and had rarely noticed any of the clients using it.

"Want to show you something," Kuvic said as he turned the television on and slipped a video into the dusty old VHS machine underneath the television. He pressed play and gestured for Brendan to sit.

"I borrowed this from my mom!" Kuvic laughed "I thought you'd like to see it."

Brendan dropped down into the chair, exhausted, and watched the video programme which appeared to have been fast-forwarded to the end.

On the screen, five white-haired children stood smiling into the camera. Their clothes looked old-fashioned as if the programme was set in the 1930's. One by one they stepped forward as their names rolled up.

Brendan squinted at the writing through exhausted red eyes.

Daniel Walker	*Jonathan Wyatt Nelson*
Joshua Hall	*Virgil Nelson*
Matthew Allen	*Clay Nelson*
Laura Cooper	*Mackenzie Nelson*
Heather Cooper	*Tyler Nelson*

Brendan's mouth dropped open as he stared in disbelief at the sight in front of him. It was a TV show. Jonathan's whole life was a TV programme. He looked away as the parents jumped playfully onto the screen, Ma and Pa Nelson with their striking blue eyes and poor farmer's clothes. The camera panned out revealing the family standing in a huge orchard on the side of a mountain. The show's title flashed onto the screen, *The Nelsons of Newsart, Virginia,* as the theme tune of Appalachian music played.

Brendan turned to look at Kuvic whose face had turned bright red as he tried to contain himself.

"The look on your face – Jesus, it's priceless!" he roared. "God, how I didn't lose it listening in on him telling you all those stories about mountain lions and apple-picking. It was the best fun I've had since I came to work in this dump! Hey, how come you never saw it anyway? I grew up watching those re-runs. That show is ancient. My mother used to watch it when she was younger!"

He cackled as he followed a stunned Brendan into the hallway.

"Hey, come on now!" he teased. "Don't you want to watch the next show? It's the one about Virgil cutting down the tree wrong and almost taking Jonathan's eye out. No? Well, guess you already know the ending!" He fell about laughing.

Brendan let himself out and walked down the steep driveway without closing the door behind him. He made his way home in a daze until he found himself outside his uncle's house. He walked down the side entrance to his apartment and wrote a note for Eileen telling her that he wouldn't be going into the centre that morning and pushed it under the patio door of the main house. He was sure his cousin wouldn't be speaking to him anyway, not when he had broken his promise to stay out of Jonathan's past or, more to the point, had got caught.

Brendan returned to his apartment and lay on his bed fully dressed. He closed his eyes tight and tried to force his mind to think of anything but Jonathan Doe but his mind would not obey.

He laughed bitterly as he lay there in the dark.

"Jonathan Wyatt Nelson, movie star!" he said aloud in the darkened room.

He thought about what a complete fool he had been and wondered if he could ever face Jonathan again, not just because he had let down and encouraged the mentally ill man but also because of the lies Jonathan had told him, all the stories that he had felt a part of, stories about places where he felt a person could be really free. He too felt let down and disillusioned at the thought of abandoning the search for the life Jonathan seemed to have known, the life Brendan thought he could sample. Disillusioned. He pondered on that choice of word because the whole story had been an illusion, a fallacy, a myth and his neediness made him a willing accomplice to the deception.

He turned over and tried to count the number of hours he had left in his community service. He reasoned that it would be pointless to look for another place to finish it and that he would have no choice but to return to the shelter and keep out of Jonathan's way. After that he could borrow money from his mother or Uncle Frank to get an apartment in New York where he would return to his life of blissful isolation, to the lonely yet pain-free life he had known.

He turned over again and looked out at the moon shining in through his open blinds. He shut his eyes and willed himself to sleep. As he drifted off he promised himself that he would never let anyone get so close to him again. Ever.

Chapter 19

Brendan heard her voice before he could see her. The loud southern twang bellowed down the pathway and in through his open window, causing his body to become rigid on his narrow bed.

"Alice?" he said to himself.

He jumped up and looked at his watch. It was a quarter past six in the evening so she must have dropped Eileen home. He could hear Coleen's voice too and realised she was directing Alice down the pathway to his apartment.

He glanced in the mirror at his rough appearance. He had not shaved or showered in two days and had barely eaten except for the meals Coleen had forced an irate and uncommunicative Eileen to take down to him.

"Well, look who's feeling sorry for hiself!" Alice wheezed as she opened his screen door.

Brendan flushed as he tried to pull on his jeans.

"Oh, don't you worry 'bout that. I raised my own boy. Seen everything there is to see!"

Brendan watched as she gasped for breath in his doorway. He beckoned for her to come in and sit down. The apartment was baking hot as it had no air conditioning.

157

"What do you want?" he asked as he pulled a creased T-shirt over his head. He filled a glass of water and handed it to her.

"Oh, I know what *I* want!" she laughed. "Point is, what do *you* want?"

Brendan frowned and shook his head in confusion. "Alice, I tried. You should have been there. He was scared out of his wits. So was I!"

"Well, yes, you did try, granted . . . and you never know . . . something might still happen for that boy. You shouldn't give up now."

Brendan smiled for a moment. He reckoned that Alice was about sixty-five or so and Jonathan was somewhere between forty-five and fifty years old. It wasn't like there was a huge age gap between them yet she referred to him as a boy.

"No, I'm done, Alice. It's over. I promised Pilar I wouldn't look into it any more. It's useless anyway."

"Well, we'll see – sometimes when we find what we were looking for, it don't look nothing like what we set out to get."

Brendan raised his eyebrows. He had never known anyone who could talk in riddles like Alice could.

"So, you coming back to us?"

Brendan tried to formulate an answer but found himself stuttering. He had intended to go back the day after they got back from New York but he knew now that the man had been badly affected by the trauma, not so much from what Eileen had told him as from the icy glare she gave him when she brought down his dinner at night, and he found he could not face him. He could not go back and allow Jonathan to see the hurt he felt at his deception, even if it was unintentional.

"I didn't think that . . ." he began.

"That what?"

"That I'd be welcome," he admitted.

Alice took a sip of water and stood. She put her hands on his shoulders and looked at him with her large, brown eyes.

"You're welcome. Don't you know that? John will come back to himself in time. Pilar will cool down . . . or maybe heat up. That gal sure needs to warm herself somewhere!"

158

"Kuvic?" he asked.

He watched Alice's expression darken.

"We found Zeb," she said.

"Oh, I was going to ask if –"

She waved her hand to dismiss his belated enquiries. "He's all right. He's home now but he was in the hospital. Badly beat up."

"Kuvic?" Brendan asked, alarmed now for Jonathan's safety.

"Nah. He's cruel all right but not like that. He likes to hurt with his words, to torture people when they're vulnerable. He put Zeb on the street in the dead of night and that poor man had to go to the park to sleep. Some gang of kids beat him up bad."

"Jesus!"

"I typed a report for Thompson. I hope he reads it well."

"Saying what?"

"Saying that Kuvic is a danger to the clients and asking that he fire the son of a b-i-t-c-h," she spelt out. "Course, I put it nicely. Mr Thompson's kind of proper. Likes things put politely."

Brendan raised an eyebrow.

"Things aren't so good at the house, Brendan. Eileen's moping around, John is drugged out of his poor mind with those tablets Dr Reiter give him and Pilar, somethin's up with that girl. Can't put my finger on it exactly. And that's just the staff!"

She stopped speaking and looked around Brendan's small apartment.

"We need you there, Brendan."

Brendan smiled shyly. He was thirty-five years old and no one had ever told him they needed him before. "Yeah, okay, I'll be in first thing in the morning."

He saw Alice to the door and grinned at how easily she had manipulated him. So much for his resolution to only worry about himself from now on and get his life back to the simple existence he had enjoyed.

Brendan showered and shaved and made his way to the house. He climbed the stairs and knocked on Eileen's bedroom door. When she opened it, he looked down at her outfit. His cousin was wearing one of the middle-aged dresses and the flat court shoes he thought he had seen the last of.

"You want a driving lesson?" he asked.

Eileen ran her tongue around her mouth as she thought about it. She peeked out the door and looked down the hallway.

"Where's Dad?"

Brendan shrugged. "Does it matter?"

"I'm annoyed with you," she said.

"I know. Come on."

"How did you come to buy this?" he asked as they sat into the car.

She grinned. "I was supposed to be at the shelter but I went to the bank and got a cheque, walked to the dealership and told them I wanted *this* car. I had nothing else to do with my money and it was building up in the bank so I decided I'd get something I always wanted. I . . . I have a disability benefit."

Brendan pretended that he did not notice her blushing.

"I had been in there so often. Jonathan, and I would wander around but I was only interested in this one."

"Why?"

Eileen thought about this for a moment. "Oh, you'll just laugh but in the showroom it shone so much more than the others . . . like it was . . . calling me." She blushed again. "Guess it was just the colour but it looked to me like . . . like a new start. Like I could get in and drive that car anywhere I wanted to and that things would be different." She looked wistful. "So I paid up and asked the salesman to deliver it."

"Wow! Just like that!"

Eileen nodded and looked pleased at his reaction.

Brendan was relieved to see that the car was automatic. After spending some time teaching her to start, brake and indicate, he directed her as she jerked out of the driveway.

He guided her slowly down the narrow street where cars were parked on either side. He noticed how relaxed she was behind the wheel and was amazed that his normally anxious cousin did not appear nervous driving for the first time.

"What did Frank do when he saw the car?" he asked after a while.

She bit her lip and glanced down.

"*Eyes on the road!*" Brendan shouted.

"Sorry! He went nuts. He forbade me to drive it, said he was going to drive it back to the showroom himself. He brought me down there . . ." She looked to the side as she recalled the memory.

"*Eyes!*"

". . . and he told them I wasn't fit to have a car, that I had problems, that they'd taken advantage of me. He held me by the arm and yelled at the manager like he'd sold alcohol to a child."

Brendan could see she was getting agitated and realised he shouldn't have mentioned Frank when he needed her to concentrate on the road. "Okay," he said, "you can tell me about it when we stop. Just focus on your driving now."

She stopped talking and followed Brendan's directions, turning into the car park of a shopping mall. She parked awkwardly and jerkily in an empty space, then sighed and turned off the ignition.

"Not bad," said Brendan. "You'll soon get the hang of it."

Eileen shrugged and smiled.

"So, go on," he said. "Tell me what happened when Frank took the car back to the showroom."

"Well, the manager looked at me and it was like he understood me in that second. He said he wouldn't take it back so Dad had to drive it all the way back here. It was before his heart surgery. He was so mad. Mom, of course, tried to pick up for me. Told him to let me keep it, so he sulked at us both for about a week. A few days later he came home looking really pleased with himself."

"Then what?" Brendan asked.

"He said he'd been to all three of the driving schools in the town and had directed them not to teach me to drive, that I might cause myself harm."

Her chin trembled but she straightened her spine and stared out the windscreen at passing cars.

Brendan placed a comforting hand on her shoulder.

"He said it was for my own good," she went on without looking at him, "that he was never going to let any harm come to me ever again. You see, Brendan, Dad thinks he is protecting me. He thinks he is saving me from all the awful things in the world but he is killing me."

Brendan exhaled loudly and the pair stared out silently for a while.

"Why didn't you leave here, Eileen? Why didn't you just take off?"

She looked at him for a moment and then rested her eyes on her hands which were clasped together firmly on her lap.

"And go where?" she asked sadly. "I knew my sisters wouldn't take me in. They wouldn't go against Dad. I've never worked so who'd give me a job? I didn't even get to finish college."

Brendan chewed on the inside of his mouth. "Come back to New York with me," he said, taking himself by surprise.

Eileen looked up at him. For a brief moment, her grey eyes lit up with excitement. He watched as the light faded and disappeared as though someone had quenched the dying flame of a candle.

"I could never leave Jonathan," she replied "But, thank you, Brendan. You being here, even for this short time, well, it's meant a lot to me."

Brendan exhaled and nodded. "If you ever change your mind . . ."

She nodded.

"Well, I guess I'll be in Frank's bad books tonight," Brendan said.

Eileen looked at her watch. "No, we have twenty minutes to get the car back. He'll be home from his bowling club then."

"Do you want to talk about Jonathan?" Brendan asked.

Eileen pursed her lips for a moment. "Reiter has him drugged up. He can hardly speak. Pilar said it's just for a couple of weeks until he gets over it but . . . it just hurts. I hate to see his beautiful mind all clouded over, see him losing his stories and just sitting there staring out."

Brendan stiffened as he tried to imagine Jonathan like that. Tomorrow was going to be harder than he'd imagined.

"I told Frank about Jonathan," he admitted. "I didn't say anything about you. I just said he was a friend of mine from the shelter. It was Frank who suggested I go to New York."

"I knew you wouldn't stop looking – even though you promised," she said curtly.

"Does he remember anything about that day in New York?"

Eileen shrugged. "Pilar sat everyone down the next day and told us all that no one is to engage him in conversation about his imaginary life. Even Henrietta was taken out of the kitchen to hear it. Pilar said it exactly like that. *Engage in conversation.* Why not say, ignore him, walk away from him, let him sit there alone, because Jonathan doesn't know how *not to* talk about his stories. It's what keeps him going, what keeps him alive!"

"I thought you didn't want anyone interfering in his life?"

"I *don't* want anybody to interfere but I want him to be able to speak to people about what he wants to talk about. They don't have to do anything, do they? They just need to listen. I don't want him to lose who he is!"

Brendan looked at his cousin and felt sorry for the situation she was in. It was clear how deeply she felt about Jonathan.

"You're in love with him, aren't you?" he asked quietly.

She looked towards her feet and pressed lightly on the brake pedal of the stationary car.

"Yes," she replied firmly. She turned her face to meet her cousin's sympathetic eyes. "Yes, I am. I've never said that out loud before. Not many people know about me and Jonathan and those that do don't take us seriously, so thank you for treating me like . . . a normal woman." She took a deep breath and looked around at passing shoppers. "Everything is going to change soon though. I've felt it coming for a long time. Jonathan has too. We're like that – sensitive, I guess. When Alice leaves, Kuvic's going to force him into one of those awful apartments that he won't last a week in. Jonathan says he's never going back into one of those places. He'll take to the road and I won't ever see him again."

"It's not definite that Kuvic will be in charge. What about Pilar?"

"Pilar doesn't think she has any hope of getting that job."

"Why? Surely it's not because . . . not because she's Hispanic?"

Eileen shrugged. "There'd be some old fogies on the board that wouldn't be too keen on a Hispanic manager, those who'd think she's not even-tempered or . . . easily controlled. You'd be surprised how people think. I've seen the way she's changed, trying to fit into what they expect. She was more passionate when she first came to the shelter. She had good fight in her. But Thompson doesn't care about her background and he has the final say. It doesn't help that he doesn't like her though. When she first arrived, she spoke out a lot about things that were wrong with the service, about how they could offer better support for those that had mental illness, and it didn't go down too well with Thompson. He's under pressure to keep the shelter open. He promised his uncle that it would always offer a home to those that needed it but funding is tight and it's getting harder for him to keep that promise. He's a good man though. He's just . . . under pressure, I guess. Alice is better at getting people to do things without them even realising it. After a few too many disagreements with Thompson and a lot of advice from Alice, Pilar settled down and got quieter, but instead of being shrewd and choosing her battles like Alice does, she just got sad and . . . kind of sour."

Brendan nodded slowly. He felt he now had a better understanding of the acerbic Latina and this new insight made her even more appealing to him.

Eileen sighed. "Anyway, what about you? Mom said you know about your dad now but that I shouldn't ask you about it – so now I'm asking. How do you feel about it?"

Brendan looked out of the passenger window and thought about her question.

"I don't know how I feel, is the answer. I . . . I guess it doesn't change much. One minute he was an Irish waste of space and now he's a Mexican waste of space. It doesn't make any difference really. I just don't know why my mother didn't tell me. That part doesn't make any sense."

Eileen pursed her lips and brooded over her cousin's words. "Are you going to ask Patricia about it when she arrives?"

Brendan shrugged. "I doubt it but . . . well . . . we'll see. Come on, let's get home before Frank skins us both alive."

After some instruction, Eileen reversed the car nervously out of the parking space and turned the car shakily towards home.

Chapter 20

The minor repair to the fire escape was the second-last thing on Brendan's repair list that he had kept in his jeans' pocket since he started working at the shelter. He had taken the ladder from the shed and set it up at the back of the house after smearing his shirtless body with sun protection in the scorching August heat. When he'd finished, he checked the roof, hoping to see some other repairs that needed doing but the slates were clean and in good condition. He looked at the last item on his list. *Fix tap in Jonathan's bedroom.* It was two o'clock and he had not seen the man yet that day. Henrietta informed him that since his little skirmish in New York, Jonathan had spent most of the time in his bedroom or sitting in the garden, and that it broke her heart to see him so sad. Her words cut through Brendan but he could see that she meant no malice. She was just another person who cared deeply for the disturbed man.

By three thirty he could not put off his visit to the attic any longer. He gingerly climbed the wooden steps and knocked nervously on the door which was slightly ajar. When he received no answer, he pushed the door slightly, hoping that Jonathan had left the room, but he was there, sitting under the blistering heat of the round window in a large armchair, his half-closed eyes fixed on the wall as if he was watching a movie.

"John?" Brendan said.

Jonathan looked up and rested his eyes on Brendan for a moment. Slowly, an expression of recognition washed over his face.

"Brendan? Where have you been?" he slurred. "I need to tell you something."

Brendan looked away as saliva ran down Jonathan's chin and onto his woollen vest. He entered the room and hunched down at his friend's chair.

"I'm sorry," he said, "I really am. I didn't know that . . ."

Jonathan raised his head and tried to steady it. He focused his eyes on Brendan and tried to speak but his head fell forward on his chest. Then, with effort, he looked dozily up again. Brendan reached out, took Jonathan's heavy head in his hands and gently lowered it towards the back of the chair.

"I want to tell you that –" Jonathan said.

"It doesn't matter. You are sick. I understand that now."

"No!" Jonathan spat angrily. "Brendan, it's not . . . I'm not . . ." His head fell forward again and his eyes began to close.

Brendan knelt down and faced his friend. "What is it, John?"

Jonathan opened his eyes and focused on Brendan. "My name is *Jonathan*."

"Ssh, don't upset yourself."

Jonathan tried to speak again. His mouth opened but his eyes closed slowly and his head fell forward as he drifted into a comatose sleep.

Brendan stood and stared at the sad sight before him. Guilt cut into him as he watched his friend slumped in an old armchair in an attic on a sunny day. This was entirely his fault and he was going to think of a way to make up for it. He would keep his promise not to delve any more into the man's past – the sight before him convinced him that it was not worth putting Jonathan through it. He was going to find a way to give him new memories and new experiences that might make up for having lost what he once knew. He looked towards the tiny makeshift bathroom but for some reason he couldn't bring himself to finish that last job.

167

He went downstairs and stood by Alice who was helping Eileen in the laundry.

"Can I help?" he asked.

"Sure! I was hoping you would."

Brendan began folding sheets roughly until he was given a lesson from the two amused women.

"That's it for the repairs," he said, "but I've roughly –"

"Eighty-seven hours yet to do," Alice cut in, finishing his sentence and looking at her watch simultaneously.

Brendan grinned at her and picked up another sheet to fold as per their strict instructions.

"Nothing to say you can't stay on when it's over," she said with raised eyebrows. Pilar came into the room and dropped another load for washing.

Brendan shrugged. "I've nothing really to keep me here when it's finished."

Alice looked from Brendan to Pilar and back. "Uh-huh," she said. "Well, we'll see about that. Well, here's Thompson so I got to go." She threw a sheet down onto the counter. She glanced at Eileen and gave her a nod as though the two women were up to something.

Brendan looked at the open door which led to the back garden but he could not see Thompson or his car. He opened the door that led to the hallway and glanced down the open area but there was no one there. Suddenly the doorbell rang and Kuvic, dressed in a black suit and immaculately polished shoes, came out of nowhere to answer it.

"How did she know Thompson was about to ring the bell?" Brendan asked.

Eileen laughed. "Alice can hear the grass growing."

"What's Kuvic doing here?" he whispered.

"The board is meeting today to decide on Alice's complaint. They're in the lounge. Kuvic will get a chance to talk his way out of it though."

Brendan closed the door and lifted another sheet to fold. He hadn't heard from his probation officer for a few days now.

Robert Hensen went a long way back with his uncle and it seemed that they talked more often than Brendan and Robert did. He briefly wondered if Kuvic had complained to the police about their little brawl but decided that Hensen would have been in touch by now if he had.

Eileen folded her last sheet and washed her hands in the sink. "I'm going up to read to Jonathan now."

Brendan nodded.

"Alice wants you to feed Zeb," she said.

"Feed him? Me?" he asked, alarmed at the notion of doing anything so personal for someone else.

"Well, he has two broken arms so he can't do much for himself. Oh, and Alice said to help Zeb downstairs in" – she checked her watch – "exactly twenty-five minutes. That's important – twenty-five minutes exactly – okay?"

Brendan shrugged. "Okay."

He made his way to the kitchen where he collected a tray for the injured man. He climbed the stairs and opened the door to the dorm where Zeb was sitting up in his bed under a window.

Brendan hardly recognised the man. He was showered and freshly shaved and if it hadn't been for his blackened eye and large plaster casts Brendan would have thought he was in the wrong room. He thought about Eileen's comments and how Pilar wanted to do more for the clients. Despite the beating he received in the park, the old man definitely looked better being cared for all day than when he was put out each morning to fend for himself.

"Hi, Zeb," he said as he sat on the side of the bed.

"Hi, Brendan."

Brendan shuddered as he lifted each spoon of soup and placed it into the man's mouth. He had few teeth left and his breath was awful.

"It's nice. Thank you," he said appreciatively after each spoonful until the brown liquid was all gone.

Brendan looked at his watch. "Alice said I've to take you downstairs right about now," he said.

"Yeah, I know," Zeb said as he rose unsteadily to his feet. "Alice has got plans," he added knowingly. He tried to tip his nose but gave up and winked at Brendan instead.

Brendan pulled a dressing gown around Zeb's shoulders and they slowly set out.

When they were halfway down the stairs, the lounge door opened and the board members spilled slowly into the hallway. Brendan looked down at them and was unsure whether he should go back up with Zeb or try to hurry him down.

"Zeb!" Alice exclaimed as though she had not planned on seeing him painfully making his way down the stairs. "How nice to see you out of bed! How's the pain?"

Zeb began to whimper. "It's real bad, Alice. I'm just coming down to see if Pilar can get me something for it," he sniffled.

Brendan scanned the entrance hall where several middle-aged people stood in horror at the sight of the poor man.

Alice turned to face them.

"This is the man I was telling you all about," she said as they shook their heads and tut-tutted.

Out of the corner of his eye Brendan could see Kuvic slink down the hallway and into the back of the house, to hide from their disapproving eyes.

"And this awful thing happened when you were put out of here?" one woman asked as she pointed at his arms.

"Yes, ma'am."

"Well, we will have to make sure that doesn't happen again!" she exclaimed loudly.

Brendan looked behind the group to where Thompson stood. He could see tears in the man's eyes, real tears of concern for Zeb who had been coming to the centre when Thompson's uncle was still alive.

"And this," Alice said loudly, "is Brendan, a first cousin of our dear Eileen here."

Two of the women clapped their hands as though Brendan was the final act in the show – like he was Alice's pièce-de-résistance.

170

"Brendan's done a fine job here and all for free. He's been visiting with his uncle here. Remember Officer Dalton? Well, this fine young man has been so helpful here. Hard to know what we're going to do without him when he's gone." And she shook her head regretfully.

"You're not leaving, are you?" another woman exclaimed.

Brendan began to answer but Alice cut in.

"Oh, the Big Smoke is calling but, nice boy like that, reckon it's lonely there. Why, I'd love if he would stay here with us and, look, see how good he is with the clients?"

Brendan almost laughed at how thick Alice was putting on the whole southern-drawl act. Zeb and Brendan had hardly spoken until that very day.

Zeb continued with the role Alice had obviously given him that morning. He moved closer to Brendan and smiled up at him with his almost toothless grin.

"He's been like a son to me," he said.

"Oooh!" several of the women said in unison.

Brendan glanced at Alice and shook his head at the clever game she was playing. He helped Zeb down the last of the steps, as Alice saw the board members out, and led him towards the dining room.

As Alice shut the front door, Brendan came back down the hallway having deposited Zeb in front of the TV. He wanted to tell her that he had no intention of staying but she looked so pleased with herself that he couldn't do it – he couldn't ruin her moment.

"Well, that ought to do it!" Alice exclaimed as she reached up and placed her arms gently around his shoulders. She stood and looked around the hallway as though replaying the scene in her head. She smiled to herself, her big brown eyes shining with delight. "Yes, that ought to do it."

Chapter 21

"Fishing?" Jonathan asked from the armchair in his room.

"Sure," Brendan replied from the doorway.

Jonathan pulled the heavy wool blanket tightly around his shoulders and frowned.

"I don't know if I've ever been fishing before," he admitted.

The sadness of his tone permeated the air in the dusty, airless room. Dr Reiter's strong sedatives had done their job. They had banished Jonathan Wyatt Nelson but left in his place a hollow, aimless man.

"Neither have I!" Brendan replied "We'll be a fine pair. Probably lose my uncle's rods pulling boots out of the water!"

A small smile washed over Jonathan's face. He stood and folded the blanket neatly on the chair.

"Okay," he whispered.

Brownwood Pond was a small lake surrounded by a dense wood off Highland Avenue. The walk, which was a twenty-minute journey on foot, took almost an hour as Jonathan shuffled painfully along on his injured foot.

"You want me to go back and get Pilar to drive us?" Brendan asked but Jonathan waved the suggestion away.

"I'm fine," he replied, still in his southern drawl.

Brendan pondered on this as he set down their lunch boxes beside a disgusting box of maggots. He wondered if the accent was actually Jonathan's own but banished the thought from his mind. He was not going down that road.

"What are we hoping to catch?" Jonathan asked.

Brendan burst out laughing. "I've no idea," he said as he looked around the deserted lake.

He squirmed as he put a worm on the end of each of their lines. They cast them into the deep murky water and waited for a bite.

"I don't think Henrietta'll cook anything that we catch," Jonathan said quietly.

"*I'm* not eating anything that we catch!" Brendan replied. "We'll throw it back in."

"Seems wrong to pull the fish out of where it belongs and then just throw it back someplace else," Jonathan said.

Brendan looked at him and wondered if he was trying to say something. He'd seemed slightly more alert in the past few days. Pilar had phoned Reiter asking for the medication to be reduced, which had brought the man partially back to himself, whoever that was.

"What do you mean?" Brendan asked.

Jonathan shrugged. "Just that . . . the fish would probably get a fright being pulled up here and then thrown back in where he doesn't rightly know where he belongs. Might be hard for him to find the exact spot he had been in. Could be it looks all the same down there in the dark."

Brendan shrugged. "It's just a fish, John."

Jonathan took his eyes off his line and stared at the side of Brendan's face.

"Brendan," he said quietly, "Kuvic told me he showed you that TV programme . . . about the Nelsons. I . . . I want you to know that I didn't mean to lie to you. I believe . . . I believed everything I told you. I really did."

Brendan nodded and wound his line tighter to the shoreline.

Ever since Kuvic had shown him *The Nelsons* he'd been asking himself why Jonathan chose that specific programme. He felt there must be a reason for it but he would never know the answer to that question or any of the other questions that tormented his mind. He had promised Pilar that there would be no more of these conversations and he intended to keep his word.

Jonathan looked at his line and tried to copy Brendan's technique but instead of winding it in, he released it further into the lake.

"I also want you to know that some of the things I told you weren't lies. I spent a lot of time sitting in my room thinking on everything and I don't remember what my last name is but I know that my name *is* Jonathan and I *did* live in a clapboard house. I *did* have a sister named Cassie and friend named Nella. I *did* have a cat that spat at me and a tyre that swung from an old oak tree and I –"

"*Enough!*" Brendan roared.

Jonathan let go of his rod, panicked by the sudden noise, and stood staring at Brendan as the rod disappeared into the deep water.

"Enough, John," Brendan said quietly. "You've . . . we've . . . I want to be your friend but we can't have any more of these conversations, do you understand?"

Jonathan stood open-mouthed at the water's edge. He did not move.

Brendan looked down and shook his head. "It's over, John. We tried. I'm sorry but it's over."

"You're giving up? You're giving up on me?"

Brendan looked away and fixed his eyes on the water. "I don't want to but . . . where can we go from here? You have to face it, John. You're never going to be able to find home."

Jonathan moved backwards and began to shake his head.

"No! No!" he said.

Brendan moved forwards to try to calm him but Jonathan began to walk down the pathway through the woods.

"*John!*" he roared.

Jonathan stopped and turned to face him.

"Don't worry, I'm just going back to the shelter and if you can't call me by my real name . . . then . . . please . . . don't use that name. Don't call me John."

Brendan watched him as he made his way through the trees and out onto the main road. He sighed and threw the box of maggots into the water.

"Here, knock yourselves out!" he said to the invisible fish.

He decided it was useless to try to find his uncle's second rod which had disappeared into the murky water. He reeled in his line, packed up their lunch and left.

When Brendan arrived at the shelter Pilar was sitting in the hallway dressed in a dark navy suit and high heels. She was wearing make-up which he had rarely seen her wear.

"Wow!" he said.

She blushed. "Don't start – I've already had two wolf-whistles from Kuvic!" she moaned.

"Kuvic's here? I thought he was suspended!"

Pilar let out a huge breath. "He is but he still has a right to attend the interview."

"Today's the interview for Alice's replacement? Good luck!"

She nodded nervously and cleared her throat. "Brendan, do you think I have too much make-up on? Isabel said I looked like a whore when I was leaving the house!" But she was smiling as she said it.

"You look lovely," he replied, laughing. "Especially when you smile. You should do it more often."

He turned to leave but swivelled back on his heels. Pilar seemed happy which meant it was a good time to ask her something.

"I don't suppose you'd let me take you to Alice's party?"

A moment passed before she answered but it seemed to Brendan like an eternity.

"No strings?" she asked.

He raised his hands in mock horror. "No strings!" he agreed.

As he walked away, Brendan was wondering exactly what he had agreed to but guessed that it meant the night would not be ending as he'd hoped it would.

He climbed the stairs and knocked at Jonathan's door.

"Come in," his friend said meekly.

Brendan opened the door and found Jonathan sitting on his bed rubbing his foot.

"Now I know why I didn't see you on the road," he said as he looked down at Jonathan's swollen foot. "What did you do, run all the way so you wouldn't have to talk to me?"

"Something like that," Jonathan replied sourly.

Brendan sat on the bed and looked out of the circular window. "You've got a good view from here," he said absent-mindedly.

"But it's not the view that I want, Brendan. I want to see the mountains again. I want to see my family again."

Brendan sighed and went to the window. He looked out at the neat manicured lawns of the houses on the opposite side of the road.

"My mother's flying in here on Thursday and . . . I envy you your feelings towards your family. I wish I felt that way. I don't get along with my uncle – well, we're getting on better these days. That is, as long as he doesn't catch me giving Eileen driving lessons or notice that I lost his fishing-rod today! And my aunt – she's nice to me but the way she looks at me with such . . . such pity . . . I find it hard to look her in the eye because I don't want to see her looking at me that way. My cousins . . . well, I'd rather chew my arm off than spend time with them . . . with the exception of Eileen . . . Eileen I like. And my mother . . . well . . . we have nothing to say to each other. I don't even like being in her company."

"So, you're saying that I shouldn't want to see my family because you don't like yours?" Jonathan asked, a slight tone of sarcasm in his voice.

Brendan shook his head. "No, no. Just that family is not everything. There are other things . . . like friends."

"Do you have many friends?"

Brendan thought about the lads in the pub that he would never see if he didn't go into Murphy's. Not one of them had contacted him since he'd come to Dover – not that he left them with a forwarding address, he conceded, but he knew that they wouldn't have phoned him even if he had. They were drinking buddies, not friends. He hadn't even had any real friends in school where he had stood out from the pale-faced, blue-eyed Irish kids in his class.

"You're the only friend I have," he said as he stared out of the window.

Jonathan got up from the bed and hobbled over to the window.

"It's not a bad view, I guess," he said. "Maybe we'll go fishing again?"

Brendan turned his gaze from the window into the dismal room. A thought struck him. "Do you like amusements?" he asked. "You know, like dodgem cars and big wheels?"

"Em . . . sure," Jonathan replied uncertainly.

"Well, there's a place on Warren Street. Eileen could come too if she's not too busy here."

"Yes."

"How 'bout we do that? Tomorrow?" Brendan moved to the doorway.

"Tomorrow!" Jonathan echoed.

Chapter 22

The following Tuesday, Brendan helped Henrietta in the kitchen after he had finished feeding Zeb another semi-solid meal. He and Eileen had to leave early that day to welcome his mother whom Orla and Doug were collecting at JFK airport at three o'clock. He rubbed down the counter and stacked the plates into the dishwasher, breaking two in the process.

"What's got into you?" Henrietta asked.

Brendan shrugged.

"Well, somethin's up!" she snapped in her strong New York accent.

Henrietta had moved to the small town after her son transferred there and, like Alice, she could see right through him.

"It's nothing," he said.

He didn't want to tell the cook how much he was dreading his mother's visit. The image of his mother sitting across the table looking at him with her icy stare made him feel physically sick. He had taken Frank's advice to forewarn her that he was now jobless and penniless and living in his uncle's tiny annex until he completed his community work, but he could not muster the courage to phone her and had chickened out by sending her a one-page letter, leaving out the part about serving eight long days in jail that he would never forget as long as he lived. He wasn't surprised when he received no reply.

He was sorry that her visit had dampened the good mood he was in. It had been a great few days with Jonathan. They had been out every day, including the weekend – at the amusements, which Jonathan and Eileen had loved, looking in museums, walking through the mountain trails and exploring the outer regions of Dover on the days when Pilar could drive them. He had even managed to sneak in two driving lessons with Eileen when Frank and Coleen were busy shopping for their visitor.

He washed his hands and walked slowly home with Eileen. As they neared the house she stopped and faced him.

"Now, Brendan, you stay calm. No matter what!" she ordered.

He laughed at how forceful his timid cousin could be when she wanted to.

Brendan shook his head. "Why would *I* need to stay calm?"

"Just promise me, okay?" she pleaded.

When they made their way around the side entrance, Brendan peered into the patio glass at the gathering. Orla and Doug were sitting at the kitchen table with his mother who had her back to him. Frank and Coleen sat at the other end of the kitchen by the fireside, playing with Orla's two freckle-faced children whom Brendan had long since taken a dislike to. He took a deep breath and opened the door, beckoning Eileen to go in ahead of him. His mother stood and turned to greet him. He could feel the eyes of everyone in the room on them and wished he could escape, could break out of the room to the safety of his apartment. He searched her face, which was thinner and more lined than he remembered. She had the same hairstyle, light reddish-brown hair cut in heavy layers at the jaw-line to disguise its thinness. It was twelve years since he had last seen her and she looked smaller than he remembered. Only her eyes were the same. Small lifeless grey eyes that never seemed to express any emotion.

"Brendan," she said in her too-quiet voice.

He noticed how hesitantly she moved towards him and how

she glanced furtively at the onlookers before placing her short arms around his large frame.

"Mam," he said nervously as they hugged awkwardly. "Was . . . was your flight okay?"

She nodded and stepped back, turning her gaze from him to Eileen who stood in the doorway with her eyes fixed on her footwear. He noticed tears welling in his mother's eyes and was taken aback at her sudden expression of emotion. He looked at Frank and Coleen who sat silently at the other end of the room, their eyes locked on each other as though they were the only two people in the room.

"Eileen," she whispered. "Look at you!"

Heavy tears began to roll down her face. She moved forward and hugged Eileen tightly before looking guiltily in Brendan's direction.

"I'm supposed to be the image of you," Eileen said shyly.

"Isn't she? Isn't she the image of you, Aunt Patricia?" Orla asked in her shrill, annoying voice. "Everyone says so, don't they, Dad?"

Frank moved his eyes slowly away from his wife's stare. "They do," he said.

Eileen moved into the room and sat by Coleen who patted her daughter's knee affectionately.

Brendan felt like he was missing something, that there were things going on in the room that were going over his head. He sat down at the table and tried not to make direct eye contact with his mother. He pretended to listen as Doug explained to her just how bad the economy was and which investments were a sure-fire way of making a good return.

As the evening went on, he felt himself withdrawing from the group as he did when he was a child. He watched as mouths opened and closed. He saw Coleen laugh nervously and Orla and Doug take centre stage as they told the gathering about their new house in New York's more affluent suburbs. He glanced quickly at his silent mother who nodded and smiled but said very little, and at Frank whom he had never seen so detached from a conversation. Twice Eileen caught his eye and grinned shyly at him. He lost count of the number of times he checked to see if the clock was working as he calculated how much longer he would have to endure the tension that hung in every corner of the room.

At eight o'clock, his mother rose abruptly from her seat and said she was exhausted. She looked at him and said goodnight. He stood and kissed her awkwardly.

Only then did she reveal her prickly ways. As Frank began to explain which room she was in, Brendan watched her screw up her tiny face like she used to do when she was angry with him.

"I know, Francis," she said curtly, using her brother's full name. "Coleen has already shown me and, remember, that room used to be mine."

She glanced around the table and walked slowly out of the kitchen towards the stairs.

"Well," Coleen said as she stood and collected the last few plates, "that wasn't too bad."

Chapter 23

"What will he do when you have returned to New York?" Pilar asked Brendan softly as they walked behind Jonathan and Eileen on the main pathway in Turtle Back Zoo.

Brendan shrugged and watched as his friend stared at the bear enclosure beside the picnic area. "I don't know."

"Have you told him yet?"

Brendan stopped and let Eileen and Jonathan walk ahead of them.

"No. I . . . will . . . in a few days," he replied.

"How do you think he will react? He's come to depend on you."

Brendan threw a stone he was holding into the small pond and frowned. "I'll come by and see him, when I'm visiting."

Pilar looked sourly at him. "There was a volunteer at the shelter when I started there. I think Ray or Rob was his name, something like that. He took a special interest in John, took him ten-pin bowling and to baseball games. He was a real sports fan – Ray, that is, not John. Then he moved to Florida. He sent letters for a while, phoned a few times and then the contact gradually faded until John never heard from him. There were others over the years who promised to keep in touch with him but didn't. Can you imagine what that's like for him?"

"I take your point, Pilar!" Brendan snapped. "But what do you expect me to do? I can't stay here because of John!"

"I know that. I'm just saying, people come into his life and they go. They go back to their lives and take with them the good time they showed him and he retreats back into Jonathan Wyatt Nelson."

"You mean . . . he's not . . . cured? What about the tablets?"

"They'll work for a while and eventually he'll be taken off them . . . or he'll pretend he's taking them. Then, gradually he'll begin to buy maps and pin them up on his walls again. That's the first sign that he's becoming unstable. But . . . you should know that no one has ever got as close to him as you have. You mean a lot to him."

Pilar stopped and watched Eileen and Jonathan walk hand in hand towards the wolf enclosure. She leaned on the fence and shook her head.

"He's due at the housing authority next Wednesday," she said. "I was hoping that . . . you could take him?"

Brendan nodded.

"I'm hoping that he'll understand that seeing the apartments with you means that it is time for you both to move on."

"Do you think he'll settle into an apartment alone?"

Pilar shook her head. "No. It hasn't worked before but we have to try. If Kuvic gets the manager's job, he'll see to it that John is out permanently and there'll be nothing I can do about it. I guess that at least if he's living in an apartment close by, it'll be better than if he is on the street. At least we can keep an eye on him. We won't know the board's decision for a few weeks. Thompson's going out of town and they won't make the final decision without him."

Brendan exhaled loudly.

When he and Eileen had arrived at the centre that morning, Kuvic was standing in the hallway wearing his usual navy outfit and steel-capped prison-officer shoes. As they made their way to the kitchen Brendan caught Kuvic looking Eileen up and down. He moved back to grab him but Eileen reached for his arm and pleaded with him to ignore the sleazy man. She then updated him and told him that Thompson couldn't fire Kuvic without giving him a warning first and that he was now on his last chance. Brendan thought about Alice and how she seemed to think the board would fire Kuvic, but Eileen informed him that Alice knew Thompson would only issue a warning but that her hope would be that the board would see that Kuvic was not fit to manage the place and that sooner or later he'd step out of line again and that the next time would be the last.

"What if . . . what if I took Jonathan to New York with me?" Brendan asked now.

Pilar laughed sarcastically.

"No offence, but you can hardly take care of yourself!" she laughed.

Brendan frowned at the insult.

"Look, I'm just teasing you," she said, "but maybe you need to let him know that you'll be going soon."

Brendan sighed again and went to stand beside Jonathan at the cougar enclosure.

"He looks sad," Jonathan said as they stared at the wild animal behind the wire fence.

"I thought you'd like it. I mean, it's not a mountain lion but . . ."

Jonathan shook his head and looked away. "It's like he's wondering what he's doing here when he has business someplace else," he drawled.

Brendan stared at the big cat as he paced back and forward behind the mesh, growling occasionally at the spectators who stared mindlessly into his adopted home.

"Come on," he said. "Let's go see something a little less depressing."

The four walked to a nearby area and sat among the ducks. Brendan watched Eileen sitting on the grass beside Jonathan as they threw breadcrumbs at the cackling ducks by their feet.

Frank's supposedly 'good' hip was now getting so painful that he could hardly walk to the end of their street so he wouldn't be able to escort Eileen to the shelter in the future. How would she manage to see Jonathan then? In any case, if Jonathan moved away from the shelter, how would they cope?

The cousins had become even closer since his mother's arrival. In the three short days that she had been there, an atmosphere of tension had settled in the house and he was relieved that his other cousins came each day to drive Patricia sightseeing around the county, his lack of a licence thankfully prohibiting him from helping out. Each evening when he and Eileen arrived home they could both sense the friction in the house. They would arrive in the kitchen door to find Coleen busily preparing dinner and pretending as usual that nothing was wrong. His uncle would be in the garden doing unnecessary work and his mother would be sitting silently in the kitchen watching Coleen work, or lying on her bed until she was called for dinner. He couldn't understand why whatever had passed between the three people could not be aired, talked out and put to bed finally and why his uncle had allowed his mother to visit when such hard grudges were apparently still felt between them.

He hoped that tonight would be different. The entire family was coming to dinner to welcome his mother home and for once he would embrace the noise of their incessant chatter in the hope that it would drown out the sound of his mother's silent brooding. He had watched her across the table each evening, glaring at her brother as he barked at Eileen's requests to attend the trips he and Jonathan now frequently took.

Since their discussion about Jonathan, Frank had begun to show an interest in the case and had frequently asked Brendan about the progress, or lack thereof, that he had made. Not once did he suspect that there might be something between his eldest daughter and the man. He simply thought she was trying to spread her wings and he was having none of it, so she'd only been able to go on the trips that would get them home safely by six. Brendan noticed his mother flinch on more than one occasion when Frank barked at Eileen's pleading as though it rekindled a memory of their own difficult relationship when she was a young girl. He tensed as he watched her roll her tiny hands into fists and boil with rage as she looked down at her empty plate. For the first time in his life, he began to feel pity for his mother, which disquieted him. He had never felt anything but disdain for her, and the change in his attitude, however small, made him want to move to New York sooner than he had planned and put geographical as well as emotional distance between them.

When Orla called loudly for everyone to come to the table, Brendan waited for his mother to sit before he took a seat at the opposite end of the table, beside Frank in his usual place at the head. Eileen sat facing Brendan while the rest of Frank's large brood sat randomly about the extended table. His uncle said grace and peeked to ensure everyone blessed themselves before tucking into the meal Coleen had spent most of the day preparing.

Brendan glanced down the long table at his cousins. Frank's youngest daughters, twins Emer and Fiona, sat facing their boring husbands in the middle of the table while Kiera and her husband positioned themselves at the other end with their baby daughter placed on a high chair between them. Orla and Doug sat nearest to his mother and had cleverly placed their two naughty sons at the other end of the table where they hoped Eileen would spend the evening looking after them. Brendan began to eat his meal as the clatter of too many voices collided around him.

When the main course was over, Frank proposed a toast to his sister. He welcomed her to his fold as she sat stony-faced at the other end of the table. Few present were aware of the tension between the two and mistook the tremor in his voice as a poignant reminder of the man's great love for his family.

As Orla and Kiera set the table for dessert, Brendan noticed Eileen tense up. He knew she was waiting to choose her moment.

"Dad, there's a party on tomorrow night at Alice's house, for her retirement," she said at last. "I'd like to go. Brendan will take me."

She looked up for a moment and glanced nervously at Brendan. The whole table quietened as Frank narrowed his eyes at his devious daughter who did not raise her eyes from her lap where she twisted her Irish linen napkin into knots in her clammy hands. Nobody moved and it seemed to Brendan that they were all holding their breaths. He wanted to rush over to Eileen and save her from the fifteen pairs of eyes that were now fixed on her.

Without thinking, he heard himself speaking. "I'm going anyway, Uncle Frank, so that's fine with me."

Brendan jumped when Frank banged his fist down hard on the table.

"*Don't you make decisions for my daughter, boy!*" he roared, sending the baby into screaming sobs.

Kiera stood and took her screaming daughter from the table while Coleen put her head in her hands. A strange silence settled in the room as everyone sat motionless. All eyes were trained on Frank who screwed up his face in anger.

"*Let her go.*"

The voice was discharged like a speeding bullet from the other end of the table, ricocheting off the crystal glasses and landing on Frank's head like a warning shot. Nobody moved. Brendan swallowed. He did not have to look down the table to know that it was his mother who had spoken.

"*What?*" Frank yelled.

He stood and leant onto the table, his fat red face swollen in anger.

"What did you say?" he demanded.

"I said, let her go." Patricia rose up slowly from her seat.

"*How dare you!*" Frank yelled.

He left his seat and stumbled around the table until he came face to face with his sister.

Orla and Doug stood to take their children from the room but Frank yelled: "*Nobody moves!*"

Coleen went and placed her hands on his chest.

"Please, Frank. You're frightening the children!" she pleaded.

"I've had just about enough of your snide little comments since you got here, Patricia, and I'm telling you I won't put up with it! You should be thanking me, not giving orders!" he shouted, ignoring his wife's pleas and inching closer to his sister's face.

"*Thanking you?*" Patricia shrieked. "Just what the fuck would I be thanking *you* for?"

Brendan had never heard his mother raise her voice like that before. Neither had he ever heard her curse. He flushed and looked at Eileen who sat pale-faced on the other side of the table, her bottom lip pinched painfully between her teeth.

"Why, you little . . . *whore!*" Frank screamed.

Brendan jumped up from his seat.

"Uncle Frank! *Don't!*" he shouted.

Frank turned to him. "What? Have I offended you, boy? Well, you don't know what this woman did. You have no idea what Coleen and I had to put up with. What my mother had to cope with before that."

"Put up with?" Patricia snarled. "You took everything from me. You took my freedom, kept me down – you wouldn't let me have my own life – you took . . ."

Patricia's turned her gaze to the other end of the table.

"You even took my daughter from me."

A collective gasp sounded down the long table followed by fearful, furtive glances.

"You couldn't take care of her. Eileen would have starved if we'd left her in your care!" Frank bellowed.

"She was my *daughter*!" Patricia screamed. "I was eighteen years old! I made a mistake but you had no right to do that! She was *mine*!" She began to cry and lowered herself heavily onto her chair.

All heads turned to Eileen who sat motionless at the end of the table, her eyes fixed on Brendan who stared at her in disbelief, the knowledge that Eileen was his sister too hard to absorb.

Orla stood again and took her two sons out of the room. Doug followed quickly behind with the twins' husbands. Emer and Fiona nervously inched their way out of the room, glancing back at Eileen as they left.

Only Brendan and Eileen remained, their eyes locked together as they tried to come to terms with what Patricia was saying.

Frank fell into an empty chair as Coleen pretended to dust invisible crumbs from the table.

"You promised you'd never tell her, for her sake. You promised," he said, his voice quiet now.

He slumped further in the chair. His mouth drooped downward and his eyes flickered.

"Frank?" Coleen said, alarmed.

"I . . . I can't b-breathe!" he gasped as sweat began to roll down his crimson face.

Brendan moved his eyes from his sister and ran quickly to where his uncle had now fallen forward, his hand held tightly over his chest.

"*Frank!*" Coleen screamed.

"Call an ambulance!" Brendan ordered as Eileen rushed to the phone.

Patricia stood and moved to her brother.

"Francis, I'm sorry. Francis!" she sobbed but he had lost consciousness and slipped slowly onto the kitchen floor, his face still screwed up in anger as his sister knelt beside him, begging forgiveness for revealing the secret she had promised to take to the grave.

Chapter 24

The waiting area of St Clare's was a long, brightly lit room on the ground floor of the low-rise hospital building. Hard cream-coloured plastic chairs, occupied by depressed-looking relatives, lined the walls of the area and gave the room an air of quiet desperation.

Coleen Dalton sat on the first seat outside the emergency department, waiting anxiously for news of her husband. Four of her daughters sat silently beside her. Only Eileen was missing. At Coleen's insistence she had remained behind to sit with Patricia in the hope that it would give the two women an opportunity to talk about the past.

Brendan sat on a seat alone on the other side of the room, chewing over the evening's events. He glanced at Coleen who smiled at him across the hallway with watery eyes. She crossed over and sat beside him, rubbing his hands in hers.

"So," she said.

Brendan creased his brow and sighed. He had no idea where to begin with his questions.

"So," he echoed. "So, Eileen's my sister."

Coleen nodded.

"Rafael Martinez, he's Eileen's dad?"

Coleen shook her head. "It was before she met him. Your mom got a job in a bar downtown and she met this guy. They were both very young. She was, I guess, very innocent and she . . . well . . . she became pregnant. He took off, left town. Frank . . ." she began, shaking her head furiously. "Frank was so – so mad . . . and I guess disappointed. He felt he'd let his own mother down. He promised your grandmother that he would look after Patricia and felt he'd broken that promise. When she finally told us, we talked and we all agreed that it was best for everyone if Frank and I adopted Eileen so that Patricia could get on with her life. Your mom did agree to it but, you know, when Orla was born and I became a mom myself, I often thought it was wrong . . . that Patricia should have been Eileen's mom. I wondered if she'd felt she'd had no alternative but to give her up. She stayed on with us and we pretended to everyone that Eileen was mine. It must have been hard for your mom watching me raise her daughter while she went back to work in that bar every day. We all just got on with it and things seemed to settle down for a while. Then she met your dad . . . If it makes any difference to you, your mother was very much in love with Rafael."

Brendan looked at the grey linoleum floor. "I know she was pregnant when she married him. Was it so she wouldn't have to give me up too?"

Coleen sighed. "I guess. Things were very different back then. Oh, she could have gotten benefits but she didn't want to live like that and . . . I think Rafael pressurised her into it too."

Brendan looked up and watched as Coleen squirmed.

"He was illegal and Patricia was an American citizen . . . so . . ."

Brendan nodded. "I see," he replied sourly.

A doctor appeared and squinted around the room, looking for Coleen. She stood up and moved swiftly to him. One by one her daughters joined her, leaving only Brendan sitting alone on the other side of the room. Orla glanced over and beckoned for him to join them. He stood and moved to the periphery of the little group and listened as the doctor explained that Frank had only had a mild heart attack and that he would be fine in a couple of days. Brendan cringed as his cousins amazingly smiled with relief for their bullying father and pulled each other into a group hug. He wondered if this was for Coleen's benefit because he couldn't accept that his cousins loved their father as much as they seemed to.

"Now, he needs rest so you all go home now and you'll see him tomorrow," the doctor ordered.

The house was in darkness when Brendan and Coleen returned from the hospital. He was glad that Eileen and his mother had obviously gone to bed. He checked all the windows and doors for his aunt, a task his security-conscious uncle took great pleasure in doing each evening. Then he said goodnight to her and left.

As he lay on his bed in the annex, he thought about how he had a sister he never knew about and how he could now make sense of his uncle's call to his mother after Eileen had been assaulted. He could also now understand Coleen's pitying glances towards him. Even though Frank had taken over Eileen's life since her ordeal, he and Coleen had until that point offered his sister a stable, albeit over-protective home – but they felt they had abandoned him to a life of silence with his cold and indifferent mother on the other side of the Atlantic. He exhaled loudly and as he drifted off to sleep he wondered what other family secrets he was yet to discover and how many of them would vindicate his mother's behaviour and bring him closer to understanding the woman.

When he awoke late the following morning, he was relieved that his mother had remained in her room. He did not want to face her yet and was unsure what, if anything, he would say to her when she appeared. He spoke briefly to Coleen as they sat facing each other across the kitchen table. His aunt looked as though she hadn't slept and her normally coiffured brown hair hung down in straight, lank bangs around her face. But she laughed as he admitted to the driving lessons, informing him that she had noticed the car parked differently on several occasions and was thankful that Frank's extreme short-sightedness prevented him from noticing it too.

He then took Eileen on a drive to the hospital. On the way, they talked a little about Eileen's conversation with their mother the previous night and how Patricia had told her about a young romance which ended badly and how she had always felt bad for keeping Brendan when she had given her up.

"So I have a brother!" she beamed, once again taking her eyes off the road.

"*Eyes!*" he yelled, pointing to the windscreen.

"Sorry!"

"You're not angry?"

Eileen swerved into the car park and parked the car unevenly in a large space.

"I kind of knew," she admitted.

Brendan raised his eyebrows at her. "Knew?"

"Well, I knew I'd been adopted," she said sheepishly. "I suspected, though, long before I knew for sure. Sometimes . . . you just know that you don't belong somewhere. You can feel it. I always felt different, like I belonged somewhere else."

"Do you think that's how Jonathan feels?"

"I guess, but I suspect it is much worse for him," she sighed. "I thought you weren't going to call him Jonathan any more," she added.

"I don't. Not to his face anyway. So, when did you find out for sure?"

"When I was about sixteen. It was before Mom and Dad broke down the wall to make the kitchen bigger. The other end of that room used to be a study room for us. I was in there one evening doing my homework. Mom was in the kitchen talking to a neighbour who had just lost a baby. The woman was crying. She was really upset. The door was partially open and I heard Mom tell her that she lost a baby through miscarriage a couple of days after her dad died and that she felt that the shock of losing him brought it on. I just sat there stunned because I remembered her telling me that I was born five months after Granddad died and that looking after me gave her a reason to go on. So I knew then. I knew that she hadn't given birth to me. I just sat there at the table and cried as quietly as I could and I didn't move until I heard Mom walking the woman to the door. When I came out of the room I set the table and helped Mom cook dinner and I realised that nothing had changed except what I knew in my head. I decided that it didn't really make any difference. I cried a lot about it for the next few months but I never said anything. I never told her or Dad that I knew."

Brendan looked at her in amazement. "You didn't want to know who your birth parents were?"

Eileen exhaled heavily. "I was curious, how could I not be? I tried to get my original birth certificate once only to discover that the original birth certs of adopted children are sealed – that means they can never be accessed."

"Did you have no suspicion at all that my mother was your birth mother?"

Eileen looked at her lap and chewed on the side of her lip. "When everyone went on so much about how we were alike, I thought about how she might be my mom . . ." she bit her lip and looked shyly at Brendan, "but I preferred to think that it wasn't true. I mean, she kept you so why would she give *me* up? It was easier for me to believe that I belonged to a complete stranger, someone who couldn't offer me what my parents did. But deep down . . . deep down I knew she was my mom. I'd see the strange way that Mom and Dad looked at each other any time anyone mentioned how much we looked alike and I knew."

"So, you knew when I arrived here that I was your brother . . . or at least . . . your half-brother?"

Eileen smiled shyly and nodded.

"I was so excited that you were coming to stay. I felt like a part of me was coming home. That I'd no longer feel so lonely in this life. I mean, I got a good home and everything and, even with how Dad ended up treating me, I don't feel that I . . . that I wasn't wanted. I just always felt that I was on the outside

194

looking in. Patricia said she feels now that she made a mistake coming here. She thought they could all put the past behind them and perhaps she'd stay in town, buy an apartment or a house or something but . . . now she says she'll go back to Ireland as soon as she can change her flight."

Brendan felt his heart quicken at the thought of his mother returning to Ireland alone.

"I told her Dad wouldn't want that and that she should stay and work things out . . . with everyone," she said meaningfully.

Brendan walked down the long white corridor and opened the door to Frank's room where he was dozing in his bed. A heart monitor beeped loudly over his head and was attached to his bare chest by long grey wires. Eileen had never seen her tough father look so fragile and helpless. She moved to the bed and rested her hand on his arm. He opened his eyes slowly and stared at her. His loose jaw line began to quiver. She leaned in and hugged him tightly.

"Eileen!" he wept.

"Dad, it's okay," she said, embarrassed by his emotion.

Frank looked up at Brendan and gave him a nod.

"No, Dad," Eileen said. "I want Brendan to stay."

Brendan moved to the back of the room, lowered himself down on a chair and pretended to look out of the window.

"I never wanted you to know," Frank began. "I wanted to protect you. To save you from the life I felt she would have given you."

"It's okay, Dad. I knew all along," she said, trying to ease the strain on her father's heart.

He raised his face up to her in surprise.

"I always felt different, Dad. I always knew that I didn't quite . . . belong."

"You belong! You're my own blood!" he cried.

A cough racked his body and he bent forward, his fat face quivering as he tried to catch his breath.

"Shh!" she said. "It's okay, Dad. I'm glad to know that I am really related to you. I thought that . . . well, I'm glad that Patricia is my mother and that I really am part of this family."

"When . . . what happened to you in Philadelphia . . . I just thought that . . . it was happening again."

Eileen tensed and trained her eyes on the bright window beside her father's bed.

"Dad, Patricia wasn't raped. She made a mistake, that's all," she replied brusquely.

"Don't say that word, Eileen. I don't want to hear you use it."

"Why? Because it makes you feel that no one could control what happened to me? I didn't lead that boy on, Dad. Sooner or later you will have to face up to the fact that none of what happened to me was my fault."

"I just wanted to protect you."

"I know that, Dad, but you didn't protect me. You hid me away from the world, you imprisoned me. I know that you did it because you thought it was right but there was a part of you that wanted to punish me because you couldn't punish Patricia for letting you down."

Frank's chin trembled. "So . . . you think . . . it's all *my* fault? Patricia's coldness, how much she hates me, Brendan living like he's a teenager, unable to settle, to get close to anyone and *you* . . ." He shook his head.

She moved her gaze from the window. "Yes, Dad, some of it *is* your fault, but not all of it. Things happen that are outside our control, outside *your* control. You don't have to feel that you are responsible for everything – for everyone."

"I let my mother down," he said as he began to sob. "I promised her, I begged her to let me take Patricia with me to America. She was only sixteen. She should have been at school but I knew my mother couldn't control her and that she . . . she didn't like Patricia much. I thought it was for the best. I took her here and look what happened. She ran wild and I – I was powerless. I tried to stop her, I did! Look how it all ended up!" He sobbed louder now.

Eileen moved closer to him and put her hands around his

face. "I am not Patricia," she said firmly. "And Patricia had her own reasons for doing what she did. I hope you both sit down and talk about it and then . . . leave it in the past."

Frank looked at Eileen and how strong she seemed in that moment, how decisive.

"Can you forgive me? Can we start over?" he pleaded.

Eileen stood and moved to the end of the bed. She looked out the window at her silver car parked crookedly in the hospital's car park.

She sighed and turned to face him.

"I've been driving my car."

Frank's mouth opened and his eyes opened wide in alarm.

"What? How?"

"Brendan's been teaching me," she said confidentially as her cousin reddened in the background.

"Why, you no good scheming little sleeveen! When I get my hands –"

Eileen raised her hand and he closed his mouth.

"And I'm going to that party tonight whether you like it or not," she said. "I am never again going to ask for your permission to go anywhere or do anything ever again. Do you understand that?"

Frank nodded hesitantly.

The door opened and Kiera entered the room noisily, followed by Orla. Eileen noticed how bashfully they looked at her as if knowing what they now knew made her a different person. She picked her coat off the bed and moved past them.

"I'll see you tomorrow, Dad," she said as she opened the door.

He smiled.

"Eileen!" he called.

She turned.

"Have a good time tonight."

"I will," she said. "I really will."

Chapter 25

Alice Turner's house was a modest duplex in a rundown part of Dover town, where she had lived for over forty years. The three-bedroom house had become too big for her since her son moved to New York over twenty years before but she had so many memories there that she could not face leaving its familiar walls. She and her husband had only lived there together for three years before he went to war but it seemed to her like there was a memory of him in every room of the old-fashioned house. Photos of her husband hung in every corner, snaps of Theo holding their baby son in the garden or in the large living area where they had laughed and talked in the evenings while young Theo slept safely in an upstairs bedroom.

Alice looked around the open-plan room which was full of her friends and family and smiled at the success she had made of her life. Her son Theo was there with his wife Linda and their three children, Carl who was one year into his law degree, Matthew who would hopefully join him at the same university the following year and ten-year-old Naomi who was the living image of her father.

Her heart swelled with pride as she looked around the gathering. She had made friends with people from all walks of life: doctors and dustmen, solicitors and streetwalkers, white, black and yellow alike. Not bad, she thought, for a black gal from Georgia who grew up shoeless on a dirt-road farm outside of Augusta.

She went into the kitchen and took a deep puff of her inhaler, though she knew the time it could help was well past now, and made her way into the group.

Brendan was sitting on a chair by the fireside with Theo junior who he noticed could not keep his eyes off his mother as she moved confidently around the packed room.

"She's seriously ill, isn't she?" Brendan asked the quiet man who had not spoken to anyone since he'd arrived over an hour ago.

Theo nodded but did not look at Brendan.

"Is there anything they can do?"

Alice's son shook his head and his chin quivered. He exhaled and looked into his drink.

"They say she has months . . . weeks . . . they don't know for sure . . . but . . . if I know my mom, she'll hang on until she's put everything on her list to right."

Brendan grinned. "Yes, that's Alice," he agreed.

"Does she know that you know?"

Brendan shook his head.

"Then don't say anything to her," said Theo. "She doesn't want anyone feeling sorry for her. She . . ." Theo's lip trembled and he took a large gulp of his drink. "She feels she's been blessed and that it is just her time to go."

Both men watched Alice greet newcomers to the party, one of whom was Robert Hensen, Brendan's probation officer. Hensen smiled wryly as Brendan raised his glass of Coke mischievously to him.

"You're lucky, Theo. I wish I'd had a mother like Alice."

Theo nodded and raised his glass to his mouth, finishing his drink in one large gulp. He stood and made his way to his mother who was waving frantically at him, wanting to proudly show him off to her friends, he supposed.

Brendan moved to Pilar's side where she was busy talking to people he didn't know. He usually hated parties like this where he was expected to move around the room talking to people who might not have anything in common with him, which in this situation was very likely, but he had come because Alice was important to him.

He looked up just in time to see Eileen and Jonathan sneak out of the main room, her guilty eyes fixed on her escape route. He stood quickly but stopped when Pilar's arm suddenly gripped his.

"Let them go," she said softly.

He looked at her for a moment but returned his eyes to the door which was now closed, his sister gone from view. His heart pounded as his mind raced between tearing after Eileen and bringing her back to the safety of the party or sitting down and allowing her to enjoy the time she had left with Jonathan Doe. He looked longingly at the bottles of ice-cold beer on the dining table and for the first time in weeks wished he could get drunk and forget everything that had happened to him since he had arrived in Dover. He decided that it was useless trying to enjoy the party. He made his excuses to Alice and Pilar and walked the hour-long journey home.

When Brendan reached the house his mother was sitting on a bench outside, reading a book under the porch light. He walked up the driveway and sat at the other end of the bench. She glanced up from her book and looked out into the darkness.

"I forgot how hot it was here in summer," she said. "I couldn't sit inside."

Brendan nodded but knew that his mother felt uncomfortable in the house since she had disclosed the secret she had promised to keep, and was keeping out of Coleen's way.

"The party wasn't any good?"

Brendan shook his head.

"That girl who picked you up – Pilar – is she your girlfriend?"

Brendan reddened and looked away. "No," he said abruptly.

It had taken his ego a while to accept that Pilar Diaz was not interested in him that way – that the wise and well-adjusted woman could see through him and knew that she didn't need another damaged, needy man in her complicated life.

"Oh," she replied and turned her gaze back to her book.

"I know about my father," he said.

Brendan felt his mother stiffen from the other end of the hard wooden bench. She put down her book and stared hard into the darkness.

"Why didn't you tell me?" he asked. He did not look at her but heard her fill her lungs with air.

"To protect you," she replied quietly.

He heard the pain in her voice, the heartbreak. His mother sounded broken, spent.

"From what?" he asked.

"From him. From knowing about him and the sort of man he was."

"Don't you think I had a right to know? Do you think it was right that I found out his name from a stranger in an office?"

Patricia swallowed. "I understand that you're angry. Please believe me that I had my reasons."

"What were they?"

She stood and moved forward on the porch, her face shielded by the darkness.

"I . . . I can't tell you," she replied nervously.

"Can't? You told Eileen all about *her* father!" he spat.

"That is different!" Her voice was louder now, her anger awakened.

"How? How is it different?"

"Your father . . . was . . . look . . . please . . . it's better that you don't know. Please . . . leave it alone!"

She rushed past him, opened the screen door and ran inside the house, banging the door behind her. He heard her thumping her way noisily up the stairs and banging her bedroom door.

He blew out and sat for a moment. He hadn't thought much about the conversation that he knew would happen sooner or later but he had definitely not planned on it turning out this way.

He stood wearily and made his way down to his apartment and lay down on his bed. He tried not to think of Eileen and what she was doing with Jonathan Doe and was glad that Frank wasn't home from the hospital yet. It was bad enough having to deal with his mother's rage without adding his uncle to his problems.

An hour later he got up and made his way into the kitchen where Coleen was lying on the sofa watching late-night TV. She sat up and moved the blanket from her legs.

"Is the party over already? Where's Eileen?" she asked.

Brendan sat down beside her. "No, it's not. I just wasn't in the humour for it. Eileen's fine. Pilar will drop her home later." He hoped that was true.

"Was that you arguing with your mother?" she asked.

Brendan sighed. "She won't tell me about my father."

Coleen pondered this for a moment. "Did I ever tell you that my name isn't Coleen?"

Brendan grimaced, annoyed by how abruptly she'd changed the subject.

"My grandfather was Irish and my dad wanted to give us all Irish names," she went on. "I had three older brothers, all with real Irish names. They've all passed now. I was the youngest and there was a long gap before I came along. Well, my mother, she was of German descent and she wanted to call me Ingrid, not only because it was a German name but because she loved the Swedish actress Ingrid Bergman. Dad put his foot down and said he was calling me Coleen. Now, before you tell me, I know that Coleen is not a real name in Ireland and that it means 'girl' in Irish but it's a real popular name here in America and he was adamant. Anyway, when I was two days old and my father was at work, my mother sneaked down to the church and had me christened Ingrid Agnes. Well, my brother told me that Dad was furious and started calling me Coleen anyway. So it stuck. Everybody got used to it. Hey, won't they get a hell of a shock when they're burying me?"

Brendan smiled absent-mindedly. He had not been listening to the story but had been glancing at the TV, watching the credits roll up on – of all things – an episode of *The Nelsons of Newsart*.

"You want to know what my point is?" his aunt asked.

Brendan grinned, embarrassed that she had read his thoughts.

"It doesn't matter what your name is or what your background is. *You* are who *you* are."

Brendan nodded. The problem was that he had no idea who he was.

Coleen patted the sofa next to her and he obliged by moving a little closer.

"Oh, I just love this programme!" she said as Jonathan Wyatt Nelson and his brothers grinned into the camera. "It's a tape. Orla and Doug got it for me for my birthday one year and I often sit here and watch it when I'm feeling down. Course, Frank hates it. He says it's sentimental wish-wash, whatever that means."

Brendan flinched as the rest of the Nelson family waved cheerfully into the camera.

"Oh, don't tell me you don't like it either!" said Coleen. "It's my favourite. I watched this as a girl and I still enjoy it. I guess I love the old-timey feel to it, you know, when people were still polite and helpful and kids were raised properly."

Brendan nodded and reluctantly looked at the television. He watched as Jonathan and his brothers went swimming after they caught fish. He tensed as the boys jumped in and out of the deep lake. It reminded him of the day Jonathan had almost drowned in the lake in Mountain Park. It suddenly became clear to him what Jonathan meant when he said he saw himself swimming. What he meant was he had seen it on TV and for some reason he thought the actor was him. The episode suddenly stopped. He looked at Coleen who was pressing down hard on the remote.

"I saw that one a hundred times," she said.

She fast forwarded the tape and chose another episode of the same programme.

"You have them all?" Brendan cried.

"Sure. Is this bothering you? You want me to turn it off?"

Brendan shook his head as a teenage Jonathan held up his

203

rifle to a half-starved mountain lion and stood staring at her through his rifle scope. He looked away as a wave of nausea hit him. He had loved that story more than any of the others and it was a stupid soap, a ridiculous tale thought up by writers in a stuffy office in New York or somewhere like it. The credits rolled and Brendan returned his eyes to the television. He watched the golden-haired kids smile and wave into the camera one by one. He realised there was something missing but the programme ended before he could figure it out.

"Can you fast forward to another one?" he asked.

"Oh, *now* you like it?" Coleen laughed as she searched.

"Stop there!" Brendan shouted when the credits rolled up on yet another episode. He watched again as the children beamed into the cameras.

"There's no Cassie!" he said.

"Who?" Coleen asked.

"There's no Cassie. His sister, the one who's blind, she's not there!" he said, jumping from his seat and making his way to the front door.

Coleen sat up straight and stared at the TV screen.

"What are you talking about? Brendan, where are you going?" she yelled but he was already out the door, slamming it behind him as he headed towards the shelter.

He had to see Jonathan. He had to tell him that he believed him. He had to tell him that he believed that at least some of his story was real.

When he arrived at the shelter it was almost midnight and the house was in darkness. He had forgotten that Jonathan had left the party with Eileen and that they were probably in his room together. He looked up at the round window which was cloaked in darkness and was deciding that he'd come back tomorrow when he heard a low moan coming from the bushes.

"Who's there?" he called out.

He moved toward the noise and looked into the dense scrub at the front of the house just below the porch.

"Jonathan?"

He moved quickly and helped his friend to sit up. A long narrow gash ran across Jonathan's eyebrow and blood pumped from both of his nostrils. He seemed disorientated.

"What happened, Jonathan? Did you fall?"

Jonathan shook his head and struggled to stand up. Brendan helped him to his feet and supported him until he got his balance.

"It's Ei . . . it's Eileen," Jonathan said. "I – I came back here with her and we tried to . . . go to my room," he said as he turned his eyes guiltily away from Brendan. "Kuvic pulled Eileen back down the stairs and she's in there with him. He's gone mad. I tried to fight him but he knocked me around some and threw me out."

"How long ago? How long has she been in there?"

"I don't know . . . I think I blacked out. A couple of minutes maybe."

Brendan climbed the steps and banged loudly on the front door.

"Kuvic!" he yelled. "Open this door!"

He ran around the back and pushed heavily on the back door but it was locked. He peered into the back window of the kitchen and could see a faint light coming from Henrietta's pantry. He could see his sister's feet poking out of the pantry door but could not see her body.

"*Eileen!*" he yelled.

He began to push heavily on the back door. Jonathan joined him and together they rammed their shoulders against it to no avail. Brendan looked at the shed behind him and beckoned for Jonathan to help him get the ladder. Together they began to slam it into the door until it gave way.

They ran into the darkened kitchen.

Brendan felt for the switch and flipped it, showering the large room with bright fluorescent light. Kuvic lay unconscious against the oven. Long scratch-marks lined his cheeks and a large abrasion ran along his forehead. The weapon, a heavy cast-iron pot, lay beside him on the floor. A long thin stream of urine ran from his trouser leg towards the drain in the middle of Henrietta's kitchen.

Brendan ran to Eileen who was sitting puffing on the pantry floor, staring at Kuvic, the kitchen phone held loosely in her hand.

"Are you okay?" Brendan said.

She nodded. "He didn't hurt me. He didn't get a chance. I called an ambulance . . ."

Brendan looked from his tiny sister to the huge pan and began to laugh. "You lifted that yourself?"

Eileen laughed too.

Brendan helped his sister to her feet and handed her over to Jonathan who led her into the sitting room. He moved closer to Kuvic and heaved from the stench of alcohol and urine coming from the man. He checked his pulse and was slightly disappointed to find he was alive and breathing.

"Lucky bastard," Brendan said as the ambulance siren screamed into the driveway.

Shortly after, as Kuvic was being loaded into the ambulance, Jonathan turned to Brendan.

"But why . . . why did you come here?" he asked.

"I came to tell you. Cassie. I think she's real."

"You believe me?" Jonathan said weakly.

"Yes . . . I do."

Chapter 26

Brendan and Jonathan were hiking alongside a stream in Hedden Park on the outskirts of Dover town on Monday morning. They stopped for a rest and studied the magnificent scenery around them. The park was silent except for the chirping of birds perched high up in the dense wood that surrounded them and the sound of water gurgling gently as it ran over the smooth stones at the bottom of the shallow stream. They could hear the muffled sound of a waterfall pouring over the rocks in the distance as it crashed down into the river below and the gentle wind that whistled through the trees high above them.

"It's peaceful here," Brendan said.

"Thought you didn't like the quiet?" Jonathan asked.

Brendan laughed. "I don't. I'm just saying it's nice, that's all."

He exhaled noisily and sat on a large rock at the edge of the stream. Jonathan settled himself on another.

Brendan's thoughts turned inevitably to Kuvic. Thompson was out of town but, when Alice informed him about his attack on Eileen, he had arranged a board meeting for when he got back. Thompson had said that Kuvic would be fired this time.

"I'm real glad Kuvic has been banned from the house," Jonathan drawled, as if reading Brendan's thoughts.

"And I'm glad Eileen has filed charges against him. She says it's not for her sake. I'm amazed that she doesn't seem the least bit shaken by what happened. She says she's doing it so that he doesn't get a job again where he has control over vulnerable people."

"About that night . . ." Jonathan began.

Brendan squirmed and reddened. He raised his hand. "It's none of my business, Jonathan."

"No, hear me out," he pleaded. "I was going to . . . going to ask Eileen to marry me."

"*Marry* you!" Brendan said. He could hear the surprise in his voice and saw his friend flush and look away.

"Oh, I know you think I have nothing to offer her," Jonathan said, "but I can feel that a change is coming . . . I just know that I am finally going home and I intend to take Eileen with me."

"Now, look . . . Jonathan . . ." Brendan began as he watched his friend swallow nervously.

"You're calling me Jonathan again. You said you believed me."

"I do. But . . ."

"But what?"

"You don't remember your last name and you don't really remember where you are from, so how are we going to find Cassie in this huge country? She could be anywhere, in any small town or huge city from California to Virginia or from North Dakota to Texas. Do you know how many millions of people live in this country?"

Jonathan cleaned his glasses in his shirt and, as he put them back on, he squinted through a clearing in the dense woods.

"She's out there somewhere. I know it. I'm going to find her, Brendan. I'm going to find my home."

Brendan looked down and tapped the dusty earth from his boots. The hope in his friend's voice had returned and it hurt to see him so full of optimism.

"I hope so," Brendan replied. "I really do."

At eleven on Wednesday morning, Brendan ate breakfast in his own apartment before walking hesitantly to the shelter alone.

Eileen had driven with Coleen to the hospital earlier that morning to bring her father home and he did not want to sit alone with his mother, who had not spoken one word to him since their row on Saturday night.

It was a morning he was dreading. Jonathan was due at the housing department and arrangements had been made for him to view three vacant one-bedroom apartments in various parts of the town. The day before, he had tried to talk to Jonathan about the trip but his friend had refused to discuss it and only agreed to go with Brendan at Pilar's insistence.

When he arrived in the door, Pilar was sitting slumped on a chair in the hallway. She had been on night duty.

"You still here?" he asked her.

"Alice was taken into hospital late last night and, with Kuvic gone, I had to do a double shift.

Brendan exhaled sharply. "Is she okay?"

Pilar shook her head sadly.

"What about Jane or Cathy?" he asked. "Could they come in?"

"They're already doing extra shifts this week to cover Kuvic. As soon as Thompson comes back, we'll be able to advertise Kuvic's job." She looked up at Brendan. "You ready for today?"

Brendan could hear the concern in her voice. She knew he was dreading today almost as much as Jonathan was.

"I suppose so."

Brendan walked alongside Jonathan down the east section of the town's main street towards the housing authority's office. It was the first time they had walked down this end of town together and he noticed that each time a Hispanic man walked towards them, Jonathan inched closer to him and lowered his head nervously until they passed. He had noticed the same nervousness when they saw the two Hispanic men in New York and remembered how Jonathan had placed the diner's tall menu onto the windowsill to block out his view of them. Several Hispanic women passed them on the same route, going about their daily business in the same way as the men, but Jonathan did not flinch and did not appear nervous of them. He wondered if this was why his friend had been afraid of him on that first day that they met, if his dark appearance had evoked a fearful memory, but he had no way of knowing what had been going on in Jonathan's mind when the man himself could not remember why he had taken fright that day.

When the two arrived at the housing office, a tall, skinny woman dressed in a neat navy suit stood waiting for them near the reception desk. She had thin brown hair tied tightly in a bun on the top of her head and her sallow skin was disfigured by large pockmarks over her cheekbones. Brendan ran his eyes over her face as he tried to think why she seemed so familiar to him.

"Oh no," Jonathan said quietly. "That's Mila, Kuvic's cousin. I was hoping she wouldn't be working here any more."

Brendan exhaled loudly, realising now why he thought he'd recognised the woman. She was the image of her rotten cousin. "Well, this ought to go well!" he muttered sarcastically.

"Well, if it isn't Jonathan Wyatt Nelson himself!" the thin woman gloated.

Two women seated at desks in the background began to chuckle.

"I just saw your sister Mackenzie. She passed by here, tired out from a hard day's apple-picking," she twanged, imitating Jonathan's accent. "Now, you be sure to say hi to all the Nelson clan, won't you?"

The women began to laugh as John hung his head at the desk.

"*That's enough!*" Brendan roared.

The smiles from the two women in the background slid slowly from their faces as they looked guiltily in Jonathan's direction. Only Mila continued to sneer at Jonathan who had stepped behind Brendan in the airless office.

"Now, I believe you have keys for us?" Brendan snapped, anxious to get out of there.

Mila handed the keys to Brendan and gave them directions to the apartments.

"Thanks for sticking up for me," Jonathan said as the pair

made their way back down East Blackwell Street towards their first viewing which was a mere block away.

When they reached the building Brendan cringed as they stood at the bottom of the stone steps and stared at the grotty façade. Several of the tall building's windows appeared cracked or broken and noise seemed to emanate from every corner of the seven-storey building. Children were crying and music boomed out of several apartments. Two unseen men argued about money and a woman, who came rushing out of the building's main door, brushed past them, screaming and cursing at her companion, an elderly woman who shuffled slowly from behind the large chipped door. Brendan glanced at his companion who stood open-mouthed at the building's entrance.

"Brendan, do you know what 'home' means?"

Brendan thought about Jonathan's question for a moment. He ran his hands through his thick black hair and frowned. "It means, em, where you live, I guess."

Jonathan shook his head vehemently. "No, Brendan. It means where you are happiest. Home is the place where the people you love are. It's the place where you feel peace, where you belong." He glanced skyward at the shabby building.

Brendan stared at his poetic friend. He had no answer to his words because he had never lived anywhere that felt like home to him.

"Look, we'll just see what's it's like inside," he said, grasping Jonathan gently by the arm and leading the frightened man up the five litter-lined steps.

Inside the apartment a small hall led to the bedroom where an old stained mattress, left behind by the previous occupant, stood on its side, covering the window and darkening the small, dismal room. They moved to the tiny kitchen whose walls were lined with grease. The smell of cigarette smoke hung in the air of the filthy room. The hand basin sat on the floor of the bathroom, broken in pieces while the pipe leaked small amounts of water onto the chipped mosaic floor, making a rhythmic, tapping sound in the silent apartment.

211

"At least it's soundproof," Brendan joked, trying to make light of the situation. Both men moved towards the small living room. It was empty except for a purple-painted radiator under a large window that looked out onto the front of the building. The red-patterned carpet appeared wet under their feet, as though someone had made attempts to clean it.

"Probably tried to clean up the blood from a murder or something," Brendan joked but he could see that John had returned to the stupor he had been in the previous day. "Forget this place, Jonathan. There's no way you're moving in here. Let's go see the next place."

But his friend did not respond.

Brendan walked ahead as they made their way on foot down Carrol Street and swung left onto Lee Avenue. They stopped about halfway down the long narrow cul-de-sac and peered up at another block of similarly neglected housing-authority apartments. They took the lift up to the ninth floor and opened the door to the apartment which was situated at the end of a long narrow corridor. The entire apartment, which faced out onto the shaded side of the building, was covered in a shaggy straw-coloured carpet that smelled of animal faeces. An old rusted bird cage stood on top of the broken-down refrigerator, its open door hanging loosely on its hinges and a cat tray stood beside the cooker, still filled with the litter of the previous occupant's pet.

"Jesus!" Brendan said as he looked around the dingy apartment. "This place is even worse than the first!"

A loud noise shot out from the floor below them.

"Turn that TV down!" a voice screamed.

Another voice retorted and hurled abuse in colourful language.

"Nice neighbours," Brendan quipped.

"I don't like apartments. I like houses," Jonathan said, breaking the silence he had retreated into over an hour previously.

"Come on," Brendan replied. "Two down, one to go."

The final apartment was a ten-minute walk down the length of

Richard's Avenue. Brendan took out the paperwork and cringed when he saw that the cross street where the apartment stood was called Nelson Street which was a run-down road on the outskirts of the town's main drag. The accommodation was listed as a two-bedroom apartment which Brendan knew the authority would not give to a single man, so he wondered if the cruel-hearted Mila had added it to their itinerary as a joke.

When they reached the corner, they could see that the building was part of an older, low-rise apartment-block complex hidden behind the high-rise mall on Richard's Avenue. They walked down to the entrance which was unfortunately on Nelson Street. Jonathan peered up at the sign and blushed. Brendan patted his back in support.

They looked at the fifteen four-storey apartment blocks which were arranged along a semi-circular roadway facing a green area filled with washing lines and children's toys. They walked underneath the stone entrance and peered at the numbers as they tried to decide which block the apartment was in. Brendan moved along the blocks followed by Jonathan until he came to the third building in the complex.

"It should be this basement apartment," Brendan said absent-mindedly as he studied the paperwork. He looked up at Jonathan to find his face had become taut with fear. "What's the matter?"

Jonathan's eyes had become fixed on a group of Hispanic men who were sitting on stones steps that led down to one of the basement apartments.

"Jonathan," Brendan said, "come on. It's okay. I'm with you. We'll just go see it quickly. Please?"

When his friend did not respond, Brendan reached forward and shook him to try to wake him from his stupor. Jonathan raised his arms defensively. Brendan flushed.

"Jonathan, please don't start this again. It's me, Brendan. I'm not going to hurt you. Now, let's just go and look at the apartment and get out of here quickly, please?"

The men on the steps had begun to take an interest in the two strangers.

Brendan reached forward and placed his hands on Jonathan's shoulders.

"Jonathan, it's me. It's Brendan. Please move," he said. He placed his hand on Jonathan's forearm and, knowing his friend was beyond reasoning with, he began to gently guide him away from the basement apartment. Two of the men sitting by the fourth building stood and began to walk towards them. Brendan swallowed.

"*Come on, Jonathan! Let's get out of here!*" he yelled but his friend fell down on his knees and began to whimper in Spanish.

"Jesus!" Brendan whispered to himself. "Jonathan, get up! Look, we'll leave here right now. We'll go back to Pilar."

"*¡No me lastime!*" Jonathan cried.

"Speak English!" Brendan pleaded. "Please, Jonathan, please get up!" He tried to lift his friend onto his feet.

Jonathan slumped onto the ground and held his wrists together as though they were bound. "*¡Por favor, no me ponga en la caja!*" he cried as the two men joined them.

"We don't want no trouble here," one of them said in a strong Hispanic accent.

Brendan reached forward again and pulled Jonathan up onto his knees.

"He's my friend!" he said. "I'm not hurting him. I just want to get him out of here!"

One of the men bent down and looked into Jonathan's face. "This guy your friend?"

Jonathan began to scream and kick out at the Hispanic who drew back and raised his leg to retaliate. Brendan jumped forward and held his arms out, blocking the men's view of Jonathan.

"He's sick. He doesn't mean any harm," he pleaded. He knelt on the ground beside Jonathan and held his face in his hands. "Jonathan," he said softly, "come with me."

But Jonathan continued to scream. "*¡No me pongas en la caja! No me escaparé otra vez. ¡No lo haré, Rafael, no lo haré!*"

Brendan fell backwards onto the dusty pathway. His mouth dropped open.

"What did you say?" he asked.

Jonathan did not answer but continued to plead in Spanish.

Brendan turned to the men who had moved back from the madman. "Please! Ask him who he thinks I am!"

One of the men moved forward hesitantly and spoke to Jonathan who answered him through sobs.

"He says you are Rafael," the man replied.

"Rafael *who?*" Brendan screamed. His blood turned cold as he waited for the man to translate Jonathan's reply.

"He says you are keeping him a box," the man replied.

"And my last name?" Brendan asked although he had heard it. He had heard his friend say it.

"Martinez . . . Rafael Martinez."

Chapter 27

Pilar Diaz sat brooding in Alice's makeshift office on the second floor of the shelter as Brendan waited patiently for her response to Jonathan's extraordinary revelation on Nelson Avenue. She tapped her fingers against her lips and took a deep breath.

"Martinez is a very common name. It could have been someone else," she reasoned.

Brendan shook his head. "I am telling you, Pilar. He said Rafael Martinez. Uncle Frank said I look just like my father. That's why he was so frightened when he met me first. He thought I was him!"

Pilar shook her head. "It's a coincidence. Nothing more."

Brendan stood and stared hard at her. "Why can't you believe it?" he asked.

"Because it is simply a coincidence, Brendan. Accept it! Brendan, please believe me. There is no secret to Jonathan, no mystery to what happened to him. His family abused him and he ran away. He blocked it out because it was too painful to remember. He was a small child, remember? A vulnerable child who made up a fantasy world to protect himself from the awful situation he lived in. Period. He needs to accept that, Brendan. He needs to know that there is no one looking for him."

Brendan shook his head and stared wide-eyed at her. "What

happened to you, Pilar? Eileen said that when you came to work here you were passionate about making things better . . . but now . . . you seem to just want to keep the status quo. But you are wrong – things can change."

Pilar raised her eyes slowly to meet his and sighed. "Brendan, Jonathan is *ill*. Whatever true memories he has have been mixed up for so long with what he has invented that it is too late to discern what is real from what is imagined."

"*No!*" Brendan shouted. "I don't believe that. I think it could be true, Pilar. I think it is possible that he has a sister named Cassie. If she was made up, why wasn't she part of his TV family? I think she is real, Pilar, and somehow they got separated. I think that something happened and now I think my father could hold the key to finding Jonathan's family."

Pilar slumped back in her chair, her heavy eyes half-closing as she ran her eye over Alice's outstanding paperwork. Brendan studied the exhausted woman and knew there was no point in trying to convince her.

"Why don't you lie down until the clients return for the night?" he said.

"Zeb is upstairs and he needs help," she replied wearily.

"I can look after him. I need time to think about what I am going to say to my mother anyway."

Pilar raised her eyebrows. "He needs more help than just feeding. You'd need to help him use the bathroom."

Brendan felt his lunch rush up his throat at the thought of helping the old man, who could not use his arms, to use the toilet. He swallowed.

"No problem," he replied.

Pilar searched his face for a moment. She stood and stretched.

"You've changed . . . for the better," she said. She reached forward and patted his chest affectionately.

"What about Jonathan?" he asked.

"I've given him a double dose of his pills. Dr Reiter said it was okay to do that if he was very distressed. He'll sleep through the day and probably the night too. He'll need it." She shook her head, remembering the distressed state in which the man had returned to the shelter.

As Pilar settled down on a sofa in the lounge, Brendan searched for Rafael Martinez on Alice's computer, hoping to find a photo of the man. He sighed when over seven million matches flashed on his screen. He began a new search and restricted it to New York which took his hits down to just under two million. He exhaled loudly and bit the side of his mouth as he tried to think of his next move and clicked on several images of Hispanic men by that name but none of them looked like they might be his father. He pushed the chair back from the computer and stared out of the window, aware now that he had no choice but to approach his mother and hope that she would be in a more cooperative mood.

Brendan shut down the computer and climbed to the attic to check on Jonathan. He crept up to his bed and watched his friend sleep. The attic space, in the increasing dusk, felt more like a prison cell than the man's home. He stood for a while and recalled Jonathan telling the Hispanic translator that he had been kept in a box. He shuddered at what his friend might have gone through and hoped that if his father was involved in it he had not been cruel to the gentle man sleeping soundly in front of him.

He went down to the second floor to the dorm where Zeb slept and was thankful that the man did not seem to need any help in the bathroom department. He went downstairs and sat in the dining room to mull over how he would get his mother to tell him what he needed to know.

When Pilar woke, he made her fresh coffee and took the long way back to Maple Avenue but was disappointed to find his mother was not there. In the kitchen, Frank and Eileen were sitting at the table talking as they tried to forge a new relationship from their tumultuous past.

Brendan took a seat. He noticed Frank throwing occasional furtive glances in his direction and wondered if he was still annoyed about his moonlighting job as a driving instructor.

"Everything okay?" Frank asked.

It occurred to Brendan that Frank might be able to get him a photo of his father from the police computer at the station. He knew his uncle was still good friends with many of the local officers who might be willing to do him a favour. He glanced quickly at Eileen but then looked guiltily away as he began to recount the story of Jonathan Doe in the apartment block.

"So," Brendan said as he finished filling his uncle in on the story, "do you think you could get a photo of him? There must be one on the system."

Eileen feigned disinterest in Brendan's quest and left the table quickly, leaving the two detectives alone to deliberate the next move.

"I suppose I could ask Guido," Frank said.

Brendan raised his eyes in alarm. He did not want Pilar to know about this.

"What?" Frank asked. "You behaving yourself with that girl?"

Brendan raised his eyes to heaven. He hadn't touched Pilar Diaz and was unlikely to ever get near the aloof woman.

"Is there anyone else at the station you could ask?" he asked.

"Sure. I'll ask Joe Novak, he's a good buddy of mine. I'll let you know when I get it. So, you think Martinez was mixed up in something heavy like kidnapping?"

"Well, Jon–" he began and then he looked at the door and saw his mother standing there glaring at him with her pinched, gaunt face. "Mam." He stood up. "I didn't know you were here."

"So behind my back you're asking Francis for information? I'm your mother and I ordered you to leave it be."

Frank stood up. "Now, Patricia, the lad is only –"

"Mam, please," Brendan intervened before another row occurred, "will you just look at a photo of someone for me?" The last thing he needed was Frank being carted off to the hospital again.

"Of who?" she demanded.

"A boy. Look, it's important to me."

Patricia sat down slowly and narrowed her eyes at her brother as he stared at her from his seat at the head of the heavy oak table.

Brendan raced to his apartment to get the photos of Jonathan on the day he was found and rushed back, fearful that a row might have erupted in his absence.

"Here!" he panted as he shoved the photos of a wide-eyed Jonathan with the two police officers towards her. "Did you ever see this boy?"

Patricia gazed at the photos and shook her head. "No. Who is he?" She looked up at her son, her eyes wild with confusion.

Brendan sighed and sat heavily on the chair facing her. "He's a man at the shelter. That photo was taken in 1979. He was found wandering the streets with no real memory of who he was or where he was from. Today he said my father's name."

Patricia looked back at the photo. She shook her head. "He spoke about Rafael?"

"Yes."

"But . . . it's such a common name."

"I know," Brendan sighed. "I didn't want to ask you. I know how upset talking about him makes you but I need to know if my father had something to do with this man getting lost . . . disappearing from his family."

Patricia looked at her brother who lowered his eyes slowly and kept them fixed on a knot on the old wooden table. Brendan looked from one to the other, his frustration rising with every second that passed.

"In 1979," she said, "your father was serving a double life sentence in jail."

Brendan's mouth dropped open as Frank coughed nervously.

"Frank said . . . I thought . . . I thought he was a petty criminal."

Patricia sighed. "He was, once. He . . . he shot a woman and her little girl when he held up a bank in New York. They both died. He won't get out for another fifteen years."

Brendan slumped down in his chair. "He's a murderer?" he asked as he tried to absorb his mother's words.

Patricia looked up at her son in the same way that Eileen did, her head lowered but her eyes raised expectantly like a child.

"Now you know why I didn't want you to know," she whispered.

Brendan got up and paced the length of the kitchen.

"And you've never seen this boy?"

"No," she replied faintly. "Never."

Brendan ran his hands through his hair as he tried to think. There was no way of knowing how long Jonathan had been in captivity. It was possible that his father had taken him before he was imprisoned but if that was the case, who had looked after him and why didn't they bring him back to where he belonged? His only option was to show Jonathan a photo of Rafael Martinez and hope that he positively identified him as the man responsible for taking him from his family. The rest he could figure out later.

"Frank, could you bring me down to the station to get that photo now?" he asked.

Frank looked from his nephew to his sister. An exchange seemed to pass between them. Patricia left the room and ascended the stairs as Brendan waited in the kitchen. After what seemed like a lifetime she returned and handed him a small worn photo.

"This is the only one I have," she said as she placed it gently into his open palm. "It's very old. It was taken in Mexico when he was young."

Brendan stared at the photo of his father. Rafael Martinez was an incredibly handsome youth with deep brown eyes and raven-black hair slicked back with hair gel. He had straight, white teeth and a perfectly formed round brown mole that sat a little higher than Brendan's on his right cheekbone. Brendan shook head, amazed at how alike they were.

"I told you that you looked like him but that is the only way you are alike," Frank said quietly from the table. "You're a good boy, Brendan."

Brendan left the house and walked back to the shelter where Henrietta and her volunteer sister were struggling to feed the fifty men who had shown up for dinner. He greeted Pilar who looked surprised to see him back so soon. Brendan went to the kitchen and began to stack the dishwasher as he wondered how long he would have to wait until he could climb the stairs to show Jonathan the photo of his father.

At nine he finally crept up the steps to the attic room and opened the door. A tray of untouched food sat beside Jonathan's bed where he lay in a comatose state.

"Jonathan," he said as he lightly shook his friend.

Jonathan half-opened his eyes and tried to focus them on his visitor. "Huh?"

"Sit up. I want to show you something." Brendan tried to hoist his friend into an upright position.

Jonathan slumped forward and rested his heavy head onto his chest which rose and fell quickly in heavy, uneven breaths.

"Jonathan!" Brendan said, slightly louder now. "Please wake up!"

Jonathan raised his head and his eyes opened slowly. He tried to steady his head as he focused on his visitor.

"Help!" he slurred as the day's events returned to his troubled mind.

"Shhh! Do you want Pilar to hear us?" Brendan whispered. "You're safe. You're in your room in the shelter."

When his friend appeared calm, he took the photo from his jeans pocket and laid it on Jonathan's bed.

"Is this Rafael?" he said quietly.

"Who?" Jonathan asked.

"Rafael Martinez, the man who took you from your family. Is this him?"

"I don't know any Rafael," Jonathan replied sleepily.

Brendan lifted the photo and placed it closer to Jonathan's half-closed eyes. "Please, Jonathan, focus. Please look at the photo."

Jonathan glanced down at the photo and then looked back at Brendan.

"This is . . . a photo . . . of you . . ." he replied indistinctly.

"It's not me, Jonathan. This is Rafael Martinez, the man who took you."

Jonathan moved his mouth back and forward and narrowed his eyes at the snap.

He handed it back to Brendan who stood patiently by the side of his bed.

"Well?" Brendan asked.

Jonathan shrugged.

"Is this the man who you remembered today? You said the name Rafael Martinez. Is this him?" Brendan barked.

Jonathan slipped slowly down the bed and closed his eyes.

"Jonathan!"

Jonathan opened his eyes again and gazed sleepily at Brendan.

"Please, Brendan . . . let me sleep . . . I told you . . . I don't know anyone by that name," he drawled as his head fell forward again onto his chest.

"Jonathan!" Brendan yelled, his patience finally wearing. "Wake up!"

He reached forward and pulled his friend back into a sitting position.

"Concentrate on the question," he ordered. "Now, is this the man who took you from your family?"

The door opened and a stream of light sifted in from the landing.

Brendan looked up to see Pilar standing in the doorway.

"I thought you might be here!" she spat. "Can't you leave him alone?"

Brendan ignored her, focusing on Jonathan again.

"Jonathan, please look at it one last time. Is this the man who took you?"

"*No!*" Jonathan screamed as he jumped from the bed.

He staggered towards Pilar and pointed at her.

"She did!"

"She took you?" Brendan asked incredulously.

"Yes, she took me! *Melibea! Melibea!* She took me."

Pilar ran her fingers over her tired eyes and sighed heavily.

"I told you, Brendan, he is sick. For Christ's sake! I was two

223

years old when he was found and I hadn't even left Puerto Rico. How exactly could I have taken him from his family?"

Brendan exhaled heavily and bent forward on the fold-up chair in Alice's office.

He knew that was the truth but he also believed that she had evoked another memory from Jonathan's past.

"What does *melibea* mean?" he asked.

Pilar stood and leant against the window of the office.

"Melibea? It's a Spanish name, a girl's name."

"Do you think this is the name of the woman who took him?"

"No. He has called me Melibea many times when he was upset. But . . ."

"What?"

"You must have hit a nerve because he's . . . he's never accused me of taking him before. He's always spoken of Melibea as though she looked after him."

"You don't think she could have kidnapped him?"

"Kidnapped? Brendan, you are running away with yourself. There is no evidence that John was ever kidnapped. Maltreated, yes, but not kidnapped. I've told you before that I think it was his own family that hurt him and that he escaped. Believe me, I've thought about it for years and it is the only credible explanation."

Brendan sighed and shook his head. "Or is it easier for you to believe that his own family and not Hispanics hurt him?"

Pilar raised her eyebrows and folded her arms around her body. "What? Oh, so it must have been Hispanics because we are all criminals, is that it?" she spat.

"Don't forget that I am Hispanic too!" Brendan retorted.

"Hispanic? You are not Hispanic, Brendan. So what if your father was Mexican?" she shouted. "Were you ever denied a job because you looked a little too dark or because an employer feared your relatives would come to the premises at night and steal?"

Brendan thought about the children at school who made fun of his dark appearance but their teasing did not compare to the sort of racism Pilar was talking about. He looked at his feet and shook his head.

"No," he said as he stood to leave. He took a step forward to try to comfort her but she turned her back on him and stared out into the darkness.

"Pilar, there is one more thing that I want to do for Jonathan before I go back to New York. He told me that the thing he missed most was sitting around the table with his family, talking about the day over a meal. Coleen suggested I invite John to Uncle Frank's for dinner tomorrow night. She's heard a lot about him and wanted to meet him. She's invited you too. It's . . . it's my birthday and Coleen wanted to do something to celebrate it. You know what she's like. It would mean a lot to me if you'd come."

He watched her raise her hands to her face and knew that she was crying. He moved to her and turned her towards him.

"Shhh . . . it's okay," he said as he ran his hands over her black shiny hair.

"Will you come?" he asked quietly.

Pilar moved away from him and nodded. She took a tissue from her pocket and dried her eyes quickly. "I'll be there."

"Do you think he would be fit to come . . . I mean, what with the heavy medication he's on?" Brendan asked.

"Yes, I think so. I can make sure he only takes a light dose tomorrow."

Brendan left the shelter and made his way to the hospital to see Alice. When he reached her ward, a nurse raised her hand to stop him from entering her room which was directly facing the nurse's station.

"No visitors, sir. Ms Turner has had a procedure today and she's still sedated."

Brendan flashed a broad smile. "Please, I'll only be a minute. I just want to tell her something."

"Well, she won't hear you," the nurse replied.

"Alice hears everything," he said.

The nurse laughed and waved her hand for him to enter.

"Go on then. But only five minutes, okay?"

Brendan nodded and opened the door to Alice's room. He walked to her bed where she lay unconscious, surrounded by three huge beeping machines. A large needle fed fluid into a vein in her hand and an oxygen mask covered her mouth. He leant forward and smoothed her hair away from her face.

"Alice, I know you can hear me. I wanted you to know that I am close to bringing John home. I'm going to come back when I've figured it all out so you hang on. Don't you leave until I come!"

Brendan waited for a moment but his friend did not stir. He leant in and kissed her forehead which was cold and clammy.

"You hang on, Alice," he said as he slipped quietly from the room and headed for home.

Chapter 28

"How's that?" Coleen asked as she stood back from her dining table which she'd dressed in her special Irish linen tablecloth.

Brendan blushed when he saw the trouble his aunt had gone to.

"Well, I'm really looking forward to meeting your friend," she said as she rearranged the flowers for the fiftieth time. "And . . ." she said, taking him by the arm and moving him to the fridge, "I wanted to forewarn you because I know you hate the attention but I got you a birthday cake. It's for both you and your mom actually."

Brendan's blush deepened. His mother's birthday was the day before his which was now two days ago and he had forgotten to get her anything.

"Don't worry!" Coleen said, reading his thoughts and opening the cupboard over the fridge. "I got you this . . . for her."

Brendan opened the small black jewellery box which contained a gold chain with a Celtic cross encrusted with tiny white crystals and green stones.

"It's lovely, thanks, Coleen. I'll pay you back!"

"Ha, don't worry! They not real diamonds or real emeralds!"

Coleen took the cross from its box and looked appreciatively at the beautiful piece. "She had one just like it when she was younger. Your grandmother gave it to her when she left for America. Patricia lost it and I remember she was so upset. I told her it was because she wouldn't know what to do with her hands if she didn't have that necklace on. She was always fiddling with it. I remember the day she lost it. She had been out all day with you and when she came back, goodness, you'd think someone had died the way she cried about that cross. She went up to her room and she stayed there all evening and sulked for a few days after that. I tried to get her one like it at the time but I couldn't. When she said she was coming over for a vacation, I went to the jeweller's and had them order me one from Ireland." She beamed proudly.

Brendan stammered. "You've gone to such trouble. *You* should give it to her."

Coleen shook her head. "No, honey, I think it would mean more coming from you."

Brendan looked at the cross and closed the box gently. He climbed the stairs to where his mother was getting ready.

"Sorry it's late," he said sheepishly as he placed the tiny box in her hand.

She opened the gift and he watched her eyes widen in surprise. "I had one just like this. How . . . how did you know?"

Brendan smiled coyly. "Coleen," he replied bashfully.

"It's beautiful," she said as she placed the chain around her neck. "Thank you."

When Jonathan arrived with Pilar, Eileen returned to her quiet, shy ways and hardly glanced at him in the lounge where Frank held court with stories of his time in the force. Brendan glanced at Jonathan who sat on the sofa in a silent daze. He was dressed in his best wool vest and white shirt and his mop of foppish blond hair was freshly washed. Despite the lighter dose of medication Pilar had given him that day, he gazed dreamily at the group as though he was in a deep trance.

As they sat at the table to eat, Patricia joined the group and sat facing Jonathan at the end of the table. Frank, who had already had three whiskeys, raised a toast to welcome the visitor to his home. He winked at Brendan and turned his attention to Pilar, loudly exclaiming that he wished her father was alive to see her and Brendan together and that, while she'd always been part of the family, he hoped it would become official.

Coleen stood and took the glass of Jameson from him as Brendan cringed.

"What?" Frank bellowed. "Now what have I done?"

Pilar laughed, which eased the tension in the room, while Patricia sat twiddling her new chain nervously.

Jonathan sat motionless facing her and appeared to all present to be hypnotised by the light show as his eyes followed the bright beams around the table.

"I believe I've seen you before, ma'am," he then slurred.

Brendan leant forward and looked down the long wooden table to where his mother was seated.

Patricia stammered and looked furtively around the room. "I – I don't think so. I think I'd remember meeting you." Certainly she would remember this strange man who stood out at the table in his 1930's clothes and depression-style haircut.

"Oh yes, ma'am. I've definitely seen you before. You were twiddling that very cross around just like you're doing now," he drawled, now speaking more clearly.

Patricia looked around the table again and flushed. "You're mixing me up with someone else. I just got this cross tonight."

Jonathan fixed his eyes on the woman and smiled sleepily. "I'm not mistaken, ma'am. You looked real nervous . . . and you were . . . sad. You were wearing an orange top with big purple circles on it and –"

"I remember that. It was a dress!" Coleen said. "You bought it when we went shopping in Rockaway!"

"Your hair was longer and you had some of it back in a clip."

Patricia's flush deepened as she became aware of all the eyes resting on her. Brendan knocked his glass of Coke over the table and sat staring at his mother as the brown liquid seeped slowly into Coleen's white linen tablecloth.

"I'm . . . I'm sorry . . . I really don't remember you. I – I think you've definitely got the wrong person," Patricia stuttered.

Brendan stood and quickly moved to the other end of the table. He knelt by Jonathan's chair and gazed intently at him.

"What else do you remember?" he asked.

"You were real upset," Jonathan continued, still staring at Patricia who sat like a statue on the other side of the table. "You were sitting in a car and . . ."

Jonathan stopped as he tried to bring the complete memory to mind. He raised his hand and began to massage the side of his head.

"And . . . you . . . you looked like you were missing something. You kept moving your arms as though someone had taken something from you and then you crossed your arms and . . . you were crying."

"What else?" Brendan asked urgently.

"You took a bag onto your lap and lifted a baby's bottle from it and . . . you cried even more and then you leant forward and I think you opened the glove compartment of the car and . . . something in there scared you. You jumped back like there was a rattlesnake in there and you stopped crying real quickly then. You just stared out the window and looked like you were waiting on something. You didn't move your eyes until . . ."

Patricia jumped up from her seat.

"How could you know that?" she cried.

"Where were you? Tell me!" Frank demanded.

"Until what, Jonathan?" Brendan urged.

"Until he got into the car with the baby."

"Who?" Brendan demanded. "Who was it?"

Patricia looked around the room and sat back down. Her eyes clouded over as though she was lost in thought. Neither she nor Jonathan answered.

"Where . . . where were you, Jonathan?" Brendan asked.

"I . . . I was in . . . a box . . . in a box looking out of the window . . . through a small hole in the side that my grandma had made so I could see out."

230

Brendan slumped back on his heels and exhaled heavily. He looked at Pilar who sat open-mouthed at the other end of the table. He moved his gaze to his mother.

"Mam?" he said, hoping that she would speak.

Patricia moved her eyes to her brother and swallowed. "You told me he was no good and I . . . I didn't listen. He contacted me, said that he had changed. He said he had a job and an apartment in New York and asked me to come back to him. Brendan was eight months old and I was afraid that I would spend the rest of my life living under your roof with nothing that was my own. I took the train to New York with Brendan and met him. He drove me to his mother's apartment in Harlem. I had never met her. He said she wanted to see Brendan but when we got there he parked the car and took Brendan and he didn't even bring me inside. He left me in the car like he was ashamed of me or something . . . and I . . . I realised that I had made a mistake and I began to cry. I was so scared that he wouldn't bring Brendan back out. I sat there in the car and waited. After a while, I . . . he said when he left the car 'Don't you touch anything until I get back' . . . but I leant over and looked in the glove compartment. I don't know why I did that. I . . . just looked in and there was a gun and . . ." She looked at her brother and cringed. "And . . . drugs. I was terrified. Finally he came back and handed Brendan back to me. As we drove off I tried to think about how I would get away from him. I thought he'd kill me or Brendan if he suspected that I intended to leave. When we pulled up outside his apartment block, I made an excuse that I had to go to the store for baby milk but he insisted on going with me."

Patricia's breathing quickened and her chin began to tremble.

"I knew I had to make a run for it. I took off my seatbelt and he . . . he must have suspected. He said I wasn't taking his son anywhere, that I could go back to New Jersey if I wanted but that Brendan was staying put. I fumbled at the handle of the door and he tried to grab my neck but instead he got hold of my necklace and tore it off. I ran for about two blocks with Brendan in my arms. Each step I took I expected to hear a gun firing after me. I saw two police parked in a car and I stood beside them while I tried to catch my breath. I told them I'd lost my wallet and asked them for a lift to the station. When I got there I boarded the train and I think I cried all the way back to Dover."

"So that's why you were so upset that day!" Coleen said. "Imagine, I thought that it was over that stupid necklace!"

Patricia looked at her brother. "I couldn't tell you what had happened because I knew you'd think I was stupid to go there but, Francis, I wanted a life of my own. I wanted a way out and I thought Rafael could offer me that."

"What about Jonathan?" Brendan asked.

Patricia looked at the strange man and shook her head sadly. "I never knew you were in that apartment. I swear it. I would have done something. I would have helped you."

Brendan went to his apartment and returned with the photo of the basement apartment Jonathan had led the police to on the night he was found. He held the photo out to his mother.

"Was this the house?"

Patricia nodded.

Brendan shook his head, amazed that he had been in the very house that Jonathan had been kept prisoner in for God only knew how many years. There was only one person now who could tell Jonathan where he was from and how he came to be in that apartment. It was going to be a very hard thing to do but he had to go and see Rafael Martinez. He had to meet his father.

Chapter 29

The meeting with Rafael Martinez took three days to arrange with the correctional officers at the maximum-security facility which was a six-hour drive from Dover town. Frank had warned his nephew of the risks of being turned away without having met with Martinez if it wasn't set up beforehand, so he had made some calls and three days later was assured that Brendan would get a short time with the prisoner.

To Brendan's surprise, his mother insisted on going with him, stating that she did not want him to go through the meeting alone.

Convinced now that Jonathan had actually been kidnapped, Pilar agreed to drive them there.

When they turned onto the long straight driveway of the prison, the impressive entrance to the tall grey building in the distance looked more like the bastion of a medieval castle wall but, as they neared, the spotlight on the tower and the armed guards standing along the curtain wall exposed the building's true purpose. As they neared the checkpoint, Brendan's muscles became taut with tension, sending shockwaves of painful spasms from his shoulders to his trembling thighs. Pilar reached over and touched his arm gently while his mother, who had not uttered a word since they left a roadside diner in Scranton, stared out at the ominous building before them.

Despite the blistering heat, Pilar insisted on waiting in the car while Patricia and Brendan walked the last few steps to the security check point. He watched his mother baulk at the indignity of being searched and stood still while a metal detector was waved around his own body. The correctional officer studied Brendan's identification closely before handing it to another CO who stood statue-like inside the main entrance.

"Martin, huh? You can tell you're Martinez' son!" he said as he returned Brendan's passport to him. "Let's hope you're not a chip off the old block."

As they walked together through a maze of doors, Patricia suddenly stood still.

"I can't do it," she whispered.

Despite her low tone, Brendan could hear the sound of sheer desperation in his mother's voice. He had never heard her sound afraid before. He turned to face her.

"I can't see him. I . . . I just can't!" she pleaded.

"It's okay. I'll be fine," he assured her as he continued down the long polished corridor to the visitors' room with the CO close by his side.

The visiting room of Attica prison in New York State was not at all what Brendan had expected. As he had lain awake the previous night, he had imagined a small, stuffy, heavily guarded room with glass panels separating the prisoners from their visitors who could only communicate with each other through telephones perched on the wall of each cubicle. Instead, he was led into a bright, open-plan room which was furnished with several wooden tables and soft-cushioned chairs. Impressive murals lined the walls of the cheery room which, instead of the hard tiles that had reverberated under his feet on the cold corridors, was floored with a soft, straw-coloured carpet.

Brendan stood in the room for a moment and glanced around at the other visitors and prisoners in the room. On his right, a woman with five children argued with her prisoner husband while a young white man held hands with his pretty girlfriend, neither speaking but gazing sadly into each other's eyes. On his left, an old black man sat holding hands and praying loudly with two elderly black women. Beside them, a young Hispanic man and his elderly father sat facing each other. Both men looked desolately at each other but did not speak.

At the back of the room, a thin, heavily lined Hispanic man sat alone with a guard by his side. Even in the distance, Brendan felt that he could be looking at an older version of himself. Rafael Martinez looked very different to the young handsome Mexican in the photo that his mother had given him and he wondered if this was why Jonathan had not recognised the man. He walked up to the table and took the seat facing the man who sat confidently with an amused expression fixed on his wrinkled face.

"Do you know who I am?" Brendan asked nervously as he lowered himself into the seat.

"I got eyes," the man replied in a heavy Mexican accent. "Where's the other one?"

Brendan raised his eyebrows. "What?"

"The other visitor? CO said 'you got visitors' so I expected more than one," he grinned. "Patricia, she lost her nerve, eh? Figures, bitch was always spineless."

Brendan swallowed and looked at the black man whose praying had begun to reach fever pitch. He returned his gaze to his father who looked older than his years. Above his left eye, a deep cut oozed blood onto the steri-strip covering. Two of his upper front teeth were missing and the rest of his once-white teeth were stained and decaying. Both of his father's lean upper arms were heavily tattooed, one of which looked very similar to the tattoo Brendan had done since he came to America and which his uncle detested. On Rafael's left arm, a double skull tattoo with the letters *MM* was encircled by a flame. Brendan had read a little about gangs in America and knew what the letters stood for: *Mexican Mafia*. Further down his arm, a rose tattoo signified his father's honour for having assaulted an enemy.

Rafael seemed to sense his son's disapproval at his appearance and caught the younger man staring at the gash on his forehead.

"Aggression-replacement therapy is not working so well for me!" he laughed. He leant forward. "So, what do you want?"

Brendan glanced at the guard and wished he would move closer to his father.

"Don't worry, I won't hurt you. You're not a pussy, are you?" Rafael sneered.

Brendan felt a flash of anger and narrowed his eyes at his father.

"Good, that's what I like to see," Rafael said in response to his son's quick temper.

He leant back again and looked his son up and down.

"You do any time?"

Brendan looked away and shook his head.

"I can tell that you lie. What, you don't think you are just like me, like my blood doesn't run through your veins?"

Brendan clenched his fists on the table. "I am *not* like you!"

"Yes, you are!" Rafael laughed as he pushed his chair back onto its back legs and rocked backwards and forwards. A guard approached and signalled for him to return the chair legs to the floor.

"What you do time for?" he asked, ignoring the guard. "Narcotics? Guns?"

Brendan shook his head angrily. "I told you. I am not like you. I am not violent."

The smile on Rafael Martinez's face slowly disappeared. He returned his chair to an upright position and moved his face close to Brendan.

"Lot of men would pay dearly for saying less than this to me," he said. "Now, I ask you what you came here for!"

Brendan studied the man and exhaled loudly. He took the photo of Jonathan as a teenager out of his pocket and placed it squarely on the table in front of his father.

"I want to know where you took *him* from," he said.

As Rafael Martinez studied the photo, a leering smile washed slowly over his face. He folded the photo and shoved it back across the table to Brendan.

"I never see him before," he said.

Brendan opened the photo and shoved it back across the table.

"Have another look," he ordered.

Rafael Martinez stood and leant forward, grabbing Brendan's T-shirt and pulling him to him. The guard rushed forward, placing his hand on his gun.

"Sit down!" he shouted.

Martinez loosened his grip and returned slowly to his seat.

"All this man wants is for you to tell me where you took him from so he can get home. He has agreed not to file any charges against you if you give me the information I want."

Rafael Martinez stared at his son as he considered his position.

"He can place you in that apartment where he was kept," Brendan said, "and my mother can also link you to that house."

Martinez leaned back on his seat again and grinned. "I have fifteen years left of my sentence. You think I care about another few years in here?"

Brendan tensed. Threatening Martinez with more years in Attica had been his only card. "Still, it would be better to enjoy a few years of old age as a free man than die in prison, wouldn't it? Also, you could do it for my mother. You owe it to her."

Martinez folded his arms and stared at his son.

"I told you, I don't know him."

Brendan stood.

"Fine, well then we'll see what the New York police have to say when Jonathan charges you with kidnapping, assault and attempted murder."

"Murder?" Rafael Martinez said through gritted teeth.

"Yes, Jonathan has a very good memory," Brendan lied. "You locked him in a box that he could have suffocated in."

A wide grin slowly spread across Rafael's face and he laughed loudly. He lifted the old newspaper photo of Jonathan at Marcus Garvey Park.

"How did you meet him?" Martinez asked.

"Let's just say our paths crossed," Brendan replied as he sat down again.

"Well, isn't that a coincidence!" his father replied sarcastically. He looked at the photo again and shook his head. "Thought that little bastard was dead. I really did."

"Tell me what happened."

Martinez glanced at the guard who was still standing close by.

"Some privacy, please! Can I have some time with my boy?" he yelled.

The guard backed off but kept his eyes fixed on the troublesome prisoner.

Martinez turned back to Brendan. "My sister used to mind the kid on some apple farm in Pennsylvania and –"

"Not Virginia?" Brendan interrupted.

"Who is telling the story here?" Rafael snapped. "She'd worked for the family there since he was a few weeks old – mother died giving birth to him. After a while the kid's father began to hit on her and the whore started sleeping with him."

Brendan cringed at his father's coarse language. "Was she Melibea?"

"Melibea? That was a false name from a passport I got. My sister was illegal. Her real name was Mariana. She wanted him to marry her but that wasn't going to happen. No white guy was going to marry no Latina. Thing was, he knocked her up and she *had* to marry and had to do it quickly."

Rafael Martinez licked his lips as though he was savouring the good part of the sorry story.

"It was my idea to take him. I convinced her to run away with the kid to New York – you know, frighten the bastard and scare him into marrying her. The kid was about four and a right little handful. Little fucker spoke perfect Spanish. Mariana's English wasn't too good so she'd always spoken to him in Spanish. It wasn't long before he'd figured out my real name. I kept him at my mama's apartment and arranged for Mariana to hole up with a friend of mine in the Village. I kept telling her not to call me Rafael in front of him. He'd already heard business associates calling me Martinez. Little fucker was always listening from his box. Had to be careful what you said around him."

"But you lied. You lied to Melibea – or Mariana. You had other ideas."

Martinez laughed. "My sister was an idiot to have believed me anyway. What man was going to marry her after she stole his kid? The kid's father was a penniless writer on a goddamn apple farm that he ran to bring in some cash but his father-in-law, the kid's grandfather, was a senator or something. Wilson, yeah, I think that was his name, or Williams, something like that. No, it was definitely Wilson. He had his hopes set on Washington. I knew they'd pay big money to get the kid back, or at least I thought they would. Once she took him, I had it arranged that I would contact them and demand a ransom."

"So you double-crossed your sister?"

"Like I said – she should have known better – too much thinking with the heart, not enough with the head. My mother was the same. Where did it get either of them?"

Brendan wanted to ask Rafael where his actions had got him but didn't want to distract him from the story. "What happened?"

Martinez blew out and peered at the picture. "When I phoned, the old guy, the grandfather, was waiting in the kid's house. He took over and made the kid's father back off. He yelled that there would be no ransom, said he didn't believe that we would hurt the kid."

"Were the police involved?" Brendan asked.

Rafael smiled. "That was the beauty of it. There was this big election on and Wilson couldn't afford the publicity. He got a lot of sympathy when his daughter died. Do you think he wanted it going public that his son-in-law was sleeping with a wetback? He didn't need that but he still wasn't giving in. He said he'd get Mariana and me deported. Course he didn't know my real name or hers."

"Then what happened?"

Rafael's expression turned more serious. He placed the photo of Jonathan on the other side of the table. "She chickened out, phoned the kid's father behind my back and tried to smooth things over, said she was sorry and that she just wanted to bring the kid back home to safety. That she was afraid for him."

"Afraid for him?"

Rafael pulled a face. "Yeah, so I had to give the kid a few slaps, okay? The little bastard kept trying to get out of the front door. When he got older, he even managed to find his way to the park a few times. Smart little fucker he was."

Brendan lowered his face to hide the emotion he was feeling. He tried to banish the image of a four-year-old child being beaten by the man in front of him.

"He told her that it was over, that whatever feelings he had for her were gone. He begged her to do the right thing and bring the child home."

"And?" Brendan asked as his father's eyes misted over.

"She went to Mama's apartment in Harlem and took the kid. I . . . I caught up with her and . . ." Martinez lowered his head, "I got him back."

The tone of Rafael's voice was final. Brendan knew his father did not want him to push any further but he had to know. He had to know everything.

"How?"

"I took him from her!" he spat angrily.

Brendan flinched and the guard moved forward again, ensuring that Rafael could see him in the corner of his eye.

"What happened to Melibea? I mean, Mariana?" Brendan asked.

"I told her to go back to my friend's place in the Village, that I'd handle it. You should have seen the look in her eye. I think she knew then, she knew Wilson wasn't going to cave in. She also knew that I wasn't going to give him back, that I couldn't. She knew it was over."

Rafael looked away and fixed his eyes on a brilliant section of the wall mural.

Brendan waited.

"She never made it back to the house. I thought the kid's grandfather had taken her and that he was playing games with me. I phoned him from a pay phone and he said he knew nothing about her but I didn't believe him. I said, you bring Melibea back and I give you back the kid and he . . . he hung up on me!"

"And?" Brendan asked.

"We had what you call stalemate. I stayed in the house but any time I went out on business, the kid would try to run away. I told Mama not to let him out of the box but she was dumb – felt sorry for him."

Brendan tensed. "So you beat him?" he asked through gritted teeth.

Rafael studied his son for a moment.

"You think I wanted to hurt a kid? If he got out, I was going down and Mariana too. I couldn't understand what the old man was waiting for. I had his grandson! Don't you think he'd want to get the kid back? A few days later I phoned him again and I said I was going to the newspapers with the story and that if he didn't let her go, I'd kill the kid. The bastard still denied having anything to do with Mariana's disappearance."

Brendan watched as his father's eyes glazed over.

"My mother was frantic. She'd gone through a lot of danger to get us out of Mexico. She worked her fingers to the bone to pay people to get us across the border. I told her that the family were playing hardball and that we had to keep the kid until we got Mariana back. She hated us keeping the kid, felt sorry for him. Each day she'd scream at me, she'd say she was going to leave him outside a police station and I had to remind her 'no kid – no Mariana' so she shut up and kept an eye on him while I saw to business."

"Business?"

"Yeah, business!" he sneered. "Two weeks later I got arrested for supplying."

"Drugs?" Brendan asked innocently.

"No, teddy bears! What do you think, stupid? I got sent down for eighteen months. I was only in prison three weeks when I heard that a Latina's body was found floating in the harbour. Friend of mine told me but he didn't know for sure if it was Mariana but the newspapers said she had a kid's yellow jacket in her coat pocket. Sounded the same as the one the kid was wearing when she took him so I knew it was her. They searched the area for a kid but, of course, I knew they wouldn't find one."

Brendan shook his head, appalled at the end his aunt had come to.

"You . . . did you . . . arrange it?" Brendan stammered.

Rafael banged his fist onto the table. "*No!*" he yelled.

The CO started forward but Rafael held up an appeasing hand. The CO slowly stepped back.

Rafael leant towards Brendan. "You think I am some kind of animal to kill my own sister!" he hissed. "Mariana took her own life and the life of her unborn child with her. That old bastard was telling the truth about not knowing where she was. All the time I was waiting, she was at the bottom of the harbour."

He slumped down in the chair and stared at the table. "We couldn't even claim her body, couldn't give her a Christian funeral. There was no identification on her so the city police recorded her as a Jane Doe and buried her in an unmarked grave."

Brendan pondered on the irony of the story. His aunt's actions condemned her to eternity in an unmarked grave and Jonathan to a life with no identity.

Martinez sighed and glanced sideways to ensure that the

guard could not hear him. "I don't know why Mariana put that kid's jacket in her pocket. It was a pretty stupid thing to do. I suspected that the kid's grandfather had friends in all sorts of places discreetly checking on things. I'd say he got to hear about an unknown Latina being washed up under Brooklyn Bridge and that he assumed that the kid was dead."

"Then what?"

"I sent a letter to Mama using a box number. I told her to get rid of the package."

Brendan mouth's dropped open at the callousness of his father's statement and hoped he misunderstood its meaning. "By get rid of . . . you mean?"

Rafael sneered and leant forward. "What use had I for him? My sister was dead."

"Your sister was dead because you tricked her into doing something she regretted!" Brendan spat.

Rafael stood and reached for Brendan again, pulling him roughly by the T-shirt until their faces were inches apart. The CO, who had not taken his eyes of Martinez rushed over and shouted for the guard to open the door.

"Visiting time is over for you, Martinez!"

Brendan looked at the CO and pushed his father's hands away. He had yet to find out what happened to Jonathan for all those years or where he had been taken from.

"Please!" he begged the guard. "Just another few minutes! It's important!"

The CO hesitated, then signalled for the guard on the outside of the door to lock it again and Rafael Martinez returned to his chair.

"But your mother didn't do as you said," Brendan said.

Rafael looked away and focused once again on the mural beside him. "I should have known she would not do it. You cannot trust women to do what has to be done. Like I told you, too much feeling, not enough thinking. She came to see me. When I saw her in the visiting room I . . . stupid bitch!" He

243

frowned and shook his head. "I had told her, never come here. No one knew we were connected. All three of us used different names. Only I could use my real name. Thanks to your mother, I was an American citizen."

"What name did you use before then?" Brendan asked.

Martinez sneered. "None of your business."

"Was your mother using the name Rosa Soto?" Brendan asked, remembering the name of the old woman who had died in the basement apartment Jonathan had led the police to all those years ago.

Rafael nodded. "She begged me to tell her where the kid was from, said she was going to take a bus there and leave him outside. Luckily the kid had forgotten the name of the place – if he ever knew." He shook his head at the stupidity of the old woman. "I had to sit real close to her so the guards wouldn't hear. I told her that the kid could lead the police to her door which, now that she had shown up in the prison, would lead to my door."

Brendan could feel his breathing quickening as he listened to the danger Jonathan had been in.

"She said she wouldn't do it. She said that the Lord would never forgive her and that a mother could never kill a child. She blessed herself and stood in the middle of the visitor's room looking at me as if I was . . . crazy."

Rafael smoothed his hands over the table. His mouth moved silently as though he was reliving the conversation with his mother.

"She was a good person. Stupid though," he said wistfully. He sighed and returned his gaze to Brendan. "I told her I didn't know where exactly he was from. She didn't believe me but it was true. Like I said – all I knew was it was some dirt farm in Pennsylvania.

"You must have organised for Mariana to be picked up from the house. She would have been noticed travelling a long distance with a white kid."

"Mariana organised that end of things herself. I had nothing to do with the kid until he got to New York."

"I don't believe you!" Brendan spat.

Well , neither did Mama," Rafael sneered. "She also didn't believe that I didn't know the kid's name."

Brendan smiled wryly at Martinez. "You don't know his last name? You're lying."

"I don't care what you believe, boy! I knew the kid's name was Jonathan but I didn't know his last name. It didn't come up. Mariana gave me the number on a piece of paper with the kid's father's first name on it which was also Jonathan. That's what Mariana called him so that's who I asked for."

"What year was it?" Brendan asked.

"Well . . . now . . . let me see," Martinez said slowly.

Brendan slammed his fist down on the table impatiently. "You're enjoying this, you sick bastard!"

Martinez looked toward the guard. "I could call him over, tell him I'm tired of our little tête-à-tête," he teased.

Brendan flinched and raised his hands up in surrender.

"It was nineteen . . . sixty . . . nine," Martinez replied, excruciatingly slowly.

"Forty-three years ago," said Brendan. " So that would make Jonathan – em – forty-seven?"

Martinez nodded. "See you got my brains as well as my good looks."

"The phone number Mariana gave you. What was it?" Brendan asked.

"You think I remember that number after more than four decades?" Martinez snapped.

"So you can't or you won't tell me what I need to know to get him home? You're sick. You'd think you'd try to do some good to pay for all the wrong you've done."

Rafael looked down and studied the wooden table underneath his wrinkled hands.

"You could look up Wilson, the grandfather. He'd be dead by now but his name might lead you somewhere," he said as he slowly raised his eyes to his son.

Brendan nodded. "Did you know anything about his older sister Cassie? She was blind."

Rafael shook his head. "I don't know anything about no blind chick."

"So your mother didn't – get rid – of Jonathan," Brendan said, skimming over the awful words as fast as he could.

"When I got out, I wasn't surprised to find she still had him there. She was sick by then, some lung disease, and the fucking kid was actually looking after her, calling her grandma and forgetting that he could even speak English. I got back into business and any time anyone came to the house, I had to lock the little bastard in the box which he didn't take too well to. Seemed like Mama had let him free most of the time."

Brendan tensed again and looked down at the table. "Then what?"

"She understood by then that we could never take him home. She knew I'd go back to prison and that I'd rot there but she wouldn't let me get rid of him, said that if she had to make a choice, she'd rather see me back behind bars than let me hurt the child. She said she'd tell the police. She said the price she would have to pay for seeing me back in jail would be worth protecting an innocent child. She said . . ." His lip began to tremble.

Brendan looked away, embarrassed. Apart from anger, it was the first real sign of emotion his father had shown.

"She said that . . . that I was lost . . . that she couldn't save me from the evil life I chose to live . . . but that she could still save the boy."

He looked away and kept his eyes focused on the wall while he composed himself. Another prisoner glanced over at him.

"*What the fuck you looking at?*" he screamed.

Brendan flinched at the sudden noise and glanced at the guard to ensure he was still near enough to help if his father became aggressive again.

"So I let her keep him. By then, the only time I had to beat him was when I tried to get him into the box. That's when he was more likely to try to run away. Man, he hated that box but I couldn't risk him seeing the faces of my business associates when they'd call. A few times he got to the water tower in the park. I was lucky there were no cops around. Had to stick him with a needle to drug him and carry him back to the apartment. By then, he wasn't too dangerous for me 'cause he no longer knew who he was anyway."

Rafael began to laugh loudly. He slapped his hands on the table as he reminisced.

"Mama . . . she was so worried about him not speaking English any more that she sat him in front of the TV all day watching soaps. There was this one show – the stupid kid actually began to think it was his family. I mean, he wasn't dumb enough to think Mama was really his grandma and I think he knew that he'd come from somewhere else but . . . you should have heard him speaking English with that southern accent on the show and thinking those stories were things he had actually done!"

Brendan stared hard at his father, astonished at how cruel the man was.

"Anyway, a few years later, I was arrested again and I've been here ever since."

"For double murder," Brendan said angrily.

Rafael gave his son another one of his icy glares. "I did not intend to kill those people," he said curtly. "They got caught in crossfire." He said it as if this made his actions acceptable.

"*Those people* were a mother and her young child!"

"You want to hear the rest or not?" Martinez said angrily.

Brendan nodded and focused his eyes on the young couple who were still smiling at each other as though they were on a date in a fancy restaurant and not in a maximum-security federal prison.

"Mama stayed on there in that apartment with the kid. I eventually got around to telling her about Mariana. Hardest thing I ever did. I waited one day 'til I was about to leave and told her quick as I could that Mariana was never coming back and that the police thought the kid was dead. Once she knew there was no one looking for him, she wanted to keep him with her for good, especially seeing as I wouldn't be out in a long, long time and she was sick. He was all she had."

"Except he belonged to another family!"

Rafael ignored the comment and appeared lost in thought.

"I never saw her again. When I heard that she had been found dead in the apartment, I thought that kid must have got out and got himself killed somehow." He shook his head in amazement. "But seems like somehow he survived."

Rafael sat back in his chair, his story now complete.

Brendan exhaled noisily, relieved to know now what had happened to his friend and anxious to find out the last piece of information he needed to take Jonathan home. He looked at his father who stared at him from across the table.

"Why did you choose this life?" he asked.

"Choose it? You do not choose this life. It chooses you."

"What does *that* mean?"

"It means that when you are poor, when you are not white, when you are an immigrant, everything you want you have to take by whatever means necessary."

Brendan looked at the dried-up old man before him. "It didn't need to be like that. That's just an excuse, a lie you and those like you tell yourself to ease your conscience – that is, if you have one. You could have worked, bought a house, had a good life. Lots of immigrants achieve that. My mother loved you. It should have been enough."

Rafael leant forward again, the familiar glint of anger returned to his thin face.

"It was not enough. I wanted it all!"

"Well, what have you got now?"

"You know, you could have been somebody. I could have seen to it that you inherited everything I built up on the outside," said Rafael.

Brendan leant toward Rafael, his fear long since dissipated. "I *am* somebody," he said as he stood and stared at the man.

Rafael's eyes opened wide for a moment as he realised his son's visit was over and that he would probably never see him again.

"You might have to come back. Could be you need more information. Could be what I tell you don't exactly fit!" He laughed as he rocked back and forward on his chair.

Brendan made his way to the door and waited for the CO on the other side to unlock it. As the door opened, he walked halfway through and looked back at Rafael Martinez who stood open-mouthed in the room.

"I am somebody and I will never be you."

Chapter 30

Jonathan Doe lay awake on his bed, listening to Brendan as he recalled his long conversation with Rafael Martinez. When he finished, Brendan dug his hands into his jeans' pockets and waited for his friend to reply. It was almost midnight and, although exhausted from the long drive back from Attica Prison, he hadn't wanted to wait until the next day to tell Jonathan what he now knew.

When he'd left the prison and returned to the car, his mother had held onto him in the back seat and had cried openly into his chest but, by the time they reached the motorway, she had regained her familiar aloof composure. She moved away from him and he watched her through the corner of his eye as she sniffed and dried her eyes roughly with wet, torn tissue paper. She had then turned her face toward her window and hardly uttered another word for the rest of the six-hour journey.

"Are you alright?" he asked now but Jonathan did not answer.

Brendan moved closer to the bed but Jonathan turned abruptly on his side and faced away from him. Brendan could hear a low sob coming from his friend who remained motionless on his bed in the darkened room.

"I'll come back tomorrow," Brendan said softly. "We can talk about what we do next."

He quietly closed the door of the attic room and made his way home where he hoped he would fall into a deep, peaceful sleep.

The following morning, Brendan slept in and arrived at the shelter just before one o'clock. He went directly to Jonathan's room and found his friend standing by the window, staring into thin air. He was dressed in his usual corduroy trousers and heavily patterned woollen vest over a white, collarless shirt. His thick hair was neatly combed back and his rimless spectacles were perched on his nose.

"Jonathan?"

Jonathan turned around, his pale face staring at his friend. He had dark circles under his eyes, revealing a sleepless night.

"You too, huh? I didn't sleep a wink either," Brendan quipped to try to ease the tense air in the room. "How are you?"

Jonathan shrugged and looked back at the window.

"I'm okay," he said meekly.

Brendan sat wearily down on the bed.

"Did what I told you last night trigger any memories?" he asked quietly.

"Some." Jonathan cleared his throat and moved his shoulders up towards his neck. "She said 'Stay with me, Jonathan, and hold my hand until I take my last breath. When I'm gone, you run from here and don't you ever come back!'"

"Abuelita?" Brendan asked.

Jonathan nodded. "She was real sick. She could hardly breathe. She told me that when she was gone I should run as far away as I could get. She begged me not to give the police his name. Even when she was dying she was trying to protect him. She also said that he had friends, lots of them, and that even if Rafael was in prison, he'd find a way to get to me if I told. So I ran."

"That's when you were found in the park?"

Jonathan nodded. "I didn't know where else to go. I took whatever clothes I had. There weren't many, just a couple of pants and that – I threw them in a bag together with some food. I stayed there for days, afraid. I had almost nothing to eat and I slept up in that tower. I was starving so I went back to the basement to find something to eat and she was gone."

"You must have been so scared, Jonathan. I can't imagine what it was like for you."

"I was."

They fell silent for a while, Brendan trying hard to think of questions to ask – searching for anything that might be a lead, a clue.

"Did anyone else regularly call to the house?"

"Since Rafael went away, the only person that called was the landlord to collect the rent. Once in a while she'd bring him in to do repairs. She always locked me in the box then but I didn't mind. I knew she'd let me back out as soon as he was gone."

"How did she pay for the rent?" Brendan asked, suddenly curious about how the illegal Latina lived.

"Rafael left a box of money that she had hidden in the kitchen. It was almost gone by the time she died."

Brendan cringed, knowing that the money his grandmother lived on had most likely come from the sale of drugs.

"The whole apartment had been cleared out. All of her furniture, my box, everything." Jonathan blushed as another memory resurfaced. "I . . . I wanted the box back. I wanted to get into it and sit in the dark."

"What did you do then?"

"I went back to the park and I stayed there, eating from rubbish bins when it was dark. During the day I'd sit real still on the top of the tower. One night, the police were doing their rounds in the park. They found me drinking water from the pond."

"Did you tell them everything?"

"No. I was afraid. All I did was take them to the house. I hoped it would somehow help them find where I had come from.

They got hold of the landlord. None of what I said held up, that's what they said. They checked missing persons in Virginia which they said my accent came from and there were no reports on anyone missing of my description. Then they checked further afield but it was the same story. I remember this one cop saying to me – 'There's no one looking for you, kid, and with the state they left you in, you should count your blessings you got out alive.' I . . ." Jonathan blushed again and swallowed. "I told them I was Jonathan Wyatt Nelson so they . . . they phoned the psychiatric hospital and Dr Reiter took charge of my case."

"And you never mentioned Rafael?"

"How could I? There was no way I could ever mention him."

Brendan sighed and shook his head sadly while Jonathan slowly traced his breath with his finger on the windowpane.

"I remember Melibea," Jonathan finally added. "And I remember that little yellow coat."

Brendan waited.

"All night I've been thinking about her, about how it all changed on that one morning and I remembered it. I . . . I wasn't sure if I had imagined it or not. Dr Reiter said it was just another story I made up. In my memory, she said she was taking me to see the sunrise. It was our thing, something we both loved to do. Each time we'd stand there, she would tell me that the sun was also rising in her village in Mexico that she missed very much. That morning, we walked to the end of the dirt road which I knew was the wrong way. The east side of our property was surrounded by trees and the sunrise could only be seen through a small gap in the clearing. I told her she was going the wrong way but she tugged my arm and told me to walk faster. She kept looking back at the house and she was carrying my father's travel bag. I felt something was wrong. I asked her what was in the bag but she didn't answer."

Brendan looked away from his friend, unable to bear the look of disappointment in his eyes as he recalled how someone he loved and trusted had betrayed him.

"She was so kind to me and Cassie. She cared for us as well

as a mother would. I don't know why she would . . . how she could . . ."

Brendan returned his gaze to his friend. He could see the side of his face as he stood in the window and noticed his chin quivering with emotion.

"There was a car parked on a straight piece of road not too far from the end of the driveway," Jonathan went on. "It was a large black car and I had never seen it before. I remember asking Melibea who owned it and she said it belonged to a friend. She opened the back door and lifted me onto the seat. Melibea sat in the driver's seat. I suddenly became very afraid although I didn't know why. I just instinctively knew something was wrong. I shouted for my daddy and when she turned around she was crying. She opened the bag and pulled out a blonde wig that she put on her head. She also put on a woman's fur coat that had been in my father's wardrobe. Cassie would sometimes put it on and she and Nella would play games in Daddy's bedroom. Daddy'd get so mad with them and would hang that coat back up so carefully like it was priceless. I guess it must have been my mother's. It made Melibea look so different that I was frightened so I cried. She pleaded with me to be quiet and promised me that everything would be okay in a couple of days, that she had something she needed to do. She asked me to be a good boy and to be quiet so I stopped crying. Then she started the car and drove. I had never seen her driving a car before. I looked back. I remember now. I looked back at my road and everything I knew disappeared in the rear window."

Jonathan looked up and turned to Brendan with wild, large eyes.

"I remember something else!" he said, the vision of his trusted nanny in a blonde wig triggering another memory. "The first time I ran away, Rafael made Melibea dye my hair black. I guess so it wouldn't look strange when he was carrying me back to the house after I'd run away. I would look like I was his son. He dyed it himself lots of times after that until he went away. It just grew out then." He shook his head. "And you say Melibea did that to me just to make my father marry her?"

Brendan had no answer to offer.

"Do you remember Rafael?" he asked after a pause.

"Yes!" Jonathan replied sharply. "He was thin and he had tattoos all over his arms. I can't believe he is your father and that you ended up here at this shelter with me. It's like . . . like you were sent to undo the wrong that he did. Alice said that. She said you were sent here to help me."

Brendan shrugged self-consciously and looked away. Until now, he didn't really believe in fate the way that Alice did but his friend was right. It was strange that he had ended up here in the same place as Jonathan.

"Maybe," he replied sceptically.

It was still hard for him to grasp that his own family had been behind Jonathan's abduction, still less grasp the horrific life they had forced him to lead. Jonathan returned his gaze to the window.

"So Rosa was good to you?"

"Yes, she was. I thought she was my grandma."

"When she was actually *my* grandmother . . ."

Jonathan turned from the window and nodded. "It was she who sat me in front of that TV show and told me that the Nelsons were my family. I remember I was very small when she said that. She kept saying it over and over. She'd point at the TV and say: 'Jonathan – see, your family, your family!' I don't know how long I'd been there when she said that but I don't think it was very long. In the beginning, when Rafael had men calling to the house, he'd go into the kitchen and lock the door so Abuelita couldn't come in and hear them. He didn't need to worry. She hated those men coming and would hide in her bedroom until they left. Then she would shout at Rafael about how they were devil men. When I got older, I'd got to understand how long he'd be busy for so if Abuelita left the door unlocked, I'd get out and find my way to the park to climb the tower. It reminded me of the little tree house my father made me although the tower was a lot higher! I felt safe there. I'd wait and wait, hoping to see my daddy somewhere on the ground but he was never there. Rafael would find me and take me back to the house. After it happened a few times, Rafael kept me locked in the box and the only time I got out was when he went out and Abuelita let me out. When Rafael would get me back to the basement, he'd take his belt off . . . Once I bit him on the leg. I was older and I dug my teeth into him hard. It was at the bottom of the tower and he yelled out. He held onto me with one hand and pulled up his trouser leg with the other. His leg was bleeding badly. I paid for that." He fell silent for a few moments.

Jonathan's eyes opened wide as though he was watching Rafael loosen his belt for yet another beating. He exhaled loudly and ran his hands through his thick mop.

"I think I now know what Abuelita meant when she said the Nelsons were my family. The series was set on an apple farm and she wanted me to remember as much as I could about my roots and my family – about my language and the type of place where I belonged. I remember that I would shout at her and say they weren't my family. I'd cry for my daddy and she'd put me on her knee and try to comfort me the way Melibea used to do."

"Why didn't you run to the police or stop a passer-by on the street?" Brendan asked.

Jonathan shrugged. "Nothing around me looked familiar. I think I understood that I was a long way from home. Most of the people in that area were Hispanic and I thought everyone would know Rafael and would take me back to him. All that time, I thought that Melibea would come back for me like she said she would or that she'd tell my daddy where I was. I used to dream of him knocking on that door and taking me away from Rafael."

Jonathan stopped speaking and looked at his friend.

"Brendan?"

"Yes?"

"Why do you think my daddy stopped looking for me?"

Brendan shrugged and clasped his hands in front of him. "I guess he thought you were dead."

"But my family didn't know for sure. There was no body," he said worriedly.

"I'm sure we'll find out when we find them," Brendan said.

Jonathan shook his head gently from side to side as though another memory had resurfaced.

"When Rafael went away again, Abuelita sat me down and asked me to try to remember the name of the place I was from. I remember her voice sounded so . . . so . . . urgent. But I didn't know. You said I was four or so when Melibea took me. I doubt if I knew even then. I was too young."

Jonathan turned again from the window and glanced shyly at his friend.

"After a while I guess I just wanted to believe that TV family was mine. I was so afraid and sad all the time and the Nelsons were so happy and safe. Well, aside from the father spanking the kids from time to time. I wanted so badly for it to be true. I became a part of that TV show and I began to believe I was part of that life. When Dr Reiter began to see me, he called it a parocosym but I refused to believe it."

"And now?" Brendan asked.

Jonathan blushed and looked towards the ground. "I've had times before when I've accepted what he had to say . . . for a while anyway. He'd give me medication that he said would help and it did, but sooner or later those happy memories of that family would creep back in and I'd think Dr Reiter was trying to take them from me. Course, I never got this far before!"

He grinned at Brendan, then the smile slowly faded from his face. He turned his face slowly back to the window.

"Some of those memories were really mine, Brendan. They just got mixed up, that's all," he said quietly.

"My father . . . Rafael . . . he didn't know anything about Cassie," Brendan said awkwardly.

Jonathan bit down in his lip and closed his eyes tightly. "I've waited so long, Brendan. I don't think I can face the idea that there might not be anyone out there waiting for me. I really hope my sister is real."

"I hope so too."

Brendan watched as Jonathan shook his head and knew that

his friend was trying to dispel his worry that his imminent return would bring disappointment.

"I've had this dream Brendan. Ever since I was found in that New York park, I imagined the day when I would walk up the driveway to the clapboard house under a pre-dawn sky. No matter how often I dreamt it, the dream was always the same. When I'd reach the garden, I could see myself gently running my fingers along the bark of the big oak tree at the entrance. The old tyre would be still hanging on a threadbare rope. I'd sit on that tyre and I'd swing higher and higher like I did when I was a small boy until I could see the mountains through the silver streaks of the sky welcoming the morning sun. I'd let the swing of the rope slowly die down and then sit there in the silence, sucking the fresh mountain air and sweet scent of the apple blossoms in the front yard into my lungs. I would wait then in anticipation to hear her there. It was always the best part of my dream. After a few moments, I'd hear the squeak of the old screen door and then I'd see her standing there, my sister with her long dark braids and her white cane. She'd wait until she heard me speak and I'd run to her and squeeze her tight in case she'd disappear from my life again. And Nella. Nella would be standing in the background, glad to see me come home. And my father, in my dream he is an old, old man but he'd be waiting there for me to return like he has since the day I disappeared. Then we'd all sit at the large wooden table and eat breakfast together before climbing the steep ridge to the clearing where we'd sit in silence and wait for the sun to rise above the tall mountain range and when the land around us finally filled with sunlight, we'd celebrate my safe return to them. They'd tell me about all the things that had happened while I was gone and I sit there and listen, thankful to hear their voices again. In my dream I do not talk about Rafael Martinez or Melibea or the woman I called grandmother. I do not tell them of the things I endured when I was gone from them, the beatings, the drugs Rafael sometimes made me take to quieten me, the taunting from him that I would never find my way home. I never tell them about the long, lonely years that I was locked away in a tiny apartment. Instead, I talk about the future, about working in the orchard and about Eileen, the woman I love. I cherished that dream, Brendan. It is what has kept me going all these years and now that it's finally going to come true I am afraid. Afraid that it might not be as I imagined."

Brendan touched his friend's arm but did not speak. He could give Jonathan no assurance that the reunion he hoped for would be as he imagined.

"What's next?" asked Jonathan.

Brendan exhaled loudly and frowned as he remembered his father's remark that he might have to return to Attica to decipher which of the information was true and which was deliberately false to force him to return. He did not think he could endure seeing the man again and hoped that whatever leads he did have would suffice to take Jonathan home.

"We have to start with your maternal grandfather and work our way forward," he replied.

"Wilson?" Jonathan asked doubtfully.

"Yes, Wilson."

Chapter 31

Brendan stood alone in the silent garden watching the sun set slowly over Dover town. He shaded his eyes as bright rays reflected off the town's orange-tiled roofs and glinted off the leaves of the large oak trees in the park beneath him. He had spent the whole day going over everything Jonathan remembered and had written a list of the leads he would begin his computer search with.

He crept into the empty kitchen and poured himself a coffee before turning on Coleen's computer in her tiny office at the front of the house. He quickly wrote a list of the possible links to Jonathan's family beginning with his grandfather. He typed **Wilson + politician + election + 1969** but found no matches. He tried **Wilson + politician** but again came up blank.

He searched for politicians from that era whose names began with 'W' and found two possibilities but one of the men had three sons but no daughters and the other was childless. He sighed loudly and placed his chin on his hand as he tried to decide what his next move would be.

He cleared his previous search and typed in **Jonathan + author + Pennsylvania** and found sixty-three matches, most of which were reviews of books on the works of three current authors from the state. He searched for photographs of the men, hoping to see a man who resembled Jonathan Doe, but found that the authors were all much younger than Jonathan's father would be now.

He blew out and tried Jonathan + author + Pennsylvania + missing which narrowed the search to twenty-six hits. This time, the newspaper articles were reviews of one book by an author by the name of Jonathan Thomas.

He clicked on a piece from *The Philadelphia Inquirer* and quickly scanned the review of the 1970 book which was called *Lost* and was reported to be a fictional novel about a writer's search for his missing son. A side note reported that the author's own son had recently died in an accident. Brendan leant back and felt a tingling sensation run up his spine as adrenalin rushed through his system. He scrolled down and stared at the black-and-white photo of the writer at the bottom of the text. Jonathan Thomas was a tall, thin, bespectacled man of about forty with a thick mop of straight blonde hair and a shy smile. The editorial did not give an address but Brendan instinctively knew he was onto something.

"That has to be him," he said aloud.

He searched for other articles and read about the writer being a widower with two children and how the death of his young son had a detrimental effect on his wellbeing which Brendan assumed was polite 1970's code for "he went crazy". Brendan searched for works by the author after *Lost* but found that Jonathan Thomas had not published any more books after *Lost* which, according to the reviews, sold hundreds of thousands of copies in North America and was also widely sold in Europe.

He opened an article by the same newspaper whose headline alarmed him. It was written two months after the review of *Lost* and again simply referred to the writer as being born in Pennsylvania but gave no town address. Brendan read the report which listed Jonathan's maternal grandfather as one Senator William Chapman and not Senator Wilson as Rafael Martinez had suggested. He groaned aloud as he finished reading the two-page report and pushed his chair back abruptly away from the desk. He stood open-mouthed and shook his head.

"Oh, Jonathan," he said sadly. "So that's why no one was looking for you."

Brendan stood and stared out of the office window for a moment. He decided that he would not tell Jonathan what he had just read. It would be better if his sister told him. Brendan returned to the computer and forced himself to sit down and try to find the last lead he had on his friend.

"Please let there be a Cassie Thomas. Please let there be someone out there waiting for you."

He typed in Jonathan's sister's name but again got no matches. He briefly wondered if she had married and searched for a marriage record but found none. He then searched for deaths for Cassie Thomas, daughter of Jonathan Thomas, and was relieved that no matches flashed onto his screen. He checked the *White Pages* directory and then suddenly realised that her full name would probably be Cassandra. He typed in her full name of Cassandra Thomas and found there were three-hundred and twenty-two people by that name in the US. He narrowed the search to Pennsylvania and found fifteen women by that name, eight of whom lived in the Philadelphia region. Brendan decided to focus on these women first. He took the cordless phone from the kitchen and dialled the first number. The phone rang eight times before a sleepy-sounding woman answered it. Brendan swallowed and asked if she was Cassie Thomas, daughter of the writer Jonathan, who once had a brother also named Jonathan. The woman angrily said no, he had the wrong woman and told him she was a night nurse and that he had woken her from her sleep before she went on duty at nine.

Brendan looked at the clock on the corner of the computer screen. It was eight o'clock. He sighed and went into the kitchen for another coffee which he brought into the garden to drink under the darkening sky. He could feel the energy flow through his body. His quest was coming to an end, he could feel it. He just hoped it would be the ending he had imagined it would be.

He already knew from the newspaper articles that it would not be as Jonathan had hoped it would be but if Cassie was alive – if, indeed, she existed at all – he felt it would still be okay, it would still be a homecoming of a sort for his friend.

Ten minutes later, Brendan returned to Coleen's office and dialled the second number on his list which was answered by the husband of this Cassandra Thomas. Verifying that it was the woman's marriage name that was Thomas, he made his excuses to her husband and got off the line to move down his list as quickly as he could. Three more Cassandra Thomases were married women who were known by their marriage name of Thomas. Two more women were recently deceased and it had taken him ages to get off the phone as their grieving elderly husbands poured out their hearts to him.

By ten, Brendan had eight names yet to ring. Two numbers went directly to voice mail but he hung up rather than leave a stammering, confused message and made a note to ring back later.

He stood again and stared out of the window, wondering if there was an easier way to get through the last six numbers. He began to search through the addresses to see which of them would have views of the Appalachian Mountains and hoped that Jonathan was right about the geography of his home. He took an atlas from Coleen's bookcase and opened the page on Pennsylvania and compared the terrain of the region to the addresses of the remaining six Cassie Thomases in the *White Pages*. Three of the women lived near the lake at Erie in the far west of the state which was two hours away from the Allegheny plateau, which was the nearest section of the mountain range in the area and probably not that visible from their lakeside homes. He checked the remaining three women who lived near enough to have views of the Poconos, which was the name given to the section of the Appalachians in Eastern Pennsylvania.

He dialled the first number and held his breath as a middle-aged woman answered. He explained what he was looking for and held his breath while she said that, yes, she did indeed have a brother called Jonathan and offered to put him on the phone. Brendan sighed and disappointedly told her that she was not the Cassie Thomas he was looking for. He dialled the next number and a stressed-sounding woman quickly informed him that he had the wrong number and put the phone down on him.

He looked at the next number on his list and for the first time noticed that the name of the townland that the house was in. Wilsonville.

"Bastard!" he said realising that his father had probably remembered the name of the town Jonathan had been taken from all along and had deliberately misled him by pretending it was the name of Jonathan's grandfather.

He took a deep breath and dialled the number which rang about ten times before a woman answered. Brendan began by asking if she was Cassie Thomas. The woman gave him a curt "No" and waited in silence for him to speak.

"Well, can I speak with Cassie Thomas?" he asked.

"What do you want?" the acerbic voice replied.

Brendan sighed and wondered if he was speaking to Nella, the sharp-tongued childhood friend Jonathan had told him about.

"Who is this?" he asked, hopeful.

"Never you mind!" she snapped.

"I . . . I have information she might be interested in . . . about her brother."

Brendan could almost feel the woman stiffen on the other end of the phone.

"What information?" she asked.

"I'd rather tell her directly."

"Wait one moment. I'll get her," the woman replied brusquely.

Brendan listened as the woman's heels clicked off the floor as she walked away and the sound faded down what sounded like a tiled corridor. He waited for a moment and then could hear the click-clicking of a pair of shoes followed by a rhythmic tapping sound which got louder and louder until he heard a woman speak.

"Hello?" a soft voice said nervously.

"Is this Cassie Thomas?" he asked.

"Yes, it is," she answered.

"Are you the daughter of the writer Jonathan Thomas?"

"Yes, I am. What is this about?" She spoke in a voice so soft that Brendan had to press the receiver into his ear to hear her.

"And your grandfather was the senator William Chapman?"

"Yes," she said hesitantly.

"I hope you don't mind, ma'am, but I have a couple more questions for you before I can tell you why I am calling."

"Yes?"

"Did you have a brother Jonathan?"

A couple of moments of silence passed and Brendan thought that Cassie Thomas had hung up on him.

"Ma'am?"

"I'm here," she whispered.

He could hear the crackle in her voice.

"Yes, I did. He died. A long time ago."

"Ma'am?"

"Yes?"

"Can I ask you one more question? It's a bit more personal."

"Yes," she said.

"Are you blind?"

Another silence deafened Brendan as he waited for her answer.

"Yes," she finally replied. "Yes, I am."

Chapter 32

Guido Diaz listened to Brendan as he pleaded with him on the phone to wake Pilar who had just gone to bed following a double shift at the shelter.

"No way, man, she's tired out. Working double shifts and helping Isabel with the new baby. You can wait until tomorrow. I'm heading into work myself now."

"Guido, can you at least leave a note at her bed asking her to call me urgently?" He knew that Pilar, like himself, often woke during the night and found it hard to return to sleep.

"Okay," Guido said and put the receiver down.

Brendan raced to the computer and searched for road directions from Dover to Wilsonville. He shook his head as he printed out the route along NJ-15.

"Poor bastard. You were just over an hour away from home," he said to himself as he planned the journey which would take his friend back to where he belonged.

Brendan climbed the stairs to Eileen's bedroom. A light shone from underneath her door, suggesting that his sister was still awake. He knocked softly and put his ear to the door, listening as she rushed around the room opening and closing the closet doors loudly before she answered.

"What were you doing?" he grinned when his sister opened the door, red-faced and panting.

Eileen smiled shyly. "Reading," she whispered.

"You're not still hiding books?" he said incredulously.

He had thought that Eileen and Frank had sorted everything out and that his sister was now leading her life as she pleased.

"He has good days and bad days. Now that he is getting better, the bad days are starting to become more common."

She beckoned for him to come in.

Brendan sat and told Eileen the news and watched as her face revealed a myriad of emotions from happiness that Jonathan's family were real to fear that he would now obviously return to them. He told her his plan to reunite her love with his family within hours and watched with alarm as the colour drained from her face which only moments before had a healthy pink glow.

"Eileen, he wants to go home. You can't stand in the way of that," he said.

Eileen nodded slowly. "I know," she said sadly.

He watched as she creased her brow and bit down on her lip nervously.

"But, I'm coming with you," she said. "I want to see him go home."

Brendan stared at her for a moment. "Okay then, but be ready. I'm waiting for Pilar to phone me. You won't be allowed to drive on motorways yet so she'll need to drive us there. It could be in the early hours of the morning. Jonathan . . . his dream is to arrive at dawn. I want it to be as he imagined."

"We'll take my car," Eileen said loudly, startling Brendan.

"Why?" he asked.

Eileen shrugged. "Pilar always drives us everywhere. My car is in better shape. It'll make the drive more comfortable."

Brendan narrowed his eyes at his sister, wondering what she was scheming. "All right," he said as he let himself out of her room.

He walked quietly down the stairs and met his mother coming up. She looked down at her shoes as she tried to pass him on the narrow staircase.

"Mam," he said.

Patricia did not look at him but slowly raised her small grey eyes and fixed them on the wall of the stairwell.

"Are we going to talk about whatever is going on between us?" he said. "You haven't spoken to me since we left Attica."

Patricia looked briefly at him but then turned her gaze downwards and stared at the red-patterned carpet on the stairs.

When she didn't answer, Brendan shifted uneasily and tried to think of something to break the silence. It amazed him that after all their years of separation his mother's silence still had the ability to make him feel so uneasy.

"We found Jonathan's home. Eileen and I are taking him there when Pilar wakes up."

Patricia did not appear surprised by the news and remained in her usual emotionless state.

"I knew you could do it . . . but . . . I feel for Eileen . . . she will be broken-hearted," she said flatly.

"Is that what is wrong with you, Mam? Did my father break your heart?"

Patricia blushed and slowly moved her eyes upward to meet his gaze. "I am the way I am for many reasons," she replied quietly.

Brendan sighed and moved out of her way to let her pass.

"Brendan?" she said when she had climbed halfway up the steep stairwell.

He turned and looked up at her. "Yes?"

"It's a good thing you've done for that man. You should be very proud of yourself," she said.

Brendan searched her face, hardly able to believe she had said those words.

And, as though she knew what he was thinking, she added, "I'm proud of you."

She turned quickly and climbed the rest of the stairs out of view.

Brendan phoned Jonathan and told him to wait for him in the

living room as there was something he wanted to tell him. He put the phone down and left for the shelter. On the way he pondered just how he would break the news to his friend.

When he arrived at the house, breathless and soaked in sweat, Jonathan was waiting alone in the brightly lit living room.

Jonathan listened white-faced and anxious as Brendan told him that his town was called Wilsonville. He watched as Jonathan repeated the name of the town twice as though he was trying to conjure up any memories the name might bring. He then told him in too-fine detail the numerous calls he had made to all the Cassandra Thomases until he eventually reached the conversation he had with Jonathan's lost sister who was now waiting for him to return to her.

"She's real? You really found her?" Jonathan had gasped.

"Yes, she's real," Brendan had replied. "And she can't wait for you to come home."

"And my father?"

Brendan looked away for a moment before reluctantly returning his gaze to his friend.

"Jonathan . . . I'm sorry but . . . your father died."

"When?"

"Em . . . a long time ago."

"How?"

Brendan bit down on his lip. He did not want to tell his friend the awful truth. It would be better coming from Jonathan's sister.

"I'm sure Cassie will tell you the details when we get there."

Jonathan sighed and looked away for a moment, distressed that he would not get to see his daddy again and that his father would never know that his son eventually found his way home.

Then he looked back at Brendan and sobbed, "You promised you'd put the pieces together and you did it. Thank you!"

The friends then hugged until Brendan broke away and directed Jonathan not to pack everything and that they could come back for the rest of his things. He watched as his friend nodded thoughtfully and hoped that Jonathan understood what he meant. The reunion might not go as he had planned.

Brendan explained that they had to wait for Pilar to contact him and left Jonathan to organise himself. He then returned to his apartment to shower and, though he hardly thought he would, to try to catch some sleep.

While he lay on his bed and waited for Pilar to phone, he replayed his mother's words, telling him that she was proud of him. She had never said that before, even when he'd finished school top of his class or when he graduated with honours from university. He pondered this as he lay there in the dark and wondered if it was because what he had achieved for Jonathan was something that required a sacrifice on his part. Had he been selfish until now? Is that what his mother saw in him? It was possible, he admitted. He knew that until he had met the strange man, he had preferred to live a simple life of seclusion and that going out of his way for other people was something that rarely occurred to him. But that had been his mother's fault, hadn't it? Surely her aloof ways and cross nature made him shy away from human contact and retreat to the safety of his quiet isolation?

Meeting Rafael Martinez was probably the hardest thing he had ever done but he had been willing to do it for his friend. He wondered if his mother's life had been about sacrifice. There was still so much that he didn't know about her. He had no idea what she had gone through in the time she had spent with his father and felt it was unlikely that she would ever tell him. He also knew that coming back to America must have rekindled all of those lost hopes and dreams that she had as a girl in her new country – those dreams that were shattered when she became pregnant with Eileen and later with him, which resulted in a rushed, unsuitable marriage so that she could get out from under her domineering brother's roof.

At three thirty the shrill of the phone startled him. He jumped up, knocking the phone off his chest where he had placed it while he awaited Pilar's call.

"Pilar?" he whispered.

"Yes, what's wrong?" she asked.

"Can you drive me to Pennsylvania?" he asked.

"*What?*" she yelled.

"Pennsylvania. I've found Jonathan's home."

Pilar fell silent but he could hear her breathing quicken on the other end of the phone.

"Are you sure? It's definitely his family?"

"Yes. Definitely. I spoke with his sister for half an hour."

"And she sounded . . . okay . . . I mean . . . nice?"

"Yes."

Pilar did not speak and Brendan could imagine the level-headed woman working out what the repercussions of her actions would be.

"I'll call Jane. She's on duty tomorrow morning. She can try to clear it with Thompson for tomorrow afternoon."

"Pilar . . . it has to be now. He has always dreamt of returning home at dawn. Please."

"What's wrong with dawn the day after tomorrow?" she snapped.

"Now that he knows?" Brendan asked. "I went to the shelter and told him. He can't wait, Pilar. He's waited long enough."

He waited as she once again fell silent.

"Pilar?"

He heard a sharp intake of breath.

"Okay. I'll go to the shelter and explain things to the night duty – then I'll bring Jonathan with me to pick you up."

"No – Eileen is coming with us and is insisting on taking her car – so come here to the house first."

"I'll be there in half an hour," she said and hung up.

Brendan rose, and went to the main house where he knocked gently on Eileen's bedroom door and eased it open. His sister was sitting dressed on her bed, reading. She stood immediately and followed him down the stairs. He could not read the expression on her face as she stood still in the kitchen for a moment before slipping quietly down the side entrance with Brendan.

When Pilar arrived, all three stood on the sidewalk in silence as they absorbed the enormity of what they were doing and the impact that it would have on their lives. Brendan knew that Pilar could lose her job at the shelter while Eileen was losing the person who mattered most to her in the world, someone who had understood her shy introverted ways and had fallen in love with her as she had with him. Brendan knew that he too had a lot to lose. Even though he could visit Jonathan, he would be saying goodbye to the only friend he had ever truly known.

As the three silently loaded themselves into the car, Eileen sat in the back seat so that she could make this journey by Jonathan's side.

When they pulled up at the shelter he was waiting at the front door with a single bag in his hand.

Brendan got out and walked over to where his friend was standing, as Pilar hurried into the shelter to talk to the night duty.

"It's really happening," Jonathan said but Brendan could hear the questioning tone as if his friend did not really believe that he was going home.

Jonathan looked up at the solitary window of the attic.

"Brendan?"

"Yes?"

"Who's going to pick my apples?" He turned his head to his small orchard to the side of the garden.

Brendan shrugged. "I can do it."

Jonathan nodded and walked slowly to the car. Eileen leant across and opened his door. Jonathan slid in and sat beside her, holding his single bag on his lap.

A few minutes passed and then Pilar returned.

"Right," she said as she exhaled. "Let's go."

Pilar gripped the wheel tightly as she headed east towards Prospect Street before turning left into Towpath Square. After a short drive down Bassett Highway she swung a left onto Pequannock Street where she joined the NJ-15. After what seemed like an excruciatingly long drive in silence they took the 206 which took them into the state of Pennsylvania.

As they passed the state sign, Pilar and Brendan looked at each other. He could read her face. They had come this far and, whatever her misgivings, there was no going back now. Pilar swerved abruptly onto the 209 and looked into her rear-view mirror at her silent passengers who were startled by the sudden movement.

"Sorry," she whispered.

He leant over and touched her arm.

"We are doing the right thing," he whispered but she did not respond.

As Pilar drove, the tension in the car increased and settled heavily on the four silent occupants. Pilar sat bolt upright in the driver's seat with her thin brown fingers wound tightly around the black-leather steering wheel as she stared straight ahead at the grey road in front of her. Brendan sat beside her with his hands clenched on his lap. His mind flitted between the joy of soon seeing Jonathan reunited with his sister and worry that the anticipation would be better than realisation for his friend who had waited and prayed for this moment for over forty years.

In the back seat, Jonathan and Eileen sat hand in hand. Eileen's eyes rested on her lap as Jonathan sat sideways, gazing into her small pale face. Brendan turned briefly to look at them and thought about their imminent separation.

The only sound was the rhythmic noise of the wheels as they drove over the expansion joints of the highway's uneven surface.

Brendan heard a sudden cough from the back seat. He turned to look at Jonathan.

"You okay?"

Jonathan nodded, then swallowed nervously and tightened his grip on Eileen's hand.

Pilar slowed down as the car took US-6 which would lead them all the way to Wilsonville. The landscape changed and the four found themselves driving through a large forested area. Jonathan appeared to sit up straight and take notice of his surroundings.

"You recognise any of this?" Brendan asked.

Jonathan shook his head worriedly as Pilar weaved down the twisted country road. When they arrived at a T-Junction, Pilar looked back at Jonathan who shrugged.

"Now what?" Pilar asked.

"Take a right," said Brendan. "The sign says it'll bring us into Wilsonville town. Maybe there'll be someone around to ask."

Within minutes a sign for Bear Run Road appeared on the opposite side of the road.

"There!" Brendan shouted. "Cassie said take this road and keep driving until we see a small turn-off to the left."

"In the dark?" Pilar asked.

The road was surrounded by mountains to the east that blocked out the silver rays of the sunrise they had seen before they left the open highway.

Pilar slowed the car down and gingerly drove along the narrow road, squinting into the thick row of trees looking for an opening.

"*Stop!*" Jonathan suddenly shouted from the back seat.

The brakes screeched as Pilar stopped the car.

"Back up," he ordered.

She reversed the car slowly until she saw a tiny opening in the trees.

"There!" he said. "I remember," he added breathlessly. "Brendan, I remember!"

Pilar turned the car through the opening and negotiated the vehicle slowly up a steep dirt road.

"*Stop!*" Jonathan shouted again when she had driven about halfway up the incline.

The car stopped and Jonathan opened the door and stood onto the soft clay beneath him. He took a deep breath and slowly exhaled as he began to walk the rest of the way alone, his bag slung heavily on his shoulder.

Pilar undid her seat belt and got out, followed quickly by Eileen.

Brendan jumped from the car. He raced around to Pilar and caught her arm.

"Let him go," he said gently.

"I have to see what kind of people they are. I have to make sure he is safe," she said urgently.

"He is safe, Pilar. Look at him. He is home."

She ignored him and followed Jonathan on foot as quickly as she could up the steep incline.

Brendan caught up with her.

"Please, let me!" he pleaded. "Please – please, Pilar – follow slowly with Eileen in the car but give him some time to savour this moment. He has dreamed about it for so long."

She hesitated then nodded and turned to go back to the car.

Brendan followed slowly behind Jonathan. He watched him touch the trees along the roadway. At one point Jonathan turned and smiled at him then continued up the hill.

Brendan followed on and as he reached a clearing he watched as Jonathan slowly lowered himself to his knees on the soft earth beneath him. He moved forward and stood next to his friend to take in the surroundings. To Jonathan's right, a large oak housed a battered tree-house, *his* tree house which now looked empty and sad in the gloomy light. A ragged rope hung lifeless from a large branch, its tyre lying idly on the ground beneath the magnificent tree. Jonathan got to his feet and stared at the rows of apple trees in the middle of the large lawn, its crop almost ready for harvesting.

Brendan watched as his friend opened his eyes wide.

"I remember being lifted up into one of those trees and taking an apple from its branches. I remember my father's big hands around my waist. I remember him saying 'Go on, take another one!' I remember Melibea shouting to my father in Spanish. '¡No, no, no es seguro! Bájelo!' she would squeal, pleading with my father to put me on the ground where I'd be safe."

Brendan watched Jonathan shake his head, as if he was trying to shake Melibea from his mind – Melibea who had obviously loved him but who had taken him from this place where he belonged.

Jonathan walked quietly past the barn where three Rhode Island Reds clucked at him. The spiteful cat he had told Brendan about, now long since dead, was nowhere to be seen and his father's old red Ford Fairlane was sombrely stationed where their cow once spent the long winter months.

Brendan stood still as Jonathan walked slowly forward and touched the wooden veranda, tracing it with his fingers as he inched his way along the front of the house. He watched as Jonathan climbed the steps which creaked noisily under his feet and, in the absence of his tyre, sat on the swing that he and his sister used to fight over. He looked out into the garden and swung himself gently back and forth.

"I remember when I'd sit here that I could hear the click-clack sound of my father's typewriter in the room behind me and the smell of pie being baked in the kitchen and the beauty of the apple blossoms as they'd fall from their trees and blew around the garden like giant snowflakes in the warm sunshine. I remember it all, Brendan."

Behind him Brendan heard the car creep into the clearing and come to a stop. Car doors opened and closed quietly and then Pilar and Eileen came forward to stand beside him.

Jonathan blew out heavily as the emotion finally forced its way into his consciousness. He bent forward and covered his face with his hands until his breathing slowed. Then he clasped his hands together as if he was praying and watched as the sun finally made its way through the clearing, illuminating the shaded garden with brilliant rays of orange light. He leant back into the swing, soaking in the beauty before him, until he heard the sound he had obviously been waiting for, the tapping of a cane and the slow screech of the old swing door to his right.

He turned and looked downward as his sister's long white cane clicked onto the wooden veranda followed by her shoes. He did not move but traced his eyes upwards from her feet until they rested on her familiar face.

Brendan wondered if Jonathan had imagined his sister would still look like the little girl she had been when he was taken from them.

Gone were the long dark braids Jonathan had described and in their place was a thick mop of shoulder-length peppered hair.

Her dark-brown eyes shone from her deeply tanned yet unlined face. She smiled, revealing two evenly spaced dimples.

"Jonathan?"

Jonathan stood and turned to Cassie as hot, heavy tears rolled down his face. He reached forward and placed his hands gently on her shoulders.

"Is it really you? Where have you been all this time?" she cried.

"It's him all right," a voice said from behind her.

Jonathan looked in through the front door where a tall thin black woman stood on guard, watching him with narrowed, suspicious eyes. He recognised her face – those full lips and her nappy hair, cut so short that you could almost see her scalp.

"Nella?"

"Yep," she replied. She moved forward and threw her arms around him. "Look, I'm not that much shorter than you any more!" she laughed. She looked at Cassie who stood open-mouthed. "You told me, Cass. You told me that some day that boy would just come on home." She glanced at the three strangers around the yard. "Guess you'd all better come on in," she said.

Jonathan looked from Nella and his sister to Brendan who was embarrassed yet pleased by the emotional reunion. Pilar and Eileen stood side by side, their arms wrapped around each other's shoulders as they smiled at him with watery eyes.

"I am home," Jonathan whispered to no one in particular. "I am home."

Chapter 33

Inside the front door of the white clapboard house was a large-open plan, L-shaped room. Several old-fashioned armchairs covered with large dust cloths sat idly in front of an empty brick fireplace and a tall china cabinet, full of unused, dusty pottery stood just inside the front door of the chilly room. To the left of the open space, a long, narrow, country-style dining table sat in front of an old- fashioned row of worn kitchen cupboards. A fine film of dust completely covered the wooden kitchen table and the creaky oak floor beneath it.

"We don't live here as you can plainly see," Nella explained as she walked about the room, pulling the dust sheets off as she went. "We came up here before dawn, planning to have the place looking like home before you got here."

She then set about dusting the table and the chairs around it.

Brendan watched as Jonathan wandered around, peering into all three of the small rooms that led off the open area.

"Our house is close by but Cassie thought you'd prefer to meet here," Nella said.

Cassie Thomas felt her way around the room and sat on a wooden chair at the table.

"You cold, Cass?" Nella shouted from the other side of the room.

Cassie nodded and Nella rushed to light a match under the set fire.

"You all sit," Nella ordered.

Slowly, they each took a seat at the long wooden table.

"I'll get breakfast while you all catch up," Nella said. "Can't say I'm up to more crying today anyway!" She moved away from the group and set about cooking breakfast.

"Jonathan!" Brendan called as his friend wandered around the open-plan area, touching things as he went and shaking his head slowly. He looked up. "Come and sit down."

When the group were all seated, Nella placed a hot pot of coffee that she had made earlier on the table and poured a cup for each of the visitors. They watched as she lovingly placed Cassie's hands around the steaming cup to ensure her lifelong friend knew exactly where the hot liquid was situated on the table in front of her.

"Where do you live, Cassie?" Brendan asked.

"We built a house about a hundred feet from this one, behind those very trees out front. It gets more light there anyway and, when I came back here, I didn't want to live in this house with all those memories."

Brendan listened to how different her accent was from her brother's. Although Cassie Thomas spoke very slowly, she did not have the same drawl as Jonathan. Vowels seemed to roll off her tongue with velvety smoothness and her consonants were spoken crisply, each syllable accentuated by her soft, silky voice. He wondered if Jonathan felt self-conscious about his southern accent and how he might explain this to his sister.

"You went away?" Brendan asked. He glanced at Jonathan who sat staring at his sister as though she was a mirage, a dream that he might at any point wake from and find that she had disappeared.

"What happened to Daddy?" Jonathan asked, unable to wait any longer.

Cassie Thomas looked sadly in the direction of her brother who was seated beside her. "I need to tell you everything that went before that, so you'll understand, Jonathan," she said.

"Can you still see shadows?" Jonathan asked.

Cassie smiled. "Yes, if it's bright enough. What do you look like?"

She held out her hand and he took it. He placed her long narrow fingers over his face and she moved them across his visage and towards his hairline. Nella stopped her noisy whisking and put her bowl down. She came to where Jonathan was sitting and looked him up and down like he was a prize bull.

"He's the living image of your daddy, Cass. He still has that mop of beautiful white hair and those big blue eyes. Face as pale as the moon though, Lord help us. Looks like a ghost. We'll have to see to that. He's real tall and skinny and, Lord, dressed in old-fashioned clothes like he bought them in a charity shop. Another thing to see to, as if I didn't have enough for doing. And, goodness," she began to laugh, "he's still got that scar where I sewed his head myself hoping his daddy wouldn't find out about the tree that hit him!"

Cassie laughed.

"I remember that. *You* sewed it?" Jonathan asked.

"I got a needle and thread from my mama's basket. I didn't know anything about boiling the needle or anything. I got Cassie to hold onto you while I sewed it quick as I could. Boy, did you yell! You'd think I was killing you with the way you screamed. Melibea came looking to see what the fuss was about and all hell broke loose. Your daddy was furious with me. My own daddy, he smacked my backside hard for that, said it could have cost him his job at the orchard." She was shaking her head and laughing at the memory. "Course, your daddy took you to town and had the doctor sew it up properly. It got infected. You had to take antibiotics. Guess that was my fault."

Jonathan laughed. "I knew that was real. I knew that tree falling on me was real!" He glanced at Eileen and she smiled at him. There were tears in her eyes, tears of happiness for him. Then he turned back to Cassie. "What happened to Daddy?" he asked again.

Cassie sighed and put her cup down on the table in front of her.

"I better start by telling all of you about the morning Jonathan disappeared when I was six years old."

Pilar suddenly interrupted.

"Jonathan, are you sure you are ready for this?" she asked. She knew from her psychiatric training that such sudden information could be too much for someone as fragile as Jonathan to cope with.

Jonathan looked warmly at the woman who had cared so much for him. Not only in that awful psychiatric hospital but at the shelter.

"I'm fine, Pilar," he said. "I need to know."

Cassie took a deep breath.

"I woke early that morning when Melibea took Jonathan away. I heard her walking around the landing outside my room. My daddy always said I'd hear a pin drop. He said he didn't need a gander around here when he had me. I walked out onto the landing and she was there. I could smell her perfume. It was lavender. I remember she used to make it herself from some that was growing in a small patch at the back of the garden. I couldn't see any light so I knew it was still way before dawn and I wondered where she could be going at that hour. She told me she was only going downstairs to the bathroom and that I should go back to bed so I did, but a few moments later I heard her talking to Jonathan so I got back up. She told me they were going to watch the sunrise but I told her it was at least an hour 'til dawn, that's how dark it was. She used to sometimes take me with her but this time she said, 'Cassie, you'll slow me down so you go on now.' Course, she said it in Spanish. She hardly spoke any English. Daddy liked the fact that we spoke both languages fluently."

Cassie quietened and her face clouded over. She ran her fingers gently up and down her brother's hand.

"I always felt guilty that I didn't stop her, that I didn't yell for Daddy but I thought she was really going to that clearing. I didn't know that she would never be coming back or that it would be the last time I would see you. I carried that guilt around with me for years."

"You weren't to know," Jonathan replied.

Cassie shook her head and continued.

"I went back to bed and the next sound I heard was Daddy shouting down the telephone to my grandfather. He kept saying 'She's gone, William! She's gone and she's taken Jonathan with her!' Granddaddy arrived at the house with lots of other men. Mama's younger sister Prudence and her fiancé Jan arrived later on. We rarely saw Prudence but I remember they had a brand-new car that sounded so smooth as it came up the driveway. Anyway, they all sat in Daddy's tiny study talking. Nella's mama arrived over and took me to her house. I guess Daddy asked her to take me away from all the upset – and, with Melibea gone, he didn't have anyone to care for me. The next day I went back to the house with Nella to get some clean clothes and I remember Daddy arguing with Granddaddy in this very room. I didn't know what it was about until years later but Daddy kept shouting that granddad shouldn't have hung up. He was crying and, though Daddy was a soft man, I had never heard him cry before. After that, I was sent to stay with Nella's family until whatever was going on passed over."

Brendan nodded as the story began to fit in with what his father had told him. He could imagine the sort of man William Chapman was. Unyielding, stubborn and arrogant, which when matched with Rafael's Martinez' mean-heartedness was a recipe for disaster.

"I didn't come back to the house for weeks. I knew it was something to do with Jonathan and at night Nella's family prayed for him so I knew something bad had happened. Then one day, Daddy sent for me. When I got home, he was sitting at the kitchen table with Jonathan's little yellow jacket in his hand. Granddaddy was sitting by the fire, sobbing into his whiskey. Daddy grabbed me and held me so tight that he hurt me. I knew Jonathan was dead because Daddy was always real careful about suddenly touching me and giving me a fright. He always gently touched my shoulders and then drew me to him slowly. You remembered that, didn't you, Jonathan, when you saw me on the porch? You did exactly what Daddy used to do."

"Yes, I did," he said.

She blew out and shook her head. "Daddy told me it was a road accident. Guess that's the story Granddad and his campaign people came up with to save face. He said there'd be no funeral but that we'd put a stone up there on the clearing for you. I didn't know the truth until I came back here. I was eighteen then."

"Where did you go in the meantime?" Eileen asked quietly from her seat at the far end of the table.

"I'll get to that," she said softly. "But, first, Jonathan needs to know that Daddy fell to pieces when he knew he was lost to us. He began to spend his days writing in his study all day and drinking all night. That's when he wrote the book *Lost*. It made him famous which wasn't something he was looking for. It also made him rich and money was never something Daddy had much interest in. I guess that's why Momma's family never really took to him. He liked a simple life and, as far as I remember, Momma did too. It was ironic how things turned out for him with all that money and fame. All he really wanted was for you to return to us but he thought you were dead so he wrote that book as a tribute to you, to tell you how much you had meant to him. It was written in the style of a letter from a father to his son and it was really very sad to listen to when Nella read it to me. He even ended the book with the writer finding his little boy and bringing him home. It doesn't really bear any resemblance to what really happened here, but I guess he was trying to do something. He felt completely powerless so he channelled all his energy into writing."

Jonathan nodded sadly and looked at the floor.

Pilar watched his reactions carefully, ready to stop Cassie if she felt Jonathan was unable to hear any more. She looked intently into his face. He smiled to reassure her but inside, inside his heart was beating so fast he was surprised the tiny Hispanic woman couldn't hear it.

Brendan leant forward and patted his friend's knee.

"What happened next, the morning your daddy sent for you?" he asked.

"Well, when Daddy finally let go of his grip on me, he looked at Granddaddy who was sitting in the corner of this room by the fire, weeping into his handkerchief. Something about him crying made daddy snap. He just completely lost control. He ran over to Granddaddy and began to shout. He told him it was too late for crying. He said it was his fault, blamed him for Jonathan's death – which I couldn't understand at the time. He must have got a hold of Granddaddy up because I heard some men shouting for him to let go. I could hear furniture smashing and chairs falling and then Daddy pushing open the screen door and a loud thud on the porch. There was shouting, mostly from Granddaddy's campaign people. Those men seemed to go everywhere with him. I heard Daddy say 'Don't you ever come back here!' so I knew then that he had thrown Granddaddy out onto the dirt. He never did come back here, never set foot inside this house again."

"What happened then?" Brendan asked.

Cassie took a deep breath and shook her head. Nella, who had finished preparing the breakfast, came to the table and placed hot plates of scrambled eggs and bacon in front of everyone. She walked back to the tiny kitchen area and brought another pot of coffee back, placed it squarely on the table and sat on the other side of Cassie.

"Pennsylvania didn't have anti-miscegenation laws like several other states that still prohibited whites from marrying blacks or

Hispanics or Native Americans. Even so, Granddaddy had plans to get elected to Washington and he didn't want any family members of his breaking the laws of other states."

Nella huffed in disgust. "Who did he think he was?" she said.

Cassie smiled in the direction of her acerbic friend. "I think my daddy knew that there was no way he could marry Melibea. He wanted to keep the peace with Momma's family. He was a good man but he was weak so even if he'd known she was expecting his baby, he wouldn't have gone against Granddaddy. It wasn't until after she was pulled from the river that Granddaddy told him that an autopsy found she was pregnant. They rowed about it. Granddaddy told him he had let the family down and had sullied the memory of his daughter. I don't know why Melibea hadn't told Daddy she was pregnant and now we'll never know. The only reason Daddy got to know what happened to her and to Jonathan was the fact that Jonathan's coat was found on her body and, even then, Granddaddy paid off his cronies to keep her identity secret so it wouldn't affect his campaign."

Cassie sighed and leant towards her brother.

"This will be real hard for you, Jonathan, but you have to understand that Daddy was under an awful lot of stress."

Pilar tensed up and wrapped her hands so tightly around her coffee cup that she thought it would smash in her hands. Eileen could feel perspiration bead on her forehead. She longed to go to Jonathan and hold him while he heard what she assumed was going to be the worst part of Cassie's story.

Brendan looked at the ground and tensed. Apart from Nella, he was the only other person in the room who knew exactly what Cassie Thomas was going to say next.

"A couple of years before Jonathan was taken, the Supreme Court ruled that anti-miscegenation laws were unconstitutional. Slowly, other states followed with only the southern states still condemning the practice although they couldn't actually stop intermarriage. Attitudes were gradually changing. The year after

Jonathan disappeared, a very rich and influential neighbour here married a Native American woman. Granddaddy was invited to the ceremony and, because this neighbour held a lot of power, he kept his views to himself and went to the wedding. Daddy heard about it and he . . . he was drinking heavily. He had finished the book and didn't even care about the success he'd had. He had nothing to do all day except brood, even left his beloved orchard to Nella's father's care. Didn't come out to work, didn't do anything except sit in the tiny room behind us and stare at your photograph, Jonathan."

Cassie Thomas's lip trembled but she held back the tears in her deep brown eyes.

"He went to where the wedding was being held on the man's property . . . with a shotgun. I've heard people around here say that he walked right into the huge marquee where Granddaddy was seated pride of place in his white linen suit with his ivory walking cane. Daddy walked up to him. He didn't say a word, just stared at him for a moment and then he . . . he shot Granddaddy at close range. Almost emptied the whole round into him. People just stood there staring. No one tried to stop him. People later said you could have heard a pin drop and then he just walked away and walked all the way down to the creek at the bottom of our property here. Then . . ." she rubbed her brother's hand, "then he . . . he shot himself. I'm sorry to have to tell you all this, Jonathan, but I think Daddy did it for you because he realised your death and Melibea's for that matter had been for nothing."

Jonathan sat open-mouthed on the chair beside his sister. His lips moved slightly.

"He loved me," he said.

"He did . . . with all his heart. He couldn't live on after you were gone. Not even for me. It was forty-two years ago now. We put his name on the stone he set up for you on the mountain."

Cassie ran her hands up Jonathan's arms and pulled him to her.

"He would have loved to have seen this day."

"I never got to tell him, Cassie. I wanted to tell him I remembered him, that I never forgot. I wanted to say I waited for him, that I knew he was looking for me. I'm never going to get to say those things to him now."

Jonathan began to sob into his sister's hair. She gently moved him from her and felt his face, wiping his tears and shushing him as she must have done when they were children.

"I'm sure he knows, Jonathan. I'm sure he's watching us here together and that he has peace knowing that you've finally come home to us."

Brendan felt a lump in his throat as he watched his friend try to regain his composure. He could see the turmoil his friend's mind was in and wanted to put his arms around him and protect him from the awful truth.

"What happened to you then, Cassie?" he asked, trying to take the focus off his friend.

She sighed. "Until the funeral was over, I slept at Nella's house. Daddy wrote a will shortly before he died and he said if anything happened to him, I was to live with Nella's parents right here. It was the only home I'd known."

"But that didn't happen?" Brendan asked.

Cassie shook her head. "Momma's only sister, Prudence, drove back over from New York with her fiancé. She said there was no way I was living with a black family and bringing further disgrace on their good family name. She packed up all my belongings and put them into her new car and then drove me away."

Cassie's eyes glazed over and she shook her head sadly.

"I thought she was taking me to live with her in New York and the whole way there in that open-topped car, I wondered how I'd get used to a noisy place like New York city. I remember Nella running after the car the whole way down to the main road. She yelled and yelled, shouting about how she'd come to New York and get me when I was of age."

Cassie began to cry. Nella leant over and rubbed her friend's hand.

"And I did, didn't I?" she said.

"Yes, yes, you did."

"Course she wasn't taking me to her home. Her and her fiancé drove me to a place just outside Philadelphia which was an orphanage for girls. It was run by Catholics which I knew was a way of letting me know how little I meant to Momma's family because Granddaddy hated Catholics. As a matter of fact, he hated anyone that wasn't rich, white and Baptist. Also, I don't think they wanted word getting out in their own community about how badly they had treated their own niece. I remember us driving into the gates of St Jude's Hall. I could feel how tall and dark the building was because it blocked out the sun from my face. There was a cattle grid or something that made a rumbling sound as you drove into the gates. I never heard that sound again until I was eighteen years old."

"They never came back for you?" asked Brendan.

Cassie shook her head. "No, but I heard about them from time to time. My aunt was quite a society lady. She married her fiancé once he graduated from medical school, bought a big house in New York and forgot that I ever existed. My first day at the orphanage, I remember the manager telling me that they couldn't cater for blind girls and that they had no idea how to teach me. She told me that there was a private school for blind children only a few short miles away. All that money my granddaddy had and the money my daddy had left me and my aunt wouldn't spend a little of it by paying for a school where I could get an education. It wasn't so bad though. I made friends there and I got by. They eventually got someone to teach me Braille so I could read."

"What happened then?" Eileen asked.

"I had a lovely teacher there, a nun. She wrote to Nella for me, telling her where I was and, after that, every single week for almost eleven years we wrote to each other. Sister Bernadette would come to the dorm and read Nella's letter to me and then write a reply. Once, the day before Christmas Day, Nella came to see me on her own. She was only twelve and I was fourteen. She'd hitched a ride to Bethlehem and then on again to Lansdale and then another to Philadelphia. She never told me how bad things had gotten for her family then. I didn't hear about that until later. It took her fourteen hours to get here and she was soaked to the skin. She hid in my room until Christmas morning just so I wouldn't have to wake up on my own. I'll never forget it, never forget what a true friend she is."

Nella stood quickly, cleared some of the plates from the table and took them to the kitchen area. She waved her hand impatiently, embarrassed by the attention.

"Then, the day I turned eighteen, I was called to the manager's office at the front of the house."

Cassie smiled and Nella burst out laughing. This part of the story was obviously something that had brought them much joy over the years.

"I knew my way around that whole building by then and as soon as I went into the office I could sense that there was someone else in the room. The manager said: 'Ms Thomas, your aunt has sent her maid to take you home.'" Cassie faked a snobbish accent.

"Before I could say anything, I could hear Nella's voice. She put on this strong southern voice. Goodness, I almost laughed out loud. 'It's Nella,' she said. 'Your uncle said I should bring you home now that you're eighteen. He couldn't come here himself on account of his breathing problem.'"

Cassie laughed aloud and Nella raised her hands to her face as she shook her head at how audacious she had been at sixteen.

"Nella had even broken into this house which had been boarded up since Daddy died. Prudence had died by then so she typed up a letter from Prudence's husband, directing the manager to place me in Nella's care. She even signed his name. Lucky for us the manager didn't care enough to check the signature or to phone him. My uncle hadn't paid for my care for years. The manager had written to him lots of times but he

ignored the letters and sent no money. There wasn't a week that
went by that the manager didn't remind me of that.'"

"Lord!" Nella said, blushing heavily from the kitchen counter.
"Still can't believe I did that!" she said shaking her head.

"So you got home?" Pilar asked.

"Yes. We didn't have a car and we had very little money,"
Cassie said. "Turned out that Nella's family didn't even live on
the orchard any more. My aunt had written to them some years
before telling them that their tenancy was revoked! For a while
Nella's family had drifted around taking work wherever they
could. Then, her father drifted on alone and Nella and her
mother moved back to town here. Her momma was in poor
health so she died young and, like me, Nella was alone in the
world. She never heard from her father again and doesn't know
what happened to him. Anyway, when we left the orphanage, we
hitched most of the way here and I think we must have looked a
real sorry pair. When we got here, we pulled the boards off the
windows and doors and cleaned the place up. That was when I
found a letter Daddy left for me in his study, explaining
everything about Melibea and how she had drowned Jonathan
with her in New York Harbour, least that's what he thought had
happened. He left his will there, stating that his entire estate was
to be left to me when I turned eighteen. It also said that he was
leaving Prudence money so that she could manage a separate
fund for my education but she never did that and, when she died,
her husband couldn't have cared less about me. I don't know
what they did with the money that was supposed to be spent on
me. When I went to his attorney, I couldn't believe how much
money we had. Nella had taken a job waiting tables in town and
she hated it. I said to her 'Nella, you can quit now!'"

Cassie laughed and turned her face towards her brother.

"Half of that money is yours, Jonathan."

Jonathan shook his head. "No," he said.

"That's the way Daddy would have wanted it," Cassie answered.
"I've got more money than I could ever spend."

"What about the orchard?" Jonathan asked.

"I was never really interested in running it, Jonathan. I remember that you loved it, even though you were such a small boy. Nella harvests a little out front just for our own use but I'm sorry to say that most of the orchard has run wild. I don't really know why but . . . I couldn't face getting people into harvest it. It would be like letting the last piece of Daddy go. It's silly, I suppose, but that's how I felt. Daddy also told me in his letter about his relationship with Melibea and how Granddaddy had taken over when the man Melibea was with demanded a ransom. I'll show the letter to you, Jonathan. He said that his biggest regret was not standing up to Granddaddy. He believed that if he had, you would have lived. We never found out who the man was that had helped Melibea with her plans."

Brendan flushed and looked at Eileen. He was dreading telling Cassie Thomas that his father was responsible and that Melibea, or Mariana, was his aunt.

"It turned out that Melibea wasn't even her real name. Granddaddy had someone investigate quietly and Melibea Lopez was an American-born citizen who'd had her passport stolen in New York several years before that. I'm sure that hurt Daddy very much." Cassie sighed. "So, for almost two years Nella and I lived here alone while we built the house across the pathway. Nella married then –"

"Don't remind me!" Nella yelled.

Cassie laughed. "We all lived then in the new house, Nella, Robert and –"

"Told you never to mention his name!" Nella yelled. "I was only nineteen and what a mistake! That skinny fool ran off on me and left me and Cassie with two wild boys to rear!"

Cassie laughed. "They're both gone now, in New York working," she said proudly.

"Surprised they turned out any way at all with your spoiling!" Nella snapped.

"So we've been here ever since," said Cassie, "but we often

thought about you, Jonathan. We'd still go up to the clearing and place flowers at your stone on your birthday. We'd remember funny stories and try to be happy. You were never far from our thoughts."

Jonathan smiled. "I felt it. I knew you were thinking of me. I knew there was someone out there. It's what kept me going all those years."

He held his sister's hand and looked lovingly at her. There was so much to ask, so much that he didn't know.

"What happened to Momma's family – they're all dead now?" he asked.

"Yes. Prudence was the last of the Chapmans and like Momma she died young."

"What about all the money Granddaddy had?"

Cassie Thomas groaned loudly. "Well, it turned out that Granddaddy was sexist as well as everything else. His will ignored me and stated that everything was to be divided equally between you and any sons that were born out of Prudence's marriage. You see, he hadn't written a new will after you disappeared."

"Did she have a son? Brendan asked.

"As I said, Prudence was quite a socialite so there was always something to read about her in the *Inquirer*, sometimes even in the *New York Times*. Sadly, she miscarried four or five times. She was seven years married when she finally had a son but the birth was difficult and she died. The poor baby had brain damage and went into state care. That husband of hers didn't even want to care for him. You'd think being a doctor that he'd be more caring. I guess Jan Reiter is clapping his hands together now. He has complete control over that money and that poor boy wouldn't even understand what a dollar is."

There was a stunned silence.

"Did you say Reiter? Dr Reiter?" Brendan asked.

"Yes."

Pilar slammed down her coffee cup, spilling some of its contents onto the old table. "Oh my God!" she gasped.

"Do you know him?" Cassie asked.

Brendan looked at Pilar who sat with her mouth open, a stunned expression on her normally calm face.

She turned her head slowly to Jonathan. Brendan watched as her mouth opened and closed, trying to make sense of the news. She finally spoke.

"That's . . . that's why he prescribed such large doses of medication for you. I queried it but he pulled rank on me. He . . . he must have known who you were and he couldn't afford for you to figure it out. It would mean he would have to share the inheritance with you."

Jonathan stood and walked to the window. He turned and leaned on the windowsill, looking at the people in the room.

"I told him about Cassie and Nella, about this place, this house. He said it was all my imagination. He used my infatuation with the Nelsons to keep me committed there until he made me lose faith in my memories. But I never believed him. I just pretended to so he'd take me off the medication and leave me in peace with the few memories I had left."

"He knew?" Brendan said. "Jesus . . . he . . . he could have . . . you could have got home years ago. He knew!" He looked at Pilar. "What are you going to do?"

"I don't know," Pilar replied, still reeling from the realisation that Reiter had used her for his own financial gain.

"You should go to the police!" Nella yelled.

Pilar's mobile phone rang. She lifted her bag and answered it as she made her way out of the front door.

The others sat there, silently, trying to absorb the revelation.

"What happened to you, Jonathan? Where have you been?" Cassie finally asked.

Jonathan took a deep breath and recounted as best he could his years locked in a tiny basement apartment in Harlem, his time under Dr Reiter's care in a psychiatric hospital, the many foster homes that he ran away from which resulted in him being returned each time to the care of the cold-hearted doctor. He recalled how when he came of age he hit the road and spent several long lonely years searching for Cassie which had brought him to the shelter one fine summer evening. He declared how it looked so much like his home that he had stopped there and had sat on the swing in the yard like he dreamt he would do when he finally found his home. He told how Alice had taken him in and had cared for him and how he met Eileen whom he loved more than anything on this earth. He told her about Brendan and the strange coincidences that resulted in their paths crossing for a second time and how his friend had promised to help him find his way home. Finally, he told her that he never gave up on the idea that she was out there somewhere, wondering what had happened to him and that not one day had passed that he did not imagine this moment.

When he was finished, a silence settled in the room again.

"All that time," Cassie said at last, shaking her head.

Brendan stood and looked at Eileen. It was the moment he dreaded.

"Eileen, we'd better go now," he gulped.

Eileen stood and looked longingly at Jonathan.

All three walked to the door with heads bowed towards the ground.

On the porch Jonathan reached forward and pulled Brendan to him.

"Thank you," he said as he patted his friend's back.

Brendan did not pull back or flinch at the touch of another human being as he once would have done, and stood for a moment locked in his friend's warm embrace.

"You're not far away. I'll come and see you," he said. He looked at his sister and his friend. "I'll let you say goodbye."

He walked down the porch steps and over to the opposite side of the clearing where Pilar had parked the car and where she now stood, her phone conversation over. She smiled as he approached.

"Good news?" Brendan asked.

Pilar nodded. "You are now looking at the new manager of the Domus Homeless Shelter."

"Congratulations!" Brendan hugged her. "What about Kuvic?"

"He's sacked. Thompson said he'll make sure Kuvic never works with vulnerable people again and, by the time the court case is over, Eileen will make doubly sure of it. I told Thompson about Jonathan and he was surprisingly supportive of him staying here. He'll get Jane to contact the local psychiatric service today to check in on him as soon as possible. I must say – I don't like leaving him here. Thompson's agreed for me or Jane to come back every few days until the local services take over. I know Jonathan seems peaceful and happy now but unfortunately his problems aren't going to go away overnight. He is still and always will be a traumatised man, Brendan. His psychosis won't go away – he'll still be afraid of Hispanic men, he'll often think he can do things he saw the Nelsons do on TV. He'll need support and understanding. I have to be sure Cassie and Nella can handle that."

Brendan nodded. He understood what she was saying. Jonathan was never going to be the boy he had once been. He had been through so much that even with support and understanding, those memories and the awful experiences he endured would remain with him for the rest of his life.

"So . . . seems like I have a position to fill?" she grinned.

"What position is that?" he smirked.

"A job at the shelter, what did you think I meant?" she teased.

Brendan pretended to be disappointed.

"Of course, you do owe me a date," she said. "I seem to remember you coming to my house to ask me something."

Brendan raised his eyebrows. "You're only answering that now?"

Pilar laughed. "You're not going back to New York now, are you?" she asked.

Brendan shook his head. "No, I'm not. But . . . I don't know if I'll be staying in Dover. I . . . I'm really not sure where I'll go from here."

Pilar nodded, appreciating his honesty. "Well, maybe you'll have your last meal with me before you go?"

"Okay, you're on. Mexican food okay?"

Pilar snorted. "Puerto Rican food is better!" she replied.

"How about Irish food? Maybe bacon and cabbage?" he said as they fell about laughing.

As their laughter died, they heard someone approaching. It was Eileen making her way gingerly towards them.

"Pilar got the job!" Brendan shouted.

Eileen nodded and smiled at Pilar. "That's good. Congratulations, Pilar! Em . . . Brendan, can I speak to you?" She looked sheepishly at Pilar.

Pilar smiled and headed towards the house to fill Cassie and Nella in on what she felt they would need to know about Jonathan.

"I'm not coming with you," Eileen said, her voice firm but her eyes trained on the dirt road under her feet.

"Eileen!" he began but she moved a few steps backward and shook her head.

"Nothing you can say will make me change my mind, Brendan. I belong here. I belong with Jonathan."

Brendan relaxed his shoulders and looked at her. He sighed. He took her hand and led her to some rocks where they sat and looked into the beautiful forest in front of them.

"Look – just come back with me and talk to Frank. Just for a few days."

"Brendan – I love Jonathan. I want to be with him. There is nothing in Dover for me. I love Dad and Mom but . . . I need him and he needs me here. This will be strange for him, even if it is home. I can't leave him and I don't want to. I'm staying."

"Okay," he said. "But what will I tell Uncle Frank?"

Eileen laughed nervously. "Haven't you learnt anything from me these past few months? I think you can handle him."

Brendan pulled his sister to him. "I'm going to miss you!"

"I'm going to miss you too," she replied.

"What will you do here?" he said, looking around the dense woodland of the rural setting.

Eileen followed his eyes around the magnificent scenery. "I've always wanted to live somewhere like this, somewhere quiet and peaceful, where I can think. Plus, the university is only a couple of hours from here. Maybe I'll finish my degree. It doesn't really matter as long as Jonathan and I are together."

Brendan loosened his grip on her and stood up. She rose and linked his arm, and they walked towards the car.

"I'll be back for Kuvic's court date and to collect my car!" she said as she opened the boot and, to Brendan's amusement, lifted out two small suitcases and her bag of books.

"Oh, so that's why you wanted to take your car!" he laughed, shaking his head as he climbed in.

Pilar appeared, having given Cassie and Nella her contact details and told them all she felt they urgently needed to know – the rest could come later. She halted, astonished, when she saw Eileen carrying the suitcases.

"I take it you're not coming?" she smirked.

Eileen smiled and shook her head.

As the car made its way slowly down the uneven roadway Brendan waved at his sister. He saw Jonathan come to stand beside her and place his arm protectively around her shoulders.

"Brendan?" Pilar said. "You've changed so much since you first came to the shelter and for the better. But . . . you're not the only one who has changed."

The smile he had seen only moments before had vanished and she looked at him with a determined expression on her face. Brendan frowned at her, unsure what she meant.

"Never again will I stay quiet when I know something is not right. I will be who I used to be. I'll speak out and make sure that someone like Reiter doesn't make me feel like what I have to say doesn't matter."

As Pilar and Brendan drove through the outskirts of Dover town, he signalled for her to stop outside the hospital.

"Want me to go in with you?" she asked.

Brendan shook his head and walked alone to Alice's ward.

When he arrived on her ward, he stood in the corridor and peered into the small window of her hospital room. Theo was sitting on a chair looking at his sleeping mother while his eldest son sat slumped on another chair, sleeping soundly. Theo sat upright and moved to the door shaking his head. He opened the door and moved into the corridor to speak to Brendan.

"She's been waiting for you. She said you'd be coming today," he said, still shaking his head in amazement at the things his mother seemed to know.

"How is she?" Brendan asked.

"It's nearly time. That's what they said," he replied quietly.

Brendan exhaled loudly and went into the room to take a seat beside the sleeping woman. In the few days since he had last seen her, she had wasted away and looked gaunt and thin, nothing like the vibrant, vivacious Alice he had known. Theo woke his son and took him outside leaving Brendan alone with Alice.

The air inside the room was acrid and stifling. Brendan yawned and stared at his friend's frail face.

"Am I keeping you up?" she whispered.

Brendan laughed as Alice slowly opened her dark brown eyes.

"I dreamt about you, Brendan," she gasped. "My husband, my Theo, he's been here all day, marching from wall to wall in his uniform, staring at me and telling me he's been waiting. I told him, I got to wait for Brendan. 'Brendan?' he said, thinking I've got myself a fancy man. Yes, I told him and *hmm-mm* he sure is good-looking, looks a lot like that Irish movie star, what's his name?"

Brendan smiled and shrugged.

"Well, you should have seen my husband getting all irate at the thought of me looking at another man. I told him, you relax there because I'm old enough to be this boy's mama and he laughed then and said, 'I'll be here, Alice, you just tell me when you're ready.'"

Alice quietened and fixed a smile on her face as her eyes slowly closed.

"Alice?" Brendan yelped, his heart quickening.

"I'm here. I'm just resting my eyes," she replied sleepily.

"Alice, I have something to tell you. We did it, Alice. We brought Jonathan home. I found his sister and he is there now. Eileen stayed with him."

A solitary tear fell down Alice's cheek and landed on the fold of her neck.

"I knew you would," she drawled as she opened her eyes. "Are they good people?"

"The best."

"First time I laid eyes on your special soul, I said that. I said that to myself. I said 'Alice, this boy is here for a reason'."

Brendan reached into the cot and held her hand.

"Now, you don't get fresh because, look, there's my Theo at the wall again, looking at this white boy holding his wife's hand."

Brendan glanced nervously at the wall but could see nobody.

He flinched as her breathing became raspy and turned to see if her son was outside. He waved and the sad-looking man came back into the room.

"Alice, I've got to go now. Will you remember that Jonathan is home? Will you remember that we found his sister?"

"I surely will," she replied. "Brendan?"

"Yes, Alice?"

"Do you know what day today is?"

Brendan shook his head. "No."

"Why, it's my retirement day."

Alice coughed and signalled for Theo to hand her a small envelope from the drawer of her locker.

"I got something for you," she said.

She took the envelope from her son's hand and passed it to Brendan. He opened it and scanned down his record of community service with her signature on the end.

"See, we're both free now, Brendan. I'm finished and so are you. I know where I'm going but what are you going to do now, boy?"

Brendan shrugged. "I don't know, Alice, but I know that I

don't need to be in the noise any more. I think I might go to Pennsylvania to be near my sister and Jonathan. The important thing is, I don't feel like I have to hide any more. I know who I am now."

"That's a good enough answer," she said as she closed her eyes wearily.

Brendan leant forward and kissed his friend for the last time.

"Thanks for everything, Alice. I'll never forget you," he said as a smile washed slowly over her face. "Never."

Chapter 34

As the sun set gently over Dover town, Brendan slipped quietly down the side entrance of his uncle's house, hoping for a quiet hour in his apartment before he told his uncle that Eileen was not coming back. He ducked his head down as he passed under Coleen's kitchen window and moved to the edge of the house, hoping that he had not been seen.

A familiar figure stood statue-like in the garden in the very spot where he had so often stood, admiring the panoramic views over the picturesque town.

Patricia turned and looked at him, then returned her gaze to the beautiful sunset on the west side of his uncle's garden.

"I saw Eileen leave with you. She's not coming back, is she?" she asked.

Brendan shook his head.

"Good for her," his mother said. She gestured towards the view before her. "I used to love this view. When we moved here first, I thought it was the prettiest thing I ever saw."

Brendan walked across the large garden to where his mother stood and stopped just behind her, looking out at the stunning view.

"I've found a place to live," she said. "A couple of blocks on

301

the other side of town. It's a small apartment but it's enough for one person. I hate gardening anyway. I never was much use at growing things."

She turned to face him and he nodded.

"You want to know why I treated you the way I did? Why I was not what a mother should have been?"

Brendan nodded as his chin quivered slightly. He looked away from his mother and focused his eyes on the town as it disappeared slowly under the darkening sky.

"Every time I looked at you, I saw Rafael. I realised that you would be a reminder of my stupidity every day for the rest of my life."

"That didn't give you the right to treat me the way you did," he said. "It's no excuse. I was just a child, an innocent child."

"I know," she whispered.

"That's why you didn't speak to me? All those years of silent treatment, because I looked like my father?"

"No. It was because I didn't think I had anything to offer you. I . . . I hated myself."

"And therefore hated me?"

"I didn't hate you," she replied quietly. "I felt sorry for you, having a mother like me, but there was nothing I could do to change that. There was no one else to take care of you and I didn't want to leave you with Frank. The very mention of Rafael's name sent him crazy. What kind of a father would he have made you who were the living image of the man he hated? I know I can't undo what I've done but I am really sorry. I'm hoping that we can at least . . . try to be friends."

Patricia put out her small hand towards him and waited.

He searched her face and slowly raised his hand, taking her fragile hand in his.

"Yes," he answered. "We can try."

Chapter 35

The small orchard at the side of the shelter looked different to Brendan as he harvested the last of Jonathan's apples amid the falling leaves in the early November sunshine. It had been a task that Brendan had put off many times since his friend had returned to his home in Pennsylvania as though the pulling of the apples would signify the end of the adventure they had enjoyed and would tell Brendan that it was also time for him to leave, to uproot himself from this town and the people that he had begun to love. When he pulled the last apple from the tree, he walked alone along the boundary of the property and remembered how Jonathan had watched him in the late spring sunshine from behind those very trees, now laid bare in the autumn fall.

He walked into the house and wandered around the large front room and into the laundry where his sister had undertaken her labour of love for all those years. He climbed the ornate staircase and remembered how his friend had inched by him in fear as he repaired the beautiful balusters on the antique stairwell and how together they had laboured to repair the furniture in the large dorms where Zeb still fought each night with the other men for his favourite bed under the window.

He climbed the last few steps to Jonathan's tower and stood for a moment, unable to bring himself to open the door to the now empty room. He missed his needy, confused friend more than he realised, the new Jonathan growing in confidence each time Brendan drove to the clapboard house and watched the man clear out the overgrown orchards on his father's farm. Jonathan had even filed charges against Dr Reiter, not for monetary gain but to expose the well-known psychiatrist as the evil man he truly was and to bring him to justice.

Brendan walked to his mother's new car where he had stacked as many boxes of Jonathan's harvest as he could fit in the boot.

"There," he said as struggled to fit the last box in. "You'd think he had enough apples of his own where he is," he said to Henrietta who stood in the garden, watching him.

Brendan glanced at the heavy-set woman who had cooked at the shelter for more years than she cared to remember. The last time he had seen her was at Alice's funeral. His friend had died only hours after he'd told her that Jonathan had made it home. Contrary to what he had expected, the funeral had not been a sad affair. He had actually enjoyed the celebration of his friend's life, which was held in a packed-out Baptist church in Dover. True to how the woman had lived her life, people from all sections of the community had crowded in to say goodbye. When Brendan arrived he had noticed Zeb standing at the very back of the church. He invited him to come and sit with the Dalton family but Zeb had refused, telling him that he was never a churchgoing man but that he had come here to say goodbye to Alice. His casts were now gone and the old man's arms hung limply by his sides as he stood alone in the background. Mr Thompson and all the board members had also crowded into the tiny church and Brendan noticed how the usually sour man was brought to tears as he watched Alice's grandchildren bring symbols of all she held dear onto the altar, one of which was a large poster of Mr Thompson's uncle who had been a great support to Alice in her futile search for her husband all those years ago – she had never forgotten the kindness he had shown her. Pilar was there with Guido and Isabel, as was Frank and all of the Dalton family.

Jonathan and Eileen had also arrived and had announced their engagement over dinner the previous evening, Jonathan having asked Frank for his daughter's hand two days before. "It's a bit late to be asking now," Frank had responded, still seething from his daughter stealing away in the dead of night without as much as a goodbye.

Brendan was glad that he'd had a chance to speak to his uncle alone before he left the house that morning. He had found him in the front garden, pretending to plant spring bulbs.

"Thanks for everything," he had said as he stretched out his hand to Frank.

"Thanks?" Frank had asked. "You're my nephew, no need to thank me for putting you up."

Brendan flushed. "No, thank you for . . . bringing me here and for . . . for making a . . . man of me."

Frank's mouth had dropped open. "My tough love worked on someone?" he had asked, joking.

"It did."

"Will you put that in writing?" his uncle quipped to hide his embarrassment.

Brendan laughed and shook his uncle's hand as the two men stared into each other's faces. Then he instinctively pulled the old man to him and hugged him tightly.

"Hey!" Frank had said. "You'll only be just over an hour away. Anyway, I'll need someone to keep an eye on Eileen for me. I'm not completely sure about that chap she's going out with yet. Will you do that?"

Brendan nodded. "I will."

"Brendan?" his uncle asked as he glanced towards the car where Patricia, who had agreed to drive Brendan, sat waiting. "And I'll look after your mother here. I don't know why she had to move into that apartment but . . . she seems happy and that's all I ever wanted."

Brendan could hear his mother start to cry in the driver's seat. He felt he finally understood his old uncle who had been forced into manhood at an early age and had tried, albeit erroneously, to protect his family from all of the evil in the world.

Frank waved tearfully to her as she buried her head in her hands.

"We'll see you at Thanksgiving in Wilsonville!" Brendan had shouted as they drove away.

Now, as he slammed the boot of the car shut in the driveway of the shelter, he saw Pilar in the window of Jonathan's room, watching him. True to her word, they'd had dinner the night before at a Puerto Rican restaurant and they had spent a lot of time together since Jonathan's departure. He had even accompanied her to Wilsonville any time she was due to check on how their friend was doing. He waved to her and smiled when she raised her petite hand and waved back to him.

"You sure you don't want to stay here?" his mother asked from the driver's seat.

Brendan took one last look at the beautiful woman in the window and shook his head.

"I'm sure," he said hesitantly.

He looked up and gave Pilar one last wave as the car made its way onto Maple Street.

Epilogue

Kuvic's court case was swift with Eileen only having to appear once to give evidence about the terrible night he attacked her at the shelter. Mr Thompson was there to listen as a guilty verdict was read out by the jury of men and women in Dover district court. Brendan could feel Alice in the room with them and could almost hear her raucous laugh as Kuvic was led away to serve an eighteen-month prison sentence. Even in death, his friend was getting her way. Kuvic's career working with the helpless and disempowered was finally over.

Jan Reiter did not receive a prison sentence but his licence to practise medicine was revoked, which nobody believed would be any real hardship for the aging psychiatrist who had only been working part-time at the hospital so he could oversee Jonathan's long-term community care and ensure that the strange man never found his way home. More painful to Reiter was the court's decision that half of the money his son had inherited be awarded to Jonathan and that an advocate be assigned to Reiter's son to ensure the money was finally used to provide the severely disabled man with the best care money could buy.

Jonathan in turn donated a large proportion of his

inheritance to the shelter, which enabled Pilar to provide the extra services she had long since envisaged for her clients.

The now married man had also gone to great lengths to find the unmarked plots where Melibea and her mother had been buried and found that the mother and daughter had been laid to rest not far from each other in Harlem's Trinity Cemetery. Brendan accompanied Jonathan to watch as two new headstones, engraved with the women's real names, were placed at the head of their final resting places.

Brendan settled into life in the Appalachian Mountains better than he had anticipated, the quiet of the woodlands seeping into his soul as though he had always belonged there. By day, he taught literature to small groups of animated adolescents, hungry for the stories he had read so passionately as a lonely child in Ireland, and by evening he would spend time with his friend, clearing more sections of the vast orchard or climbing to the clearing that Jonathan had described to him so beautifully from a hilltop in Dover. That day now felt like it had occurred a long, long time ago. In finding his friend's lost home, he had also discovered a place where he could belong, a place where he now lived in peace.

When Jonathan and Eileen had their first child, a bridge was created which Patricia could use to heal the wounds of the past. Some evenings Eileen would organise a get-together. Frank and Coleen would visit with Patricia as would Cassie and Nella. Pilar would arrive and Brendan's heart would soar at the very sight of her. On each visit, he noticed she would stay on longer. He knew she was beginning to love the peaceful place and that the draw of Dover was slowly slipping from her. Together they would all sit at the large oak table and talk about their day. On those beautiful evenings Brendan would watch his friend's eyes moisten as he enjoyed the very thing he had missed most during his time in captivity. Then he would walk with Pilar into the dense woodlands and listen to the wind blowing through the majestic trees.

And on the nights when she was not there, he would sit in his room in the big clapboard house set high among the mountains and imagine Pilar standing in the round window, waving to him as she had done the day he left Dover. He would think about her then, her hair tied up tightly as she roamed around that big old house, checking on her charges and locking the house down for the night. And sometimes he would succeed in shaking that lonely image from his mind. He'd stand and look out of his window into the darkness of the wilderness around him where he'd see her standing barefoot on the long dirt driveway, as he knew she someday would, her hair loose around her, waiting for him to come take her from the darkness and into the light of the shaded room.

If you enjoyed
The Incredible Life of Jonathan Doe
by Carol Coffey
why not try
Winter Flowers also published by Poolbeg?
Here's a sneak preview of the first three chapters.

Winter Flowers

CAROL COFFEY

POOLBEG

Chapter 1

"Iris Fay, are you in there?" The man's voice boomed from outside the rundown shop as he knocked heavily on the door.

Iris switched on her bedside lamp, leapt from her small bed and threw an old dressing-gown around her thin body. She had not been asleep. She glanced at the clock. It was one o'clock. She rarely slept before three, spending the darkest hours lying there, thinking. She pulled the belt tight and tied it, staring at her thin pale face in the dusty bedroom mirror. In the dim light she looked older than her forty years. She raced to the door.

"Wait! I'm coming!" she called weakly.

Iris opened the door and saw a tall garda with a young boy standing beside him.

"Is this your nephew, Miss Fay?"

Iris looked down at the dishevelled boy. Her heart sank. She knew this meant trouble.

"Yes," she breathed heavily. "Luke . . . my sister's boy."

"Well, he didn't know your address or phone number and your sister wouldn't say. We had to get him to direct us here."

"What's happened . . . is my sister . . . where's Jack?"

The boy stayed silent, not knowing if he should speak. He was afraid his mother might be angry at him for coming here but he hadn't known what else to do. There were black marks on his face and he was dressed in a T-shirt and light track-suit top despite the cold night.

"The younger child is with hospital staff," the garda answered.

"Hospital – what's happened?" Iris asked loudly. Fear gripped her and she began to sway slightly.

"There was a fire. They're fine but they inhaled fumes. They'll probably keep your sister overnight. The boy will be discharged when someone comes to collect him."

"How did it happen?"

"The fire department thinks it was probably a chip pan left on a cooker that hadn't been turned off. Too soon to tell though. Do these boys have a father I can call? This one says you're their only relative. Is that true?"

"Yes," Iris replied sadly as she stroked her nephew's curly head.

She looked down at Luke and felt an overwhelming pity for him. What was going to become of the boys with a mother like theirs? It was over two weeks since her troubled younger sister had last visited her. The visit had ended in yet another row. That's the way it was for them. When things weren't going right for Hazel, she would barge into Iris's tiny flat looking for trouble.

Luke smiled sheepishly up at her. He liked his Aunty Iris. She was good to him even though she often made his mother cry and he didn't like it when people made his mother cry. Even though he was not yet eight years old, he was the man of the house and it was his job to protect his mother. It was a hard job though because she needed a lot of protecting and sometimes he needed Aunty Iris to help, times like now.

"Can you look after the lads tonight?" the garda asked doubtfully, peering in at the rundown sewing shop she called home.

"Yes," Iris replied, knowing what he was thinking. "There's room at the back. I'll collect Jack at the hospital."

"Miss?"

"Yes?"

"The younger lad has asthma?"

"Yes."

"You might tell the boy's mother that it's probably not smart to be smoking in a house with an asthmatic child."

314

Iris reddened and lowered her head. "I'll see that he gets his medication, officer. I'm a . . . I used to be a nurse . . ."

Thanking the garda, Iris moved Luke inside and closed the door slowly. She exhaled a loud breath and stood with her back against the cold glass of the door for a moment, digesting the news, then led her shivering nephew through the small shop and into her living area.

She washed his face in her tiny cold bathroom and gave him one of her own jumpers to keep warm.

"Don't worry – it doesn't look like a girl's jumper!" she said. "You hungry, love?"

"Just a bit."

In the kitchenette she set about making some toast and slicing some cheese.

Luke could feel the anger rising in her. He watched her neck redden and her lips moving silently and knew she was about to ask questions he didn't want to answer.

"Who was smoking in the house, Luke? Did your mam have a visitor?"

Iris hated this, using the child to find out what was going on but she had no choice. Hazel was never going to tell her what had happened.

He didn't answer, and that was answer enough.

She led him into the sitting room and put his plate and a glass of milk on the coffee table.

Luke sat and began to eat. He thought about lying but knew he'd only get himself into a bigger mess. It would be a sin. He was making his Communion next May and he knew he'd have to save it up for Confession.

"Mam's friend came round," he said at last, in his flat Dublin accent. "D'you 'member Pete?"

"Oh yeah," Iris replied, trying to hide her annoyance.

Pete Doyle only came around when Hazel collected her One-Parent Family Payment. He'd usually spend the night after talking Hazel into spending more than she could afford on booze, and then disappear for another week.

"Were . . . were they . . . ?" Iris hated this. She watched Luke

315

squirm as he swallowed a huge bite of toast and cheese. She stopped herself for a moment. She knew it wasn't fair on the child but decided to continue anyway. "Were they having a good night then?"

Luke looked up, unsure how to answer the question. He knew that Iris hated it when people smoked around his younger brother and that she also didn't like it when his mam had been drinking.

"Em . . . yeah," he replied nervously. "Mam was laughing for ages . . ." He stopped, wondering if that was too much information because he knew that his mam only laughed that much when she drank too much wine.

"Ah . . . that's nice," Iris said unconvincingly. "Well, finish your milk and let's go and collect your brother. He'll be worried, won't he? I've enough for a taxi so it'll be an adventure, eh?"

Luke was looking worried, already concerned that there would be another row between his mam and his aunt.

The pair huddled together as they made their way down Fairview Strand towards the taxi rank in the bitter cold. It was pitch black and there wasn't a soul to be seen.

The taxi driver didn't seem too pleased to be woken from his slumber as he sat parked on the corner and didn't say a word to either of his depressed-looking passengers, although he was slightly interested in why the woman was going to hospital with a child at this hour. He didn't look sick. Skinny maybe, but not sick.

When they pulled up in front of the old inner-city hospital he muttered the fare and found that his passengers were as dour as he was. He watched as they walked with bowed heads towards the large wooden doors of the formidable building. Maybe they've received bad news about a relative, he thought, suddenly feeling guilty, before turning the car back towards his rank. Ah well, if I'm lucky I'll get a couple of hours' kip before the day job starts.

A&E on the ground floor of the hospital had a long miserable line of old iron trolleys that should have been replaced years before. Iris could see Hazel before the nurse pointed her out. Hazel's long narrow body almost made it to the end of the trolley while her thick fair hair covered the pillow.

Iris approached her sister gingerly. She didn't want another row although she did intend to find out eventually what had happened.

Iris cleared her throat, anxious not to say the wrong thing and God knew it was easy to say the wrong thing to her highly strung sister. "How are you?" she asked quietly. She leaned in to kiss Hazel but pulled back quickly when her sister turned her face away. Iris sighed. "I've brought you some toilet things and a couple of nightdresses. They're mine, hope they fit you . . . might be too short though."

She knew Hazel loved to gloat about the difference in their appearances. Although both women were considered pretty when they were younger, Iris was short and dark while Hazel was very tall with long straight fair hair. They both had their mother's eyes: large round blue eyes that made them look constantly surprised, or scared.

Iris placed the bag she was carrying on the trolley and stood with her hands in her pockets. She looked at Luke who stood like a frightened rabbit, his brown eyes narrowed beneath his curly brown hair that was badly in need of a cut. Both boys looked like their father whom they never saw and didn't remember.

"Hazel," she said softly, "I'll take the boys to my place tonight. The nurse said you'll probably be out tomorrow. Jack's in the children's ward but they said to take him – that he's fine but keeps crying – and he –"

"No! You're not taking my kids anywhere!" Hazel shouted loudly, her sudden rage frightening the entire A&E including her sister and her son whose lip began to quiver slightly.

A nurse began walking towards Hazel's bed.

"Hazel, please . . ." Iris said as softly as she could. "If they don't come with me the hospital will ring Social Services." She moved closer to the trolley to avoid Luke hearing her. "You don't want that, do you?" she whispered.

Hazel jumped from the bed and, tearing off the nightdress the hospital had supplied, began putting her clothes on. She swayed and almost fell as she was pulling her jeans on but seemed unaware of her son's acute embarrassment.

"Don't you tell me what I want for my kids!" she screamed, before coughing loudly.

"Hazel!" the nurse called out. "Get back into bed, please – your breathing is still laboured."

Hazel ignored the nurse and began walking towards the door of the ward.

"I'm signing myself out. I feel perfect now," she said sharply to the nurse, raising her voice in a mocking intonation. "That okay with you?"

The nurse had met plenty like her before. They came in looking for help, worse for wear, and then up and left without as much as a thank you. Well, she didn't care either way. One less to look after through the night.

"You'll have to sign a discharge form," she replied dryly as she watched the woman sway.

At the nurses' station she quickly filled in a form and handed it to Hazel to sign.

She looked at the young child and then at Iris. "You staying with her tonight?"

Iris nodded.

"Good luck," she said as she snapped the signed discharge form from Hazel and directed the sisters to the children's ward.

Jack slept soundly in the taxi on the way home. Iris knew not to ask how bad the fire was and whether or not they could actually sleep there tonight. These questions were pointless with Hazel when she was like this. When the taxi pulled up in the small cul-de-sac outside the house, Iris couldn't see any external damage.

They got out and walked to the front door, Hazel struggling to carry Jack, unwilling to let her sister help. She opened the door and stepped inside, then pulled Luke angrily into the hallway before slamming the door loudly in Iris's face.

Iris stood, rooted to the spot. Her shoulders dropped forward. She had used the last of her cash on the taxi. She pulled her coat around her and looked up at the dark sky as she turned to walk the three-mile journey home.

Chapter 2

The narrow sitting room which sat directly behind Iris's modest clothes-repair shop was darkly decorated with cheap furniture, some of which had been her mother's. A small television sat on a low table and faced a worn two-seater sofa-bed and equally worn armchair, a coffee table in front of them. A silver-tasselled lamp stood tall on a side table which was adorned with a photo of Hazel and the boys on one side and one of Iris and Hazel as children on the other. A small wooden kitchen table was pressed up against the wall directly behind the shop as there was no room for it in the kitchenette. To the left of the sitting room was the door to Iris's tiny bedroom which consisted of a single bed with a wardrobe and side table and looked more like a convent cell than a single woman's bedroom. A door in the far wall of the sitting room led into the kitchenette which had room only for an old gas stove, small fridge and sink. Two painted cupboards stood over by the window that faced onto a small concrete yard. Iris's cat, Marmalade, sat on the window ledge, looking in at her as she prepared her modest evening meal. It made periodic meowing sounds, hoping to get inside from the cold breeze that blew around the yard. A bathroom jutted off the kitchenette with a small shower cubicle, toilet and hand basin. It obviously had been added onto the old building as an afterthought. It had no radiator and Iris dreaded showering there in the winter.

She looked about the flat and, while she knew she didn't have to live this meagrely, she liked it. It was a simple life. She did not need much and found that she preferred to give any extra cash she had to Hazel for the boys than spend it on material things for herself.

Iris pondered the day's event as she ate while watching *EastEnders* which was her favourite programme.

Hazel had come into the shop that day, almost two weeks after slamming the door in her sister's face, all smiles and cheerfulness, as if nothing had happened. But that was Hazel. Iris was used to it and, while she liked seeing her sister, she enjoyed a strange sort of peace when Hazel was fighting with her. Even though it could be lonely, life was predictable. She would get up each morning early and walk for about an hour before spending the day repairing clothes for her few regular customers or occasionally making new dresses for young brides or debutantes who knew nothing of what life was to bring, God help them. She didn't have to worry about her sister flying off the handle about some slight comment she might make.

Yet the sisters depended on each other. Their parents had not had a happy marriage and rowed constantly. Hazel was too young to remember much about either of their parents and anything she did recall was through rose-coloured glasses. When their dad failed to return after yet another row, their mother had sat the sisters down and told them that he had been killed in a car accident. Three years later their mother died, a needless death caused by alcoholism. It haunted Iris to this day and caused great bitterness. All her mistakes, she felt, were down to that one selfish act. It had led her to this place, to this life.

Iris sighed. Tomorrow was Friday and she had agreed to take the boys for the weekend while Hazel went to Galway with some friends. Where her sister got the money to go away she didn't know, but she said nothing. As usual, she kept her mouth shut when she didn't approve – and anyway she loved having the boys. Luke was a handful, though, so she was even happier when Hazel returned for them and she could return to her peaceful, predictable existence.

Iris looked up at the clock on the wall above the television. There was nothing good on and it was only eight o'clock. She sat in silence for a few minutes and wondered what to do with herself. She could hear the rain start to fall heavily against the window. The flat was cold and she rose to get another cardigan to put around her shoulders. She hoped that Hazel had lit the fire for the boys and wondered if she'd remembered to fill the prescription for Jack's regular inhaler. She almost phoned Hazel to remind her but stopped herself in time. She stood and walked back into the shop. May as well use the time to work, she thought. She sat down at her sewing machine and hummed as she began to work.

Chapter 3

After Hazel dropped the boys off to her sister for the weekend, she raced back to her house and began dolling herself up. She hadn't wanted to lie to Iris, telling her she was going to Galway with friends, but her sister would never understand if she said Pete was coming around. The woman lived like a nun. Hazel didn't know how Iris didn't get lonely like she herself did, but they had always been so different. Iris was always the strong one while Hazel was the emotional one, crying or laughing and nothing in between.

The three-bedroom red-bricked house that Hazel lived in was the most constant thing in her life. It had been her parents' house. She had grown up there and, except for the years when she and Iris had to go into care, she had never lived anywhere else. The house was only minutes away from the Botanic Gardens, which she loved. She couldn't understand why Iris didn't want to live there with her, preferring the grotty little flat. It was a modest house that was in need of some redecoration but it was a decent size and what Hazel loved most about it was the large back garden where her father used to tend his beloved plants. It was where he was happiest, Iris had said, although Hazel didn't really remember him. Even the photos of him looked somehow foreign to her. There was one particular photo of him, standing alone by an old-fashioned motor car, taken in Sussex where he was born and where her parents had met when her mother went to work there. He was young and handsome, smiling into the camera with a confident air. When she was a teenager she used to spend hours looking into the photo, hoping for some memory to come to her, anything at all, but it never did. He was a stranger whom she was told had loved her dearly. Hazel knew that her father had walked out during a row with her mother. Although her memories were few, she remembered her mother telling them a few days later that he had died in an accident – she remembered because Iris had screamed when she heard and had cried all night in her bed and Hazel had rarely seen Iris crying. She often wondered at how different their lives could have been if he'd come back and sorted out the problem with their mother. He wouldn't have been driving that car in England and he'd be alive. She thought of her boys and wondered how anyone could walk out on their children but then she only had to look at her sister to see that it was possible. After what Iris did, Hazel wondered if it was somehow genetic, something inherited that made you just walk out without as much as an explanation. Hazel knew she wasn't the world's greatest mother – but to abandon her kids! She'd never do it, never. No matter how bad things got, and they often got really, really bad.

She wasn't brushing the boys off now because of Pete. She wouldn't do that. It was just easier if they weren't there. She needed some time alone with Pete. It would be nice. He shouted a bit much at the boys anyway so they probably preferred to be with Iris who would spoil them, she reasoned to herself. It wasn't Pete's fault – he wasn't used to kids, that's all. If it worked out between them, he'd get used to the boys. They were good kids. All in good time, she thought, as she dressed in the skimpiest dress she could find. She applied some bright red lipstick and stood back to look at herself in the mirror. "Gorgeous!" she said, laughing. She looked great and had regained her figure despite putting on almost three stone during her pregnancies. She thought fleetingly about Gerry, the boys' father, and wondered where he was now. Probably still married to his wagon of a wife who he wouldn't leave to be with her. Bastard. He hadn't actually told her he was married until she was pregnant with Luke. He promised he'd leave his wife, start a new life with their son and she believed him. She should have known better. She was twenty-nine at the time, not a kid. Gerry was older than her, a lot older, but she didn't mind – she liked it actually. It made her feel kind of safe, protected. While Gerry was filling her full of lies about buying a house in the country where she could plant a garden as good as her dad's, she fell pregnant again with Jack. She threatened him to make him leave his wife, said she'd tell. She even begged him when she became desperate but he walked away, just like her dad – only this time she would remember it. The thought of being a single mother of two children depressed her. She was no snob but she knew she could have done better and couldn't understand why she had settled for this. It puzzled her to this day. Well, it was all history now. The boys were getting big and she hadn't had any luck with any of her boyfriends since, and there had been a lot of boyfriends, lots of losers who promised her the stars and took more than they gave in return. She felt that Pete was different. For one, he had never been married so didn't come with any baggage. Even if it didn't turn into any fairytale wedding, she had fun with Pete. He took her out of her dead-end life and made her laugh. She needed him; she needed anyone who did that for her. She was suffocating in her monotonous existence and if she had to settle for short bursts of happiness, then that would have to do. Hazel peered closer into the mirror and inspected the frown lines that appeared each time she was thinking like this, thinking like Iris did – worry, worry, worry.

The doorbell rang and Hazel glanced in the mirror again, making final touches to her make-up. It rang a second time as she quickly adjusted her dress and took one last look at herself. As she raced downstairs to open the door, Pete was already ringing the bell impatiently for the third time.

"Come on. Open the bleedin' door, will ya – it's freezing!" he shouted.

Hazel stood for a moment on the last step. She hoped Pete wasn't in a bad mood. She took a deep breath before swinging the door open. She smiled nervously.

"Sorry, Pete . . . sorry."